HOLIDAY WITH THE BEST MAN

BY
KATE HARDY

First Published in Great Britain 2016
By Mills & Boon, an imprint of HarperCollins*Publishers*
1 London Bridge Street, London, SE1 9GF

© 2016 Pamela Brooks

ISBN: 978-0-263-91977-6

23-0416

Kate Hardy has always loved books and could read before she went to school. She discovered Mills & Boon books when she was twelve and decided this was what she wanted to do. When she isn't writing, Kate enjoys reading, cinema, ballroom dancing and the gym. You can contact her via her website: www.katehardy.com.

To Gay, the best stepmum in the world

PROLOGUE

ROLAND'S FACE ACTUALLY ached from smiling, but he knew he had to keep it up. Apart from the fact that it was his best friend's wedding day—and of course Roland was delighted that Hugh had found the love of his life—he also knew that half the guests were remembering that Roland's wife had been killed in a car accident nearly two years ago, and were worrying that he was finding it hard to cope with today.

As he'd said to Hugh at the altar, today had brought back good memories of his own wedding day. Roland just hoped that Hugh and Bella would have a lot more years of happiness together than he and Lynette had had—and none of the misery that they'd both kept secret, even from their family and their closest friends.

He knew he ought to make the effort to go and dance with the chief bridesmaid. Even though his friend Hugh had opted to have two best men, and Tarquin—the other best man—was dancing with Bella's sister right now, Roland knew that he couldn't use that as an excuse. If he didn't dance with Grace, everyone would assume that it was because he was thinking of Lynette, and the last thing he wanted right now was another dose of pity. He'd had more than enough of that after the crash.

One dance. He could do that. All he had to do was ignore the fact that the ballroom in the Elizabethan manor house was full of fairy lights, creating the most romantic mood. And to ignore his misgivings about the chief bridesmaid, because it wasn't his place to judge her—even though the little he knew about her pressed all the wrong buttons. Grace had been so drunk the first time she'd met Hugh, that she'd thrown up over him in the taxi; plus she'd cancelled her wedding at the last minute. Sure, everyone had an off day or made mistakes, but to Roland it sounded as if Grace was a spoiled princess who liked alcohol too much.

And a spoiled, princessy drunk driver had shattered Roland's life with her selfishness, nearly two years ago. Having to be nice to a woman like that for even a few minutes really stuck in his craw. But he'd do it for his best friend's sake. His best friend who, even now, was dancing with his bride—and Roland was pretty sure that the glow around Hugh and Bella was due to more than just the fairy lights. This was real happiness.

Which left him to man up and do his duty. Right now Grace looked perfectly demure in her dark red bridesmaid's dress with its ballerina skirt and sweetheart neckline, and she was even wearing flat shoes rather than spindly heels so she didn't tower over the bride. Though her dark hair was in a sophisticated up-do with wisps of hair curled into ringlets that framed her face—a seriously high-maintenance style—and her eyelashes had most definitely been enhanced. So maybe Roland was right about the princessy tendencies. And even Tarquin—who saw the good in everyone—had admitted that Grace was nothing like sweet, bubbly little Bella.

One dance, he reminded himself. Do your duty and don't let your best friend down.

At the end of the song, he walked over to Grace and Tarquin. 'As the other best man, I believe the next dance is meant to be mine,' he said, forcing himself to keep smiling.

'It is indeed,' Tarquin said, and clapped him on the shoulder. 'See you later, Grace.'

'See you later, Tarquin,' she echoed, then turned to Roland. 'I don't think we've been properly introduced yet. I'm Bella's sister, Grace. You're Roland, aren't you?'

'Yes.'

'Nice to meet you.' She held out her hand to shake his.

Thinking, oh, please, just hurry up and let us get this over with, Roland took her hand and shook it. And he was truly shocked to find a prickle of awareness running down his spine.

Close up, Grace Faraday had the most incredible eyes: a deep cornflower blue. Her mouth was a perfect cupid's bow. Her complexion was fresh, almost dewy. And there was something that drew him to her. Something that made him feel protective.

And that really threw him.

Based on what he'd heard from the two people whose opinion he trusted most in the world, Roland had expected to dislike the woman. Instead, he found himself attracted to her. Attracted to someone he'd been sure was the last woman he'd ever want to date. And he really didn't know what to do about it.

'It was a lovely wedding, wasn't it?' Grace said. 'And that song Hugh wrote for Bella—that was amazing.'

'Mmm,' Roland said, too confused to string a coherent sentence together, and gave her his best attempt at a smile.

* * *

Grace was shocked by how different Hugh's two best friends were. Tarquin had been sweet and funny, and she'd felt really comfortable with him; Roland was taciturn to the point of making Grace feel awkward and shy, the way she usually was with strangers.

It didn't help that she'd felt a weird prickle of awareness when he'd shaken her hand. By any standards, Roland was good-looking, and the tailcoat, dark trousers, dark red waistcoat and matching cravat he wore emphasised it even more. His dark hair was brushed back from his forehead, and his slightly olive skin was clean-shaven. He could've been a model for a wedding suit company, and Grace wasn't sure if she found that more attractive or intimidating.

Maybe if she treated this as work—if she was professional and sensible with him, the way she'd be with a client—they could get through this dance without it being a total disaster.

Not having a clue what to say to him, she went through the motions of dancing with him and really hoped that pinning a smile to her face would be enough to get her through the next song. Just as well she'd talked Bella into letting her wear flat shoes; if she'd worn heels, she would probably have tripped over Roland's feet and made a complete and utter fool of herself.

Though it felt odd to be dancing with someone who was six inches taller than she was. Howard, her ex-fiancé, had been five foot eight, so she'd always worn flat shoes to make him feel less self-conscious about the fact that she was the same height as he was. Roland was broad-shouldered, where Howard had been slight. Being in his arms made Grace feel petite and feminine—something she wasn't used to. She was sensible, no-nonsense, and way too tall to be treated as if she was fragile.

She noticed that Roland's dark eyes were watchful. Why did he look so wary? Grace wondered.

Then she realised with a sinking heart just why she was feeling so awkward with him: because Roland was looking at her in exactly the same way that Howard's mother always had. Rather than smiling back at her, his lips were thinned. It was pretty clear that he'd judged her and decided that she wasn't quite good enough.

No wonder he wasn't chatting to her, the way Tarquin had. The guy clearly disliked her—even though he'd never met her before.

Well, that was his problem. She'd be polite and dance with him to this song, fulfilling their duty as the chief bridesmaid and the best man. Then she'd make sure she stayed out of his way for the rest of the evening, spending her time with her parents and Hugh's family.

And as for that weird prickle of awareness just now—well, that was just how weddings made everyone feel. Especially a glitzy wedding like this one, held in the grounds and ballroom of a manor house that had been in Hugh's family for generations. Yet behind the glamour was a warm-hearted, loving family who adored Grace's bubbly, slightly unconventional baby sister for who she was. And Grace had seen Roland hugging Bella earlier—with a proper smile on his face—so clearly he liked Grace's sister.

But this taciturn, slightly forbidding man clearly wasn't going to extend that warmth to Grace. And she absolutely refused to let it get to her. Why should his opinion of her matter? She didn't know anything about him, other than that he was Hugh's other best friend from school and was a sleeping partner in Hugh's record label. But, even if Roland was single, he was the last man Grace would even consider dating. She wasn't going to repeat her mistake with Howard. The next man she dated would be one who made her heart skip a beat and who'd sweep her off her feet. Someone who'd make her feel good about herself.

Which meant absolutely not Roland whatever-his-name-was.

Even if he was one of the most good-looking men she'd ever met.

CHAPTER ONE

Two days later

YET AGAIN GRACE missed Bella. Her little sister was the person she most wanted to call and talk to about her job interview today. But Bella was in San Francisco right now with Hugh and, even without having to take into account the eight-hour time difference, Grace had no intention of interrupting her baby sister's honeymoon. She'd wait for Bella's daily 'postcard' text, and casually mention in her reply that she thought the interview had gone OK. And hopefully later in the week she'd be able to report good news.

Please let her have got the job.

Temping was fine, but Grace knew that she functioned at her best with a solid structure in her life, and when she was able to plan more than just a couple of days ahead. The last couple of months, since she'd called off her own wedding, had changed her entire life. Not only had her relationship ended, she'd lost her job and her home because of it, too.

Bella was the bubbly one who coped just fine with change and seizing the day, always living life to the full; whereas Grace was more cautious, weighing things up and doing the sensible thing every single time. Even though calling off the wedding had been the right thing to do, it had caused her a huge amount of heartache and guilt. Bella had stood by her, as had their parents. But Grace hated the ensuing chaos.

At least she had a flat of her own again now. She'd been let down at the last minute with the flat she'd managed to find, but Bella as usual had been a bit scatty and forgotten to give her landlord her notice on time. And it had all worked out perfectly for both of them, because the landlord had agreed to let Grace take over the lease; she was just awaiting the paperwork. So that was another little bit of her life rebuilt.

Trying to push away the thought that she wasn't adjusting terribly well to her new life so far, Grace opened the front door of the house that had been converted into three flats—and saw with horror that the hallway was an inch deep in water. *Water that was coming from underneath her front door.*

OK. Forget the panic and work with your common sense, the way you always do, she told herself. Turn off the water supply at the mains to stop any more water gushing out from wherever the leak is, turn off the electricity to avoid any problems there, run the taps to make sure the system drains fully, and *then* find out where the leak is coming from and call the landlord to organise a plumber.

Fortified now she had a plan to work to, Grace opened the flat's front door to find water everywhere. The carpet was soaked through and she could see from the change in the colour of the material that the water was soaking its way up into the sofa, too. What a *mess*. She took a deep breath, took off her shoes, and put them on the kitchen table along with her handbag and briefcase so they'd be out of the way of the water.

Stopcock. Where would the stopcock be? The house had been converted into flats, so there was only a fifty-fifty chance that the stopcock would be inside her flat. But, to her relief, when she opened the cupboard under the sink in the hope that it was the most likely place to find the stopcock, the little wheel on the water pipe was clearly visible. She turned it off. Another switch dealt with the electricity supply, and when she went into the bathroom to turn on the taps to drain the system she could see the problem immediately: water was gushing through a burst pipe underneath the sink.

She grabbed the washing up bowl from the kitchen sink and put it there to catch the water that was still gushing from the burst pipe, then turned on the taps in the bath so the system would start to drain.

Those were the most important things. Now to call the landlord—and she really hoped that he'd be able to send an emergency plumber out to fix the pipe tonight. Though, even when the pipe was fixed and the water supply was back on, Grace knew that she was still going to have to find somewhere else to sleep tonight, because the flat was too badly flooded to be habitable. She'd also have to find somewhere to store all her stuff.

Although part of her wanted to burst into tears of sheer frustration and anger and misery, she knew that crying wasn't going to solve anything. She needed to stick with the practical stuff. Once she'd sorted that out, she could start weeping. But absolutely not until then.

There was a note in Bella's handwriting underneath a magnet on the door of the fridge, with a telephone number and the words, *Call if any problems.* Obviously this was the landlord's number; Grace was truly grateful that for once her little sister had been organised, despite spending the last three weeks knee-deep in plans for her whirlwind wedding to Hugh. Grace grabbed her mobile phone from her bag and called the number on the note.

Roland didn't recognise the number on his phone's screen, so he let the call go through to voicemail. A cold caller would give up as soon as Roland's recorded message started playing, and anyone who really wanted to talk to him could leave a message and he'd return the call when he had time.

There was an audible sigh on the answering machine. 'Hello. This is Grace Faraday.'

Bella's sister? Roland frowned. Why on earth would she be calling him?

'Please call me back urgently.' She said her telephone number slowly and clearly. 'If I haven't heard from you within thirty minutes, I'll call an emergency plumber and assume that you'll pick up the bill.'

Why did she need an emergency plumber? And why on earth did she think that *he'd* pay for the cost?

Intending to suggest that she called her landlord or her insurance company instead, he picked up the phone. 'Roland Devereux speaking.'

There was a stunned silence for a moment. 'Roland? As in Hugh's other best man Roland?' she asked.

'Yes.'

'Um, right—if you didn't catch the message I was in the middle of leaving, it's Bella's sister Grace. There's a flood at the flat and I need an emergency plumber.' Her voice took on a slightly haughty tone. 'I assume that you, as the landlord, have a list of tradesmen you use.'

So *that* was why she thought he'd pay the bill for an emergency plumber. 'I'm not the landlord.'

'Ah. Sorry.' The haughtiness disappeared, and there was the slightest wobble in her voice. 'I don't suppose you know the landlord's contact details?'

Why on earth would he know something like that? 'No.'

'OK. Never mind.'

And there it was.

The tiniest sob. Muffled quickly, but he heard it.

It brought back all the memories of Lynette. Her heart-wrenching sobs every single month they'd failed to make a baby. The guilt about how badly he'd let her down and how he'd failed her at the last.

Plus Grace was his best friend's sister-in-law. If Roland's sister had called Hugh for help, Hugh would've come straight to Philly's rescue. So Roland knew he had to do the right thing.

'I'm sorry to have bother—' she began.

'Grace. How bad is the flood?' he cut in.

'You've just told me you're not the landlord, so don't worry about it.'

He winced, but he knew that he deserved the slightly acidic tone in her voice. But there was one thing that was bothering him. 'Where did you get my number?'

'Bella left me a note on the fridge—a phone number for emergencies.' She sighed. 'Again, I apologise. I assumed it was the landlord's number. Obviously I was wrong.'

That didn't matter right now. He was focused on the flood. 'Have you turned off the water?'

'Yes. I'm not an airhead,' she said drily. 'I also turned off the electricity supply to prevent any problems there, and I'm currently draining the system to try and stop any more water coming through. I need a plumber to fix the burst pipe, and I also need to tell the people in the flats upstairs, in case the problem in my flat has affected their water supply, too.'

He was surprised that Grace sounded so capable and so organised. It didn't fit with what he'd been told about her. But she'd said there was a burst pipe, and clearly she didn't have a number to call for help—apart from his, which Bella had left her in case of emergencies. He could hardly just hang up and leave her to it. 'What's the address?' he asked abruptly.

'Why?'

'Because you just called me for help,' he said.

'Mistakenly,' she said crisply. 'For which I apologise. Yet again.'

'Bella obviously left you my number in case of emergencies—and a burst pipe counts as an emergency.' Although Bella had forgotten to tell him she'd given Grace his number, that wasn't Grace's fault. 'Where are you?'

'Bella's flat.'

'I don't actually know the address,' Roland explained.

'Oh. Right.' Sounding slightly reluctant, she told him the address.

'OK. I'm on my way.'

'Are you a plumber or something?'

'No, but I know a good one. I'll call him on the way and have him on standby in case you can't get hold of the landlord.'

'Thank you,' Grace said. 'I appreciate this.'

Roland called his plumber from the car, warning him that it was possibly a storm in a teacup but asking him to stay on standby. But, when he turned up at the flat, he discovered that Grace had been underplaying the situation, if anything. The water had clearly been gushing for a while and the carpets were soaked through; they'd need to be taken up and probably replaced. The sofa also needed to be moved, because water was seeping into it. And he felt another twinge of guilt as he noticed that Grace looked as if she'd been crying. Although she was clearly trying to be brave, this had obviously upset her.

'Did you manage to get in touch with the landlord?' he asked.

She shook her head. 'His details are probably somewhere in Bella's shoebox—but I'm not blaming her, because I should've checked everything properly myself before she and Hugh left. I live here now, so it's my responsibility.'

'Shoebox?' he asked, mystified.

'Bella's not really one for filing,' Grace explained. 'She has a shoebox system. Business receipts go in one shoebox, household stuff in another, and you just rummage through the shoeboxes when you want something.'

'That sounds a bit chaotic.' And it was definitely not the way Roland would do things. It wasted way too much time.

Grace shrugged. 'At least she has the shoeboxes now. It took a bit of nagging to get her that far.'

What? This didn't fit, at all. Wasn't Grace the drunken, princessy one? And yet right now she was wearing a sober grey suit and white shirt; plus that looked like a proper briefcase on the kitchen table, along with a pair of sensible black shoes and an equally sensible-looking handbag. Her nails weren't professionally manicured, her dark hair was cut simply in a long bob rather than being in a fussy high-maintenance style like the one she'd had at the wedding, and her make-up was minimal.

Maybe he'd got her totally wrong. More guilt flooded through him.

'The neighbours aren't home yet, so I've left a note on their doors to tell them what's happened,' she said. 'And I really need to find the landlord's details and check the insurance.'

Again, there was that tiny wobble in her voice.

'Are you OK?' he asked, hoping that she wasn't going to start crying.

'I've had better days.' She lifted her chin. 'And worse, for that matter. I'll live. Sorry. I would offer you a cup of tea but, as I don't have water or electricity right now...' She shrugged. 'I'm afraid I can't.'

'It's not a problem,' Roland said. 'My plumber's on standby, so I'll call him again to get him up to speed with the situation—and we need to shift that sofa in a minute before it soaks up any more water, to try and minimise the damage.'

'And the bookcase. And the bed. And...' She blew out a breath. 'It's just as well my car's a hatchback. I'm going to have to move everything I can out of here until this place dries out. And find somewhere for storage—though, as all my friends have flats just as tiny as this and none of them have a garage I can borrow, even temporarily. It's probably going to have to be one of those lock-up storage places.'

'Give me a moment.' Roland went outside and made a swift call to his plumber and then to one of the restoration specialist firms he'd used in the past. He also remembered seeing a café on the corner as he'd driven here; he made an executive decision to grab two takeaway black coffees, packets of sugar and two chocolate brownies. It would give them both enough energy to get through to the next stage. And if she didn't drink coffee—well, now would be a good time to start.

Grace had talked about finding a lock-up place to store the stuff from the flat. At this time of the evening, she'd be lucky to find somewhere to sort it out. And he had more than enough space to store her stuff. Even though part of him didn't really want to get involved, part of him knew that if something like this had happened to his sister, he'd want someone looking out for her. Grace was his best friend's sister-in-law. So that kind of made him responsible, didn't it?

On the way back to her flat, he called one of his team and asked him to bring a van.

She was already loading things into the back of her car when he got there.

'Coffee,' he said, and handed her one of the paper cups. 'I didn't know if you took milk or sugar, so I got it black and there are packets of sugar.'

'Thank you. How much do I owe you?' she asked.

He shook his head. 'It's fine. And I have a van on the way. Do you have some bags, boxes or suitcases I can start filling?'

'A van?' she asked, looking puzzled.

'The flat's small, but we're not going to be able to fit its entire contents into your car and mine,' he pointed out.

'So you hired a van?' Her eyes widened. 'Actually, that makes a lot of sense. I should've thought of that. Thank you. Obviously I'll reimburse you for whatever you've paid out.'

'There's no need—it's my van,' he said.

She frowned. 'But this isn't your mess, so why…?'

'Because you're Hugh's sister-in-law,' he said. 'If this had happened to my sister when I was out of the country, Hugh and Tarq would've looked out for her. So I'm doing the same, by extension.'

'Considering that you and I didn't exactly hit it off at the wedding,' she said, 'this is really nice of you. And I appreciate it. Thank you.'

Roland was beginning to think that he'd seriously misjudged Grace. If she'd been the spoiled, princessy drunk he'd thought she was, she would've been wailing and expecting everyone else to sort out the mess for her—most probably while she swigged a glass of wine and wandered about doing nothing. Instead, while he'd been away, she'd been quietly and efficiently getting on with moving stuff out of the flat. Not liking the guilt that was beginning to seep through him, he handed her a brownie. 'Chocolate. My sister says it makes everything better.'

Then she smiled—the first real smile he'd seen from her—and he was shocked to discover that it made the street feel as if it had just lit up.

'Your sister sounds like a wise woman.'

'She is.'

Roland Devereux was the last person Grace had expected to come to her rescue, but she really appreciated the fact that he had. And today he was very different from the way he'd been at the wedding. This time, he didn't make her feel the way that Howard's mother always made her feel. He treated her like a human being instead of something nasty stuck to the bottom of his shoe.

Fortified by the coffee and the brownies, between them they had most of Grace's things outside in boxes and bags by the time Roland's van arrived. And in the meantime, Grace's neighbours had returned, offering sympathy when they saw the mess and thankfully finding the landlord's number for her.

She called the landlord, but there was no answer, so she left a message explaining what had happened and giving him her mobile number, and continued moving stuff out of the flat.

Roland's plumber arrived and took a look at the burst pipe.

'It's very old piping around here,' he said. 'The system probably got blocked somewhere along the line, and this pipe had a weaker joint that couldn't cope with the extra pressure.'

'So it wasn't anything I did wrong?' Grace asked.

'No, love—it was just one of those things. I can do a temporary repair now, and then sort it out properly tomorrow.'

She nodded. 'Thank you. Let me have an invoice and I'll pay you straight away.'

'No need—the boss is covering it.'

'The boss?' she asked, mystified.

'Roland,' the plumber explained.

What? But it shouldn't be Roland's bill. OK. Right now she didn't have time for a discussion. She'd sort it out with him later.

She'd just left the plumber when a restoration specialist turned up and introduced himself. He took photographs of everything, and asked her to hold a metal ruler against the wall to show the depth of the water. 'For the insurance,' he explained. And then he brought a machine from his van to start sucking up the water.

'I really appreciate everything you've done to help me,' Grace said to Roland. 'Just one more thing—do you happen to know the number of a good lock-up place as well?'

He shrugged. 'There's no need. You can store your things at my place.'

She blinked. 'But you don't know me. You only met me once before today. For all you know, I could be a thief or a fraudster.'

He shrugged again. 'You're my best friend's sister-in-law—that's good enough for me.' He paused. 'You really can't stay at the flat until it's dried out properly.'

'I know.' She grimaced. 'Hopefully I can persuade one of my friends to let me crash on their floor tonight, then I'll find a hotel or something to put me up until the flat's usable again.'

It was a sensible enough plan, and if Roland agreed with her he wouldn't have to get involved.

But something in her expression made him say, 'I have a spare room.'

She shook her head. 'Thank you, but I've already imposed on you far too much.'

'It's getting late,' he said, 'plus your stuff's all in the back of your car, my car, and the van. You can't do anything else here until the landlord calls you back and the insurance assessors turn up—which won't be until at least tomorrow. And you said yourself that none of your friends have the room to put you up, let alone store your stuff as well. So come and stay with me.'

'That's—that's really kind of you.'

He could see her blinking back the tears and lifted his hands in a 'stop' gesture. 'Don't cry. Please.' He didn't cope well with tears. He never had. Which had been half the problem in that last year with Lynette. He'd backed away when he shouldn't have done. And she'd paid the ultimate price.

Grace swallowed back the threatening tears and scrubbed at her eyes with the back of her hand. 'OK. No more tears, I promise. But thank you. I owe you.'

CHAPTER TWO

ONCE THE RESTORATION man had finished getting rid of the worst of the water and Grace had locked the flat, she programmed Roland's address into her satnav in case she got stuck in traffic and lost both him and the van on the way, then followed him back to his house—which turned out to be in a swish part of Docklands. Once she'd parked behind his car, outside what looked like a development of an old maltings, Roland and the van driver helped her transfer her things from their cars and the van to his garage.

'Everything will be safe here for tonight,' he said when they'd finished.

'And dry,' Grace added. 'Thank you.'

There was a row of shops on the ground floor of the building, and Grace assumed that Roland had a flat on one of the upper floors; to her surprise, she discovered that his house was at one end of the building. And when he showed her into the townhouse itself, she saw that the entire back of the house was a glass box extension. It was incredibly modern, but at the same time it didn't feel out of place—and the views over the river were utterly amazing.

'This place is incredible,' she said.

He looked pleased. 'I like it.'

'But—' she gestured to the floor-to-ceiling windows '—no curtains? Don't you worry about people peering in?'

'I have a little bit of trickery instead. It's much cleaner, design-wise. And I loathe frills and flounces—my idea of hell is those swags of fussy fabrics.'

And those were just the kind of thing Grace had in mind for her own dream home—a pretty little Victorian terraced house, with sprigged flowery wallpaper and curtains to match, and lots of cushions in cosy armchairs.

He flicked a switch and the glass became opaque, giving them complete privacy.

'Very clever,' she said. And although she would've preferred the kind of curtains he hated, she could understand what he liked about it. 'Did you have an architect design this for you?'

'That,' Roland said, 'would be me.'

Grace stared at him in surprise. 'You're an architect?'

He nodded. 'I designed Hugh and Tarquin's offices,' he said, 'and I had a hand in remodelling Hugh's place so it's soundproof—for the sake of his neighbours, if he gets up in the middle of the night and starts composing on the piano.'

'This is amazing.' She shook her head. 'What an idiot I am. I thought you were some sort of builder, given that you had a plumber and a van.'

He smiled. 'You weren't that far off. I'm in the building trade, and I was pretty hands-on with this place. I guess this was my prototype.'

'How do you mean, prototype?' she asked, not understanding.

'My company makes eco-prefab buildings—either extensions or even the whole house. They're all made off site, and they can be put up in a matter of days.'

'You mean, like the ones you see on TV documentaries about people building their own houses or restoring old industrial buildings and turning them into homes?' she asked.

'They've been featured on that sort of programme, yes,' he said.

'That's seriously impressive.'

He inclined his head in acknowledgement of the compliment. 'I enjoy it. Let me show you to the guest room.'

Like the rest of the rooms she'd seen so far, the bedroom was very modern, simply furnished and with little on the walls. But, with one wall being pure glass, she supposed you wouldn't need anything else to look at: not when you had a whole panorama of London life to look at. Water and people and lights and the sky.

There was a king-sized bed with the headboard set in the middle of the back wall, a soft duvet and fluffy pillows. The bed linen was all white—very high maintenance, she thought. The en-suite bathroom was gorgeous, and was about six times the size of the bathroom in Bella's flat; Grace still wasn't quite used to thinking of Bella's old place as her own flat.

She took the bare minimum from her case—it seemed pointless to unpack everything just for one night, when tomorrow she'd be moving to a hotel or whatever alternative accommodation the insurance company offered—and hung her office clothes for the next day in the wardrobe so they wouldn't be creased overnight. Just as she was about to go back downstairs in search of Roland, her phone rang; thankfully, it was the landlord, who'd spoken to the insurance company and could fill her in on what was happening next.

Roland was sitting at the kitchen table, checking his emails on his phone, when Grace walked into the kitchen, looking slightly shy.

'Can I get you a drink?' he asked.

'No, thanks. I'm fine,' she said. 'The landlord just called me. He's talked to the insurance company and they're getting a loss assessor out to see the flat—and me—tomorrow morning at eleven.'

She sounded a little unsure, he thought. 'Is getting the time off work going to be a problem for you?'

She wrinkled her nose. 'I'm temping at the moment—but if I explain the situation and make the hours up, I'm sure they'll be fine about it.'

He was surprised. 'Temping? So you're what, a PA?'

'An accountant,' she corrected.

Which made it even more surprising that she didn't have a permanent job. 'How come you're temping?'

'It's a long and boring story. It's also why I've moved into Bella's flat.' She flapped a hand dismissively. 'But it's not because I'm a criminal or anything, so you don't need to worry about that. I just made some decisions that made life a bit up in the air for me.'

He wondered what those decisions had been. But she was being cagey about it, so he decided not to push it. It was none of his business, in any case. 'You can keep your stuff here as long as you need to, so that isn't a problem.' He glanced at his watch. 'You must be hungry. I certainly am, so I was thinking of ordering us a takeaway.'

'Which I'll pay for,' she said immediately.

'Hardly. You're my guest.'

'You weren't expecting me,' she pointed out. 'And I'd feel a lot happier if you let me pay. It's the least I can do, considering how much you've done for me this evening.'

He could see that she wasn't going to budge on the issue. In her shoes, he'd feel the same way, so he decided to give in gracefully. 'OK. Thank you.'

'And I'm doing the washing up,' she added.

'There's no need. I have a housekeeping service.'

She scoffed. 'I'm still not leaving a pile of dirty dishes next to the sink.'

A princess would've taken a housekeeper for granted. Grace didn't, and she clearly wasn't playing a part. How on earth had he got her so wrong? 'We'll share the washing up,' he said, feeling guilty about the way he'd misjudged her. 'What do you like? Chinese? Pizza?'

'Anything,' she said.

So she wasn't fussy about food, either.

And, given the way she was dressed…it was almost as if she was trying to blend in to her surroundings. Minimum fuss, minimum attention.

Why would someone want to hide like that?

Not that it was any of his business. He ordered a selection of dishes from his local Chinese takeaway. 'It'll be here in twenty minutes,' he said when he put the phone down.

It felt very odd to be domesticated, Roland thought as he laid two places at the kitchen table. For nearly two years he'd eaten most of his evening meals alone, except if he'd been on business or when Hugh, Tarquin or his sister Philly had insisted on him joining them. Being here alone with Grace was strange. But he just about managed to make small talk with her until the food arrived.

His hand brushed against hers a couple of times when

they heaped their plates from the takeaway cartons, and that weird prickle of awareness he'd felt at the wedding made itself known again.

Did she feel it, too? he wondered. Because she wasn't meeting his eyes, and had bowed her head slightly so her hair covered her face. Did he fluster her, the way she flustered him?

And, if so, what were they going to do about it?

Not that he was really in a position to do anything about it. He'd told Hugh and Tarquin that he was ready to date again, but he knew he wasn't. How could he trust himself not to let a new partner down, given the way he'd let his wife down? Until he could start to forgive himself, he couldn't move on.

'Don't feel you have to entertain me,' she said when they'd finished eating and had sorted out the washing up. 'I've already taken up more than enough of your time this evening, and I don't want to be a demanding house guest. If you don't mind, I'm going to sort out Bella's shoeboxes for her so all her papers are in some sort of order.'

So Grace was the sort who liked organisation and structure. That made it even stranger that she'd call off her wedding only three weeks before the big day. There was a lot more to that story than met the eye, Roland was sure; but he didn't want to intrude on her privacy by asking.

'I'll be in my office next door if you need me. Feel free to make yourself a drink whenever you like. There are tea, coffee and hot chocolate capsules in the cupboard above the coffee machine.' He gestured to the machine sitting on the work surface.

'Thanks.' For the first time, she gave him a teasing smile. 'Now I've seen your house, I'm not surprised you have a machine like that.'

'Are you accusing me of being a gadget fiend?' he asked.

'Are you one?' she fenced back.

He grinned. 'Just a tiny bit—what about you?' The question was out before he could stop it, and he was shocked at himself. Was he actually flirting with her? He couldn't even remember the last time he'd flirted with anyone.

'I use an old-fashioned cafetière and a teapot,' she said. 'Though I might admit to having a milk-frother, because I like cappuccinos.'

Tension suddenly crackled between them. And Roland was even more shocked to find himself wondering what would happen if he closed the gap between them and brushed his mouth very lightly over Grace's.

What on earth was he doing? Apart from the fact that his head was still in an emotional mess, Grace was the last person he should think about kissing. He'd just rescued her from a burst pipe situation. She was as vulnerable as Lyn had been. He needed to back off. Now. 'See you later,' he said, affecting a cool he most definitely didn't feel, and sauntered into his office.

Though even at the safety of his desk he found it hard to concentrate on his work. Instead of opening the file for his current project, he found himself thinking of a quiet, dark-haired woman with the most amazing cornflower-blue eyes—and he was cross with himself because he didn't want to think about her in that way. Right now he couldn't offer a relationship to anyone. Who knew when he'd be ready to date again—if ever.

Grace sorted through the contents of Bella's shoeboxes at Roland's kitchen table, putting everything in neat piles so she could file them away properly in a binder. She tried to focus on what she was doing, but the mundane task wasn't occupying anywhere near enough of her head for her liking. It left way too much space for her to think about the man who'd unexpectedly come to her rescue.

And now she was seeing Roland Devereux in a whole new light. He'd been cold and taciturn when she'd first met him. She would never have believed that he was a man with vision. A man who could create such a stunning modern design, which somehow didn't feel out of place in its very traditional setting; he'd merged the old and the new perfectly to get the best of both worlds.

She couldn't resist taking a swift break and looking him up on the Internet. And she liked what she saw on his company website, especially the way they paid attention to detail. Although the houses they built were prefabricated, the designs didn't feel as if they were identikit; from the gallery of pictures of the finished houses, Grace could see that Roland's company had added touches to each one to make it personal to the families who'd wanted to build them. And not only was he great at design, he'd worked with conservation officers on several projects. One in particular involved an eco extension that had enhanced the old building it was part of, rather than marring it, and he'd won an award for it.

There was much more to Roland Devereux than met the eye.

And she had to push away the memory of that moment when he'd flirted with her in the kitchen. Right now, her life was too chaotic for her to consider adding any kind of relationship to the mix. And, although Roland seemed to live alone, for all she knew he could already be committed elsewhere.

So she'd just put this evening down to the kindness of a stranger, and consider herself lucky that her brother-in-law had such a good friend.

Roland had already left for the day when Grace got up the next morning, even though she'd planned to be at her desk by eight. He'd left her his spare door key along with a note on the table asking her to set the house alarm, giving her the code. He'd added, *Call me if any problems.*

She texted him to say that she'd set the alarm and thanked him for the loan of his key, then headed for the office. At work, she explained the situation to her boss, who was kind enough to let her reorganise her work schedule so she could meet the loss assessor at the flat.

But the news from the loss assessor wasn't good. It would take a couple of weeks to dry out the flat, even with dehumidifiers, and there was a chance they might need to take all the plaster off the walls to stop mould developing, and then re-plaster the walls. Which in turn would take time to dry. And the landlord would probably have to look into replacing the plumbing completely in the very near future. And that meant even more disruption.

How could a burst pipe cause so much chaos?

And she could hardly invite herself to stay with Roland for an unforeseeable amount of time. Her parents lived too far out of London for her to be able to commute from their place, and she knew her friends didn't have the room to put her up, so she'd just have to find a room in a budget hotel. Hopefully Roland wouldn't mind her leaving her stuff in his garage for another day or so until she could organise storage.

She called in to a specialist wine shop to buy a thank-you gift for him on her way back to the office, then worked through her lunch hour and left late that evening to make up the time she'd had to take out to meet the assessor. When she returned to the house in Docklands, Roland was in the kitchen, making himself a coffee.

'Hi. Coffee?' he asked, gesturing to the machine.

'Thanks, but I'm fine. Oh, and I got this for you.'

She handed him the bottle bag, and he blinked in surprise. 'What's this?'

'To say thank you,' she said. 'I have no idea if you prefer red or white wine, so I played it safe and bought white.'

'That's very kind of you,' he said.

But she noticed that he hadn't even opened the bag to look at the wine. 'Sorry. Obviously I should've gone for red.'

'Actually, I don't drink,' he said.

Grace wished the ground would open up and swallow her. 'I'm so sorry.' And she wasn't going to ask him why. It was none of her business.

'You weren't to know.' He opened the bag and looked at the label. 'Montrachet is lovely. I know a certain woman who will love you to bits for bringing this.'

His girlfriend? Grace squashed the seeping disappointment. So not appropriate. And it raised another issue. 'I hope your girlfriend doesn't mind me staying.'

'No girlfriend. I was talking about my little sister,' Roland said. 'Just because I don't drink, it doesn't mean that I make everyone else stick to water.'

And the little rush of pleasure at discovering he was single was even more inappropriate. 'Uh-huh,' she said, knowing she sounded awkward, and wishing yet again that she could be as open and spontaneous as her sister.

'So how did it go with the loss assessor?' he asked.

'Not great.' She told him what the loss assessor had said. 'So if you don't mind me staying here again tonight, I'll sort out a hotel room for tomorrow night onwards. I'll find a storage place, and it shouldn't take me too many trips to ferry all my stuff there.'

'Why go to all that trouble when I've already said you can stay in my spare room and store your stuff here?' he asked.

'Because I can't impose on you for an open-ended amount of time,' she explained. 'I know you're my brother-in-law's best friend, but this is way beyond the call of duty, and I'd rather stand on my own two feet.'

'Noted,' he said, 'but you said yesterday that you'd made some choices that made life a bit up in the air for you. I think we all have times like that, when we could maybe use a friend.'

'You're offering to be my friend?'

He looked at her, his dark eyes full of questions, and suddenly there didn't seem to be enough air in the room.

Was he offering her friendship...or something else? She didn't trust her judgement to read the situation properly.

And then Roland said, 'Yes, I think I'm offering to be your friend.'

'But we don't know each other,' she pointed out.

'I know, and I admit I took you the wrong way when I first met you.'

She frowned. 'Meaning?'

He winced. 'Meaning that I've been a bit judgemental and I can see for myself that you're not what I thought you were.'

'You're digging yourself a hole here.'

'Tell me about it,' he said wryly. 'And I'm sorry.'

'So what did you think I was?' she asked.

'Are you sure you want to hear this?'

No, but she'd gone far enough to have to keep up the bravado. 'I wouldn't have asked otherwise.'

'OK. I thought of you as the Runaway Bride,' he said.

He'd thought *what*? Obviously he knew that she'd cancelled her wedding quite late in the day—but he'd assumed that she was some kind of spoiled brat? She narrowed her eyes at him. 'You're right, that's judgemental and that's not who I am—and, for your information, I didn't leave my fiancé at the aisle or even close to it. In fact, I hadn't even bought a wedding dress.'

It was his turn to frown. 'But Hugh said you cancelled the wedding three weeks beforehand. And I've seen by the way you've dealt with the flood that you're organised. This doesn't add up. Why didn't you have a wedding dress that close to the big day?'

'It's a long and very boring story,' she said.

'I don't have anything better to do—do you?' he asked.

She blew out a breath. 'Maybe, maybe not. And I guess if I'm going to stay with you, you probably need to know why my life's a bit chaotic.'

'Let's talk over pizza,' he said, 'and maybe a glass of wine. We could open this bottle now.'

'You just told me you didn't drink.'

'I also told you I don't make everyone else around me stick to water.'

'I don't actually drink that much,' she admitted.

He looked at her. 'But the first time you met Hugh…'

Oh, no. Well, he was Hugh's best friend. Of course he'd know about what happened. 'I threw up over Hugh because I'd drunk three glasses of champagne on an empty stomach. Which is more than I would usually drink in a month.' Shame flooded through her at the memory. 'Does *everyone* know about that?'

'Tarq and I do.'

'Tarquin never mentioned it when he met me.'

He gave her a wry smile. 'Probably because Tarq's nicer than I am.'

'I'm reserving the right to stay silent.' Because Roland had come to her rescue, and he was offering her a place to stay. But she was still annoyed that he'd thought so badly of her without even waiting to hear her side of the story. Maybe she'd been right in her first impression of him, too, and he was firmly in the same box as Cynthia Sutton: cold, judgemental and obsessed by appearances.

He raised his eyebrows. 'Isn't the rest of that speech along the lines that if you want to rely on something later in court, you have to speak now?'

'Am I on trial?' she asked.

'Of course not.' He shook his head. 'Pizza it is, then. And mineral water.'

'Provided I pay for the pizza. I don't want you thinking I'm a freeloader as well as being the Runaway Bride and a lush to boot.'

The slight colour staining his cheeks told her that was exactly what he'd thought of her. Which was totally unfair—he'd jumped to conclusions without even knowing her. If it wasn't for the fact that he'd come to her rescue last night and been kind, right at that moment she would've disliked him even more than she had at the wedding.

'I know now that you're none of those things. And you insisted on paying last night, so this is on me,' he said.

'If you buy the pizza,' she said, still cross that he

thought she was one of life's takers, 'then I want an invoice for the use of your van yesterday.'

'How about,' he suggested, 'we go halves on the pizza?'

She folded her arms. 'I'd prefer to pay.'

He met her glare head-on. 'Halves or starve. That's the choice.'

And how tempted she was to choose the latter. On principle. Except she was really, really hungry and it was pointless spiting herself. 'OK. Halves. But I do the washing up. And, tomorrow, I cook for us.'

'You can cook?' He looked taken aback.

She could guess why. 'I love my little sister to bits,' she said, 'but Bella's a bit of a disaster in the kitchen. If she's cooked for you, then I understand why you're surprised—but her culinary skills don't run in the family.'

'She hasn't cooked for me. But Hugh told me how bad her stir-fry is,' he admitted.

'In her defence, she does make great pancakes and cupcakes.'

He smiled. 'But you can't live on pancakes and cupcakes alone.'

'Exactly. Is there anything you don't eat, or do you have any food intolerances or allergies?'

'No—and you can use anything you like in the kitchen.'

'I'm glad you said that, because your kitchen is gorgeous and it'll be a pleasure to cook here.' She gestured round. 'So do I take it that you're a cook, too, or is this just for show?'

Roland thought back to the times when he and Lynette had cooked together. Never in this kitchen—he'd still been renovating the place when the drunk driver had smashed into his wife's car. And he hadn't had the heart to cook since. Most of the time he lived on sandwiches, takeaways or microwaved supermarket meals; apart from when his family and his best friends insisted on seeing him, he filled the time with work, work and more work, so he didn't have the space to think. 'I don't cook much nowadays,' he said.

'Fair enough.' To his relief, she didn't pry.

'But if you can text me and let me know what time you want to eat tomorrow,' she added, 'that would be helpful.'

'I'll do that,' he said. Though it felt weirdly domestic, and it made him antsy enough not to press Grace about the reason why she'd moved to Bella's flat—just in case she expected him to share about his past, too. The last thing he wanted was for her to start pitying him—the poor widower who'd lost his wife tragically young. Especially because he didn't deserve the pity. He hadn't taken enough care of Lyn, and he'd never forgive himself for that.

Grace's phone pinged. 'I'm expecting something. Can I be rude and check my phone?' she asked.

'Be my guest.'

She glanced at the screen and smiled. 'Oh, I like this. Today's Bellagram is the Golden Gate Bridge,' she said, showing him the photograph of Bella and Hugh posing with the iconic bridge behind them.

'Bellagram?' Roland asked, not quite understanding.

'Postcard. Telegram—the modern version,' Grace explained. 'Bella likes puns.'

'She texts you every day?'

Grace nodded. 'We always text each other if we're away, sending a photo of what we've been doing. Bella forgot about the time difference for the first one, so it woke me at three in the morning.' She laughed. 'But that's Bella for you. It's great to know they're having a good time.'

'Have you told her about…?'

'The flood? No. I don't want her worrying. I just text her back to say I'm glad she's having fun and I love her,' Grace said.

Which was pretty much what his own family had done when he and Lyn had sent a couple of brief texts from the rainforest on their honeymoon, purely to stop everyone at home worrying that they'd got lost or been eaten by piranhas. Another surge of guilt flooded through him. He'd taken care of Lyn then. Where had it all gone so wrong?

He was glad when Grace was tactful enough to switch the subject to something neutral and kept the conversation easy.

Though later that evening Roland still couldn't get her out of his head. He lay awake, watching the sky through the glass ceiling of his bedroom—a ceiling that wasn't overlooked by anyone or anything—and thinking of her.

What was it about Grace Faraday?

He'd misjudged her completely. Far from being a spoiled, princessy drunk, Grace was a capable and quietly organised woman with good manners. She was a little bit shy, very independent, and *nice*. Easy to be with.

Which was why he probably ought to find somewhere else for her to stay. Grace Faraday was dangerous to his peace of mind. She was the first woman in a long time to intrigue him. Or attract him. And for someone like her to call off a wedding only three weeks before the ceremony… Something had to have been very wrong indeed. Even though it was none of his business, he couldn't help wondering. Had she discovered some really serious character flaw in her husband-to-be?

She'd been going to tell him about it, and then they'd been sidetracked. Maybe she'd tell him tomorrow.

And maybe that would be the thing to keep his common sense in place and stop him doing something stupid.

Like acting on the strong pull he felt towards her and actually kissing her.

CHAPTER THREE

THE FOLLOWING EVENING, Roland opened his front door and stopped dead. It was strange to smell dinner cooking; he could definitely smell lemons, and possibly fish.

Then he realised he could also hear music; clearly Grace had connected her MP3 player to his speakers in the kitchen. Odd; he'd half expected her to like very formal classical music, but right now she was playing vintage feel-good pop songs. And she was singing along. He smiled as she launched into 'Build Me Up, Buttercup', ever so slightly out of key.

But were the song lyrics a warning to him that she didn't want her heart broken? Not that he should be thinking about a relationship with her anyway. His smile faded as he went into the kitchen. 'Good evening, Grace.'

'Oh! Roland. Hello.' She looked up from whatever she was doing and smiled at him, and to his shock his heart felt as if it had done a somersault.

When had he last reacted to someone like this?

Then her face went bright red as she clearly thought about what she'd been doing when he'd opened his front door. 'Um—I apologise for the singing. I'm afraid I can't hold a tune.'

'That's not a problem,' he reassured her. 'You can

sing in the kitchen if you like—though actually I had you pegged for a classical music fiend.'

'The boring accountant who likes boring stuff?' she asked with a wry smile.

'Not all classical music is boring. Have you ever heard Hugh play Bach on the piano? It's amazing stuff.'

'No—and, actually, I do like classical music. Not the super-heavy operatic stuff, though,' she said. 'I've always wanted to go to one of those evenings where they play popular classical music to a background of fireworks.' She paused. 'Not that you want to be bored by my bucket list. Dinner will be about another ten minutes.'

Why did Grace think she was boring? Though Roland wasn't sure how to ask her, because she seemed to have gone back into her shell. Clearly she was used to being the shy, quiet older sister, while Bella was the bubbly one. He fell back on a polite, 'Something smells nice.'

'Thank you. I wasn't sure if you'd prefer to eat in the dining room or the kitchen, so I guessed that here would be OK—though I can move it if you like.' She gestured to the kitchen table by the glass wall, which she'd set for two.

It was definitely less intimate than his dining room would be, he thought with relief. He wasn't sure if he could handle being in intimate surroundings with her, at least not until he'd got these weird, wayward feelings under control. 'The kitchen's fine,' he said. 'Is there anything I can do to help?'

'Everything's pretty much done,' she said. 'Can I get you a coffee or something?'

'It's fine. I'll make it,' he said. 'Do you want one?'

'That'd be nice.' She smiled at him and went back

to scooping the flesh and seeds out of passion fruit. 'Thank you.'

This felt dangerously domesticated, working in the kitchen alongside her. Roland made the coffee in near silence, partly because he didn't have a clue what to say to Grace. His social skills outside work had really atrophied. Right now, he felt as gauche as a schoolboy.

'How was your day?' she asked.

'Fine. How was yours?'

'As exciting as any temporary accountancy job can be,' she said with a smile.

'Are you looking for something permanent?'

She went still. 'Roland, if you're just about to offer me a job out of pity, please don't. I'm perfectly capable of finding myself a job.'

'Actually, I don't have anything right now that would match your skill set,' he said. 'But if I did and I offered you an interview, then I'd expect you to be better than any of the other candidates before I offered you the job.'

'Good,' she said. 'And I guess it was a bit previous of me to jump to the conclusion that you were going to offer me a job—but you've already rescued me this week and...' Her voice trailed off and she looked awkward. 'Sorry.'

'And sometimes rescuers don't know when to stop and let someone stand on their own two feet. I get it,' he said. 'And no offence taken.'

'Thank you. Actually, I did have a job interview the other day. And I think it went well.' She wrinkled her nose. 'But then I came home to find myself flooded out, so I haven't really thought about it since then.' She shrugged. 'I probably haven't got the job, or I would've heard by now.'

'That depends on how many they're interviewing,' Roland said.

'I guess.' She brought a jug of what looked like sparkling elderflower cordial over to the table, and then two plates. 'I thought we could have fig, mozzarella and prosciutto skewers to start.'

'Impressive,' he said.

She laughed. 'There's nothing impressive about threading things onto skewers.'

'It's nicely presented, anyway.' He took a taste. 'And it's a good combination.'

She inclined her head in acknowledgement of the compliment. 'Thank you.'

The citrus-glazed baked salmon with sweet potato wedges, caramelised lemons, spinach and baby carrots was even nicer. 'Now this you did have to cook. Don't tell me this isn't impressive.'

'Again, it's much simpler than it looks. I was kind of guinea-pigging you,' she confessed.

'Guinea-pigging?'

'I'm going to teach Bel to cook,' she said. 'So the food needs to look pretty—but it also has to take minimum effort and not involve planning the cooking time for more than two things at once.'

He smiled at her. 'You're obviously a foodie—so why are you an accountant rather than, say, running your own restaurant?'

Because numbers were safe.

Though Grace didn't quite want to admit that. 'I was good at maths when I was at school, and accountancy has good employment prospects,' she said. 'Plus that way I could study for my qualifications in the evenings while I earned money, rather than ending up with a pile of student debt. It made sense to choose accountancy as my career.' And that was who she was. The sensible, quiet older sister who was good at sorting things out.

'Do you enjoy your job?'

She smiled. 'Bella always groans and says she doesn't get why, but actually I do—I like the patterns in numbers, and the way everything works out neatly.' She paused. 'What about you? Why did you become an architect?'

'Because I love buildings,' he said simply. 'Everything from the simplest rural cottage through to grand Rococo palaces.'

She looked at him. 'I can imagine you living in a grand Rococo palace.'

He smiled. 'They're not all they're cracked up to be. They're very cold in winter.'

She blinked. 'So you've stayed in one?'

'The French side of the family owns a chateau or two,' he admitted.

She felt her eyes widen. 'Your family owns *castles*?' Roland had a posh accent, but she hadn't realised just how posh he was. Way, way outside her own social circle.

'Chateaux tend to go hand in hand with vineyards, and our French family produces wine,' he said. 'Christmas in France when I was young was always magical, because there was always the most enormous Christmas tree with a silver star on the top, and there were roaring open fires where you could roast chestnuts and toast crumpets.'

Now she knew he was teasing her. 'Since when do they eat crumpets in France?'

He spread his hands. 'What can I say? We tend to mix the traditions a bit in my family, so we get the best of both worlds. But, seriously, that was probably where the architecture stuff started. Apart from the fact that I liked the lines and the shapes of the buildings and I was always drawing them as a boy, waking up in a freezing cold bedroom with ice on the inside of the windows made me think about how it could be made better. How we could have all the modern conveniences we were used to in London, but without damaging the heritage side of the building.'

'And that's how come you're so good at mixing the old and the new,' she said. 'The front of your house is an old maltings, but the back half is as modern as it gets.'

'All the new stuff is eco,' he said, 'and all the old building is maintained properly.' He shrugged. 'Perhaps I'm greedy, but I like having the best of both worlds. All the comfort and convenience of the modern stuff, and the sheer beauty of the old.'

She smiled and brought over dessert—passion fruit cream with almond *cantuccini*.

'This is seriously nice,' he said.

'Thank you.'

When they'd finished eating, he made them some more coffee.

'You were going to tell me yesterday,' he said, 'why your life got turned upside down. It's a bit unexpected for someone who likes order and structure to make a decision that makes everything messy.'

This time, he didn't sound judgemental, and Grace felt comfortable enough with him to tell him. 'I don't like myself very much for what I did. I know I hurt Howard and I feel bad about that.' She grimaced. 'But if I'd married him it would've been so much worse.'

'For what it's worth,' he said, 'I've already worked out that you're not a spoiled princess. Not even close. So that must've been a serious case of cold feet.'

She nodded. 'If I'm honest, I'd been feeling that way for quite a while, but I thought I could still go through with it.'

'So what happened to change your mind?'

She took a deep breath. 'The Fifty Shades of Beige party.'

Roland almost choked on his coffee. Had he just heard right? 'The *what*?'

'Howard—my ex—it was his parents' golden wedding anniversary,' Grace explained. 'I wasn't looking forward to the party, and Bella drew me this cartoon to make me laugh. She called it "Fifty Shades of Beige".'

He smiled. 'From what Tarq says about her, I can just see Bella doing that.'

'Except the awful thing was that she was right,' Grace said. 'I was the only woman there not wearing beige.'

'And it was a problem?' he asked.

'Not for me. For… Well.' She grimaced. 'Don't get me wrong—I did love Howard. But that's when I finally realised that I wasn't in love with him.'

'And there's a difference?'

'A very big difference,' she said. 'It wasn't fair to marry him, knowing that I didn't love him enough—I didn't love him the way he deserved to be loved. I think we were each other's safe option. We were settling for each other instead of looking for what we really wanted.'

'Why did you need a safe option?' He only realised he'd spoken the question aloud when he saw her wince. 'Sorry. That was intrusive and you don't have to answer,' he said hastily.

'No, it's fine. Just don't tell Bella any of this, OK?'

He frowned. From the way Grace talked, she was clearly very close to her sister. 'Why doesn't Bella know?'

'Because,' Grace said, 'she's my little sister and I love her, and I don't want to burden her with it. Basically, my dad's really unreliable and I didn't want to be like my mum. I wanted my partner to be someone I could trust.'

Roland frowned. 'But I met Ed at the wedding—he seemed really nice and not at all unreliable.'

'Ed is utterly lovely. He's Bella's biological dad, but he's my stepdad and he adopted me after he married Mum,' Grace explained. 'I think of him as my real dad, and he's been a better father to me than my biological dad could ever have been. But the first time round my mum married a charming man who let her down over and over again. He was terrible with money and he never kept his promises. He hardly ever turned up when he'd promised to be there to see me. We've pretty much lost touch over the years. I just wanted to avoid making my mum's mistake.'

'And in the process you made your own mistake,' he said. 'Picking someone who was reliable but not right for you.'

She nodded. 'Howard's a nice man. He's kind and gentle.'

'But?'

'But he made me feel like part of the furniture, and I probably did the same to him,' she admitted. 'I never once felt swept off my feet. And I think we both secretly had doubts—after all, we were engaged for four years.'

In the twenty-first century, that was an unusually long engagement, Roland thought. 'Were you saving up for a house?'

'Avoiding it, I think, if I'm honest,' Grace said. 'We didn't even live together. And if we'd really loved each other, the wedding and everything else wouldn't have mattered—we would've been together regardless. But we weren't.' She dragged in a breath. 'The truth is, if I'd married Howard, his mother would've run our lives—right down to the tiniest detail.'

'Ah, the old cliché—the interfering mother-in-law.'

'Sadly,' Grace said drily, 'in this case Cynthia more than lived up to the cliché. She wanted us to get married on her fiftieth wedding anniversary, and she wasn't very pleased when I said that I thought she ought to be the centre of attention on her special day rather than having to share it with her son's wedding.'

So Grace was tactful and kind, too, Roland thought. Rather than throw a hissy fit at the idea of sharing her wedding day, she'd tried to make the older woman feel important.

'And,' Grace added, 'I wanted my sister to be my bridesmaid.'

Roland blinked in surprise. 'She didn't want Bella to be a bridesmaid?'

'Cynthia didn't like Bella. She said Bel was too head-strong and too quirky.'

'Bella's a free spirit, yes—and she's great,' Roland said. 'I'm beginning to dislike your almost-mother-in-law.'

'Bella didn't like Cynthia, either. She called her "Mrs Concrete Hair".'

'Because it was never out of place?' Roland had to stifle a grin.

Grace nodded. 'Cynthia prided herself on always being turned out immaculately. And she wore a lot of beige.'

'Did you like her?' he asked.

Grace wrinkled her nose. 'Do I have to answer that?'

'Yes.'

She smiled wryly. 'I think Cynthia and I didn't meet each other's expectations. I wanted a mother-in-law who's like my own mum—someone who's warm and supportive, who'd be there if I needed help, but who would always encourage me to stand on my own two feet. Someone I could be friends with and who'd make me feel part of the family.'

Roland thought of his own parents. That summed up their relationship with Lynette—and his own with Lynette's parents. He'd assumed that was completely normal, but maybe they'd both been lucky.

'And what did Cynthia want?' he asked.

Grace looked away. 'Someone who'd keep up appearances at all times and do whatever she told them to.'

'Which doesn't sound like much fun.'

'It wasn't,' Grace said, her voice so quiet that he could barely hear her. 'I hated being judged all the time, and always falling short.'

Which was what he'd done to her. No wonder she'd been so prickly with him, at first.

And now he was beginning to understand her. Grace was the quiet, sensible sister. The one who'd thought she'd wanted her partner to be completely the opposite of her unreliable father. And yet what she'd really wanted was to be swept off her feet…

An idea was forming in his head.

A really crazy idea.

But maybe it could work. Could he ask her?

Should he ask her?

'Obviously cancelling the wedding shook up your life a bit,' he said, 'but why did it mean that you became a temp and you taking over the lease of Bella's flat?'

'Because I worked for Howard's family's accountancy practice,' she said. 'I could hardly keep working there when I'd just cancelled my wedding to the boss's son. I couldn't ask them for a reference, in the circumstances, so temping was my only real option. Plus I'd already given notice to my landlord, and he'd leased my flat to someone else.'

So cancelling the wedding had cost Grace her job and her home, too. Now he understood what she meant about a decision turning her life upside down. And it was a decision she clearly hadn't made lightly.

'So what are you looking for, Grace?' he asked carefully. 'Marriage?'

'Maybe, maybe not. I've just come out of a long relationship, and I guess right now I need to find out who I am and think about what I really want.' She wrinkled her nose. 'I just wanted to be swept off my feet once in a while. Which I know isn't going to happen, because I'm very ordinary—I'm not free-spirited and brave like Bella is.'

The crazy idea suddenly seemed that little bit less crazy. Maybe Grace—quiet, sensible Grace—could help him move on, haul him out of the limbo where he'd spent two long years. 'What if you had the chance to be swept off your feet? Would you take it?' he asked.

'That's *really* not going to happen,' Grace said. 'I have friends who've joined online dating sites or gone speed-dating, and they've all ended up disappointed.'

'What if,' he asked carefully, 'the date was with someone you know?'

'Such as?'

'Me.'

'You?' She stared at him, looking shocked. 'But you don't even like me.'

'I was obnoxious to you at the wedding because I'd jumped to some very wrong conclusions about you,' Roland said. 'I've got to know you better over the last couple of days and I've realised how wrong I was. And I apologise for that.'

'Thank you. I think.' She frowned. 'You're actually suggesting that we should date?'

'That we should help each other out,' he corrected. 'You want to be swept off your feet, and I need to practise my dating skills.'

She frowned. 'Why do you need to practise your dating skills?'

Grace had been brave enough to tell him about her life. Roland guessed he owed it to her to be brave back. 'I assume Bella didn't tell you?'

'Tell me what?'

'That my wife was killed in a car accident nearly two years ago—a year before I moved in here.'

She reached across the table and took his hand briefly, squeezing it gently for just long enough to convey sympathy, then letting his hand go before the contact dissolved into pity. 'I didn't know her, and it's a horrible cliché, but I'm really sorry you had to go through losing someone you loved like that.'

'It was hard,' he said. 'And I miss Lynette. A lot.' Mostly. Apart from the one sticking point in their marriage—the thing that had made him jump at the chance to get away for a few days and be rid of all the pressure. And he still felt guilty about it, even though he knew that the accident hadn't been his fault. But part of him still felt that if he'd been here instead of a couple of thousand miles away, maybe Lynette wouldn't have gone out in the car, and she wouldn't have been hit by the drunk driver. Or, even if the accident had still happened, at least he would've been by her side when she'd died, later that night.

He pushed the thought away. 'But missing her won't bring her back—and there isn't such a thing as a time machine, so I can't go back and change the past. Though, if I could, I'd stop the other driver from guzzling her way through a bottle of wine and several cocktails and then getting behind the wheel of her car.'

Now Grace understood why Roland didn't drink—and why his house was immaculate but didn't feel quite like a home. Because he'd lost the love of his life to the selfish actions of a drunk driver. 'That's so sad,' she said.

He said nothing, but gave a small nod of acknowledgement.

'But I still don't get why you're asking *me* to help you practise your dating skills.'

He reached across the table and took her hand, then drew it up to his mouth and pressed a kiss into her palm.

And Grace tingled all over. Nobody had ever kissed her hand like that before.

'My friends,' he said, 'and my family have tried to find me someone suitable to heal my broken heart.'

'Too soon?'

'Partly,' he agreed. 'But I know Lyn wouldn't have wanted me to spend the rest of my life on my own, mourning her. She would've wanted me to share my life with someone who loves me as much as she did.'

For a moment, a shadow crossed his expression. It was gone before she could be sure it was there. Maybe she'd imagined it, because hadn't he just pretty much told her that Lynette was the love of his life? Or maybe that shadow had been grief that he was still trying to be brave about.

'So,' he said, 'I'm going to start dating again. Put my life back together. But I'm finding it hard.'

'Because you're not ready to move on?'

He dragged in a breath. 'And I'm out of practice. I need to date someone who won't mind if I make mistakes and will help me get better at dating. And you want to be swept off your feet, just for a little while. So that's why perhaps we can help each other out. For two weeks.'

'Until Bella and Hugh are back from honeymoon. And no strings?' she checked.

'No strings. We could just clear our diaries outside work for those two and a bit weeks and spend time together.'

'Like a holiday?'

'I guess,' he said.

A holiday with the best man. Part of Grace wanted to say yes; but part of her wondered just how sensible this was. Roland Devereux wasn't the surly, barely civil man she'd met at Bella's wedding. He was kind and sensitive—and this side of him was seriously attractive. But he still had a broken heart; and, even though he thought he wanted to try looking for love again, that made him vulnerable.

She knew that she was vulnerable, too. Her life was still all up in the air. She wanted to stand on her own two feet and work out what she wanted from life. And did she really want to take the risk of dating someone who wasn't going to be available and maybe falling in love with him? Or would this be the thing that changed her life and made everything right again? 'Can I have some time to think about it?' she asked.

'Of course. Maybe you could tell me your answer tomorrow?'

'All right.' Sitting here at the kitchen table with him didn't feel casual and easy any more; Grace felt hot and bothered, remembering the touch of his mouth against her skin. For the last four years—and for longer than that, if she was honest—she hadn't felt anything like this. Like a teenager about to go on her first date, with her heart pattering away and butterflies dancing a tango in her stomach. 'I'd better do the washing up,' she said, taking the coward's way out of facing him.

'I'll help.'

Which would put them at even closer range. She couldn't risk that. 'There's no need,' she said brightly.

'There's every need,' he corrected. 'It's my kitchen—and I'm not the kind to make other people do my share of the chores.'

She had no answer to that.

But, as they worked by the sink, they ended up brushing against each other. Grace tingled all over—which was ridiculous, because they were both fully clothed and, technically speaking, his shirtsleeve had touched her dress, which was nothing like his bare arm against her bare torso.

And then she really wished she hadn't thought of that, because now she was imagining what it would be like if Roland was skin to skin with her. She went very still, and looked at him. He was exactly the same: still and watchful. So had he felt that strange connection between them? Was he tingling all over, too?

Grace couldn't help glancing at Roland's mouth. His

lips were slightly parted, revealing even, white teeth; how had she not noticed before how sensual the curve of his mouth was? When she looked up again, she realised that he was looking at her mouth, too.

And then he leaned forward and kissed her. It was the lightest, gentlest, most unthreatening brush of his mouth against hers, and it sent shards of desire all through her. She couldn't ever remember a kiss making her feel as hot and shivery as this before.

'Tell me tomorrow,' he whispered.

She shook her head. 'I can give you the answer right now.' Even though part of her knew this was crazy and she ought to be measured and sensible about this, the way she always was, a stronger part of her couldn't resist the challenge. And maybe taking a leaf out of Bella's book—living life to the full, instead of being sensible all the time and holding back—would be good for her.

Two weeks. No strings.

Time to take the leap.

'Yes.'

CHAPTER FOUR

THE MIDDLE OF the next morning, Roland texted Grace.

Do you have a posh cocktail dress?

She thought about it. Was he planning to take her
to a cocktail bar or something? Given that Roland was
six-foot-two, she could actually wear her one pair of high
heels without being taller than he was and making him
feel embarrassed. She could team them with a little black
dress, and maybe put her hair up.

Yes. Why?

Taking you out for dinner tonight. Need you to be ready
for seven. Does that fit in OK for work?

Which meant she had absolutely no idea where they
were going; all she knew was that the dress code meant
posh. It could be anything from a private dinner party in
a castle somewhere—given that Roland's family owned
chateaux in France and he mixed in very different circles
from her own—to dinner at Claridge's. Was this what it
felt like to be swept off your feet, not having a clue about

what was happening? Grace was used to being organised and in charge, and right now she felt a bit out of her depth. But she brazened it out.

Sure, can be ready.

Good. Any allergies or things you can't bear to eat?

No to both.

Excellent. See you at seven.

Where are we going? she texted, though she had a feeling that he wouldn't tell her.

Out, was the reply that she'd half expected, leaving her none the wiser.

Roland wasn't at the house when Grace went back to Docklands after work. But he'd asked her to be ready for seven, so she showered, changed and did her hair to make sure she'd be ready. As she started applying her make-up, a wave of nervousness swept through her. This was their 'date'—and it had put her in a complete spin. She knew this wasn't a real relationship, but Roland had promised to sweep her off her feet, and she'd promised to let him practise his dating skills.

Did that mean he was going to kiss her again? And those feelings she'd had last night—would they get to the point of overwhelming her common sense? Would she end up making a fool of herself?

She tried to put the thought from her mind and concentrated on getting ready. By the time she'd finished, it was ten to seven and Roland still hadn't come back from work. Given that he'd asked her to be ready for seven, if he turned up in the next few seconds it wouldn't leave him much time to get ready to go out. But surely if he'd been held up at work or in traffic he would've called her?

Had she just made a huge mistake and agreed to a ridiculous deal with someone who would turn out to be as unreliable as her father? Someone charming who would let her down? That would mean she'd gone from one extreme to the other: from thinking of marrying a sensible man who didn't make her heart beat faster, to dating one who'd break it without a second thought. That wasn't what she wanted. At all.

Maybe she should call the whole thing off and find herself somewhere else to stay until Bella's flat had dried out.

She was about to start looking up hotels when the doorbell rang. Even though it wasn't strictly her place to answer the door, maybe it was a delivery or neighbour who needed something and she really ought to answer. When she opened the door, she saw Roland standing on the doorstep. He smiled and handed her a single red rose. 'Hi.'

'Thank you,' she said. Then she noticed the way he was dressed. He was wearing a formal dinner jacket, with a bow tie—and she was pretty sure that wasn't what he'd normally wear to the office. 'But—but…'

'But what?' he asked, his dark eyes glittering; clearly he was enjoying the fact that she was completely wrong-footed.

She gestured to his suit. 'You didn't come back here to get changed.'

'I can hardly sweep you off your feet if you see all the domestic stuff first,' he pointed out with a grin. 'I came home at lunchtime to pick up my clothes and I got changed in the office.'

'Oh.' Feeling stupid and vaguely pathetic, Grace stared at the floor. Why hadn't she thought of that? And that was why he was here at precisely seven o'clock—the time when he'd asked her to be ready. Of course he wasn't unreliable. She'd jumped to conclusions and been as unfair to him as he'd been to her.

Roland reached out, gently put the backs of his fingers under her chin and tilted her chin until she met his gaze. 'Hey. This was meant to make you feel special, not awkward,' he said. 'But I did warn you my dating skills are rusty. I'm sorry I got it wrong.'

If this was Roland in rusty mode, heaven help her when he was polished. 'It's not you, it's me being stupid,' she mumbled. 'I'd better put this rose in water—and it's lovely. Thank you.' And now she was babbling like a fool. He must be really regretting making that deal with her.

As if he could read her mind, he said quietly, 'Grace, just *relax*. This is about having fun.' Then he leaned forward and brushed his lips very lightly against hers, which sent her into even more of a tizzy. Every nerve end in her lips tingled and her knees felt as if they'd turned to soup.

'You have two minutes,' he said.

She just about managed to get her head together enough to ask, 'Where do you keep your vases?'

'Um—I don't have any, which is a bit pathetic given that my sister Philly is a florist.' He flapped a hand dismissively. 'Just use a glass for now and we'll sort it out later.'

The momentary confusion on his face made her feel a bit better. She put the rose in a glass of water in the kitchen, then joined him again at the front door.

'Your transport awaits, madam.'

She had no idea what she'd been expecting—but it certainly wasn't the gleaming silver Rolls-Royce that waited for them by the kerb, with a chauffeur at the wheel wearing a peaked cap.

'A Rolls-Royce?' she asked.

'In design terms, I prefer this to a stretch limo,' he said with a grin, and helped her into the car.

'Are you quite sure your dating skills need polishing, Roland?' she asked when he joined her in the back of the car. 'Because I think you've already swept me off my feet tonight more than I've ever been swept in my entire life so far.'

He inclined his head in acknowledgement. 'Good. That's the plan.'

They stopped outside a restaurant in Mayfair. The chauffeur opened the passenger door for her, and then Roland was by her side, tucking her arm into his elbow and leading her to the restaurant.

Grace recognised the name of the place as one of the best restaurants in London. It had two Michelin stars and the food was legendary—and it was so far out of her budget that she'd never even dreamed of booking a table here for a special birthday. Yet she noticed that the *maître d'* greeted Roland as if he was very well known here, then ushered them over to an intimate table for two.

She drank in her surroundings. This was definitely a once in a lifetime opportunity. The room was very light and airy, and was decorated in Regency style. There were Venetian glass chandeliers suspended from the ceiling, with beautiful art in gilded frames and a huge antique mirror hanging on the duck-egg-blue walls. The carpet was in a slightly darker shade than the walls, and her feet actually sank into it as she walked. The dark wood chairs had blue-and-cream-striped seats; the tables were covered with plain white damask cloths and were set with silver cutlery, with a simple arrangement of roses and a candelabrum in the centre.

'This is amazing,' she whispered when the *maître d'* had seated her and left them to look at the wine menu, 'but don't you have to book a table here months in advance?'

'Usually,' Roland agreed with a smile.

Which meant there was a reason why Roland had been able to book a table at the last minute. 'So did you go to school with the owner or something?' she asked.

He shrugged. 'I just did a little bit of renovation work for them, about four years ago.'

'They have one of your glass boxes here?'

'Sadly not. Though I do like the idea of a glass wall between the restaurant and the kitchen so the customers can see their food being cooked,' he said. 'Possibly not for here, though, because it wouldn't work with the architecture. I've booked the tasting menu for us, by the way. I hope that's OK?'

'More than OK, thank you. I've always wanted to do something like this,' she said shyly.

'And don't feel that you have to stick to water just because I don't drink,' he added. 'I'm perfectly happy for you to have the paired wines with each course if you'd like them.'

'I don't drink a lot,' she said, 'so it'd probably be a waste for me to do that. Maybe I could have one glass of wine, if they can recommend something?'

He spoke to the sommelier, who returned with a single glass of champagne and a bottle of water.

'Thank you,' she said quietly. 'That's really lovely.'

'What I like about this place is the attention to detail,' Roland said. 'Maybe it's the architect in me, but I like the fact they've kept the Regency styling right down to the glassware.'

She looked at the glass; the stem was sturdy and the bowl was conical, with an engraving of wine leaves just below the rim. 'This is an antique glass?'

'Reproduction—but a good one,' he said.

The waiter brought out the *amuse bouche*—a sunflower seed crisp with a braised artichoke and a bay leaf cream. Grace had never seen anything so beautifully presented; it looked more like a work of art than a dish.

But the first mouthful was even more amazing; the combination of the tastes, the textures and the scent stunned her.

'I've never had food this good before,' she said in almost hushed tones. 'The way the whole thing is put together and presented—it's incredible.'

Roland looked pleased. 'I hoped you'd enjoy this, seeing as you're a foodie.'

'Hey, I'm strictly amateur,' she said ruefully. 'But I like this very much indeed. Thank you so much for bringing me here.'

He smiled. 'That's what tonight's about, doing something we both like. It's nice to come here with someone I know will get this as much as I do.'

Grace wondered, had Lynette not liked this sort of thing? But she didn't ask; it was too intrusive and might spoil Roland's enjoyment of the evening. And Grace was determined to enjoy being swept off her feet, because she knew she'd never eat at a place like this again. Roland's world was in a completely different league from her own.

Course after course followed, all cooked to perfection and plated beautifully. The staff were friendly and attentive without being over the top, and Grace started to lose her shyness and relax with Roland.

'I hope you've got stamina,' he said with a grin. 'There are eight courses.'

'Eight? That's *so* greedy.' But she grinned back. 'Bring it on. I love everything about this. And, as you say, it's nice to do something like this with someone who gets it.'

'So what else do you like doing?' he asked.

She thought about it. 'Curling up on the sofa with a good book, walking in the park, going to the cinema with friends, and dance aerobics class with Bella. You?'

He considered it. 'I probably spend too much time at work. But I like wandering round museums. Especially ones in gorgeous buildings.'

'Where you look at the architecture and think what you'd do if you were given a free hand?'

'Busted,' he said with a grin.

Grace found herself relaxing with Roland, chatting easily about the food. 'A pre-dessert dessert? What a fabulous idea,' she said when the waiter brought a terrine with lemon verbena cream layered with orange curd, and served with the lightest and crispest almond *tuile*. Even better was the dark chocolate *pavé* with fresh blueberries and shards of dark chocolate. And then there was the cheeseboard, with a selection of cheese, tiny crackers, walnuts and black grapes, all served on a long slate board.

'That was utter perfection,' she said with a sigh. 'And right now I feel like a princess. A very greedy, full-to-bursting one, but definitely a princess.'

'Good.' Roland smiled at her. 'I'm glad you're enjoying this.'

While they had coffee and *petits fours*, the chef came out to see them.

'Ro. It's been too long,' he said, clapping Roland on the shoulder. 'And this is…?'

'Grace Faraday, my friend,' Roland said. 'Grace, this is Max Kleinman.'

'Delighted.' Max shook her hand warmly.

Max Kleinman was the equivalent of a rock star in the culinary world, and Grace felt incredibly shy. She knew Bella would've been in her element here and chatted away to him, and not for the first time she wished she had her sister's people skills. But she was the one who was quiet and sensible and good with numbers. All she could think of to say was, 'Your food is amazing.'

To her relief, Max looked pleased rather than embarrassed. 'I'm glad you liked it. I hope this means you'll come back.'

In my dreams, Grace thought, but she smiled. 'I hope so, too.'

Finally, the Rolls-Royce took them back to Roland's house. Grace was shocked to realise that it was almost midnight; they'd spent nearly four hours at the restaurant. She'd never lingered that long over a meal before.

Roland gestured to his coffee machine. 'Decaf cappuccino?'

'I think I'm too full to eat for another week, let alone drink coffee now,' Grace said. 'Thank you, but I'm fine.'

'So was it OK?' Roland asked.

'More than OK. I've never eaten such amazing food in my life,' she said. 'Thank you so much for spoiling me.'

'My pleasure,' he said, sounding utterly sincere rather than being polite.

'Though I have to be honest,' she said. 'I do feel as if

I'm cheating you. The deal is that I'm supposed to help you brush up your dating skills while you're sweeping me off my feet, but as far as I can see you don't need any help with your dating skills at all.'

'I think that's because of you,' he said. 'You made me feel comfortable enough to be myself with you. You're easy to talk to. Maybe—I don't know—maybe next time you can be a bit awkward with me so I have to work harder at it?'

She flushed at the compliment, pleased by the idea that she'd made this complex man feel relaxed with her. 'I'll try. And I'm organising tomorrow night. Though I'm afraid my budget won't stretch to anything as fabulous as tonight was. That is, if you want to do something?' Given that he didn't really need to practise his dating skills, it was a bit forward of her to suggest it.

He frowned. 'You don't have to organise anything. The idea is for me to sweep you off your feet.'

'Yes, I do,' she corrected, 'because I'm not a freeloader and I'm going to feel horrible if you pay for everything and sort everything out. And if I feel horrible, then you're not sweeping me off my feet. Quite the opposite.'

'You're stubborn.' To her surprise, he reached out and stroked her face. 'OK. We'll play it your way and you can organise tomorrow night. We agreed to clear our diaries so I won't be working late. I can make any time after seven.'

His touch made her feel all shivery. His eyes went dark and for a moment she thought he was going to dip his head and kiss her. But then he took a step back. 'It's late and we both have work tomorrow. I'd better let you go to bed.'

Grace was relieved and disappointed at the same time.

And she couldn't get to sleep for ages, tossing and turning and thinking about the situation. She was horribly aware how easy it would be to fall for Roland Devereux. But this wasn't real, and besides she'd only just come out of a long relationship. She needed to stand on her own two feet for a bit, not just fall for the first man to smile at her.

This was a temporary arrangement. She should just enjoy it for what it was and not be stupid enough to want more.

The next morning, Grace spent her entire journey to work looking up something unusual to do with Roland. Finally she found the perfect thing. She texted him swiftly.

Meet you at seven at Docklands. We're going by Tube. Dress code casual. Do you mind maybe eating a bit late?

It took him a while to reply.

Is fine. What are we doing?

She felt brave enough to text back, Wait and see.

Intrigued, he texted back. Bring it on.

She met him back at the house, but managed to keep him guessing about what they were doing until they were standing in the queue for the pop-up rooftop cinema.

'We're seeing *Back to the Future*?' He smiled. 'Considering what Hugh told me about Bella's first meeting with his family, I should consider myself lucky this isn't *The Sound of Music*.'

'I love that film, but no.' She smiled at him. 'Though you very nearly got *Jaws*.'

He laughed. 'I wouldn't have minded. Actually, I really like the idea of a rooftop cinema.' He eyed the sky. 'Though I hope those are threatening clouds rather than actual rainclouds.'

'They give out ponchos if it's wet,' she said. 'I checked the website.'

He brushed his mouth lightly against hers. 'That doesn't surprise me. You're good at organising things and you pay attention to detail.'

The compliment warmed her all through; and the kiss made her shivery at the knees. She was going to have to be so careful and keep reminding herself that she and Roland weren't really dating. This was simply a practice run for him.

There was a bar selling film-themed cocktails—including a James Bond martini, the White Russian from *The Big Lebowski*, and a Cosmopolitan from *Sex and the City*.

'It's my bill, tonight,' she said firmly. 'Have whatever you like.'

Roland glanced down the list of non-alcoholic cocktails. 'A Shirley Temple for me, please,' he said.

She joined him; they had a brief argument over whether sweet or salted popcorn was better, and ended up sharing a tub of each.

The film was as feel-good and fun as she remembered it. And when Michael J. Fox hitched a ride on his skateboard, she nudged Roland and whispered, 'I can't ever imagine you on a skateboard.'

'No, but I can play the guitar badly enough to make Hugh and Tarq cry—does that count?' he whispered back.

She smiled. 'Just.'

And then the butterflies in her stomach started stampeding as Roland took her hand and laced his fingers through hers. Was this still a practice run? Or did he mean it? He held her hand through the whole film, and she still hadn't worked it out when the first raindrops spattered down.

The ushers swiftly handed out ponchos to the audience, who passed them along the rows of chairs. Grace couldn't help laughing when the ponchos that reached them were pink.

'Hey. I'm comfortable enough with my masculinity to wear pink,' Roland said, and helped her with her poncho before putting on his own.

'Uh-huh.' She was still smiling.

He looked at her. 'What?'

'You, looking all pretty in pink. I should so grab a picture of that for Hugh and Tarquin,' she said with a grin.

In response he kissed her until she was breathless.

And her concentration was totally shot to pieces.

After the film, they went for a burger. 'I'm afraid this isn't going to be anywhere near up to the standard of last night's food,' Grace said ruefully.

'You're comparing apples and pears,' Roland pointed out, 'and I'm as happy with a burger as I am with gourmet food.'

She scoffed. 'You don't seriously expect me to believe that.'

'I eat out sometimes for work,' he said, 'or when Hugh and Tarq drag me out for our regular catch-up and suggest we go for a curry or a burger. But most of the time for me it's a ready meal at home or a takeaway because I don't really have the time or the inclination to cook.' He looked at her. 'But that meal you cooked me—it was very obvious that you cook on a regular basis.'

'I like cooking,' she said simply. 'It relaxes me.'

'You're really good at it. Did you ever think about going into catering rather than accountancy?'

'You asked me that before.' She shook her head. 'I'm happy with my job—or I will be, if I get offered the one I had the interview for the other day.'

'I'll keep my fingers crossed.' He paused. 'And if you don't get it?'

'Then I'll keep applying until I get a permanent job. But in the meantime the temping tides me over,' she said. 'Anyway, I don't really want to talk about work tonight. Though I guess work is a good topic for a first date when you're trying to get to know someone.'

'As we're sorting out my rusty dating skills, what other topics of conversation would you suggest for a first date?' he asked.

'Things you like and don't like. Say, what kind of films do you normally watch?' She looked at him. 'I'm guessing action movies?'

'Actually, no. I like the old ones that rely on good direction and acting rather than special effects.'

'Like Hitchcock's films?' she asked. '*Vertigo* and *Rear Window* are two of my favourites.'

'Mine, too,' he said. 'So does this mean you're a film snob at heart?'

She raised an eyebrow. 'Would a film snob go to singalong musical showings?'

He groaned. 'No. Please. Tell me you don't.'

'Oh, I do—that's one thing where Bella and I definitely see things the same way,' she said with a grin. 'You can't beat singing along to *Grease*, *Mamma Mia* or *The Sound of Music* with a cinema full of people.'

'So I really did get off lightly, tonight.'

'You don't like musicals?' she asked.

He grimaced. 'Lyn used to make me watch these terrible rom-coms. I put up with them for her sake, but…' He grimaced again. 'I'm sorry if you think rom-coms are wonderful, too, but they're really not my thing. Musicals aren't quite my thing, either.'

'I'll remember not to drag you along to a rom-com or a musical,' she said. 'Though you're missing out. Doris Day, Gene Kelly—that kind of film is the best thing ever for cheering you up when you've had a bad day.'

'No. That would be going to a gig performed by one of Hugh's pop punk bands,' he corrected. 'Standing right in the middle of the front row, yelling the songs along with them and letting the sound drive everything else out of your head.'

'Pop punk? I'm sure you look great wearing guy-liner,' she teased.

'Oh, please. At thirty, I'm way too old for that.' But he was laughing, and he held her hand all the way to the Tube station—and all the way back to Docklands.

They walked hand in hand along the river frontage in easy silence, watching the play of lights on the water. Grace thought wistfully, if only this was real. But that wasn't the deal, and she needed some space to stand on her own two feet again. So for now she'd just enjoy the moment. Two weeks of being swept off her feet. Wanting more was just greedy.

'I had a really good time tonight,' Roland said.

'Even though it's not the glamorous kind of stuff someone like you is used to?' she asked.

'It was fun,' he said. 'You put a lot of thought into it and came up with something original and different that I really enjoyed. Anyway, it doesn't have to be super-glamorous or cost a lot of money for it to be a good time—like now. There's nothing better than walking by the river at night watching the lights on the water, and that doesn't cost anything.'

'True,' she said. 'I can see why you live here.'

'Is this the sort of area where you'd live, if you had the chance?' he asked.

'Are we talking about my dream home? That would be a pretty little Victorian terraced house, filled with the kind of curtains and cushions you hate most,' she said. 'If I won the lottery, I'd want a place that overlooked somewhere like Hampstead Heath, or have one of those gorgeous houses in Notting Hill that have access to a pretty garden.'

He stopped and turned to face her. 'Like the one in the film where the movie star kisses the ordinary guy?'

'I guess,' she said, and she couldn't help staring at his mouth. Except he wasn't an ordinary guy and she wasn't a film star.

She only realised she'd spoken aloud when he said, 'I'm ordinary enough,' and leaned forward to kiss her.

Time seemed to stop. And she was super-aware of his nearness—his clean male scent, the warmth of his skin, the way the touch of his lips made her skin tingle.

A cat-call from a passing teenager broke the mood, and he took a step back. 'Sorry.'

'It's fine to kiss your date in public,' she said, striving for cool. 'Except maybe not as, um…' How could she tell him that he'd made her feel feverish, without giving herself away? 'A little cooler might be more appropriate,' she said.

'Noted.' But his pupils were huge. Was that because of the darkness around them, or had kissing her affected him the same way it had affected her? She was way too chicken to ask.

And she was even more relieved when her phone pinged. 'This might be my daily Bellagram,' she said. 'Oh, look—they took a cable car ride today.' She showed him the photograph. 'Trust Bella to hang off the running boards like Doris Day.'

'Wouldn't you do that, too?' he asked.

She gave him a rueful smile. 'I'm the sensible one. I'd be thinking of health and safety.' And missing out on the fun.

'Nothing wrong with being sensible. Do you have plans for tomorrow?' he asked as they headed back to his place.

'No.' Even if they hadn't already agreed to clear their diaries for these next few weeks, she didn't have anything planned.

'You do now—and, no, I'm not telling you what. Dress code is whatever you like. Something comfortable. But bring something warm in case it turns chilly, and I'll bring a golfing umbrella in case it rains.'

They'd be doing something outdoors, then, she guessed. 'What, no pink poncho?' she teased, trying to keep the mood light and not let him guess about how much his kiss had affected her.

'A golfing umbrella is much more appropriate,' he said, unlocking the front door.

'We're playing golf?'

'No—and stop asking questions. It's meant to be spontaneous.'

Spontaneous wasn't how she usually did things. Roland was definitely pushing her out of her comfort zone.

'See you in the morning,' he said. 'And thank you for tonight. I really enjoyed myself.'

'Me, too,' she said.

And although part of her was disappointed that he didn't want to sit with her in his kitchen, drinking coffee and talking about everything under the sun, part of her knew this was the sensible option. She'd nearly lost her head as it was when he'd kissed her. If he kissed her again…

Two weeks, she told herself. She might like the way Roland made her feel, but she was his practice date. This wasn't permanent. Wasn't real. And she'd better remember that.

CHAPTER FIVE

THE NEXT MORNING, Roland was horrified to discover that there was only one firework display set to music in a fifty-mile radius of London—and, worse still, all the tickets to it were already sold.

Oh, for pity's sake.

This was the sort of summer evening event that was often held in the park of a stately home, or possibly in a municipal park or seaside resort as part of a week's carnival event. He couldn't believe that there was only one event available that evening. Surely there had to be others?

He widened the radius for his search, and discovered that the nearest music and fireworks event with a few tickets remaining was being held a hundred miles away. A two-hour drive each end wouldn't be much fun for either of them. So much for sweeping Grace off her feet with something that he actually knew was on her bucket list and she'd really love to do.

Even though he didn't usually use the 'get me a ticket at the last minute' type websites, it looked as if that was going to be his only option. To his relief, he managed to get two tickets for the venue he'd wanted in the first place. That was the hardest bit done, he thought, and headed out to the local deli for part two of his plan. A few minutes later, everything was sorted to his satisfaction.

Roland was sure that this would be the perfect way to sweep Grace off her feet. Even if the weather wasn't on his side and it poured with rain, it wouldn't matter. The fireworks and the music would still go on. And he could set the scene for it, starting right now.

He checked the breakfast tray. Coffee, croissants, freshly squeezed orange juice, granola, Greek yoghurt and a bowl of perfect English strawberries. Philly would forgive him for not buying the sweet peas from her; he'd seen them in a shop window on the way back from the deli and they'd just reminded him of Grace, all sweet and shy. And he hoped that Grace wouldn't mind the fact that the flowers were propped in water in a juice glass rather than in a proper vase.

It was almost nine o'clock. He didn't think that Grace was the sort who'd stay in bed all day; but at the same time she would still have had the chance to relax and sleep in a bit longer than she could on a weekday. Hopefully she wouldn't mind him waking her now. He tucked the newspaper under his arm and carried the tray to her room; he balanced the tray between himself and the wall and knocked on the door. 'Grace?'

'Yes?' Her voice sounded sleepy and he felt a twinge of guilt. Maybe he should've left waking her for another half an hour.

'Can I come in? I've brought you some breakfast.'

'I…sure.'

He walked in to the room. She was sitting in the middle of the king-sized bed, nestled into the duvet, with her hair all mussed and her eyes all sleepy, and his mouth went dry. Oh, help. This wasn't in the plan. He wasn't supposed to react to her like this. He was meant to be sweeping her off her feet, not the other way round. And he definitely needed to keep his eyes off her pretty camisole pyjama top. He absolutely couldn't walk over there, slide the straps from her shoulders and kiss her bare skin. Even though his body was urging him to do exactly that.

'I, um, didn't know what you like for breakfast, but I hoped this would be OK. And I brought you the Saturday paper.'

'Thank you. That's really kind of you. And flowers. That's so lovely.'

Her smile was sweet and shy and genuine, and it made him feel warm inside. 'Pleasure.' He handed her the tray. 'I, um…' How come he was suddenly so flustered and inarticulate? He was known for being as good with words as he was with building, and he could talk anyone through even the most complex project so they understood the plan and loved the concept as much as he did. But, in Grace's presence, all his words seemed to have turned into so much hot air. 'I know we said we'd clear our diaries, but I need to nip into the office and do a few things this morning,' he improvised. 'Would you mind amusing yourself?'

'Roland, you really don't have to entertain me all the time,' she said. 'You're already being kind enough to put me up while the flat's drying out. I don't expect you to run around after me as well.'

'OK.' He couldn't take his eyes off her hair; he wanted to twine the ends round his fingers and see if it was as soft and silky as it looked. So he'd better leave before he did something stupid. 'See you later, then.'

She smiled at him. 'Have a good morning. And thank

you for breakfast. This is such a treat. I can't remember the last time someone brought me breakfast in bed.'

Hadn't Howard done that for her? Then again, she'd said they hadn't lived together.

Did that mean they hadn't slept together, either?

That was a question Roland knew he couldn't ask. Not without going into very dangerous territory indeed. Sleeping with Grace... He really had to get that idea out of his head. Fast. Because that wasn't part of the deal he'd made with her. This was about helping her to feel swept off her feet, and helping him to move past the guilt and misery so he could truly live again.

He changed the subject to something safer. 'We need to leave here at about four, if that's OK with you,' he said.

'I'll make sure I'm ready.'

And he knew she'd do exactly that; she prized reliability in others, and that meant in turn that she was always reliable too.

But even when he drove to the office, he found it difficult to concentrate on work instead of thinking about Grace. His foreman, Charlie, who'd come in to the office to debrief him on a project, teased him about being on another planet.

Possibly Planet Crazy, Roland thought, because he just couldn't get Grace Faraday out of his head.

When Roland drove back to London later that afternoon, he had just enough time to drop into the deli to pick up his order and then change into a fresh shirt and a pair of chinos. Grace was ready on time, as he'd expected; her idea of 'smart casual' turned out to be smart black trousers and a pretty strappy top. One which made him remember that pretty camisole top she'd worn in bed that morning, and heat spread through him. 'You look lovely,' he said, meaning it. And somehow he'd have to find that tricky balance between sweeping her off her feet and losing his head completely.

'Thank you,' she said, smiling in acknowledgement of the compliment.

Then he noticed just how sensual the curve of her mouth was. He itched to kiss her, but he managed to hold himself back. Just. 'Ready to go?' he asked, hoping that his voice didn't sound as croaky to her as it did to him.

'Sure.'

He kept the conversation light as he drove Grace to the stately home on the edge of London. Then she saw the banners on the wrought iron fence. 'A classical music and fireworks spectacular? We're actually going to this, right now?'

'You did tell me this sort of thing was on your bucket list,' he pointed out, enjoying the fact that her excitement had sounded in her voice.

'I know, and this is utterly wonderful—but telling you the sort of thing I'd love to do really doesn't mean that I expect you to actually take me to all my dream places,' she said, her face a mixture of delight and guilt.

'But isn't that what you're supposed to do when you sweep someone off their feet? Take them to their dream places?' he asked.

'Maybe.' She bit her lip. 'And that banner says it's sold out.'

'Uh-huh.'

'Don't tell me.' Her voice was dry. 'You called in a favour because you did some work for the people who live here?'

He laughed. 'No. Actually I got our tickets from one of those "get me in at the last minute" sites.'

'What? But they always put a massive mark-up on ticket prices!' She sounded horrified. 'Roland, I need to reimburse you for my ticket.'

He groaned as he followed the car park attendants' direction to a space on the grass. 'Grace, I know you like to be independent, and I appreciate the offer, but you're supposed to be being swept off your feet. Right now, it seems to me that you have both feet very firmly on the ground, so I'm failing miserably.'

She flushed. 'In other words, I'm being an ungrateful brat.'

'No—just a bit difficult,' he said.

'You did tell me that you wanted me to be awkward with you, so you could practise your dating skills on being smooth,' she reminded him.

'Are you telling me you're being difficult on purpose?' His eyes narrowed. 'So how do I know when you're acting and when you're not?'

She spread her hands. 'You tell me.'

He resisted the urge to kiss her until she was breathless—mainly because he knew he'd end up in a similar state, with his head in a spin. Instead, he said, 'Let's go and get set up.' And then maybe the fresh air would help bring him back to his senses. This was meant to be practice dating, not the real thing. She'd made it clear that she didn't want to be let down—and he couldn't trust himself not to repeat his mistakes and let her down.

Roland took a picnic blanket, umbrella, two small collapsible chairs and the wicker picnic hamper from the back of the car.

'What can I carry?' Grace asked.

'Nothing. It's fine.'

'It isn't fine at all. You're totally laden—and there's a big difference between being swept off your feet and being a poor, helpless female who can't carry anything in case she breaks a fingernail.'

He laughed and she narrowed her eyes at him. 'What's so funny?'

'A week ago, I would've said you were exactly that type.'

'Helpless and pathetic? Well, thank you very much.' She scowled at him.

He winced. 'Grace, I've already told you that I know how much I misjudged you. Though this is particularly bad timing.'

'How do you mean?' she asked.

'Because you're right,' he said. 'I'm fully laden. I'll have to put something down before I can kiss you to say I'm sorry for getting you so wrong.'

'You want to kiss me?'

He moistened his lower lip. 'Firstly to say sorry. And then because…'

Her heart skipped a beat. 'Because what?'

He waited until she met his gaze. 'To say I like you.'

And even though they were outdoors, standing in lush parkland, it felt as if there wasn't enough room to breathe.

'I like you, too,' she whispered. Even though she hadn't expected to. And even though she really didn't want to feel this way about him. She wanted to be independent. She couldn't possibly fall for someone this quickly. Especially someone who'd made a deal with her that he'd sweep her off her feet in exchange for her brushing up his dating skills—because she knew that everything he was saying to her was dating practice, not for real.

'I'm glad you like me,' he said, his voice slightly husky.

Grace knew she ought to leave it there, make him give her a couple of things to carry, and keep it light. But Roland was staring at her mouth, and it was a little too much to resist. She closed the gap between them, stood on tiptoe, and reached up to brush her mouth against his.

When she stepped back, she could see a slash of vivid colour across his cheeks and his eyes had gone all dark.

'If we weren't in a public place...' His voice cracked.

'But we are,' she said. 'And you need to let me carry something.'

In the end, he let her carry the umbrella and the picnic blanket. They found a nice spot on the lawns with a good view of the stage and the lake—where the fireworks were going to be set off—and between them they spread out the blanket, set up the chairs and opened the picnic basket.

When Grace had gone on picnics as a child, the food had consisted of home-made sandwiches stored in a plastic box, a packet of crisps, an apple and maybe a cupcake or some sausage rolls; there might have been cans of lemonade or cola for her and Bella to drink. Everything had been stored in a cool box, and they'd eaten without plates or cutlery.

This was a whole new level of picnic. Roland's wicker basket had storage compartments for plates, glasses, cutlery, napkins and mugs as well as for the food. And when she helped Roland unpack the food, she discovered that it was on a whole new level from the picnics of her childhood, too. There was artisan seeded bread and butter curls; cold poached chicken with potato salad, watercress and heritage tomatoes; cocktail blinis with cream cheese and smoked salmon; a tub of black olives; oatcakes with crumbly Cheddar, ripe Brie and black grapes; and then strawberries, clotted cream and what looked like very buttery shortbread.

There were bottles of sparkling water, a Thermos which she guessed was filled with coffee, and there was also a tiny bottle of champagne.

'I thought you might like some bubbly to go with your fireworks,' Roland said.

Given what she knew about the tragedy in his past, she felt awkward. 'Are you sure about this?'

He smiled at her. 'I did say I'm fine about other people drinking.'

'Then thank you. This is the perfect size for a treat. Plus it means I won't wake up with a monumental hangover or ask you to make me some banana porridge when we get home,' she said with a smile.

Then she realised what she'd said. *Home.* But the house in Docklands wasn't her home; it was his. She really hoped he hadn't noticed her gaffe.

But he seemed happy enough as he shared the picnic with her.

'So what do women expect to talk about on a date?' he asked.

'I'm probably not the best person to ask, given that I haven't dated that much apart from Howard and...' She let the sentence trail off and grimaced. 'Sorry. I'm not living up to my part of the deal. Let me start again. I guess it's about finding out about each other, and what we've got in common.'

'How do you do that?'

She was pretty sure he already knew that. There was absolutely nothing wrong with his social skills. But she'd go with it for now. 'I guess it's the same as you'd do with any new friendship or even a business relationship—you start with where you are and work from there. If you'd met your date at a swimming pool, you'd ask her how often she came for a swim, or whether she preferred swimming in the pool to swimming in the sea, or where was the nicest place she'd ever been swimming. That sort of thing.'

He smiled. 'So, as we're at a musical event, this is where I ask what sort of music you like? Even though actually I already know that you like popular classical music, and you sing along to the radio.'

She smiled back. 'And then I ask you what you like, even though you already told me yesterday that you like loud pop punk.'

'I do.' He thought about it. 'I like popular classical music as well as indie rock. And I've never been to the opera, but I've been to a few good gigs in my time. Especially since Hugh set up Insurgo.' He paused. 'So that's covered what we listen to. If I extend that to actually playing music—I did about a term's worth of violin lessons before my parents gave in and begged me to stop. What about you?'

'Apart from singing Christmas carols at the infant school nativity play—oh, and playing the triangle for "Twinkle, Twinkle, Little Star" one year and doing it in completely the wrong place—no,' she said. 'None of my friends are musical, either.'

'Some of mine are.' He shrugged. 'But you already know that my best friends own an indie recording label and Hugh's an amazing producer. And your sister gave him his music back. It's great to see him with his heart and soul back in place.'

'I think Hugh and Bella are good for each other,' she said. 'Which reminds me—today's Bellagram.'

Roland burst out laughing when he saw the photograph of Hugh by the railings on Fisherman's Wharf, posing like a sea lion clapping its front feet together, with a crowd of sea lions behind him. 'That's priceless.' He looked at Grace. 'Are you sending her Bellagrams back?'

Grace shook her head. 'If I did, she'd start asking questions—and our deal is just between us.'

'True.' He paused. 'OK. That's music done. What next? I know you can cook, and you know I don't bother. We both like good food.'

'And, even though you might not cook something yourself, you make great choices. This cheese is amazing,' she said, helping herself to another slice of the Cheddar with an oatcake.

'Food, music. Next topic.' He looked thoughtful. 'Travel?'

'I haven't travelled that much,' she admitted.

Because she was scared of flying? Or had she just never had the chance to travel?

If it was the latter, Roland thought, this was a definite sweeping-off-feet opportunity. The perfect way to end their time together, even. He knew exactly where he was going to take her. He'd book it later tonight.

'Do you have a passport?' he checked.

She nodded.

Good, he thought. That was the biggest barrier out of the way. Then he remembered that she'd called off her wedding very recently and grimaced. 'Sorry. Did I just put my foot in it? Had you booked an amazing honeymoon in Hawaii or something?'

She shook her head. 'Howard wasn't really one for long-haul flights—or even short-haul, really. We were going to drive down to the south of France. Cynthia had asked a couple of her friends to lend us their flat.'

Who on earth organised their son's honeymoon, unless it was a special surprise and something that the happy couple couldn't afford to do for themselves? Roland wondered. And although a borrowed flat in the South of France would be very nice for a short break, he didn't understand why a qualified accountant who worked for the family firm—and therefore had to be on a pretty decent salary—couldn't afford to book something a little more special for his honeymoon. So either Howard and his family were very mean with money, or his mother was a control freak who refused to let her son make his own decisions. Either way, it sounded as if Grace had had a lucky escape.

'The South of France is nice,' he said carefully.

'But not where you'd choose for a honeymoon?' she asked, picking up on his hesitation.

'No,' he admitted. 'And definitely not a borrowed flat if I could afford to pay for somewhere myself.'

'Where did you and Lynette go?' she asked. Then she bit her lip. 'Sorry. That was nosey. I didn't mean to bring up memories.'

'They're good memories,' he said. And, surprisingly, it didn't hurt to talk about Lynette to Grace. It was actually nice to remember the times when they'd been happy. Before the baby-making project had put so much pressure on them both and their marriage had started to crack under the strain. 'We went to the rainforest in Brazil and stayed in a treetop hotel.'

'That sounds amazing,' she said wistfully.

'It was a kind of private oasis,' he said. 'We could sit out on the balcony and watch the monkeys and hear the macaws. There were wooden catwalks through the canopy of trees, so walking between our suite and the dining room was amazing. There was even a treetop swimming pool.'

'That's really exotic,' she said.

'I've never been anywhere like it—swimming with all these tropical birds flying just over your heads. And the food was great; every night we had fresh grilled fish, beans and rice and amazing bread, and exotic fruit. The day I remember most was when we took a boat trip on the Amazon and swam with the pink freshwater dolphins.'

'That sounds perfect,' Grace said wistfully.

'It was the trip of a lifetime,' he said. 'We'd both always wanted to see the rainforest, and it more than lived up to our expectations. I'm not sure whether I liked the sunrise or the sunset most, or just looking up into the sky and seeing a different set of stars, so bright against the darkness of the sky and so very different from London.' He paused. 'So what about you? What's your dream trip?' The one that her ex-fiancé hadn't made come true.

'It's a bit nerdy.'

He smiled. He'd expect nothing less from Grace. 'Nerdy's good. Tell me.'

'I'd love to go on the Orient Express,' she said, 'all the way from Paris to Istanbul.' She shrugged. 'But that particular trip is only scheduled once a year.'

If Roland had been planning to get married to Grace, he would've arranged their wedding so they could start their honeymoon with the train journey from Paris to Istanbul before venturing further afield. Why hadn't Howard done that? Didn't he like trains? Or had he never bothered to find out what made his fiancée tick?

Not that it was any of Roland's business. And he wasn't planning to get married any time soon. This was practice dating, he reminded himself. Talking to his date and finding out more about her. 'Where else would you like to go?'

'Do you mean my fantasy travel wish-list—the really wild stuff that I know I'm never actually going to do?' she asked. At his nod, she continued, 'I'd like to go to Australia and see the stars in the outback, and to Alaska to see the glaciers and the whales, and maybe the Antarctic to see the penguins, and to walk along some of the Great Wall of China.' She paused. 'How about you?'

'Actually, I like the sound of all of those.' He was faintly shocked by how much their tastes dovetailed. Only a few days ago, he would've said that they had nothing in common. But it looked as if some of her dreams were very similar to his own.

'You haven't already done them?' She looked surprised.

'No. Lyn really liked city breaks, so I've been to all the big cities in Europe,' he explained, 'plus New York, Boston, San Francisco and LA. And I've travelled pretty extensively on business, with conferences and the like; I always try to spend a day looking round wherever I'm based.'

'So where would you go for your fantasy travel list?' she asked.

'I'd like to see the Victoria Falls, and swim in the Blue Lagoon in Iceland,' he said. 'And visit Yosemite, to see the hot springs and waterfalls.'

'So it's water that draws you?'

'I've never thought about it that way, but yes, I suppose it is,' he said, surprised. 'Venice is one of my favourite places ever, and I love the sea. There's nothing better than walking on the cliffs with the waves crashing below and sending spray everywhere. Or strolling on a flat sandy beach in the moonlight with the sea all calm and just lapping at the shore.'

'Plus you live right on the Thames,' she pointed out.

'And you could never keep me off the lake as a boy.'

'Would this lake be at one of the chateaux?' she asked.

'No. At my family home in Kent,' he admitted.

'You had a lake?' She blinked. 'So are you telling me that you grew up somewhere like this?' She gestured to the stately home in front of them.

He squirmed. This felt like bragging—and that wasn't who he was. 'It's not as big as this. But, um…yes, I guess it's this sort of thing. Though it's been in the family for generations, and the roof is a total money pit, to the point where Dad's opened the gardens to the public, and we're turning the boathouse at the lake into a café.'

'And would I be right in guessing that his favourite architect,' she asked with a grin, 'is going to suggest having a glass wall all along the side of the building that faces the lake?'

'You are.' He smiled back at her. 'Though I guess that was obvious.'

'Not necessarily. Do you have another brother or sister who's an architect?'

He shook his head. 'Will's the oldest, so he's pretty much involved with the estate because he'll take over from Dad. Actually, he's already doing his own projects—he's sorting out a licence so we can hold wedding ceremonies. I'm the middle child, and I get hauled in to look at the roof from time to time and give my professional opinion on any renovation work that crops up.

And Philly's the baby—she basically adopted the head gardener as her honorary uncle when she was a toddler and moved up to nagging him to let her have a corner of the greenhouse all to herself by the time she was ten. So it was always obvious that she'd end up being either a landscape gardener or a florist. And she's brilliant. Really gifted.'

'You sound close to your family,' she said.

'I am.' He smiled. 'And you're close to yours.'

'I'm lucky,' she said simply.

He could tell that Grace was thinking about her almost-in-laws. What he didn't understand was why on earth her ex-fiancé's family hadn't liked her. She was sensible, kind and tactful. And, once you got past her shyness, she was fun. Yes, she had a nerdy streak, but that meant she looked at things from a different viewpoint—and in turn that made him look at things differently, too.

Though this dating thing was a temporary deal. And she'd just come out of a long relationship; she'd made it clear that she didn't want to rush into anything new. He didn't want to rush into anything, either. So he needed to keep these burgeoning feelings firmly under control, because they just weren't appropriate.

The orchestra began playing on stage, so he was saved from further conversation. But every so often he sneaked a glance at Grace to check that she was enjoying herself. And once or twice he caught her sneaking a glance at him, too. In the darkening evening, her cornflower-blue eyes were almost navy. Hypnotic.

As the fireworks began, he found himself sliding an arm across the back of her chair. If she asked, he'd say it was because he was worried she might be cold—English summer evenings weren't that warm. He certainly wouldn't tell her that it was because he wanted to be close to her. 'OK?' he asked.

'Very OK,' she said with a smile. 'This is absolutely gorgeous—the music, the fireworks and the reflections. It's the perfect combination. Thank you so much for bringing me.'

'My pleasure,' he said, meaning it. He couldn't remember when he'd relaxed so much, just enjoying his surroundings and chilling out. And he knew it was all down to Grace. Her quiet calmness made him feel grounded.

Maybe, he thought, he should suggest turning this from a practice run to a real relationship. See where it took them. But would she say yes? Or would she back away?

He managed to keep his thoughts under control during the fireworks, and driving home in the dark meant that he needed to concentrate and didn't have the headspace for thinking. But once they were back in Docklands he found the question buzzing through his head again.

Should he ask her?

Or should he do the sensible thing and back away?

In the end, Grace made the decision for him, by kissing him on the cheek. 'Thank you for tonight, Roland. It was every bit as fabulous as I dreamed it would be. And it was even nicer because it was a total surprise.'

'My pleasure,' he said automatically. She'd kissed his cheek, not his mouth. Meaning that he needed to back off.

Before he could suggest making a drink so he could linger in her company just that little bit longer, she said, 'I'll see you in the morning, then. Good night.'

'Good night,' he said. 'Sleep well.'

Though he had a feeling that he wouldn't. Grace was stirring feelings in him that he thought were long buried. And, even though he was usually so sure about what he

was doing, right now he felt as if he was walking blind-
fold along a path littered with lumps and bumps and
holes, having to feel his way to make sure he stayed on
his feet.

Maybe he'd manage to get his common sense back
into place overnight.

Maybe.

CHAPTER SIX

GRACE'S MOUTH WAS soft and sweet, and Roland couldn't get enough of it. Yet he wanted a deeper intimacy, too. He'd just unzipped her dress when he heard something banging.

Then he realised it was the door.

His bedroom door.

And he was completely alone in bed. It was Sunday morning, and he'd been dreaming about making love with Grace. Heat rushed through his cheeks.

'Roland? Can I come in?' a voice called.

Grace.

The heat in his face intensified. No way did he want her to have any idea what he'd just been thinking about. On the other hand, he didn't have a valid excuse to tell her to go away. 'Uh—yeah,' he mumbled, hoping that he'd be able to think on his feet, and sat up.

She walked in carrying a tray. 'No sweet peas, I'm afraid. But I hope you'll like this.' Then she looked at his bare chest and blushed. 'Um. Sorry. I didn't realise…'

'I'm wearing pyjama bottoms,' he said hastily. But he was very glad that the duvet was piled in his lap and hid his arousal. He didn't want to embarrass either of them.

When she handed him the tray, he realised that she'd

brought him coffee and Eggs Benedict. It looked and smelled amazing.

'Is that home-made Hollandaise sauce?' he asked.

'Yes.'

'If you ever get tired of working with numbers,' he said, 'I guarantee you'd have a fantastic career if you opened your own restaurant.' He still didn't get why she wasn't using her talent. Why she was hiding behind numbers.

'I like cooking for fun,' she said. 'Cooking as a business would be a totally different ballgame. And it'd be sad if something I really enjoy doing turned out to be something I felt I was forced to do. Not to mention the unsociable hours I'd need to work; I wouldn't get to see enough of my parents and Bella.'

'I guess,' he said. And it was a logical explanation, one he couldn't argue with.

'It's my turn to organise things today,' she said. 'That is, if you'd like to do something with me and you don't have to work?'

Maybe he should grab this opportunity to put a little distance between them.

Except his mouth wasn't working from the same script as his head and using his usual cast-iron excuse of working on some architectural design or other, because he found himself saying, 'I'd like to do something with you.'

'Great. Maybe we can be ready to leave in an hour?' she suggested.

'I can be ready before that. What are we doing?'

'Something immensely nerdy, but I hope you'll enjoy it,' she said with a smile. 'See you later.'

He watched her walk out of the room, noting the sway of her hips. He was definitely going to need a cold shower after breakfast. And it had been a while since he'd had such a graphic dream.

So did that mean that he was ready to start to move on? With Grace?

But she'd only just come out of a long relationship where she hadn't been happy. And although she'd said that she'd wanted to be swept off her feet, the Grace he was beginning to get to know liked structure and organisation. She was very far from being the sort to rush into things. He needed to be careful with her.

Which meant not giving in to the urge to sweep her off her feet, literally, and carrying her to his bed.

The cold shower was enough to restore some of his common sense. He shaved, got dressed, and found her in the kitchen doing a number puzzle in a magazine.

He smiled. 'Would this be your Sunday morning guilty pleasure?'

'Busted,' she said ruefully.

He glanced over her shoulder at the page. 'That doesn't look like the kind of thing you see in the newspaper supplements.'

'I suppose it's for people who like, um, really nerdy puzzles. My parents buy me a subscription to this magazine every Christmas,' she admitted.

'Don't hide your light under a bushel,' he said. 'Most people couldn't do these sorts of puzzles. Be proud of yourself because you can.' And why was she so diffident about her abilities? That was really bugging him. He'd actually met her family and liked them. They weren't the sort who'd do someone down to boost their own ego. So who had made Grace feel bad about herself and hide who she was? 'Would I be right in guessing that your ex didn't like you doing them?'

'No.'

But she looked away, and he guessed that yet again her ex's disapproving mother had been the sticking point.

'Not everyone likes puzzles,' she said, still not meeting his eye.

'Which doesn't mean you should take away the fun from those who do.' And it made him wonder why Grace's ex had put up with the situation. If his own mother had been difficult with Lyn, he would've taken his mother to one side and gently explained that he'd made his life choice and he'd prefer her to respect that and treat his partner with a bit more courtesy—even if they couldn't be close friends, they could still be civil to each other. Though Roland's mother wasn't the cold, judgemental type who placed importance upon appearances above all else, and he knew that his whole family would adore Grace. She would adore them, too.

Not that he intended to introduce them to each other. This was way, way too soon.

She closed her magazine. 'I'll just do the washing u—' she began.

'No,' Roland said, and put everything from his tray in the dishwasher before she could argue. 'Didn't you say you wanted to leave soon?'

'Yes. And it's my trip, so we're going in my car.'

'Yes, ma'am,' he teased.

As he'd expected, Grace turned out to be a very competent driver, but he didn't have a clue where they were going until she turned off at Bletchley Park. 'I should've guessed you'd plan to visit somewhere like this,' he said.

'Why?'

The expression on her face was fleeting, but he'd noticed it. Expecting that she'd be judged—and judged harshly. Although Roland didn't believe that violence solved anything, he would've liked to shake Howard's mother until her teeth rattled. Grace had been engaged to Howard for four years, so they'd probably dated for a year or so before then—meaning that the woman had had five years to crush Grace's confidence. And how. The fact that Grace had still had the guts to walk away from the situation was a testimony to her strength. 'You like numbers, so this place must be fascinating for you,' he said. 'If you'd been alive in those times, I think they would've asked you to work here, given that you're good at puzzles.'

'And if you'd been alive in those times, you might've been working on the architecture for the Mulberry harbour or something like that,' she said.

'Or working with the guy who was trying to find an alternative material to build the Mosquito planes when there was a shortage of balsa wood,' he said thoughtfully. 'There was a chemist who was working on making a foam from seaweed that dried into planks that would be as strong as wood.'

She glanced at him. 'A plane made from seaweed? I assume you're teasing me?'

'No, I'm serious,' he said. 'I read an article about it in a professional journal. Apparently one of the seaweed "planks" is in the Science Museum in London.'

'What an amazing story,' she said. 'I'm going to have to go to the Science Museum now to see it for myself.'

'Maybe we can go together.' The words were out before he could stop them. This was dangerous. He wasn't supposed to be finding shared points of interest for the future. They'd agreed to help each other out, not fall for each other.

'Maybe we can go next weekend, or on one of the evenings when they open late.' She gave him another of those shy smiles, then parked the car. 'We don't need to queue, by the way. I bought tickets online while you were in the shower this morning, and I've already downloaded the multimedia guide to my phone,' she said.

Typical Grace, being organised and thorough. 'Sounds good.' He took her hand and they wandered round, enjoying the sunshine and exploring the different code-breaking huts.

'I love the way they've done this so you can actually feel what it was like to work here—even down to the sounds and smells,' he said.

'Me, too,' she said. 'I hoped you'd like this—you said you liked museums and buildings, and this is… Well.'

'It's brilliant. And I'm going to be totally boring when we get to the displays about how they restored the buildings.' He kissed her to reassure her that he was happy with her choice of date, but kept it swift so he could keep his feelings in control.

They lingered in the display about the Enigma machines, and the Bombe machine that finally cracked the code. He could see how interested she was, and how her eyes lit up. If he was honest with himself, she fascinated him as much as this place fascinated her. He hadn't met anyone quite like her before. Lyn had been outgoing and confident—at least, until the baby-making plan had gone wrong—and Grace was quiet and shy and kept a lot of herself hidden. Yet something about her drew him. He wanted to take down all her barriers and let her shine.

They stopped for lunch in the site's café. 'So when did you know you wanted to work with numbers?' he asked.

She shrugged. 'I just always liked numbers. Dad found

me trying to do the number puzzles in the Sunday supplements, so he started buying me puzzle magazines. My favourite ones were where you have to fit a list of numbers instead of words into a grid. Then I moved up to logic puzzles and Sudoku. I, um, won a competition at school for being the fastest at solving them,' she added shyly.

'And you never thought about going to university to study maths?'

'One of my teachers tried to get me to apply to Oxford,' she said, 'but I don't think I was cut out to be a teacher. It seemed a bit pointless spending three years studying and getting into debt when I could've been learning on the job and making progress in my professional exams.'

Sensible and measured and reliable: that was Grace. Though he wondered what would've happened if she'd let herself have the chance to work with the more abstract branches of mathematics—how far she would've soared.

'And that's where you met Howard, when you were training?'

She shook her head. 'I qualified in a different firm, then moved to Sutton's because there was an opportunity for promotion. I never expected to fall for the boss's son, but we worked together on an audit when I'd been there for six months and he asked me out.'

Roland had the feeling that Grace had concentrated on her studies rather than on partying. He wouldn't be surprised if Howard had been her first serious boyfriend.

'And you liked him?' he asked.

She nodded. 'He was sweet and kind—and I guess I was a bit naive because I thought that his parents would eventually warm to me. I'm not a gold-digger.'

'Of course you're not,' he said. But clearly Howard's

parents had treated her as if she was. It made Roland understand where her insistence on being independent and doing her fair share came from. Clearly she'd had to prove herself over and over and over again. But why hadn't her ex stood up for her? And why had it taken her so long to realise that she was worth more than the way his family treated her?

'How about you?' she asked. 'How did you meet Lynette?'

'We worked together,' he said. 'I was an architect and she was a PA at the practice. We danced together at an office Christmas party, and that was it.'

'So you knew straight away that she was The One?'

'I guess.' He nodded. 'We moved in together fairly quickly, but she insisted on a long engagement when I asked her to marry me.'

'But not four years?' Grace asked wryly.

Roland smiled. 'Just one. And that was long enough. Though I guess she was right; it gave us time to get to know each other properly and be really sure we were doing the right thing. And we were happy.' Until that last year of their marriage, when Lyn's friends all seemed to fall pregnant the very first month they started trying, while he had to comfort his wife every month when her period arrived. The doctors had all said they were young and it was too early to think about fertility treatment, and advised them both just to relax and keep trying; but sex in those last six months had been all about making a baby and not at all about expressing their love for each other. Lyn had charts and ovulation kits everywhere, and every time they'd made love it had been carefully timed rather than simply because they wanted each other.

Roland had started taking every opportunity to work

away, or to give a paper at a conference, just to take the pressure off and make him feel less like a machine. And that was why he'd bought the house at the maltings—something that would take over his head completely. Something he could escape to.

Not that he'd told anyone about it. Not his family and not his closest friends. How could he tell them that he'd felt a failure as a husband, that he'd let Lyn down every single month?

And the cruellest irony of all had been when the doctor at the hospital had told him...

He dragged in a breath. Not now. He wasn't going to think of that now.

She laid her hand against his cheek. 'I'm sorry, Roland. I didn't mean to bring back bad memories for you.'

Yeah. They must've shown on his face. But he didn't have the words to tell anyone about the worst bit. He hadn't even told Lyn's parents. Which made him a seriously bad person, because he really shouldn't have kept it from them. Or maybe it had been kinder not to tell them. 'It's OK. But I could do with changing the subject,' he admitted. He still found it hard to handle the guilt. Although he knew it wasn't his fault that the drunken driver had crashed into Lyn's car, and it was entirely possible that the crash could've happened even if he'd been at home, he still couldn't forgive himself for not being there at the end—or handle that last, unkindest cut of all.

'Let's go and look round a bit more,' she said.

And funny how comforting he found it when her hand curled round his as they walked round the site. She didn't push him to talk; she was just there, offering quiet support and kindness.

If he wanted to make this thing between them real,

he'd have to tell her the truth. All of it. Including the stuff he didn't let himself think about. He didn't think she'd pity him, and she definitely wouldn't judge him. But he still wasn't ready to talk, and he wasn't sure if he ever would be. Maybe brushing up his dating skills was a bad idea. Or maybe he'd work out some way to move things forward between them without opening up that world of hurt.

On Monday morning, Grace picked up a text from Roland during her break.

Can you get Wednesday to Friday off this week?

Why? she texted back.

Sweeping-off-feet stuff was the response. Which told her nothing.

I'll see what I can do, she said.

Possibly because it was still June, before the summer holiday season started in earnest, the office where she was working was happy for her to take the time off.

'Excellent,' Roland said when she told him the news.

She coughed. '"Sweeping-off-feet stuff" is all very well, but if we're going away somewhere I need to know what to pack.'

'A couple of nice dresses and something for walking about in,' he said.

'Walking about—do you mean walking boots, waterproofs and insect repellent?' she asked.

'Nope. Smart casual.'

'So it's urban and not country, then?'

He sighed. 'Grace, I can hardly sweep you off your feet if you know all the details.'

'But if I don't know enough, I'll need three suitcases so I can be prepared for every eventuality,' she countered.

He smiled. 'Minimal luggage would be better. OK. It's urban. I'm not planning to make you walk along most of Hadrian's Wall—though,' he added, 'if you're up for that…'

Grace pushed away the thought that she'd go anywhere with him. Because this thing between them wasn't permanent. 'Uh-huh,' she said, hoping that she sounded polite enough but not committing herself to anything. 'Got it. Minimal luggage, a couple of smart dresses, and smart casual stuff with shoes I can walk in.' Quite what he had in mind, she had no idea.

'And your passport,' he said.

'My passport? Bu—'

He silenced her protest by the simple act of kissing her. 'It's sweeping-off-feet stuff,' he reminded her gently. 'And my bank balance can definitely take it, before you start protesting or feeling guilty. It's a place I'd like to show you, so please just give in…' He laughed. 'I would say gracefully, but, given your name, doing something "Gracefully" means asserting your independence and being stroppy.'

She nodded, simply because that kiss had wiped out anything she'd intended to say. And he just smiled and kissed her again. 'Sweeping you off your feet. That was the deal,' he said.

And how.

CHAPTER SEVEN

'REMIND ME NEVER to play poker with you,' Grace grumbled as they got on the Tube. 'You have to be the most…' She shook her head, unable to think of the words.

'Poker-faced?' Roland teased.

'Annoying,' she retorted.

Roland just laughed. 'If I told you where we were going, then I wouldn't be sweeping you off your feet. Trust me. It'll be worth it.'

Grace wasn't so sure—until he led her to a platform at Victoria station and she realised what was standing in front of them. An old-fashioned train, with the staff all lined up in front of it, wearing posh livery.

'This is the London starting point of the Orient Express.' She caught her breath. He couldn't mean this—could he? 'We're going on this? Now? Really?'

He looked utterly pleased with himself. 'Yup. I was paying attention when we talked at the fireworks, you know.'

And how. This was something she'd dreamed about doing for years and years, and never thought she'd ever actually do. When she'd mentioned it to Howard, he'd clearly discussed it with his mother because he'd told her the next day that it was way too extravagant and there were much better, cheaper and more efficient ways of going to Paris than the Orient Express.

Not that she'd ever been to Paris. Since she'd been dating Howard, they'd always been too busy at work to take off more than a couple of days at a time, which they usually spent in a cottage somewhere in England—even though Paris was only two hours away from London on the Eurostar.

And now Roland was taking her on her dream trip. Although they weren't going all the way to Istanbul—because that particular journey was only scheduled for once a year, and even Roland couldn't change that—they were still taking a slow train to Paris, the City of Light. The most romantic place in Europe.

He was really sweeping her off her feet.

She realised that he was waiting for her to say something, but right now she was so overwhelmed that she couldn't think straight, let alone string a proper sentence together. 'Roland, I don't know what to say.'

'"Thank you, Roland, it's nice to tick something off my bucket list" would do,' he teased.

'It is, and it's fabulous, and I'm stunned because I never expected you to do anything like this, but—'

As if he guessed she was about to protest about the cost, he cut off her words by kissing her.

'Grace, I wouldn't have booked this if I couldn't afford it,' he said, 'and I'm actually quite enjoying sweeping you off your feet. Do you have any idea how good it makes me feel, knowing that I'm able to make one of your dreams come true?'

It was something she knew she'd like to do for him, too. Except Roland hadn't really shared his dreams with her, so she had no idea what she could do to make him feel this same surge of delight. She took a deep breath. 'OK. Brattish protesting about the cost all swept to one side. This is really fantastic and I'm utterly thrilled. I can't believe you've done something so amazing and lovely for me, but I'm really glad you have.' And she meant that, from the bottom of her heart. 'Thank you so much. This is the best treat ever.'

'I'm glad you're enjoying it.' He took her hand. 'Let me escort you to our seat, *mademoiselle*.'

Roland had said that there was a French branch of his family, and given that his surname sounded French she could entirely believe it; but this was the first time she'd ever heard him speak the language. Admittedly, it was only one word, but it was amazing how much sexier he sounded in French.

And then she made the mistake of telling him that.

He grinned and launched into a rapid stream of French.

She coughed. 'My French is limited to schoolgirl stuff, and that's pretty rusty. I understood maybe one word in ten out of that. Even if you said it all again at half the speed, I still wouldn't understand much more.'

'Maybe,' he said, 'I'll show you later instead.'

And, oh, the pictures that put in her head. Heat rushed through her and her face felt as if it had turned a vivid shade of beetroot.

He simply gave her the most wicked and sultry smile.

Not only was Grace feeling swept off her feet, she was in severe danger of losing her head as well. And, even though she was loving every second of this, part of her felt way out of her depth. So she'd just have to remind herself that she was sensible and this was two weeks of sheer fun—he didn't expect her to fit into this environment permanently.

When they got to their carriage, it was nothing like the trains she normally used outside London. There was plenty of space, and the plush, comfortable seats were placed opposite each other in pairs, with the small table in between covered by a white damask cloth.

'I forgot to ask if you get travel sick,' Roland said, suddenly looking horrified. 'Sorry. Would you prefer to face the direction we're travelling?'

'I don't get sick, exactly,' she said, 'but yes, please— if that's OK with you?'

'Of course it is.'

But the luxury didn't stop at their seats. The waiter came to serve them their drinks—freshly squeezed orange juice for Roland, and a Bellini for Grace.

'This is so decadent,' Grace said with delight, giving herself up to the pleasure of being pampered.

Brunch was even nicer—fresh fruit salad, followed by crumpets with smoked salmon, caviar and scrambled eggs, then pastries and coffee. And everything was slow and unhurried, as if they had all the time in the world. So very different from the usual rush of a working life in London.

At Folkestone, they were met by a band serenading them, and then took the bus through the Eurotunnel to Calais. At the station, they were met by another band playing; and on the platform where the vintage blue and gold train was waiting, the staff were lined up in their smart blue uniforms and peaked hats. The restaurant staff were clad in white jackets with gold braid, black trousers and white gloves.

'I feel like a princess,' Grace whispered.

'Good. That's the idea.' Roland squeezed her hand.

'Now for the real thing,' he said with a smile. 'The Orient Express over mainland Europe.'

One of the uniformed staff took them to their cabin; it was cosy yet beautifully presented, and Grace had never seen anything so luxurious in her life.

Again, the pace was slow and unhurried. If they'd taken the express train from St Pancras, they would've been in Paris already; but the slow journey through the French countryside was so much nicer, giving them time to look at their surroundings.

'So tell me about the French side of your family,' she said. 'Didn't you say they have vineyards?'

He nodded. 'They're all in the Burgundy area. One branch of the family produces Chablis, and the other produces Côtes de Nuits.' He grinned. 'They're horribly competitive—but luckily because one specialises in white wine and one specialises in red, they're not in competition with each other. But there's a kind of race every year about how many awards and glowing reviews they can get.'

'But I bet they're the only ones allowed to be rude about each other, right?'

His eyes glittered with amusement. 'Right.'

'So do you see them very often?'

'Not as often as I'd like,' he admitted. 'It's very pretty in Dijon, with all the old narrow streets and houses built of honey-coloured stone. The whole area is lovely and the views from the chateaux are amazing. Actually, I really ought to go and visit them soon, because I've been getting pleading emails about difficult roofs and I did promise to go and have a look.'

'Do all old buildings have problematic roofs?' she

asked, remembering what he'd said about the roof in his family home.

'It's not just that—there's damp, dry rot, death watch beetle, subsidence…' He spread his hands. 'And if someone hasn't been careful enough to use the right materials when working on an old house—using modern plaster instead of lime, for example, or replacing a wooden floor with concrete—it can create more problems than it solves.' He smiled. 'But I'm not going to drone on about restoration work.'

'Or glass?' she teased.

'There's one glass building I'm definitely taking you to see in Paris,' he said. 'But don't ask me what. It's a surprise.'

'No asking. I promise,' she said.

'One thing I was wondering about you, though,' he said. 'Why do you worry about the cost of things so much?'

She grimaced. 'This stays with you? You're not going to say a word to Bella?'

'It stays with me,' he promised.

'I guess it stems from when I was little,' she said. 'My father wasn't just unreliable about time—he wasn't very good with money, either. I can remember the bailiffs coming round when I was about three, and it was pretty scary. I remember my mum crying her heart out when she thought I was asleep. I don't ever want to be in that situation again.' She shrugged. 'Which is why I'm always very careful with money. I'm being sensible.'

'I wasn't accusing you of being a Scrooge,' he said swiftly. 'But don't you ever feel you've missed out, sometimes?'

'No.' But her denial was too swift, and she could see in

his expression that he thought so, too. And, yes, she knew she'd missed out on things in the past because she'd been too sensible and too careful. Just as she would've missed out on this trip today if she hadn't for once thrown caution to the wind and agreed to his suggestion of helping each other out. 'Can we change the subject?' she asked, feeling antsy and cross with herself because she was ruining the mood.

'Sure.'

'Tell me about Paris,' she said. 'The first time you went there and what you really loved.'

'That's easy,' he said. 'My parents took all three of us, on the way down to Bordeaux. I must've been about five. It was Christmas, and we went to the Galeries Lafayette. The Christmas tree there was the tallest one I've ever seen in my life—before or since—and it was covered in lights and shiny red apples. And we went to a café for hot chocolate that had a cinnamon stick in it—something I'd never really seen in England—and we all had a slice of chocolate cake from the *bûche de Noël*. And my mum bought poinsettias.' He smiled. 'Philly of course loved the fact they're called *étoile de Noël* because the leaves are star-shaped and red, gold and green are the colours of Christmas in France. She always does them up the French way in her shop at Christmas.'

Grace relaxed again as Roland chatted easily with her about Paris and Christmas and how his family mixed both French and English traditions.

'It's nice to include both bits of your heritage, though—the English and the French.'

'Yes, it is,' he agreed.

They dressed up for an early dinner in the dining car— Grace was really glad she'd bought a new cocktail dress during her lunch break the previous day—and every course was sumptuous and exquisitely presented, from the lobster to the tournedos Rossini, the platter of French cheeses, and then a cone of coconut sorbet with a delicate slice of fresh pineapple that had been caramelised.

'This is beyond what I dreamed it would be like on the Orient Express,' she said to Roland when their coffee arrived. 'Thank you so much.'

'Je t'en prie,' he said.

'Um—I don't remember what that means.'

'You're welcome,' he said. 'And we haven't reached Paris yet. I hope you'll like what I've planned.'

'If it's even one per cent as fabulous as this,' she said, 'I'll love it.'

Roland had arranged for a plush car to meet them at the station and take them to the centre of the city. Grace drank in their surroundings in total silence as they drove through the centre of Paris, not wanting to break the spell; she'd had no idea just how pretty the city was. The wide boulevards, the pretty buildings, the light and airy feel of the place.

The outside of their hotel was beautiful, a five-storey white building with long narrow windows and wrought iron balconies—just what she'd imagined a Parisian hotel to look like. Inside, it was even better: the lobby was all white walls with gilt-framed pictures, red and white marble chequered flooring and wrought iron chandeliers. At the end was a marble staircase with a wrought iron and gilded balustrade. She'd never seen anything so glittering and gorgeous.

When the concierge took them up to their floor, her pulse speeded up. So this was it. Sharing a room with Roland.

As if he'd guessed her sudden nervousness, he said, 'We have a suite. There are two bedrooms and two bathrooms. I'm not taking anything for granted.'

So he wasn't expecting her to sleep with him. 'Thank you,' she said.

But, even though they hadn't known each other for very long and they weren't in a permanent relationship—and weren't planning to be in one, either—Grace knew that if he asked her to make love with him while they were in Paris, her answer would be yes. How could she resist him in the most romantic city in the world?

Her bedroom was gorgeous, with a pale blue carpet, cream walls, and tall windows that opened onto a balcony with an amazing view of the Eiffel Tower. Her bed was wide, with plenty of deep, fluffy pillows; and the bathroom was all cream marble and gilding. When she came back into the living room between the bedrooms, she noticed that there were comfortable chairs and sofas upholstered in old gold, and there was a vase of fresh flowers on the coffee table.

'This is amazing, Roland,' she said.

He smiled. 'Yes, it's pretty good.'

Had he stayed here before? Did this bring back memories of his late wife? But she didn't want to hurt him by asking.

He didn't seem to notice her awkwardness, because he said, 'And now we have an evening in Paris.'

An evening in Paris. It sounded incredibly romantic. And he said he'd planned things. 'What do you have in mind?' she asked.

'Come with me,' he said.

He'd retained the plush car from before. 'It would take us an hour to walk where I'm taking you, and the Métro journey means a lot of messing about, so that's why we're taking a car now,' he explained. 'We can walk through the city and explore tomorrow.'

'OK,' she said.

They ended up at what he told her was the fifth *arrondissement*. 'This is Quai St Bernard,' he said, 'and it's the perfect place for a summer evening.'

There was a mini amphitheatre on the side of the Seine. People were sitting on the side of the river, picnicking or drinking wine and listening to the DJ playing what sounded like tango music; and there was a crowd of people dancing.

'Tangoing in Paris?' she asked. 'Roland—this is fabulous, but I'm afraid I don't know how to tango. Though I'm very happy to watch the dancing,' she added swiftly, not wanting him to think she was ungrateful. 'I can still soak up the atmosphere and enjoy it.'

'I know you do dance aerobics with Bella, so you can follow a routine,' he said. 'Don't worry that you've never danced a tango before. You'll pick it up. Just follow my lead.'

And what could she do but give in to the steady, hypnotic beat and dance with him? He held her really close, sliding one thigh between hers and spinning her round, and it was his nearness rather than the dancing that took her breath away.

When he bent her back over his arm, his mouth skimmed the curve of her throat and she went hot all over. If there hadn't been so many strangers dancing around them—if he'd danced with her like this in the privacy of their hotel suite—she knew this would've been the prelude to a much deeper intimacy. She could see from the expression in Roland's dark eyes that right now he felt exactly the same way. And although part of her felt shy about it, part of her revelled in it. In being totally swept off her feet, dancing the tango by the river in Paris at night.

The music changed to a salsa—something she did know, from her aerobics classes—and Roland smiled as she segued into the step-ball-change routine, side to side and back to front.

'What?' she asked, aware that he was watching her.

'It's lovely to see you letting go,' he said.

'Are you saying I'm uptight?'

'No. More that you hide yourself. But tonight you're *la belle étoile.*'

Her schoolgirl French was enough to let her translate: he thought she was a beautiful star?

She realised she'd spoken aloud when he stole a kiss. 'Right now you're shining. And you're beautiful.'

Tears pricked her eyelids. 'Thank you. *Merci beaucoup.*'

'Je t'en prie,' he said, and spun her round so they could salsa together, holding her close enough at times so she could feel his arousal pressing against her, and at others standing facing her and shimmying along with her.

The DJ changed to playing slower, sultrier music, and they ended up swaying together, dancing cheek to cheek. Grace felt cherished and adored—something she wasn't used to, and something she had a nasty feeling she could find addictive.

She really had to keep it in mind that this wasn't real. Roland saw this as dating practice, nothing more. Wishing it could be otherwise was the quickest route to heartache. She needed to remember her fall-back position: being sensible, the way she always was.

When the music finally ended, they took the car back to their hotel.

'That was fantastic,' she said. 'I enjoyed that so much.'

'Me, too.'

'Obviously you know the city well.' She swallowed hard. Time for a reality check. 'I assume you've done that before?'

He shook his head. 'I've been to Paris a few times with Lynette, yes—but we didn't stay at the hotel where we are tonight and I'm not retracing our footsteps.'

Which made her feel a bit better; and she was impressed that he realised she'd been worrying about that. 'So how did you know about the dancing?'

'You want the truth?' he asked. At her nod, he laughed. 'The Internet is a wonderful thing. I looked up romantic things to do in Paris. And that one struck me as being a lot of fun.'

'It was.' And she loved the fact that he'd gone to that much trouble for her. 'Your dating skills really don't need any practice, Roland. That's absolutely the way to melt someone's heart. To think about what they might like and surprise them.'

His fingers tightened around hers. 'That's what these couple of days are about. Exploring and having fun. I'm not trying to recreate the past. This is just you and me.'

As they pulled up at the hotel, he gestured across the river. 'Look.'

'The Eiffel Tower's sparkling!' she said in delight. 'I had no idea it did that at night.'

'It sparkles on the hour,' he said.

Grace was so tempted to take a photograph of the Eiffel Tower on her phone and send it to Bella—but then her sister would call her and ask why she was in Paris, and it would get too complicated. Pushing back the wist-fulness and disappointment that she couldn't share this with the one person she knew would understand how much she was enjoying the chance to travel, she said, 'This is just like I imagined Paris to be. The City of Light.'

'I'll show you more tomorrow,' he promised.

Despite what he'd said on their arrival, Grace won-dered if Roland expected her to share his room that night. But he kissed her at her bedroom door. 'Good night, sweet Grace.'

It took the pressure off; but, at the same time, she felt disappointment swooping in her stomach. She lay awake, wondering if she had the nerve to walk into his room. If she did, would he open his arms to her? Or would he re-ject her? In the end, she didn't quite have the nerve, and she fell asleep full of regret.

The next morning, she felt a bit shy with him; but he was relaxed and easy. 'Are you up for a lot of walking?' he asked.

She nodded. 'Bring it on.'

After a breakfast of excellent coffee and the best crois-sants she'd ever had in her life, he took her to the Tuileries and they wandered through the pretty gardens. 'I know this is a bit touristy, but we can't miss it.'

'With you being a glass fiend, you're going to show me the pyramid at the Louvre, right?' she guessed.

He laughed. 'Not just the one everyone knows about in the courtyard. This is a bit of a whistlestop tour. I hope you don't mind.'

'No. It's fabulous,' she said, meaning it.

They walked through the museum itself, and Grace was stunned to come across pieces of art she'd known about for years, just casually dotted through the building. It didn't seem quite real, and she pinched herself surreptitiously.

And then Roland took her to the other pyramid.

'And this is what I love, here. The perfect symmetry of glass,' he said with a grin, and took a selfie of the two of them on his phone, standing under the inverted pyramid with a rainbow of light shining across their faces.

'You and your glass,' she teased.

From the Louvre, they walked to the Place des Vosges. 'It's the oldest planned square in the city,' he told her. 'Victor Hugo lived here when he wrote *Les Misérables.*'

It was utterly beautiful: a terrace of redbrick houses with tall windows and blue-tiled roofs, and little arcades running along the bottom storey. Grace was enchanted, and even more so when they wandered through more of the Marais district. 'This is lovely,' she said. 'All cobbled streets and medieval crooked lanes.'

'It's how Paris was before Napoleon razed most of it and built all the wide avenues and huge squares,' Roland said. 'What I like about it is the way you've got old-fashioned *boulangeries* mixed in with art galleries and wine shops and jewellery designers.'

'You could just lose yourself here,' she said.

He nodded. 'It's the best way to explore.'

They ended up at Place du Marché-Ste-Catherine, a cobblestoned square with pretty plane trees and lots of cream-coloured four-storey eighteenth-century houses. On three sides of the square there were little cafés with parasols and sunshades on; there were wrought iron benches in the centre, and a couple of buskers playing Bach on the violin.

'Time for lunch,' Grace said. 'And I'm going to order

for us. Even though it's a long time since I've spoken French.'

'Sure you don't want me to help?'

'Nope. I'm going outside my comfort zone,' she said. 'And I've got you to thank for making me that brave.'

'OK,' he said. *'Allons-y.'*

Grace's schoolgirl French was just about up to ordering two coffees and quiche, though she had to resort to sign language and a lot of smiling to order the lamb's lettuce salad, and Roland couldn't help smiling. Grace was oh, so sweet. And wandering through one of the prettiest districts of Paris with her had soothed his soul.

He'd called her a beautiful star, the night before. And even in the daytime she seemed lit up. He loved the fact that she was throwing herself into the whole Parisian experience, enjoying every single moment and sharing his delight in the glorious architecture. And a corner of his heart that he'd thought would stay heavy for ever suddenly seemed lighter, just because she was with him. But he knew she wanted someone who wouldn't let her down. His track record wasn't good enough. Falling in love with Grace Faraday wouldn't be fair to either of them.

That evening, they had dinner in the Michelin-starred hotel restaurant—another treat he knew she'd enjoy as much as he did—and then he took her to the Eiffel Tower. 'This is the best way to see Paris by night,' he said, 'with all the streets lit up.'

He showed her the broad boulevards radiating outwards; the River Seine was like a black silk ribbon with its bridges lit up. 'This is the Champ de Mars,' he said, showing her the south side of the tower, 'with the military school at the end.' He pointed out the shiny gold dome of the Hôtel des Invalides, and the Trocadéro gardens.

'This is amazing,' she said. And, to his shock, she threw her arms round him and kissed him.

Time seemed to stop.

And although there were plenty of other tourists enjoying the view from the platform, he felt as if the two of them were alone in a little bubble of time and space.

When Roland finally broke the kiss, he felt almost giddy and had to keep holding her tightly. And then he recovered his customary aplomb and told her more about the tower and pointed out more of the landmarks in the city. Just because if he kept talking, then he'd be able to stop himself kissing her stupid.

Back at the hotel, he had to damp down the urge to carry her across the threshold and straight to his bed. That wasn't the deal. And, even though he was pretty sure she wouldn't say no, it wouldn't be fair to her. So he kissed her good night at the doorway to her room— making very sure he kept the kiss short enough so it didn't play havoc with his self-control—and went to bed alone.

And he spent the next couple of hours lying awake, thinking of Grace.

What if she was the one who really could make him live again?

But the biggest question was, what did she want? And, if they did try to make a go of things, would their relationship splinter in the same way that his marriage had? Would she want children, to the point where nothing else mattered?

It was a risk. And he wasn't sure he had the strength left to take that risk.

So he'd stick to the rules.

Despite the fact that he really wanted to break them.

CHAPTER EIGHT

How DID YOU sweep someone off their feet without losing
your own head in the process? Roland still didn't have
any clearer ideas the next morning. But after breakfast
he took Grace to Montmartre. As he expected, she was
charmed by the gorgeous Art Deco Métro signs, loved
the beautiful church and the amazing views over the city,
and enjoyed walking through the crowded square where
the artists sold their wares and did charcoal portraits of
tourists. He got her to pose on the steps next to the fu-
nicular railway and took a photograph of her; when a
passing couple offered to take a photograph of them together, he enjoyed the excuse to wrap his arm round her
shoulders and for her to wrap her arm round his waist.

They stopped at one of the street vendors for a cinnamon crêpe, then wandered further through Montmartre,
looking for the plaques to show where the famous turn-
of-the-century artists had once lived or painted.

'Bella would love it here,' Grace said.

And for a moment Roland could imagine the two of
them coming here with Hugh and Bella, Tarquin and
Rupert, lingering at a table outside one of the cafés and
talking and laughing until the early hours of the morning.

He shook himself. That wasn't going to happen. His

next step was dating again, not finding his true love. And who was to say that he would find The One? Maybe one chance was all you got, and he'd already had that with Lynette. Wanting a second chance was greedy. And he had to look at it from Grace's point of view, too; even if he wanted to try making a go of things with her, she wasn't ready to rush into another long-term relationship.

So he kept it light and fun and did touristy things with her for the rest of the afternoon until it was time to catch the Eurostar back to London. This time their journey was swift and businesslike rather than slow and romantic, the way the Orient Express had been. Which was a good thing, because the brisk and businesslike feeling would stop him doing something stupid.

'Thank you, Roland,' she said when they were back in Docklands. 'I've had the nicest time ever.'

'My pleasure,' he said, meaning it.

He used the excuse of catching up with work for Friday evening and the whole of Saturday, in an attempt to cool his head again; but on Sunday afternoon, when she diffidently suggested that maybe they could go to the Science Museum in search of the seaweed 'plank', he found himself agreeing. And again he ended up holding hands with her as they walked round.

Disappointingly, they couldn't find the plank.

'Let's go next door,' he said.

'Because you want to see the dinosaurs? Or because it's one of the most gorgeous buildings in London and you want to drool over the architecture?' she asked.

He loved it when she teased him like this. Grace really seemed to get who he was and what made him tick. 'Both?' he suggested.

'Pfft. It's the brickwork all the way, with you,' she said

with a grin. 'But let's go and see the dinosaurs as well, because I loved those when I was a child.'

'And I bet you used to count the bones,' he teased back.

'Absolutely. And I could always talk Dad into getting a dinosaur head on a stick for Bella and me—you know, the sort with a trigger on the end so you can make the mouth snap shut. We used to pretend to be T-Rexes and chase each other round the garden. Bellasaurus and Graciesaurus, that was us.'

Grace, all young and carefree and letting herself shine. When had that stopped? he wondered. He'd really, really liked the carefree Grace who'd danced the salsa with him on the banks of the Seine. Could she be that Grace back in London? And could she take a risk with him?

When they queued up to see the dinosaurs, the little girl in front of them was scared when one of the large animatronic dinosaurs roared unexpectedly, and burst into tears. Her father immediately swung her up in his arms to comfort her.

'Poor little lass,' Grace said.

Roland gave her a sidelong look. Was he being over-sensitive and paranoid, or did she have the same kind of broody expression that he'd seen permanently on Lynette in that last year?

'Do you want children?' The question was out before he could stop it.

She stared at him and blinked. 'That's a bit abrupt. Why do you ask?'

'Just wondering.' Stupid, stupid. Why hadn't he kept his mouth shut?

'I don't know,' she said.

'But you were engaged to Howard for four years. Surely you talked about having a family?' He knew he should shut up and leave the subject well alone, but his mouth was running away with him. Big time.

'Actually, no,' she said. 'We didn't. What about you? Did you and Lynette…?'

The question made him flinch inwardly, but he knew it was his own fault. He'd been the one to raise the subject. 'I was still getting my business off the ground.' That was true. Up to a point. But oh, yes, Lynette had wanted a baby. More than anything.

'But did you want to have children when the business was more settl—?' She stopped herself. 'Sorry. I'm probably bringing back difficult stuff for you.'

Yes, she was, but not in the way she thought. Roland had never spoken to anyone about the way he and Lyn had struggled and struggled, and how their love had got lost somewhere under her desperate need for a child. Or about the shock news the doctor had given him at the hospital. 'It's OK,' he said. Even though it wasn't and it hurt like hell.

'Sorry, anyway,' she said, and squeezed his hand.

Change the subject. Change it now, he told himself.

But it was like prodding a bruise to see if it was getting better yet. And the words just spilled out before he could stop them. 'I can imagine you as a mum.' She'd bring her child somewhere like here, to point out the wonders of the big blue whale and the dinosaurs and the fossilised lightning and the beautiful colours of the gemstones. And he had a sudden vision of himself at the seaside, building sandcastles with a little girl who had her mother's earnest blue eyes and shy smile.

'I think I'd like to be a mum,' she said.

And that was the sticking point.

Roland had wanted to be a dad—but not at the expense

of his marriage. He'd wanted their life to grow and expand, not for some of it to be excluded.

'But there are no guarantees,' she said.

It was the last thing he'd expected her to say and it surprised him into asking, 'What do you mean, no guarantees?'

'Apart from the fact that I'd need to find someone I wanted to have a family with in the first place, not everyone can have children. I've got friends who couldn't, even after several rounds of IVF,' she said.

That figured. Grace would take the sensible, measured point of view. But then again, he'd thought that Lyn would take that point of view, too, and maybe look at alternative options when things hadn't gone to plan. But, once her biological clock had started ticking, Lyn's views had changed. She'd become obsessive, almost. And, instead of running away and hiding in work, he should've done more to help her. He should've found a middle way that worked for both of them.

'Not everyone can,' he said, and hoped that Grace couldn't hear the crack in his voice, the way that he could.

She didn't comment on the fact he was quiet for the rest of the afternoon, but she bought him an ice cream in the museum café, and she got him talking about the amazing architecture of the Natural History Museum.

Funny how she understood him so well and knew what was balm to his soul.

'I never thought to look it up,' she said, 'but is there a museum of architecture?'

'Actually, there's something really amazing here in London,' he said. 'It's the house of Sir John Soane—the architect who designed the Bank of England, and the Royal Hospital in Chelsea. He arranged for the house to become a museum for students and people who loved architecture, after his death. They do candlelit tours in the evening so you get the feel of what life was like there, nearly two hundred years ago.' He smiled at her. 'Actually, if there's one next week, would you like to go?'

'Yes, but haven't you been there already?'

'Several times,' he said, 'but I see something new every time I go. It's a total maze of rooms with all these hidden compartments and corridors. The collection's arranged by pattern and symmetry rather than by period, and it's a total magpie's nest—everything from Egyptian relics to old clocks and period furniture and incredible art.' And it would be nice to share it with someone. Someone who understood what made him tick.

She smiled back. 'Sold.'

'Great.'

They visited the shop on the way out; Roland used the excuse that he wanted to pick up something for his five-year-old niece, but when Grace wasn't looking he secretly bought one of the dinosaur heads on a stick she'd told him about. Later that evening, he wrote a note on the outside of the paper bag and sneaked it into her briefcase, hoping she'd enjoy it when she found it.

On Monday morning, Grace opened her briefcase at her desk and discovered an unfamiliar paper bag resting on the top of her things.

In Roland's precise handwriting was a note.

Saw this and thought of you. Rrrr.

Intrigued, she opened the bag, and she burst out laughing when she saw the dinosaur head on a stick.

It was the last thing she would've expected from the man she'd met at Bella's wedding. But the Roland she'd got to know over the last few days had a keen sense of humour—and he made her feel more light-hearted and carefree than anyone she'd ever met. Like the teenager she'd never really been, because she'd always been the serious type.

Roland made her feel different.

And she liked that feeling.

Smiling, she texted him.

Thanks for the T-Rex. Am sure it will scare the numbers into behaving.

On impulse, she added a kiss to the end of the message, and sent it before she could chicken out.

Pleasure, came the immediate response.

Checked and is candlelit evening at museum tomorrow. Entry limited to first two hundred so we need to be there by five p.m. latest. Can you make it? R x

The fact that he'd sent her a kiss at the end of his own text made her heart flutter. It would be so easy to lose her heart to him. But that wasn't what he was looking for, and she needed to remember that. This was their last week together. They'd just enjoy it, and part as...well, hopefully, friends.

On Tuesday evening, Roland met Grace at Lincoln's Inn Fields and they joined the queue—early enough to guarantee their admission, to his relief.

He took her to the catacombs in the crypt, so she could see the sarcophagus by candlelight; there was lots of dramatic up-lighting. 'This is the spooky bit,' he said. 'It always feels like being in the middle of a gothic novel.'

'Your architect liked drama, then,' she said. 'I can't believe this is all a private collection. Imagine living here with this in your basement.'

'And this is probably how he would've lit it,' he said.

She shivered. 'It's a little bit too spooky for me.'

'Come and see my favourite bit,' he said, and took her to the model room.

'Oh, I can see why you love this,' she said with a smile.

'My favourite one is the Pantheon. I loved the model, when I was a child—and then, when I visited the real thing in Rome, I was totally blown away by it. I think it's my favourite building in the whole world.'

'So what is it about it that grabs you most?' she asked.

'The dome. It still amazes me how they constructed that dome nearly two thousand years ago, without all the modern equipment we have now. It's the most incredible feat of engineering.'

'It's impressive,' she agreed.

'I used to come here a lot when I was a student,' he said. 'Soane used to open these rooms up to his students before and after lectures, so they could get more of a feel for the subject. I could just imagine being taught architecture here with these models.' He guided her round to see the miniature Parthenon. 'These models are incredible. Even the acanthus leaves on the Corinthian capitals here are accurate copies of the real thing. It's like being on a mini Grand Tour.'

'Have you actually done the Grand Tour?' she asked.

'I did think about doing it, the year I graduated,' he admitted, 'but a real Grand Tour could last anything from several months to several years. That wasn't really an option if I wanted to get my career up and running, so I did the whistlestop version, concentrating on Italian architecture and pretty much missing out the art and sculpture.'

'What was your favourite building? After the Pantheon, that is,' she added.

'The Coliseum's a close second,' he said, 'and the Duomo in Florence is something else, especially if you go inside the dome.'

'So would you think about building something with a dome?'

'Maybe.' He smiled at her. 'I guess I could pitch to Dad and Will that we ought to have a folly—as in a mini Pantheon—in the grounds, but I have a feeling they'd both laugh until they collapsed.'

'I thought your family supported your architecture?'

'The serious stuff, they do. A mini Pantheon is pure fantasy.' He laughed. 'And if they actually let me do it, in two hundred years' time people would point at it and refer to me as Roland "the Mad Architect" Devereux. Though I guess it'd make us stand out from the crowd if we could offer weddings held in the English Pantheon.'

'I have a nasty feeling that I could be a bad influence on you,' she said.

He tightened his fingers around hers. 'And that's probably a good thing.'

They'd planned to go to the cinema the following evening; but at lunchtime Grace found a text on her phone from Roland.

Sorry, something's come up at work. I need to sort it out. Going to be late home. Can we take a rain check on the movie?

Sure, she texted back, burying her disappointment. She knew he wouldn't cancel without a good reason, and he'd given her as much notice as he could.

She texted him just before she left the office.

Have makings of stir-fry in fridge, so if you don't get time to eat I can cook you something in five minutes flat tonight.

It was a while before he replied to thank her, and he didn't get home until almost nine.

'Sit down and I'll make you a drink. Have you eaten?' she asked.

'No. I'm too tired to eat,' he admitted.

'You need to eat,' she said, and ushered him to the kitchen table. 'Give me five minutes.'

As she'd promised, five minutes later, there was a plate of chicken, stir-fry veg, sweet chilli sauce and noodles in front of him.

'Thank you. This is good,' he said after the first mouthful.

'You're very welcome. Did you manage to get your problem sorted out?' she asked.

He sighed. 'We're getting there. It's a problem with an eco extension we're doing. The team started digging foundations this morning and it turns out there's an old well shaft right in the middle of the new build site. It wasn't on any of the plans of the area, so we need to talk to the building regs inspector and the planning department about how we're going to deal with it. We can cap it and build over it, or we can make a feature of it say with a partial glass floor, but either way it's going to affect how we deal with the foundations.' He grimaced.

'I'm probably going to be tied up dealing with this until the weekend, and it means I'll be working late as well. Sorry, Grace. It isn't what we agreed and I feel bad that I'm letting you down.'

'It's not your fault,' she said, 'and it's clearly not something you can delegate so it's fine. I can amuse myself.'

'Thank you.' He reached over to take her hand and squeezed it. 'I really appreciate you being so understanding. And don't worry about cooking for me for the rest of the week. I'll grab something with the team.'

'If there's anything you need, just tell me,' she said.

The rest of the week dragged. Grace was shocked to realise how quickly she'd come to look forward to her dates with Roland. So maybe his problem at work was a good thing; it would bring her common sense back and stop her making a fool of herself by falling for him.

On Friday evening, she went to the flat after work to see how things were going and pick up any post, and discovered there was a letter waiting for her. The job she'd been interviewed for on the day of the flood was hers, and they wanted her to start the week after next.

Given that she'd resigned herself to having to keep looking for a job, she was thrilled by the news. She texted Bella swiftly.

Got the job. Celebrate when you get back. Love you lots. x

And then she called her parents.

'Oh, darling, that's wonderful,' her mother said. 'I'm so pleased for you.'

'Can I take you and Dad out to dinner tonight to cel-ebrate?' she asked.

'That's so lovely of you,' her mother said, 'but your dad's booked us a surprise break and we're heading out to the airport in about ten minutes. But we'll take you out the day we get back.'

'OK. That'll be lovely,' Grace said, swallowing her disappointment. 'Hey. I'd better let you go and finish getting ready. Have a great time, and text me to let me know you arrived safely.'

'We will. Love you, Gracie,' her mother said. 'And I'm so proud of you.'

'Love you, too, Mum,' Grace said.

She tried calling her three closest friends, just in case any of them might be free to celebrate her news with her, but their phones were all switched through to voicemail. By the time she got back to Docklands, Grace was feel-ing just a bit flat; she had some seriously good news, but nobody to celebrate with. For the first time since she'd broken up with Howard, she felt really alone.

And it made her question all her decisions. Had she done the right thing in cancelling her wedding? Should she have settled for a man who was kind but made her feel like part of the furniture?

She shook herself. No. Of course not. She'd done the right thing for both of them. She and Howard hadn't loved each other enough, and eventually they would've made each other miserable. She just had to get used to her new life. And she had a new job to look forward to—a challenge to meet. Everything was going to be just fine.

'Nothing fazes a Faraday girl,' she reminded herself out loud.

She knew Roland was busy, but texted the news to him

anyway. He didn't reply, and she was cross with herself for being disappointed that he hadn't even had time to text her back saying 'congrats'. Talk about being an ungrateful, needy brat. 'Get a grip,' she told herself crossly, 'and stop being so selfish.'

Half an hour later, the doorbell rang. A woman stood on the doorstep, holding a gorgeous hand-tied floral arrangement and three helium balloons.

'Grace Faraday?' she asked.

Grace blinked. 'Yes.'

'These are for you.' The woman—who looked strangely familiar, even though Grace knew they hadn't met before—handed her the flowers and balloons. She opened the card to find a message from Roland saying, *Well done! Congrats. R x.*

'That's amazing,' she said. 'How can he arrange something as gorgeous as this at such short notice—especially as practically everywhere is shut at this time of night?'

The delivery woman said drily, 'Because if your sister's a florist, you can talk her into doing things out of hours.' She looked Grace straight in the eye. 'He's kept you very quiet. I had no idea he was even seeing someone, let alone *living* with someone.'

This was Roland's little sister? 'You're Philly?' Grace asked, shocked.

'Phyllida Devereux of Philly's Flowers,' she confirmed.

Now Grace realised why the woman had looked familiar. Because she looked like Roland; she had the same dark eyes and the same gorgeous smile.

And Philly thought that Grace was living with Roland? Oh, help. She needed to do some damage limitation. Fast. 'We're not living together. This isn't what you think.'

Philly tipped her head to one side. 'Care to try me with an explanation?'

Roland wasn't here but, from the way he'd spoken about Philly, Grace was pretty sure they were close. 'Look, if you're not already on your way somewhere, come in for coffee and I'll explain.'

'All right.' Philly followed her inside.

Grace played for time while she made coffee. 'Have you eaten yet tonight?'

'No.'

'Then, if you're free, why don't you stay and have dinner with me?' She rummaged in the fridge. 'Do you like gnocchi with tomato and mascarpone sauce? I apologise in advance that it's shop-bought rather than home-made.'

Philly smiled. 'It sounds lovely—and Ro never cooks anyway. If I come here, either he orders something in or he makes me cook for us.'

'And I guess at least this is quick.'

'Is there anything I can do?' Philly asked.

'Lay the table?' Grace suggested, pretty sure that Roland's sister knew her way around the kitchen.

'Deal,' Philly said.

Ten minutes later, they were sitting at Roland's kitchen table with dinner in front of them.

'All righty. I'm not living with Roland—I'm staying in his guest room,' Grace said. 'I'm Bella's sister. There was a burst pipe in my flat—which used to be hers—and Bel left me Roland's number in case of emergency. He said if something like that had happened to you, he knew Hugh and Tarq would look after you, so he was going to do the same for me, as I'm Hugh's sister-in-law. And he offered me a place to store my stuff and stay until my flat dries out.'

'I get that's why you're staying here, but what I *don't* get is why he's sending you flowers.' Philly flapped a dismissive hand. 'Well, obviously as he asked for helium balloons that said "New Job" and "Congratulations" and I wrote the message on the card, I realise you've just got a new job. But this is my brother we're talking about and he hasn't sent a woman flowers since—' She stopped and narrowed her eyes. 'I assume you *know*?'

'About what happened to Lynette? Yes, he told me,' Grace said.

Philly looked thoughtful. 'And it's something he doesn't talk about very much. So are you seeing each other?'

How could she explain? 'It's complicated,' Grace prevaricated.

Philly folded her arms. 'Which tells me nothing. Spill, or I'll make his life a misery until you do—and, trust me, only little sisters can be that annoying.'

Grace smiled. 'Mine isn't annoying. She's lovely.'

'I can be lovely. But I'm definitely the annoying variety,' Philly said. 'Explain complicated.'

'We're helping each other out for a few weeks. Which are practically at an end.'

Philly frowned. 'What do you mean by helping each other out? And why is there a time limit?'

Grace knew that this was going to sound bad. 'He's practising his dating skills on me.'

Philly looked suspicious. 'And what do you get out of it?'

'Being swept off my feet.'

'And what happens at the end of these few weeks? You're going to be just good friends?' Philly added quote marks with her fingers round the last phrase.

Grace felt herself blush. 'Yes.'

'And you'd swear that in court?'

'I'd swear that he doesn't think of me romantically.'

Bad move. Because Philly honed straight in on what Grace hadn't said. 'But *you* think of *him* that way.'

'It's not going to happen,' Grace said. 'I went into this with my eyes open. To be honest, although he says he wants to start dating again, I think he's still in love with Lynette. But if I can help him take those first steps into coming back unto the world, then I'm glad I can do that.'

'You're in love with him,' Philly said.

'We barely know each other. We only met briefly at Hugh's wedding and we've known each other a little over two weeks,' Grace protested. But she had a nasty feeling that Philly was right. Even though it wasn't the sensible thing to do, she'd let herself fall for Roland. A man who wasn't available. Which was as stupid as it got.

'A little over two weeks is long enough.' Philly paused. 'He's seemed different whenever I've talked to him recently. Now I know why. I think you might be good for him.'

'It's not going to happen,' Grace repeated. 'I'm not what he's looking for.' And, even though a part of her really wished that she could be what Roland was looking for, she was sensible enough to know that she didn't fit into his world. She wasn't glamorous and exciting; she was sensible and slightly dull.

Philly had left by the time Roland returned, that evening.

'Thank you for the flowers and balloons,' Grace said.

'My pleasure.' He inspected them. 'Philly did a good job.'

'I like your sister.' Grace paused. 'I hope you don't mind, but she stayed for dinner.'

'And interrogated you?' he asked wryly.

'To be fair, she was delivering flowers to a woman at your house. If I'd been in her shoes, I would've been asking questions, too.' She smiled. 'Philly's nice.'

'Yeah, she is.' He paused. 'What did you tell her?'

'That you're putting me up while the flat dries out.'

'And she didn't ask anything else?' He looked sceptical.

Best to admit the truth, Grace thought. 'She did. So I told her about our deal.'

'Uh-huh.'

She wasn't going to tell him about what Philly had guessed. Because that was way outside the terms of their deal and he didn't need to know about that. 'She gets it. I think she's glad you're…' She grimaced. 'Sorry. That's not tactful.'

'Planning to get back in the land of the living,' he said. 'It's fine. I'm sorry I was working and couldn't take you out tonight to celebrate your new job. The flowers were sort of an apology as well as a congratulations.'

'The flowers are absolutely lovely,' she said.

'And Bella's away, so you couldn't celebrate with her.'

'And my parents are going on holiday; they're on their way to the airport now. Plus my friends are all busy. So, actually, I was pretty glad that your sister came round,' she admitted. 'It stopped me feeling completely like Billy-No-Mates.'

'I intend to make this up to you tomorrow—that is, if it's not going to mess up any plans you've made?' he asked.

She shook her head. 'We agreed to keep ourselves

free until Hugh and Bella got back, so I haven't made any plans.'

'Good. It's going to be an early start, so can you be ready for six?'

'Sure.'

'Pack for a night away. Nothing bigger than a case you can take in the cabin of a plane. Shoes you can walk in, something dressy, a hat, sunglasses and your passport. And don't ask where we're going.'

'Because you're not going to tell me.'

'Humour me. I want to see your face when we get there.' He wrapped his arms round her. 'Congrats again. I knew you'd do it.'

'Thank you.' She hugged him back. Funny how the world felt all right again when he was this close to her. But she'd have to get used to being on her own from next week onwards. So she needed to start putting that little bit of distance between them from now on.

CHAPTER NINE

THE NEXT MORNING, Grace was ready to leave at six. And Roland refused to tell her anything about where they were going until they were at the airport and their flight was called.

'We're going to Venice?' Her eyes grew wide in wonder. 'You're taking me to Venice just for the *day*?'

'And night,' he corrected. 'We fly back to London late tomorrow afternoon.'

'Venice,' she said again, seeming unable to quite take it in.

'It's my favourite place in the world,' he said.

Then he saw the wariness creep into her expression. He could guess why. 'Yes, I've been there a few times with Lyn,' he said, 'but you're not going to be following in her footsteps. This is just you and me. We're celebrating your new job.'

The beginning of her new life. And ending their deal on a high note. He didn't say it, but he was pretty sure she was thinking it, too. He was sticking to the plan. Sweeping her off her feet—and then saying goodbye.

Venice.

Who else but Roland would think about going to Venice just for one night? Grace thought.

And she had a feeling that he'd planned this right from the beginning, when she'd first told him that she hadn't travelled much. It would be the perfect end to their perfect few weeks together.

She was very aware that tomorrow was the last day of their agreement. And, as soon as Bella came back from honeymoon and discovered what had happened with the burst pipe, no doubt she'd insist that Grace came to stay with her and Hugh until the flat was habitable again. There was no reason for Grace to remain at Roland's house.

Unless he asked her to stay.

Somehow, she didn't think that was going to happen. Roland's job meant that he was used to planning in advance and working to a schedule. This was no different, really. It had been a short-term project to brush up his dating skills and sweep her off her feet. Mission accomplished, just before the deadline.

So she'd just enjoy this weekend for what it was.

The end.

Roland held her hand all the way on the plane, and when he walked with her to the end of the jetty at the airport. 'I thought we could take a water taxi into the city,' he said. 'It's the best way to see Venice for the first time.'

Once they were on the lagoon, Grace understood why he'd suggested bringing a hat and sunglasses. The reflections of the sun on the water were so bright that she would've been squinting without them. 'Right now, I feel like a princess,' she said.

'That's the idea,' he said. 'Watch the horizon.'

The water was pure turquoise and she couldn't make anything out at first. But then she saw rooflines, all spires and domes. As they drew closer, she could see that there were houses packed in tightly along the shoreline, with bridges arching over the entrances to the waterways running through the city.

'Venice rising from the water—this is one of the most beautiful things I've ever seen,' she whispered.

Roland's fingers tightened around hers. 'And it gets better. Watch.'

As they grew closer, she could see the architecture more clearly. There were shutters at the windows of the houses; plaster peeled away from some of the brickwork, while other houses looked as if they'd been recently restored.

Their driver took them under a bridge, and now they were really in Venice.

'I've never been in a city without any traffic noise, before,' she said. And it was odd to hear the swish of the waves and hear people talking where she'd usually expect to hear engines revving and horns blasting.

'What's that building?' she asked. 'All that latticed plaster reminds me of the icing on a wedding cake.'

'That's the Palazzo Ducale—the Doge's Palace,' he said. 'And that tall tower opposite—the one with the red bricks and green roof—is Galileo's Tower.' He smiled at her. 'We'll walk through St Mark's Square later, so you can have a closer look at them.'

'Thank you,' she said. Coming here was a treat—but coming here with someone who knew the place and could help her to find all the most interesting bits was better still. And the fact that that someone was Roland...

When their driver moored at the jetty, Roland helped her from the boat.

'I still can't get over this,' she said. 'I've seen documentaries and photographs of Venice in magazines, but the real thing is beyond anything I'd dreamed about. I think,' she added shyly, 'I like this even more than Paris.'

He looked pleased. 'I hoped you'd like this. Let's check in, and then we can go exploring.'

The hotel was part of an old palazzo; the decor was all cream and navy and gold, with marble flooring and a fountain in the reception area. Roland had booked them a suite with two rooms. Because they were only staying for one night, Grace managed to unpack her overnight case very swiftly.

The streets outside were crowded, yet at the same time it was so much quieter than she was used to in London, without the traffic noises. Gondolas and small rowing boats glided through the narrow canals; there were bridges everywhere, with the sunlight reflecting off the water and dappling the undersides of the bridges.

Shops crowded against each other, offering glass and Venetian masks and marbled paper; tourists posed for photographs on the bridges and in the little squares. 'All the signs seem to point either to the Rialto or San Marco,' she said in surprise.

'In this part of the city, they're the two main destinations and all the streets lead to them—though sometimes it's the long way round,' he said with a smile. 'Let's start at the Rialto. There's a gorgeous view of the Grand Canal from the bridge.'

The marble on the bridge had been worn shiny by countless hands skimming across it; and Grace leaned against the bridge to watch the traffic on the canal go by. When they finished crossing the bridge to go into the marketplace itself, she discovered that it was a sheer delight, full of colour—selling everything from fresh seafood glistening in the sunlight through to tiny wild strawberries and fragrant herbs sold by the handful.

'This is amazing,' she said.

He glanced at his watch. 'Wait a second.'

And then suddenly bells were pealing all over the city.

'Is it a special occasion, or does this happen every day?' she asked.

'Every day. In the summer it's like aural sunlight; in the winter, especially if it's foggy, it's a little spooky,' he said.

'I can see why Venice is one of your favourite places,' she said. 'It's amazing.'

They walked hand in hand through the narrow streets, enjoying all the bustle around them and stopping to buy a *piadina* from one of the street vendors to keep them going over lunchtime. Grace stopped to take photographs of the figures outside some of the mask shops—the terrifying plague doctor with his hooked beak, and the pretty harlequin—and took a selfie of Roland and herself standing on a bridge with a gondola gliding behind them. 'Do you mind me being horribly touristy?' she asked.

'Not a bit.' He smiled. 'Actually, I'm enjoying seeing how much you like Venice.'

'It's gorgeous,' she said. 'I know I keep saying it, but it's like… Venice is just like nowhere else I've ever been.'

'If you don't mind us doing a whistlestop tour,' he said, 'we can go take a look at the basilica and the Doge's Palace.'

'But you've seen it all before,' she said.

He shrugged. 'You know I never pass up the opportunity to look at architecture. And besides, you can't come to Venice and not see the *quadriga*—the four horses. They've been in Venice for more than eight hundred years.'

Grace thoroughly enjoyed their tour of the cathedral and the palace, especially as Roland turned out to be a mine of information about the buildings. And she loved the fact that he took a selfie of them on the loggia of the basilica, next to the replicas of the four bronze horses.

Right now, she thought wistfully, this felt like a honeymoon. Though she knew she was being ridiculous. Roland hadn't given her any signals that he wanted their relationship to continue past their agreement, let alone anything more. They'd known each other for only a few weeks; it was way, way too soon to fall in love.

Stop being greedy, she reminded herself. Just enjoy every second of this and stop wishing for something you're not going to get.

'I thought we'd have dinner early,' he said, 'because there's something else you absolutely have to do in Venice.'

'Bring it on,' Grace said with a smile.

Roland found a little tucked away restaurant. 'My Italian's a bit scrappy,' he said, 'but I can get by. What would you like to eat?'

'A Venetian speciality,' she said.

'Let's ask the waiter what he recommends,' he said. 'But for pudding I'd say it has to be tiramisu in the area where it was invented.'

The waiter recommended *sarde in saor*—sardines in a sweet and sour sauce—followed by *polenta e schie*—tiny Venetian shrimps on a bed of white polenta. And the tiramisu was the best Grace had ever, ever tasted.

'This is perfect,' she said. 'Thank you so much.'

But the best was what Roland had arranged for after coffee.

'I wanted to eat early,' he said, 'so we'd get to see the sunset.'

And then she discovered where he'd planned their viewpoint to be: from the seat of a gondola.

Their gondolier wore the traditional black trousers, striped jersey and straw hat; he guided them through the narrow waterways, using his pole to propel them and pushing his body against it to help them turn the odd corner. To Grace's delight he actually serenaded them in a mellow tenor voice.

The sunset itself was the most romantic thing she'd ever seen: the sun sinking, the sky turning shades of orange and apricot with the domes and towers of the city silhouetted against it, and the turquoise waters of the Grand Canal changing to reflect the deep tones of the sky.

She was too moved to say a word; she leaned her head against Roland's shoulder, drinking in the view and enjoying his nearness. He held her close, and again this felt so much like a honeymoon.

The gondolier took them through the narrow waterways again, which had turned almost inky to reflect the darkened sky; reflections from little globe-shaped lamps flickered on the water. 'This is so pretty,' she said. 'Thank you so much.'

'My pleasure,' he said, and stole a kiss.

They lapsed back into companionable silence; then, as a covered walkway rose in front of them, Roland said, 'This is the Bridge of Sighs. It's traditional to kiss underneath it.'

What else could she do but kiss him as the gondola glided underneath the bridge?

'This was the perfect end to a perfect evening,' she

said as the gondolier tied up the boat at the jetty by St Mark's Square and helped them off the gondola.

'We haven't finished quite yet,' Roland said. 'Remember tangoing by the Seine? Now we're going to do the same in St Mark's Square. Well, not necessarily dance the tango—it depends what they're playing.'

As they walked into the square, lit by more of the pretty globe-shaped lights, Grace realised what he meant. There were tables and chairs outside Florian's and Quadri's, the two oldest *caffès* in the city, and a couple of small bands played on stages underneath gazebos.

Roland spun her into his arms and began to dance with her. Other couples were doing the same, she noticed, so instead of protesting that they were going to make a spectacle of themselves, she relaxed and gave herself up to the sheer pleasure of being held by Roland.

Grace looked so beautiful in the soft light of the square, Roland thought. Tonight, she was really shining—relaxed, happy, enjoying the music and the dancing and the sheer romance that was Venice.

And he, too, was being seduced by the place. To the point that when they got back to the hotel and he'd unlocked the door to their suite, he actually picked her up and carried her across the threshold.

Then he realised what he was doing, and set her back down on her feet. 'Sorry. I got a bit carried away.'

She smiled and reached up to stroke his face. 'I think you were doing the carrying. Literally. And the answer's yes.'

He sucked in a breath. Was she saying…? 'But—'

She pressed a finger lightly against his lips. 'No

strings,' she said. 'That's what we agreed. And tonight's just you and me and Venice.'

'Are you sure about this?' he asked.

Her eyes were almost navy in the low light. 'I'm very sure.'

'Grace, you don't owe me anything. I didn't bring you here expecting you to sleep with me in exchange for the trip.'

'I know, and that's not why I'm saying yes.' She took a deep breath. 'It's because I want to. I know there are no strings and this is just temporary between you and me—but you've swept me off my feet this far, so let's go the whole way.'

He needed no further encouragement. He picked her up and carried her across the threshold to his bedroom.

And then he got to live out the dream he'd had the previous weekend. Unzipping her dress, sliding it off her shoulders, kissing every centimetre of skin he revealed—and finally losing himself in her warm sweet depths.

That night he fell asleep with his arms wrapped round her and her arms wrapped round him, feeling more at peace with himself than he had in way too long.

The next morning, Roland woke first. Guilt flooded through him. He really had let the romance of Venice carry off his common sense, last night. Even though Grace had told him that she was sure, he shouldn't have let things go this far.

So what now? Would her feelings have changed this morning? Would she regret it? Would she want things to be different? Or would they both be able to blame it on the romance of the sunset and the music?

She was shy with him when she woke, and he knew he had to break the ice.

'I'm sorry,' he said. 'I, um…I guess last night shouldn't have happened. I apologise.'

'Don't apologise. It was just as much my idea as yours,' she said. 'It wasn't part of our deal. We got carried away by—well, by Venice. So we can pretend it didn't happen.'

If she'd wanted last night to be the start of something more, now was the perfect time to say so. The fact that she hadn't made it clear to him that she intended to stick to the terms of their arrangement.

So today was their very last day together.

This was going to be goodbye.

As far as he knew, the landlord hadn't contacted her any more about the situation with the flat, so she might still need to be his house guest for a while. But Bella and Hugh were due back from their honeymoon tomorrow, and it was more than likely that as soon as Bella learned what had happened, she would insist on Grace moving in with her.

And then he and Grace would be polite and distant strangers.

That was what they'd agreed, so why did it make him feel so antsy?

'I, um— There was something I wanted to show you this morning,' he said. 'Shall we go exploring straight after breakfast?'

'That sounds good,' she agreed.

A shower helped him get some of his equilibrium back. Strong Italian coffee helped even more.

And then, with the help of a map, he found the Soto-portego dei Preti. 'This is what I wanted to show you,' he said. 'It's the *cuore in mattone*—the heart in the brick.'

'I should've guessed it would be something architectural,' she said with a smile, looking at the brick just below the lintel. 'A heart-shaped brick is very appropriate for Venice. What's the story behind it?'

'You're meant to touch it and make a wish—so the legend goes, if your wish is respectful and harms no one, it will be answered within the year,' he said.

'So have you known about this for years, or was this like the tangoing in Paris?'

'Like the tangoing. I looked it up on the Internet,' he admitted. 'Shall we?'

They touched the brick together and made a wish. Roland couldn't help asking, 'So what did you wish for?'

'I imagine it's like the wish you make on a star or when you blow out the candles on your birthday cake,' she said. 'So I can't tell you, or it won't come true.'

'I guess.' And that meant he didn't have to tell her what he'd wished for, either.

For love to fill his life again. For this thing between them to become real.

They took the water bus over to Murano to see all the pretty painted cottages and to see a glass-blowing demonstration.

'You and your glass,' she teased afterwards.

He spread his hands. 'You can't come to Venice without seeing glass being blown or lace-making.'

'I guess. And it was pretty spectacular—I've never seen anything like that before. Do you mind if I take a quick look round the shop?'

'Sure. Though shopping's not really my thing, so I'm going to sit in the sun while you're looking round. Don't rush,' he added. 'Just come and find me when you're ready.'

* * *

Grace was glad that Roland wasn't planning to shadow her in the shop, because she'd hoped to find a gift for him to thank him for taking her to Venice. And there was a beautiful modern paperweight that was absolutely perfect. Better still, the sales assistant wrapped it beautifully for her, so he wouldn't have a clue about it.

Roland found a little *osteria* that sold *cicheti*—Venetian tapas—for lunch, and the choice was breathtaking: tiny *polpette*, stuffed olives, tomato bruschetta, white asparagus wrapped in pancetta, baby octopus in lemon, slices of grilled polenta with salami, *arancini*, spider crab, *zucchini* stuffed with tomatoes and cheese, and marinated artichokes. Between them, they tried a little of everything, sharing a plate and feeding each other little morsels; again, it felt like being on a honeymoon, and Grace had to remind herself to keep her feet on the ground. To go back to being sensible, quiet Grace.

But on the flight back to England, Roland went quiet on her.

And that in turn gave her time to think. Today was the last day of their arrangement. Their last day together. Grace and Roland had agreed that once Bella and Hugh returned tomorrow, from then on they'd be polite strangers.

A few weeks ago, that had seemed perfectly reasonable. But, last night, they'd made love. So would he still want to stick to their original deal, or would he suggest that they try to make a go of things?

She knew what she wanted. She'd wished on the heart-shaped brick that things would be different—that this thing between them could turn out to be real. But she wasn't quite brave enough to bring it up. This morning, she'd woken to find him looking full of panic, clearly having second thoughts. What else could she have done but pretend everything was just fine and let him off the hook?

It was pretty clear that her feelings were one-sided. Last night, they'd simply got carried away with the romance of Venice, the gondola and dancing through St Mark's Square. It hadn't been real.

So it was better to leave this situation with her dignity intact.

And she'd get over this.

She would.

Back in the airport at London, she switched on her phone to find that it was dead. 'I must've left an app on that drained the battery,' she said.

'You can use my phone if you need to,' Roland offered.

'Thanks, but I didn't tell my family I was away so they won't be worrying. It can wait,' she said.

Back at Roland's house, there was a pile of post. He set his coffee machine working, then sat at the kitchen table to go through his mail, while Grace plugged in her phone and waited for it to charge for long enough that she could switch it on again, then checked the messages that came through.

She was about to tell Roland the good news when she noticed that his face had blanched. 'Is everything OK?' she asked instead, concerned.

'Sure.' But he didn't move. He just sat there, staring at the table.

She finished making the coffee and brought his mug over to the table. 'You don't look sure,' she said gently.

'I…' He sighed and gestured to one of the envelopes. 'This came from Mindy, Lyn's best friend from school.

They're moving house and she found these photos and thought I might like them.'

'That was kind of her,' Grace said. Or was it? He looked as if someone had ripped his heart out. Roland had clearly loved his wife deeply. Despite the fact that he'd said he was ready to move on, from his reaction to getting those photographs Grace didn't think he was. Was he feeling guilty that he'd taken her to Venice— as if he'd betrayed Lyn's memory? Though asking him would be like stomping over still-fresh wounds, and she didn't know what to say.

In the end she reached over to squeeze his hand. 'I didn't know Lyn, but you said that she wouldn't want you to be sad. Why don't you look at the photos and re-member the good times?'

'I...' His voice sounded thick with emotion. 'But you...'

'We had a deal,' she said. 'It finishes today. And I'd like to think that we've become friends.' More than that—they'd been lovers, and it had shown Grace ex-actly what she'd been missing in her life. How wrong she'd been when she'd thought she could settle for nice enough instead of the real thing.

Roland could so easily have been her real thing.

But she knew that he wasn't ready to move on, and she wasn't sure if he ever would be.

'Friends,' he said.

'I'd like to see the photos,' she said. 'Talk to me, Ro-land. Tell me about Lyn. Tell me about the good times.'

Roland knew he ought to tell Grace the truth. About the bad times. But he didn't want her to think badly of Lyn. Or of him.

He took the photographs out of the envelope. 'They're from years ago. Just a weekend at the beach with friends.'

'She looks nice,' Grace said. 'As if she was fun. And you both look so happy.'

They had been. Once.

'Yeah.' His voice cracked.

Grace pushed her chair back and walked round the table to wrap her arms round him. 'Don't focus on the fact that she's gone. Focus on the fact that you were together and you loved each other.'

And it hadn't been enough. But how could he explain?

'Grace, I wish…'

As if her thoughts were totally in tune with his, she held him just that little bit tighter. 'Roland, these past few weeks have been amazing. You've swept me off my feet—but, better still, you've shown me that I don't have to settle for being sensible all the time. That it's OK to dream and to reach for those dreams. And your dating skills are just fine—but I don't think you're ready to move on. Not yet.'

No. Because his guilt still held him back, making him feel that he didn't deserve a second chance. Not when he'd messed up so badly. 'I guess,' he said.

But, even if they could get over that hurdle, there was another sticking point. The one that had cracked his marriage. He and Lyn had had trouble conceiving, and he didn't know if the problem had lain with him. What if Grace wanted children—and, just like it had happened with Lyn, their love got bogged down in the problems of conception? He couldn't bear to go through that nightmare again. And, even though he knew Grace was sensible and down to earth, even the most sensible person could be sideswiped by emotions.

He had to let this go. For her sake as well as for his own. He had to get out of her way and let her find the happiness she deserved. Even if it was with someone else.

'Those messages that came through—one was from my landlord,' she said. 'Thanks to your restoration expert sucking up the water and putting a dehumidifier in early, the flat's all dried out now. It seemed they don't need to strip the plaster back after all, so I can move my stuff back whenever I like. Which is perfect timing,' she said brightly.

Meaning she was going to walk out of his life. Roland didn't want her to go—but he knew she was right. He wasn't ready to move on. It wasn't fair to ask her to wait indefinitely.

'I'll get a couple of the guys to move the heavy stuff for you in the morning if you don't mind lending me your key,' he said.

'Thank you.'

'No problem,' he said. 'And thank you. You've helped me, too, these last few weeks.'

But not enough, Grace thought. Not enough for him to be able to move on from the sadness of his past and ask her to stay.

'Great,' she said. 'I guess I'd better start getting my stuff together—and let you get on.'

'Uh-huh.' He gave her an awkward smile. 'Let me know if you need anything.'

She did. She needed him. But it wasn't fair to put that extra burden on him. 'Sure,' she said.

'I'd better check my emails,' he said.

'Yes. So life goes back to normal tomorrow for both

of us,' she said. 'You get your space back. And I get to stand on my own two feet again.'

'Well—good night.'

'Good night. And thanks for everything.' This time, she didn't hug him—because it would hurt way too much to let him go. Instead, she had to go back to the fall-back position. Sensible Grace.

If only it could've been otherwise.

CHAPTER TEN

GRACE SPENT THE morning moving her things back to the flat. Just as Roland had promised, he'd sent a van and two of his workmen to move the heavy stuff for her, and she'd bought them both a case of beer to thank them for their help.

When she'd put the last of her things in the car, she took the gift-wrapped paperweight she'd bought in Venice from her bag and went into Roland's office. She put the parcel in the top drawer of his desk, along with the card she'd written earlier, and closed the drawer again.

Once he'd finished grieving for Lynette, he'd make someone a wonderful partner.

If only it could've been her.

But he wasn't ready to move on; and she was still up in the air after her break-up with Howard. Being the one who'd called everything off didn't mean that she'd escaped any feelings of hurt and loss. She still needed to work out what she really wanted from life.

Besides, it was way too fast for her to have fallen in love with Roland. She'd just responded to the way he'd swept her off her feet, that was all. She couldn't possibly be in love with him.

She set the alarm and locked the door behind her, then

posted his door key through the letterbox. Have locked up and left your key, she texted.

Back in her own flat, she spent her time cleaning the place from top to bottom and then moving everything back into its rightful place. She called in to see Bella and Hugh with a bottle of champagne, and thought she'd managed to fool Bella into thinking that everything was fine; though the next evening her sister turned up unexpectedly, bearing a seriously good walnut cake from her local bakery.

'Spill,' Bella demanded.

Just like Roland's sister had demanded last week, Grace thought wryly.

'There's nothing to tell,' she said, giving her best fake smile.

Bella coughed. 'You look worse now than when Mrs Concrete Hair used to do a hatchet job on your confidence with her sly little insinuations. So what's happened? Has Howard had an epiphany and asked you to go back to him, and Mama Dearest has stuck her oar in?'

'No to both,' Grace said. 'And I'm not going back to Howard. We wouldn't make each other happy. And he's a nice guy, Bel. He deserves to be happy.'

'And he needs to grow a backbone, but OK,' Bella said. 'So if it's not Howard, it's someone else. You might as well tell me, Gracie, because you know I won't shut up until you do.' Bella cut them both a large piece of cake.

Grace knew that her sister meant it, so she gave in and told Bella about her deal with Roland. 'And it's fine,' she said. 'We both did what we promised. He swept me off my feet and I helped him with his dating skills. End of story. If we see each other again, we'll be polite but distant strangers.'

'Which obviously isn't what you want.'

Grace denied it, though she knew full well that Bella wasn't going to believe her.

'Just call him,' Bella said, rolling her eyes. 'Tell him how you feel. What have you got to lose?'

'Bel, he's still in love with Lynette. I can't compete with a memory,' Grace said. 'And don't get any bright ideas about inviting us both to dinner and trying to fix us up. It'll just be embarrassing. I'll be fine. I've got my new job to look forward to, and that'll keep me busy.'

And if she kept telling herself that, eventually she'd believe it.

Over the next couple of days, Roland threw himself into work and refused to admit to himself how much he missed Grace. How empty the whole place felt without Grace around.

She thought he couldn't move on because he was still in love with Lyn. It wasn't true. But he'd let her go because he came with baggage and he hadn't wanted to drag her down with it.

Had he made a mistake?

If he'd opened up to her properly, told her the whole truth instead of just parting, would she have understood? Could she have helped him start his life all over again—give him a second chance?

He shook himself. No. He was being selfish. He'd done the right thing—even though it hurt.

He tried distracting himself with a magazine. On one page, he saw a photograph of the heart-shaped brick he and Grace found in Venice. According to the paragraph beneath the photograph, Roland had got the legend completely wrong. It wasn't about wishes coming true. Allegedly, if you pressed the brick you fell in love immediately; if you pressed it together, you'd be devoted for ever.

And he and Grace had touched the brick at the same time.

A pretty story. That was all it was. He tried to put it out of his head and started on some preliminary sketches from his latest design brief. When the point of his pencil snapped, he opened his desk drawer to grab a new lead; but there was something he didn't recognise in the drawer. A wrapped parcel, next to a card. The handwriting on the envelope was Grace's. When he opened it, the card showed a picture of Venice at sunset, very similar to the one they'd seen on the gondola. Inside, she'd written, *Thank you for sweeping me off my feet.*

The parcel contained a beautiful paperweight in shades of turquoise and blue. The sort of thing he would've chosen for himself. He handled the smooth glass thoughtfully. She'd thanked him for sweeping her off her feet and she'd bought him the most perfect present.

She understood him.

Would she understand if he told her the rest? And would she be prepared to take a risk on him?

There was only one way to find out. He called her. Her phone went through to voicemail, so he assumed that she was busy. 'Grace, it's Roland. Please call me when you get this message.' He left his number, just in case she'd mislaid it.

And now it was up to her.

Why was Roland calling her? Grace wondered.

Maybe she'd left something behind and he'd just discovered it. Of course he wasn't calling her to say he'd changed his mind about the terms of their deal. It was ridiculous to hope.

When she was quite sure that she wasn't going to make a fool of herself and blurt out something inappropriate, she returned his call.

He answered on the second ring. 'Roland Devereux.' He sounded as cool and impassive as he'd been the first time she'd called him. When she'd mistakenly thought he was her landlord. And now...

'It's Grace,' she said. 'Returning your call.'

'Thank you.'

'What did you want? Did I leave something behind?' Despite her best intentions, hope flickered in her heart.

'Yes.'

The hope sputtered and died. 'Sorry. Let me know when it's convenient to come and pick it up.'

'I'll come over.'

'I can't put you to all that trouble,' she protested.

'It's no trouble. I'll be in the area anyway.'

Why? Work? But it wasn't her place to ask. 'OK. Thank you. Let me know when, and I'll make sure I'm here.'

'Now,' he suggested.

Now? As in...right *now*? Then she realised he was waiting for her answer. 'I—um, yes, sure. I guess at least this time you won't be helping me shift furniture out of a flooded flat.'

'Indeed. See you soon.'

It took all of ninety seconds for her to tidy the flat.

And then what? Would he stay for coffee? Was this the beginning of them becoming friends? *Could* they be friends, after their fling? Or would the memories always get in the way?

When the doorbell rang, her heart leapt. She took a deep breath and reminded herself to act cool, calm and collected. 'Hello, Roland,' she said as she opened the door. Then she noticed that he wasn't carrying anything. She frowned. 'I thought you said I left something behind?'

'You did.' He paused. 'Me.'

'What?' She couldn't quite process this. 'I don't understand.'

'We need to talk.'

She frowned again. 'But I thought we'd already said it all. We had an agreement. You swept me off my feet and I can rubber stamp your dating skills. And now it's all done and dusted.'

'There's a lot more to say,' he said, 'but I don't want to do it on your doorstep.'

Her head was in a whirl. 'Sorry. I'm being rude. Come in. Can I get you a drink or something?'

He shook his head. 'I just want to talk.'

She gestured to the sofa. There wasn't anywhere else to sit, unless she opted for one of the metal dining chairs at the small table in the kitchen part of the flat, so she sat next to him.

'I don't know where to start,' he admitted.

'Try the beginning,' she said. 'Or wherever you feel like starting and you can go back and forth.'

'Then I'm going to tell you something I've never told anyone—not even my family or my best friends.' He took a deep breath. 'It's about Lyn. Everyone thinks I've been mourning her for the last two years.'

'And you haven't?' she asked, surprised. But Lynette had been the love of Roland's life and he'd lost her in horrible circumstances. Of course he'd been mourning her. He didn't even have any of the wedding photographs on display in his house because it clearly hurt too much. And the way he'd reacted to the photographs Lyn's friend had sent had signalled very clearly that he was still in love with Lyn.

'More like nearly three,' he said.

He'd mourned her for a year before she'd died? But why? Grace bit her lip. 'Was she ill but you hadn't told anyone?'

'Sort of.' He sighed. 'She wanted a baby.'

Which wasn't remotely the same as being ill. Or did he mean a different sort of problem? But Roland hadn't seemed the selfish type. She didn't understand. 'I take it from that, you didn't want a baby?' Grace guessed.

'No, I did,' he said, 'but I always thought love would expand along with my family. With Lyn, it narrowed. Right from the moment we first talked about it and started trying, she changed. All her friends who started trying fell pregnant the very first month, which made it even harder for her when she didn't.'

'Did you talk to a doctor about it?'

He nodded. 'He said we were both young and they wouldn't even consider offering us fertility treatment until we'd tried for at least another year. And it broke her, Grace. Every month when her period started, it was like the end of the world. And every time we made love, it was timed by her ovulation chart. I tried taking her away for the weekend and being spontaneous to take her mind off things, but nothing worked. She was driven. It was as if our relationship was only there for the sole purpose of having a baby, and I hated that I was letting her down all the time.'

She took his hand. 'Hey. You tried. You were there for her.'

'Not enough,' he admitted, 'and that's the really shameful bit. I don't like myself very much, Grace.'

'Hey. We all have things that make us feel that way,' she said gently. 'I'm not squeaky clean, either. I broke off my engagement three weeks before the wedding day, remember?'

'Which was the right thing to do,' he said. 'Whereas I…' He sighed. 'We stopped seeing my family. Will and Susie have a little girl, Matilda, and when Lyn couldn't get pregnant she couldn't handle being around children. It made her feel a failure, even though I tried to tell her that she wasn't a failure and nobody was ever going to judge her. But I couldn't exactly explain to everyone why Lyn didn't want to be anywhere near Tilda, not without telling people the truth—and she'd sworn me to secrecy because she didn't want anyone pitying her or judging her. So we used my work as an excuse, saying I was too busy for us to see people.' He grimaced. 'My mum even rang me to say she was worried about us—she said that I was neglecting Lyn for work and she asked if she could do anything to help. I hated having to lie to my family.'

'But you weren't neglecting Lyn—you were trying to protect her,' Grace protested.

He shook his head. 'Actually, my mum was right. Because it got to the point where I was glad to have an excuse to be away. I did end up neglecting Lyn. I accepted invitations to give lectures abroad so I didn't have to face all that pain. And that's why I was away when the accident happened.'

'The accident wasn't your fault, Roland.'

'I know,' he said. 'And I keep telling myself that, even

if I had been in London, the accident might still have happened. But at least then I would have been there to say goodbye to her before she died, instead of being thousands of miles away.'

'I'm sure Lyn knew that you loved her.'

He nodded. 'And I did, even though our marriage was cracking at the seams. But the very worst bit was what the doctor told me, something I couldn't bear to tell anyone because it was just so...' He caught his breath.

She squeezed his hand. 'Roland, you don't have to talk about this. And it's understandable that you're still in love with Lyn.'

'I'm not,' he said. 'I miss her. But I missed her for a year before she died. I missed the closeness of being with someone. And it's taken me a while to work through all the guilt and misery I've been feeling. I wasn't sure that I'd ever be ready to put my life back together again, but...' He drew her hand up to his mouth and kissed the backs of her fingers. 'I've worked out for myself that the only way to finally get past the pain and heal again is to talk about it. I don't want to have any secrets from you, Grace.' He closed his eyes for a moment, and her heart bled for him. He'd been through so much. 'I haven't been able to say this to anyone, because—well, I know what Lyn meant about not being able to face all the pity. I've been there. But I know you won't pity me.'

'I won't pity you,' she promised. 'But I do reserve the right to give you a hug.'

'OK.' He dragged in a breath. 'Lyn was pregnant when she died. It was so early on that she probably didn't even know. But how different things might've been,' he finished wistfully.

Roland would've been a father and Lyn would've had

the baby she'd longed for so badly. And his marriage might have healed. But the driver who'd crashed into Lyn had taken away all those possibilities. No wonder Roland had locked himself away. 'I'm so sorry,' she said, still holding his hand.

'And that's partly why I haven't really dated since she died. Part of me wants to move on, because I can't spend the rest of my life in mourning. The Lyn I married wouldn't have wanted me to do that—just as I wouldn't have wanted her to be on her own if I'd been the one who was killed and she was the one left behind,' he said. 'But it went sour for us because she wanted a family so desperately. And that's what's stopped me moving on. I don't want to go through that again, to lose the woman I love a little more each day and know I can't do anything to help.'

'I can understand that,' Grace said.

'But then I realised something,' he said. 'These last few days I've been running away again, burying myself in work so I didn't have to think or face things—but I'm ready to face them now.'

'Face what?' she asked.

'The fact that…' He took a deep breath. 'I love you, Grace. And I want to be with you. And I should've told you that as soon as we got back from Venice, instead of letting you come back here on your own.'

'I don't get it,' she said.

'You don't believe I love you?'

'I don't get why you're saying this to me now. Nothing's changed since we came back from Venice.'

'Oh, but it has,' he corrected. 'I've had time to think. Time to miss you. And what finally made me realise was when I found the paperweight—and you thanked me for sweeping you off your feet.'

So did that mean...? The hope she'd ruthlessly squashed earlier flickered back into life.

'And I think you swept me off my feet, too,' he said. 'In just over two weeks, you taught me to have fun again. You taught me how to reconnect.'

'But I didn't really do anything,' she said. 'You're the one who did all the big romantic stuff and took me to places I'd always wanted to see. I don't even know what your dreams are, so I couldn't even begin to start making any of them come true.'

'I didn't know what my dreams were, either, but I do now,' he said. 'I want to live, really live, with the woman I love. A woman who's brave and funny and sweet.'

He couldn't possibly be describing her. 'But I'm not brave. Or funny. I'm just *ordinary*.'

'You're quiet and sensible and grounded,' he said, 'which is all good. But there's more to you than that. There's also a part of you that shines. The woman I danced with on the bank of the Seine, and who was brave enough to order lunch in Paris in schoolgirl French. The woman who likes to plan everything but who put herself out of her comfort zone for a few weeks. The woman who makes my world so much brighter just by being there. And I want you in my life for good, Grace. As my wife.'

But he'd been there before and it had all gone wrong. She couldn't just sweep that under the carpet. 'What about children?' she asked.

'Yet more proof that you're brave,' he said wryly, 'since you're not scared of dealing with a subject that would make most people shy away. Especially because you're the only other person in the world who knows the whole truth about Lyn and me.' He looked at her. 'I admit, part of me is scared to death about it. I've had one marriage go sour on me—and it's something I can't really talk about, because Lyn can't speak up for herself now and I don't want people to think badly of her.'

'Absolutely,' she agreed. 'And, just so you know, I don't think badly of her either.'

'Thank you.' He took a deep breath. 'I'm not confusing you with Lyn. I'm not seeing you as her replacement—I'm seeing you as you. But, even though I want to be with you, it scares me that I might end up repeating the same pattern.'

'How?' she asked.

'I don't want to see you get hurt and bogged down,' he said. 'When I asked you in the museum if you wanted children, you said there were no guarantees.'

'Because there aren't,' she said.

'I don't know if the problem was with Lyn or with me,' he said. 'If it was with me, then you and I might not be able to conceive. I hate the idea of going through all that again, knowing month after month that I've let you down. But,' he said, 'if having children is really important to you, I'll take that risk. I just need to know that…' He stopped. 'I'm making a mess of this.'

'You need to know that our relationship is about more than just having children,' Grace said. 'I get it.' She paused. 'Do you want children, Roland?'

He nodded. 'But not at the cost of my marriage. I love you, Grace, and I want to marry you. But wanting everything is greedy.'

'You taught me something,' she said. 'You taught me that it's OK not to settle for things, not to stick rigidly to my fall-back position of being sensible. It's OK to dream. But you need to balance it with real life and you need to keep it in perspective. If having children naturally doesn't work for us, we can look at other options. Being a biological parent is no guarantee of being a good one. Ed isn't related to me by blood, but he's the best dad I could ever have asked for.'

'I agree with you. OK. So what happened to me and Lyn—that won't happen to us,' he said.

'Definitely not,' she confirmed. 'We won't let it.'

'You know when we touched that heart-shaped brick in Venice?'

She nodded.

'What did you wish for?'

'You asked me that before—and if you tell a wish it doesn't come true,' she reminded him.

'Actually, I got the legend wrong. Apparently, the real one is that if you touch the brick, you fall in love. If you touch the brick at the same time as someone else, you'll be devoted to each other for the rest of your days.' He paused. 'We touched the brick at the same time, Grace. I remember that very clearly.'

She felt the colour heating her cheeks. 'Yes.'

'And I fell in love with you. I think I fell in love with you before then, but that was when it hit me.' He raised an eyebrow. 'Do you want to know what I wished?'

'What did you wish?' Her words were a whisper.

'I wished that our arrangement was more than that. That it could be real. And carry on for the rest of our lives.'

Exactly the same as her own wish.

'So will you marry me, Grace?' he asked. 'Will you make my dreams come true?'

Every nerve in her body was urging her to say yes. To go for her dream. But her common sense still held her back. 'We've known each other only a few weeks, and

you really think we can make a go of it?' She shook her
head. 'But I'd known Howard for eighteen months before he proposed—six months as a colleague and a year
as my boyfriend.'

'So you don't want to marry me?' His face went in-
scrutable.

'My heart's telling me to rush in and say yes,' she
admitted, 'but I'm still scared. Like you, I've been there
before and it's gone wrong. I was engaged to Howard for
four years, Roland.'

'And you still hadn't bought your wedding dress, three
weeks before the big day—when I know you're the super-
organised type who likes planning things in advance,' he
pointed out. 'So maybe you knew deep down that marriage wasn't the right thing for you and Howard, and you
let it go as slowly as you could.'

'Maybe.'

Again, he lifted her hand to his mouth and kissed the
backs of her fingers. 'His parents didn't like you, and
they made you feel as if you were a worthless gold-digger. So I'm guessing that you're worried my family will
feel that same way about you, too.'

She swallowed hard. 'Yes.'

'My family isn't like Howard's,' he said. 'They're not
judgemental. They're eccentric and they have bossy tendencies—well, you've met Philly so you already know
that bit for yourself—but they're warm and they'll love
you to bits as soon as they meet you. And I definitely
like everyone I've met in your family.'

'Uh-huh.' She bit her lip. 'Roland, I'm not very good
about being spontaneous. And I know you're good at
sweeping me off my feet, but that wouldn't be right—not

for this. Can I have some time to think about it? Time to sort my head out?'

'Yes,' he said, 'but I'm not giving you time to worry about things. Come and meet my family tomorrow, so you can see for yourself that it'll be fine.'

She looked at him, horrified. 'That's not giving them much notice.'

He smiled. 'Are you telling me you wouldn't ring Bella or your parents on the spur of the moment and ask if you could drop in for a cup of tea? Or that they wouldn't drop in on you unexpectedly?'

'They're my family. That's what families do.'

'Exactly. And it's the same for me. So you'll come and meet them tomorrow?'

She didn't have any arguments left. And she knew she was right: the only way to get over her fears was to meet them. 'OK.'

'Good.'

'But I need you to know that I'll never come between you and your family. If they don't like me, then I'll fade out of your life,' she warned.

'Deal,' he said. 'And I need you to know that I'm absolutely certain that won't happen. They'll love you, Grace. They'll see you for who you are and they'll love you.' He kissed her lingeringly. 'More to the point, *I* love you.'

'I love you, too,' she said shyly.

'But you're worried that the past is going to repeat itself and you need to be sure it won't. I get that.' He smiled. 'And I'll wait until you're ready to give me an answer.'

CHAPTER ELEVEN

THE NEXT MORNING, Grace woke in Roland's arms. She lay there for a moment, just enjoying being close to him; but gradually she grew antsy.

Today was the day she was going to meet his family.

He'd said it would be light and easy. Just coffee. And he was sure they'd love her.

But what if they didn't? Howard's parents had never thought she was good enough for their son. And Roland's background was very different from her own.

She knew that if she lay there, she'd get more and more miserable, and she'd start fidgeting. She needed to be active; but she also didn't want to wake Roland and start whining at him.

When life gives you lemons, she thought, you make lemon drizzle cake.

And maybe that would be a good way to break the ice with Roland's family. She could take them some home-made lemon drizzle cake to go with the coffee.

Gently, she extracted herself from Roland's arms, shrugged on her dressing gown, crept out of the bedroom and quietly closed the door.

She'd just finished putting the hot lemon and sugar solution on the cake, letting it sink in, when Roland walked out of the bedroom.

'Sorry—did I wake you with all the noise?' she asked.

'No. But something smells amazing.'

'I thought I could take some cake with us,' she said.

He wrapped his arms round her and kissed the top of her head. 'Stop worrying. It'll be fine. But cake is good. You didn't make any spare, by any chance?'

'You'd eat cake for breakfast?'

'French family rules,' he said.

She laughed. 'Made-up rules, more like.'

'Busted.' He held her close. 'Grace, it's going to be fine. I promise.'

He took her mind off things by having a shower with her.

But her nerves returned, doubled, when he drove them to his family home and she could see the enormous house at the end of the long drive.

'Roland—this is a stately home!'

'It's not open to the public. Well, the gardens will be and we're going to do teas and weddings, but...' He shrugged. 'It's not a big deal.'

Yes, it was. She bit her lip. 'Roland, I come from a very ordinary background—and I'm not like Bel. I'm not all bubbly and bouncy and easy to love.'

'Your background is absolutely not an issue—and you're not ordinary, you're the woman I love,' he said firmly. 'Yes, I know you're a bit shy and it takes time to get to know you—but you're more than worth getting to know, and my family's perceptive. They'll see that straight away.'

Grace, remembering Cynthia Sutton's judgemental sneer and her habit of muttering disapproving comments behind the swing of her perfect bob, wasn't so sure. By the time Roland opened the front door, she was feeling physically sick.

But then two dogs came romping down the hallway, barking madly, with their tails wagging nineteen to the dozen.

'Morning, beasties. Coco's the poodle, after Chanel, and Napoleon's the basset hound,' Roland explained. 'French dogs, French names, yada-yada-yada.'

Grace made a fuss of the dogs, who insisted on licking every bit of her they could reach.

'Paws off the cake, beasties,' Roland said with a grin. 'Most of that is mine.'

And then the hall was full of people. Roland introduced them swiftly.

'Grace, these are my parents, Henry and Joanna; my brother Will and sister-in-law Susie; my sister Philly you've already met; and this is my niece, Matilda.'

'Hello,' Grace said shyly, holding out a hand.

But, to her shock, instead of shaking her hand, they all hugged her in turn; and that included little Matilda.

This was so very different from Howard's family; and so much more like her own.

'Coffee's ready,' Joanna said. 'Would you prefer to sit in the drawing room or the kitchen, Grace?'

Grace looked to Roland for an answer, but his face was impassive.

'The kitchen, please,' she said. 'And, um, I made you some cake. I hope that's OK.' She handed the plastic box to Joanna.

'Told you she was a keeper,' Philly said in a stage whisper.

'Shut up, Philly,' Roland said, in the same stage whisper. 'Sorry, Grace. But you've already met my sister. You know she's bossy.'

'Runs in the family,' Philly retorted, and put her arm round Grace. 'What kind of cake is it?'

'Lemon drizzle.'

'Yes! That makes you my new best friend,' Philly said with a grin.

'Actually,' Joanna said, 'I think the men should go and sit in the drawing room while we go and sort out cake and coffee in the kitchen.'

'Good idea,' Susie said with a smile.

'Hang on,' Roland began, his eyes widening. 'No interrog…'

But it was too late. Joanna swept Grace off to the kitchen along with Philly, Susie and Matilda. When Roland came in to try and rescue her, his mother just waved him away and said, 'This is a girls-only chat. Off you go, and close the door behind you.'

Roland gave Grace a helpless look, mouthed 'sorry', and did as he was told.

'We really are glad to meet you, Grace,' Joanna said, putting the cake on a plate. 'And this smells gorgeous. Did you make it this morning?'

'Yes. I, um—when I'm nervous, I bake,' Grace admitted.

'And meeting all of us for the first time is pretty scary,' Susie said. 'I remember what it feels like.'

'Though it's not all of us for the first time. You already know me,' Philly pointed out.

'And we feel we know you,' Joanna said, 'because Philly's told us about you.'

'There isn't actually that much to say about me,' Grace said. 'I'm very ordinary.'

'Tell us about you in your own words,' Susie invited.

This felt like a job interview, but she also knew that it was the most important interview she'd ever have in her life. If Roland's family couldn't accept her, then she'd fade out of his life—for his sake. 'I'm an accountant, I have a clean driving licence and I like cooking,' Grace said. 'I think that covers it.'

'I think there's something quite important you forgot to say,' Joanna said quietly. 'You've put the smile back into Roland's eyes. And to do that takes someone very out of the ordinary.'

'Seconded,' Philly said promptly.

'Thirded,' Susie added.

'Fourthed,' Matilda said, beaming at her. 'Can you make cupcakes, Grace? They're my favourite.'

'Chocolate or vanilla?' Grace asked.

Matilda thought about it. 'Both.'

Grace laughed. 'Good choice. Yes.'

'Are you going to marry Uncle Roland?'

Susie swept her daughter up and plonked her on her lap. 'We're not supposed to ask that, sweet-pea.'

'Why not? I like Grace. So does Coco. I think she should marry Uncle Roland and then I can be the flower girl at the wedding,' Matilda said.

Susie groaned. 'I'm so sorry, Grace. She's obsessed with being a flower girl.'

'My best friend's been a flower girl three times already,' Matilda confided, 'and she's got a tiara with sparkly butterflies on it.'

'That sounds lovely,' Grace said, smiling.

'I think you should go and tell Daddy the cake's coming soon, Tilda,' Susie said, and Matilda slid off her lap and scampered out of the kitchen. 'I really am sorry about that,' she said to Grace.

'It's fine. Really,' Grace said.

'Out of the mouths of babes,' Philly said with a grin.

Then it hit Grace. This wasn't anything like her first meeting with the Suttons. Roland was right. She hadn't been judged and found wanting. His family was eccentric and bossy—and utterly lovely. And it felt as if they'd already taken her to their hearts.

'This,' she said, 'feels exactly like my parents' kitchen would if I had a brother who'd brought a girlfriend home to meet them for the first time.'

'Is that a good thing?' Joanna asked carefully.

Grace nodded. 'Because, although I don't have a brother, I do have a mother and a sister I love very much. And the best stepfather in the world.'

'That sounds good to me.' Joanna lifted her mug of coffee in a toast. 'We really are pleased to meet you, Grace. And I'm sorry for the interrogation.'

'No, we're not,' Philly admitted, not looking in the slightest bit abashed.

'Of course you're not,' Grace said, laughing back. 'Just as I wouldn't be in your shoes.'

'If it's any consolation, they did it to me, too,' Susie said, giving her a hug. 'And they're all right, this Devereux lot.'

The ice was well and truly broken then—especially when they re-joined the others in the drawing room and everyone tasted Grace's cake. 'You're officially in charge of cake from now on,' Will said. 'And we are so going to pick your brains for tea room suggestions.'

'Yes—Roland ought to show you the boathouse after

lunch and tell you what he's planned,' Henry added. 'He can explain them better than any of us can.'

'Actually, I have new plans,' Roland said. 'I know exactly how we can make ourselves stand out for the wedding business.'

Grace had a feeling she knew what was coming next, and hid a smile.

'We could,' he suggested, 'build a folly. A mini-Pantheon.'

Merciless teasing followed.

'This lot has no vision,' he sighed theatrically. 'Grace, tell them you think it's a great idea.'

'I think I'll stick with what you said originally,' she said. 'In two hundred years' time, visitors to the house will be told that you were Roland the Mad Architect.'

'She's got your number, little brother,' Will said with a grin.

After lunch—and after Grace had absolutely insisted on being allowed to help with the washing up—Roland took Grace out to the boathouse and explained what they were planning to do.

'It's got the perfect outlook,' she said. 'And you're right. That wall of glass will give a spectacular view of the lake.'

On the way back to the house, he took her on a detour into the rose garden.

'Oh, now this is pretty,' she said in delight. 'And I've never smelled anything so lovely.'

'You'd need Philly to talk you through all the names and their history,' he said. 'But.' He paused by the sundial. 'You've met my family now.'

'Yes.'

'Do you like them?'

She smiled. 'They're lovely. And they remind me a lot of my family.'

'Good.' He paused. 'I know I said I'd give you time to think—but I really hate waiting. I'm sure that my life with you will be good. And, now you've met my family, I hope all your fears are set to rest, too.'

'They are,' she said.

He took something from his pocket and dropped to one knee. 'Grace. I love you. Will you marry me?' He opened the box and held it out to her.

Set on a bed of purple velvet was the prettiest ring she'd ever seen: a solitaire diamond set in a star-shaped mount.

'A star,' he said, 'because you're *ma belle étoile*. And I really, really love you.'

Grace swallowed hard.

She'd asked him for time. But she didn't need it any more. 'I love you, too. Yes,' she whispered.

He slid the engagement ring onto her finger, then stood up, picked her up, whirled her round, and then kissed her until she was dizzy.

'I hope you're prepared for what happens next, because my family have a really bad habit of taking over,' he said.

'I'm with you, so I can be brave.' She smiled. 'Bring it on.'

It took Matilda all of five seconds to spot the difference when they walked in. 'Your hand—it's all sparkly!' she said in delight. 'Oh—it's a ring. And it's like a star!'

And Roland slid his arm round Grace's shoulders, clearly enjoying the spectacle of seeing his closest family stunned into silence. 'This has to be a first,' he said, laughing.

Everything suddenly went high-octane, with everyone talking at once.

'So when's the wedding? And it has to be here—every Devereux gets married here,' Will said.

'I have a friend who makes amazing dresses,' Susie said.

'*Croquembouche.* We need a proper *croquembouche* wedding cake,' Henry said. 'With sparklers. Lots of sparklers.'

'The flowers are mine, all mine,' Philly said, rubbing her hands together. 'I can't wait to make you the most beautiful bridal bouquet in the world.'

'And I can be the flower girl and have a sparkly tiara with butterflies!' Matilda crowed happily.

'Wait,' Joanna said, walking into the middle of the room and holding her hands up for silence, for all the world like a headmistress in the middle of a noisy assembly hall.

Grace felt her stomach drop. Had she made the wrong decision? Would Joanna feel the same way that Cynthia had—that Grace wasn't good enough for her son?

'Listen, you lot. I know this is the best news ever, but we have to remember that it's Grace and Roland's day,' Joanna said quietly. '*They're* the ones who make the decisions, not us. And we are absolutely not talking wedding plans without Grace's family being part of those discussions.'

So very unlike the way the Suttons had seen things, Grace thought with relief.

'OK. We'll have a planning meeting tomorrow—or as soon as Grace's family can get here,' Will said.

Roland coughed. 'Did you not hear what Mum said? And I agree. It's Grace's choice.'

Everyone stopped and looked at her.

They all wanted to be involved in her wedding, Grace

realised. Not because they wanted to take over, the way that Howard's family had, but because they wanted to be part of it and make her and Roland's day truly special.

She knew without a doubt that, unlike Cynthia, they'd be more than happy for Bella to be her bridesmaid. Just as Grace would be very happy to ask Philly and Susie to be her bridesmaids and Matilda to be the flower girl—complete with her sparkly butterfly tiara. And butterfly wings, if she wanted them.

'My parents are in Italy right now,' she said, 'but they're due home next weekend. A planning meeting sounds good to me. And your house is beautiful. I can't think of anywhere nicer to get married.'

'In our private church,' Will said. 'Or in the house—I'm doing the paperwork to get licensed to hold weddings right now, and I'm sure I can rush it through if you need me to.'

'Or I could build the mini-Pantheon in the grounds,' Roland suggested. 'That'd be a really spectacular wedding venue.'

Everyone groaned. 'Roland. *No!*'

'Spoilsports,' Roland grumbled. But he was laughing.

'And, whatever anyone suggests, Grace gets the casting vote,' Henry added.

Coco and Napoleon barked, as if agreeing.

They were all on her side.

And Grace knew that this time everything was going to be just fine.

EPILOGUE

Three months later

ON A PERFECT Saturday afternoon in September, Grace got out of the car at the gates leading to Roland's ancestral home, and let her stepfather help her up into the old-fashioned coach pulled by four perfect white horses.

'You look beautiful, Gracie,' Ed said. 'Like a princess.'

'Thank you,' she said shyly.

'I know I'm not your real dad, but I'm so proud of you.'

She squeezed his hand. 'You're not my *biological* dad,' she corrected, 'but as far as I'm concerned you're my real dad and you have been ever since you came into my life. I'm a Faraday girl through and through. And you're the only person I would ever consider asking to walk me down the aisle.'

Moisture glittered in his eyes. 'Oh, Gracie.'

'Don't cry, Dad,' she warned, 'or I'll cry too, and Bella took ages doing my make-up—she'll kill us both if it smudges.'

'I love you,' he said, 'and I'm so glad you're marrying someone who loves you and will always back you.'

This was so very different from what she'd planned before. And even making the plans had been different this time, too: because both families had arranged things together.

The horses pulled the coach up the long driveway. Grace's mother, the bridesmaids and the photographer were waiting outside the little private church where every member of Roland's family had been married for the last three hundred years.

The photographer took shots of her in the coach with Ed; then Ed helped her out and her mother made last minute adjustments to her veil and dress.

'You look wonderful,' she said. 'Now go and marry the love of your life, with all our love and blessings.'

Grace's smile felt a mile wide as she entered the church.

The string quartet—Hugh's latest signing—struck up the first movement of Karl Jenkins's *Palladio* as Grace walked down the aisle on Ed's arm. The chapel was filled with old-fashioned roses chosen by Philly from the formal gardens at the house, and the arrangements were echoed in the simple but elegant bouquets carried by Grace and her bridesmaids. Matilda walked in front of them, wearing her sparkly butterfly tiara and scattering rose petals. Grace could see Roland waiting for her at the aisle, and saw his brother Will nudge him and whisper something just before he looked round.

As he saw her walking down the aisle towards him, he smiled and mouthed, 'I love you,' and the whole world felt as if it had just lit up.

She couldn't stop smiling through the whole service. Finally, the vicar said, 'You may now kiss the bride.' And Roland did so lingeringly.

There were more photographs outside the church and in the rose garden; then they finally walked down to the lake, where the boathouse was newly renovated and ready to host its first ever wedding breakfast. The wall overlooking the lake was completely glass, giving perfect views across the lake; and as they looked out they could see swans gliding across the water.

'This is so perfect,' Grace whispered.

Roland kissed her. 'It certainly is.'

The tables were set with more beautiful arrangements of roses and the last of the sweet peas. 'Like the first flowers you ever bought me,' she said to Roland with a smile. 'Philly's really done us proud.'

Everything was perfect, from the meal to the speeches and the music from Hugh's quartet. And Grace knew that it was going to get even better; they had a band for the evening reception, and Roland had planned a display of fireworks just behind the lake.

And there were fireworks indoors, too: because to Henry's pleasure they'd gone with his suggestion of using a tradition from the French side of the family, and instead of a tiered wedding cake they had a *croquembouche* with a spiral of white chocolate roses curled round it. At the top of the cone, instead of a sugar crown there was an array of indoor sparklers; as soon as they were lit, everyone oohed and aahed.

'It's magical,' Grace said.

'Absolutely. And that's how it's going to be for the rest of our life,' Roland agreed. 'With our whole family behind us, helping us to make our dreams come true.'

She raised her glass of sparkling elderflower cordial to toast him. 'For the rest of our life.' She paused. 'Roland, do you think we can sneak out for a moment without anyone noticing?'

'Why?'

'Because…' She needed to tell him something, but she wanted to tell him in private, and so far she just hadn't found the right moment. 'I need a moment with you. Alone.'

'And you want us to sneak out, given that all eyes are on the bride and groom?' He grinned. 'Well, hey. We're a team. We can do anything.' He put her glass down on a nearby table, and waltzed with her over to the corner of the room, then quietly danced with her until they were at a side door. 'Righty. Let's slip out.'

Once they were outside, he found them a quiet spot by the lake. 'OK. From the look on your face, it's not just because you want to be on your own with your new husband. What's wrong?'

'Nothing's wrong. But… What you were saying about us being a team. A team means more than two, or it can mean a pair.'

'You're splitting hairs, but OK,' he said. 'You and me. Two. We're a pair, then.'

She coughed. 'I'm trying to tell you something. We're a *team*.'

'You just said we were a pair.'

'But,' she said, 'we went to Venice just over three months ago. We made love for the first time.'

'Ye—es.' He frowned. 'You're talking in riddles, Gracie.'

'No, I'm not.' She stroked his face. 'I thought architects were good with figures? And have an eye for detail?'

'We do.'

'So did you notice that I toasted you in elderflower cordial, not champagne?' she asked. 'And alcohol is off the menu for me for the next six months. Along with soft cheese and lightly cooked eggs.'

She saw the second that the penny dropped. 'Are you telling me…?' he asked, hope brightening his face.

'I know we didn't plan it, but we're definitely Team Devereux,' she said. 'I didn't want to tell you until I was completely sure—and I wanted you to be the very first to know. I thought I might be a bit late just because I've been rushing about sorting out wedding stuff. Not because I was stressed, because our joint family is brilliant, but just because…it's a wedding.' She spread her hands. 'And it's not that. Because I did a test this morning.'

'And it was positive?'

'It was positive,' she confirmed.

'I don't care that we didn't plan having a baby. It's the best wedding present ever,' he said, picking her up and whirling her round. 'I love you—both of you.' He set her back down on the ground and cupped his hand protectively over her abdomen. 'Team Devereux. You, me, and a baby that's going to have the best family in the world.'

'The best family in the world,' she echoed.

* * * * *

"No." April twisted her fingers together. **"You don't understand."**

"You're right. I don't. And, honey, at this moment I don't really want to." There was a lot of lust in the look he settled on her.

"And I don't really want to tell you. But, like I said before, you set a high bar for full disclosure. So whether you want to or not, you have to hear this."

"Okay, then. If I agree to listen, can we pick up where we just left off?"

"Trust me. You're not going to want to do that." When Will found out she was a scheming, under-handed, devious witch, he wouldn't want anything to do with her.

"Let me be the judge of that. Because right now I want to kiss you more than anything. And unless you tell me you're a man, which I know for a fact isn't true, there's not much you could say to change my mind." His blue eyes turned darker and focused a lot of intensity on her mouth.

* * *

**The Bachelors of Blackwater Lake:
They won't be single for long!**

HOW TO LAND
HER LAWMAN

BY
TERESA SOUTHWICK

First Published in Great Britain 2016
By Mills & Boon, an imprint of HarperCollins*Publishers*
1 London Bridge Street, London, SE1 9GF

© 2016 Teresa Southwick

ISBN: 978-0-263-91977-6

23-0416

Our policy is to use papers that are natural, renewable and recyclable products and made from wood grown in sustainable forests. The logging and manufacturing processes conform to the legal environmental regulations of the country of origin.

Printed and bound in Spain
by CPI, Barcelona

Teresa Southwick lives with her husband in Las Vegas, the city that reinvents itself every day. An avid fan of romance novels, she is delighted to be living out her dream of writing for Mills & Boon.

To Kate Carlisle, Christine Rimmer
and Susan Mallery, the best plot group ever.
You make it so much fun to play "what if?"

Chapter One

Will Fletcher would rather face an armed felon than have the conversation he was about to have with his exgirlfriend. But, as the saying went, this town wasn't big enough for the both of them. For better or worse, this summer he was the acting sheriff in Blackwater Lake and she was a freelance photographer who occasionally did work for the department. She also had a studio on Main Street across from his office.

There was no way he wouldn't see her and the sooner this confrontation was behind him the better.

He'd been watching the Photography Shop all morning, waiting for her to be alone, and now stood on the sidewalk in front of the sheriff's office ready to head over. Hesitation was costing him a hell of a lot of time when there was work to do. He looked left, then right before crossing the street. Her window had big, fancy letters telling the establishment's name, then smaller print in the right hand corner proclaiming April Kennedy, Photographer. There was a list of services in the right corner—Portraits, Family Sittings, Weddings and Special Occasions.

Will stared at the displayed dance-hall girl and gambler forms with cutouts where the tourists put their faces for a fun souvenir picture of a visit to Blackwater Lake, Montana. Technically he was a visitor but definitely not a tourist. Born and raised in this town, he was only here to help out and would go back to being a detective for Chicago PD in three months when his dad, the real sheriff, got a clean bill of health to resume his job.

"Man up, Fletcher," he muttered. "What's the worst that could happen?"

She could cry. The thought made him cringe.

He'd seen her do that and it ripped him up. But that was a lot of years ago. He didn't know whether or not she'd still be angry but the first face-to-face since then was no doubt going to be awkward.

Will braced himself and pushed open the glass door. The bell above it rang as he walked inside. There was no one in the front but a familiar female voice called out, "I'll be right with you."

It was cheerful and sweet and the sound echoed inside him, stirring the cobwebs of tucked-away memories. It was impossible not to notice the framed photos displayed on the walls, examples of her skill as a photographer. There were individuals, families, babies. Some were black-and-white portraits, dramatic and really good. There'd always been something about April that people responded to, something that made them relax and allowed the camera to capture a special look or smile. The only black-and-whites he usually saw were cop cars, so this was a pleasant change.

"I'm so sorry I kept you waiting—" April Kennedy

came through the open doorway and froze in her tracks when she saw him.

"Hi," he said.

At one time they'd practically been engaged, but Will felt as if he was seeing her for the first time. Her shiny long brown hair was pulled into a ponytail with wisps coming loose around her face. She was wearing jeans and a purple Photography Shop T-shirt that clung to every sweet curve. Big hazel eyes stared back at him and right now they were more green than brown, which meant she wasn't happy to see him. He couldn't blame her.

"Will."

"You look really good, April."

"Thanks. So do you."

"I'm pretty sure you didn't want to tell me that, so I'll take it as a compliment."

"Gotta be honest." She shrugged.

"And I've always liked that about you."

"I heard you were coming back to Blackwater Lake."

He didn't have to ask how she'd heard. April was best friends with his younger sister, Kim. She and her teenage son lived with their dad and Will had moved into his old room for the summer. One big happy family again. The backyard of April's little house was separated by an alley from his dad's rear yard. Hank Fletcher had watched over April and her single mom because it was the neighborly thing to do. And, unlike himself, his dad had been there when April's mom died of breast cancer. The Fletchers had kind of unofficially adopted her, so of course they would warn her that he was coming back.

"The thing is, this is a small town," he started.

"As opposed to Chicago." Her voice was as icy as a Windy City blizzard.

"Right. There's no way we won't run into each other

and I wanted to make sure the first time wasn't public and uncomfortable for you."

He'd checked one out of two boxes. This wasn't public but she had to be as uncomfortable as he was.

"Kim told you to do this." She wasn't asking a question.

"My sister mentioned that it would be better if the first time we saw each other it was just the two of us, without a big crowd of people looking on. And talking about it." Because the only thing folks in Blackwater Lake were better at than being neighborly was gossiping.

"Still, you didn't have to take her advice. It's actually very thoughtful of you, Will." Her tone implied his consideration was unexpected.

Or maybe it just sounded that way because his conscience was passing the words through the guilt filter. Either way, he figured it was a good idea to clear the air. "I don't think I ever apologized for what happened in Chicago."

"You mean the time I came to surprise you and a woman answered the door wearing nothing but your shirt?"

"Yeah. That." He was staring at her mouth, the way she pressed her lips together. It had always made him want to kiss her and unfortunately now was no exception. Normally it was comforting knowing things didn't change but this wasn't one of those times.

"You tried to apologize, actually." She met his gaze directly. "But I wasn't speaking to you, so that made it kind of hard."

"Well, let me say it now. I'm sorry for what happened."

"Let it go, Will. I have. That was a long time ago. It was my idea not to be exclusive when you went to Chicago and entered the police academy. It seemed the right thing to do since I couldn't go with you and everyone knows long-distance relationships are a challenge. We found out the hard way how true that is. Technically we didn't have a relationship and it still fell apart."

Will remembered trying to talk her into going to Chicago with him, but her mom had just been diagnosed. April had never known her dad and wouldn't abandon the mother who had raised her daughter alone and always put her first. She'd suggested they date other people but keep in touch and after a year reevaluate things between them. He was glad she hadn't forgotten that.

"I didn't expect you not to date," she said. "And you did."

"For what it's worth, you were right about everything."

"Things happen for the best. Water under the bridge. Let bygones be bygones. And any other cliché you can think of to put this behind you." She shrugged as if it made no difference to her.

"Okay, then."

Will felt oddly dissatisfied with her response. Maybe the altitude was getting to him. That was the best explanation he could come up with for why he wasn't completely relieved that she didn't scream or cry or seem the least bit emotional about what had happened. Or maybe he was simply an egotistical jerk who expected her to still be a little bothered about something he'd done six years ago.

Possibly his reaction was colored by the fact that he'd married the woman wearing nothing but his shirt and it had been a failure. On top of that, he'd always had the nagging feeling that what he'd done to April was the biggest mistake he'd ever made. For a man who hated to fail, doing it twice at the same time didn't sit very well. And it was kind of annoying that she seemed completely at peace with how things had turned out.

"So, if that's all—" She cocked a thumb over her shoulder toward the back room, where a camera sat on a tripod.

"Just so you know, I'll be here until the end of summer while Dad is recuperating from his open-heart surgery."

"That was a scare." She put her hand to her chest. The first honest emotion she'd exhibited since he'd walked in. "First the heart attack, then surgery. It was like watching the Rock of Gibraltar crack. Your sister has been his diet-and-exercise drill sergeant ever since he got out of the hospital and started cardiac rehab."

"Kim is hard to say no to." He was here talking to April, wasn't he? "The sheriff has always protected the citizens of his town first and himself a distant second. Maybe he saw God when the doc put him under for the procedure because right after he got out of the hospital he asked me to fill in for him. Then he got the mayor and town council to approve my temporary appointment."

"It would be just like him to push himself to go back to work too soon. I'm sure your family is glad to have you here." Her tone said she felt differently. "And a good thing you could take extended leave from your job."

Maybe the job needed time off from him. Between that and his sister nagging him to not be an ass and do it for Dad, he had decided to take one for team Fletcher. All he was willing to say was, "I have a lot of days on the Chicago PD books."

"So you're the sheriff now." She folded her arms over her chest.

"Acting, but yeah. And I wanted to make sure I can count on you for freelance work when needed." Sometimes there were multicar accidents that required photos with more detail than an untrained photographer could capture with a cell phone. Insurance companies were funny that way when a settlement was involved. Mug shots were part of the official record.

"Of course I'll continue the arrangement. It's important that Hank knows everything will go smoothly in his absence. Just as if he was at the wheel."

"So you're doing it for Dad."

"Absolutely. After you and I didn't work out, you got what's-her-name, but I got your family. I'd do anything for them."

"They're lucky to have you."

"No." She shook her head and her ponytail swung from side to side. "I'm the lucky one."

The weird feeling in his chest felt a lot like envy. He was jealous of her loyalty to his dad, sister and nephew even though he'd given up any right to her commitment. He might not have cheated officially but it was a betrayal of spirit. And he still didn't feel as if the air was cleared.

"I should have told you I was dating someone, but I didn't want to hurt you."

"And that worked out so well." She smiled, but it didn't turn her hazel eyes from green to warm. They went almost chocolaty brown. "Golly, this has been fun, but I have someone coming in for a sitting and need to get things set up."

"Okay. I didn't mean to keep you."

"No problem. I appreciate you stopping by. Now when we run into each other it won't be awkward at all. See you around, Will." She turned and walked into the back.

"Bye, April."

He left her shop and felt like gum on someone's shoe. Kim had said seeing her would take the heat off, but she couldn't have been more wrong. The heat was on and it had nothing to do with their history and everything to do with the beautiful, sexy woman April Kennedy still was. And when had she gotten so confident and sassy? So independent?

That was different. She was the same—but different.

Man, it was going to be a long, hot summer.

* * *

April heard a knock on the sliding glass door in her kitchen and hurried to answer it. Kim Fletcher was standing on the back porch and she yanked the other woman inside.

"Thanks for coming. I'm glad you didn't have plans with Luke."

"I'd have canceled if I did. You said it was vital that we talk. What's up?"

Her friend was engaged to be married this summer to another teacher at Blackwater Lake High School, where she worked in the English Department. Luke was the football coach in addition to teaching science. Her son, Tim, played freshman football and approved of the man his mom was going to marry. She'd found her happily-ever-after and April was glad at least one of them had.

"Did anyone at home know you were coming over here?"

Kim gave her a "really?" look. "News flash. My father, brother and son are guys. They don't pay any attention to me. I could announce that I was going to be a fire eater in the circus and they'd say 'Have a good time.' I'm invisible to them."

"Okay." With Will in Chicago all this time, April had forgotten how inconvenient it was that her best friend and her ex were siblings. Who now temporarily lived together under the same roof. All she'd thought about was her own personal emergency and made an SOS call to her bestie. "I need to talk to you and the conversation calls for wine."

"Twist my arm." Kim held it out. "I promise I won't say no."

Kim Fletcher was pretty and for a long time April hadn't thought about how much she looked like her brother. Same blue eyes and brown hair, although her friend's was heavily highlighted, making her look more blonde. The thought of manly, masculine Will with highlighted hair almost made her smile.

After April poured Chardonnay into the two wine-glasses waiting on the kitchen island, they carried them to the family room and sat on the sofa.

Kim scooted back and tucked her legs up beside her. "You saw Will."

April sipped her wine then nodded. "I'd say you're psychic except that he admitted the meeting was your idea. To avoid an awkward, public encounter."

"You're welcome," Kim said.

"Hold it. I'm not on the gratitude train yet." April had been jittery and uneasy ever since seeing him again. She liked status quo and really wanted it restored but wasn't quite sure how to stuff all the emotional junk back in the jar. "It might have been better to take my chances. Maybe I wouldn't have run into him at all."

"Seriously?" The other woman gave her a you're-kidding-yourself look. "This town is the size of a postage stamp. The sheriff's office is right across the street from your shop. He's living not very far from your back door. If you really believe your paths won't cross in the three months he'll be here, you're in serious denial."

"I know. And you're right. But I wish you'd warned me."

Kim shook her head. "Surprise was better. Your reaction had to be natural. Unscripted."

April wanted to crawl into a hole when she thought about how it had gone seeing Will again. She hadn't been prepared and preparation was her thing. When she got in the car, she mentally plotted the route to her destination. Writing a grocery list started on aisle one and ended at produce. For a photography sitting she always had cameras, lenses, backdrops and props ready.

Even though he lived in Chicago, she knew Will would return to Blackwater Lake from time to time because his family was here. Kim had always warned her when he was visiting and she'd successfully avoided him. In fact she hadn't seen him at the hospital when his dad had surgery, but she knew he'd been there. She managed to stay out of his way. None of that stopped her from picturing how a meeting between them would go and in her imagination she'd always been less tongue-tied, her wit sharp as a stiletto. Her moment to make him sorry he hadn't waited for her.

"I don't know about unscripted," April said ruefully, "but it was unsomething."

"How was it? Seeing him again, I mean?" Sympathy gathered in Kim's eyes.

"He looks good." Really good. April hated to admit it, but he'd been right that she hadn't wanted to tell him so. "And it's nice of him to put his life on hold and come back to help the family."

Kim nodded absently. "Don't get me wrong. I love my brother. But I think there's something going on with him. Career-wise, I mean. There have been family crises—God knows I was one. Being an unwed teenage mother certainly qualifies for family-crisis material. Mom was killed in that car accident not long after he entered the police academy. It's not to say he doesn't care because I know he does. But he never put work on hold to be here for us before."

"Has he said anything?"

The other woman shook her head. "No. He just seems edgy, tense. Different. I don't know. Maybe I'm seeing ghosts where there aren't any."

"Maybe you should talk to him about it." April didn't have the right to be involved in his life and it annoyed her that she couldn't shut off her concern. "Get him to open up."

"You know better than anyone that my brother doesn't talk about stuff. Right now getting Dad back on his feet is the most important thing. Will stepping in for him as sheriff means Dad won't worry about this town and can focus on getting strong again."

"That's true." But April's life would be far less complicated if the sheriff trusted someone besides his son. No matter how well Chicago PD trained its officers. On top of that Will knew Blackwater Lake inside and out. There was no doubt he would take good care of the town. "I just wish I knew how to get through the next three months with Will here."

Thoughtfully, Kim tapped a fingernail against her wineglass. "A statement like that makes me think you're still in love with my brother."

"No. You're wrong. It's been a lot of years." April rejected that suggestion with every fiber of her being. "That would just be stupid. Fool me once shame on you. Fool me twice, shame on me."

"Hmm." The woman stared at her. "Where there's smoke, there's fire."

"A cliché? From Blackwater Lake High School's favorite honors English teacher?"

"Clichés work because they convey a lot of truth. In this case, you seem to have strong feelings about seeing Will again. That doesn't happen if you don't care." She finished the wine in her glass. "Hence, smoke and fire."

"I can assure you that what I feel for Will isn't love. It's ancient history. I've had relationships since him."

"But you make sure they never work. You always find an excuse to not take things to the next level. As soon as a guy even hints at getting serious, you shut down and blow him off completely."

April shrugged. "So sue me. I want something special, to be swept away. Settling for less isn't an option for me. And you have to kiss a lot of frogs…"

"Maybe." Kim didn't sound convinced. "Or maybe you need closure with the first frog. Maybe you never moved on after Will hopped away."

"Finding him with another woman seemed like closure to me." But, darn it, today he'd looked genuinely sorry about what had happened.

"Then why did you call me over here to talk? What's the problem?" Her friend didn't sound annoyed as much as frustrated that she couldn't help.

"I guess the problem is that I really want to hate him. That would make this summer so much easier and less awkward. Hate is simple, straightforward and sensible. I can deal with hate. But he was *nice*."

"Rest assured I'll give him a stern talking-to about that." There was a teasing look in Kim's eyes.

"You know what I mean," April protested.

"I do. And I still say your problem is about closure."

"I wish I could be the opposite of a bear and hibernate in the summer. Go to sleep and wake up after Labor Day. If I haven't gotten closure by now, I'm never going to."

"Maybe there's a way." Her friend had a familiar expression on her face, the one that hinted inspiration was knocking on the door.

"Enlighten me." April's interest was piqued.

"Seduce him."

"What? Are you crazy?"

"In the best possible way, or so my fiancé says. That Luke is a keeper," she said with a sigh.

"No argument. But can we go back to where you just told me to seduce your brother in order to find closure?"

"And then dump him. Did I leave that part out?"

"Yes." April sat up straighter. "How does that give me closure?"

"Your last breakup was situational and one-sided. Your emotions are stuck in neutral. Flirt with him. Have a fling. When he's putty in your hands tell him Jean Luc, your winter-ski-instructor-lover, is due to arrive any day and you have to end your summer dalliance."

"On top of the fact that there is no Jean Luc, I don't think I can do that."

"Don't you see?" Kim said, warming to her proposal. "You finally have your chance for revenge. Of course you can do it."

April shook her head. "I'm not that person."

"Look, I know you're really nice. It's why I love you and why we've been best friends forever. But, trust me on this, you need to get some perspective and the best way to do that is to take control."

"But he's your brother," April protested.

"All the better. I give you my permission. If I approve no one can judge you harshly."

"But I'm not very good at seduction."

"You'll be fine. And I have a feeling it won't take much effort or finesse. You need this and revenge is swift and satisfying. Humility would give Will a little character."

April was starting to weaken. "But he married Miss Naked-Under-His-Shirt. And now they're divorced." Surely she could be forgiven for feeling the tiniest bit of satisfaction about that. "I would think that gives him a lot of character credits."

"No. He left her, remember?" Kim made a face. "I never liked that woman."

April loved her for that. "Still, it seems inherently dishonest. Because it is inherently dishonest."

"If you flirt with him and he responds, how is that dishonest? It would be if you hated him, but you said you can't do that."

This whole scene tipped into weird territory because that actually made a twisted sort of sense. "So you really don't think this is a despicably underhanded thing to do? Intentionally flirting with every intention of dumping him? That's the very definition of premeditated."

"You're so overthinking this." Kim sighed. "Just get my brother in bed, then say goodbye. He's moving back to his life in Chicago at the end of the summer anyway. The two of you have a good time and it ends. Things will work out. Trust me."

Famous last words.

But a lot of what her friend said made sense. It was a proactive way to deal with the problem. If he felt nothing for her, no way would there be sex. That in itself would be confirmation they'd never have worked out. Pretty much all she had to do was be nice to him and see what happened.

She leaned over and hugged her friend. "That's why I needed to talk to you."

"Happy to help."

"You definitely did," April said.

And now she had a plan.

Chapter Two

April pulled the chicken casserole out of the oven and smiled at the cheerful bubbling around the edges of the perfectly browned noodles. The crispy parts were her favorite.

"Okay, then," she said to herself, "Operation Poke the Bear is officially under way."

And officially time to get in touch with her inner flirt. Hopefully she still had some of that mojo although that would presuppose she ever had any in the first place. Anything too obvious would be, well…too obvious. It would be a dead giveaway if she walked up to him and said, "Hey, Mr. Sexy Pants, come on up and see me sometime."

When she started to hyperventilate it was a signal that she needed to get a grip. Less than twenty-four hours ago Kim had floated this idea. A slow start didn't mean she'd lose the race and as long as she didn't do anything out of character, no warning flags would be raised.

"Okay. Here goes." She put a lid on the dish, then slid the whole thing into a casserole carrier and food warmer.

April grabbed the dish and went out her kitchen door, stepping onto the patio. She looked around at her neatly trimmed grass and the flowers in cheerful bloom. A sidewalk led to the alley and she smiled, remembering that her mother put it in because there was already a worn path in the grass from April going to Will's house. Or him coming here.

That seemed like a lifetime ago, but still a stab of sadness went through her. She still missed her mom and probably always would. Seeing Will again had stirred up a lot of memories, some good but a whole lot of them not.

Sighing, she walked across the alley, up the three steps to the Fletchers' back door and knocked loudly.

Moments later it opened and Will stood there. "April. Hi."

"Hey. I made a casserole for your dad. And everyone." Oh, God, her mind was going blank. "I've gotten in the habit of doing this since he got out of the hospital. It was a helpless feeling not being able to do anything for him, so I made food and brought it over. This is heart-healthy. Low fat. Whole-grain noodles." She was babbling.

When the horrifying thought sank in, she pressed her lips closed and ground her back teeth together. And oh, right, she was supposed to be flirting. So she batted her eyelashes.

"This is very nice of you." Will took the container she held out and met her gaze. Frowning, he asked, "Is there something wrong with your eyes?"

"Oh. No. I mean—" She blinked furiously. "I think there was something in one, but it's fine now."

"Good."

Doggone it! This flirting thing wasn't easy. It just felt

awkward and dishonest. She should cut her losses and run for cover. "Okay, then. I'll see you around."

"Come on in." Will moved the door open a little wider with his shoulder. "Unless you've got plans."

"No." Jean Luc was busy tonight, so she was free to flirt.

She walked into the house that was as familiar to her as her own. The door opened into the family room with a leather corner group and a flat-screen TV mounted on the wall. On the other side of a granite-covered bar was the kitchen with its large square island, stainless-steel appliances and plentiful oak cupboards.

She looked around. "It's awfully quiet. Where is everyone?"

"Kim is out with Luke." He set the casserole on the island and looked at her. The expression on his face said his sister and her fiancé weren't out so much as staying in and having sex.

April's already pounding pulse kicked up a notch. "What about your dad and Tim?"

"They went to a movie."

"Okay." The house was empty. In theory that worked for her plan except that she wasn't very good at flirting. "Well, then, now you have dinner. Enjoy."

He slid her a questioning look. "Have you eaten yet?"

"No."

"What are you doing for dinner?" he asked.

"Oh, I have a frozen thing in the freezer." She cocked a thumb over her shoulder, indicating the general direction of her house, freezer and the frozen thing.

Will leaned back against the countertop and folded his arms over his chest. The tailored long-sleeved khaki-colored sheriff's uniform shirt fit his upper body like a second skin. Matching pants showcased his flat stomach and muscular legs to male perfection. She was the one with a seduction plan, but if this was being in control, she'd be better off flying by the seat of her pants.

"So," he said, "you put in time and effort on this food and you're going to eat something that's been in a state of suspended animation for God knows how long?"

"Yeah, pretty much. I do it all the time." She could have bitten her tongue clean off for saying that. How pathetic did it sound that she often ate by herself? Next he'd be asking how many cats she owned.

"Not tonight you won't," Will insisted. "You're going to stay and have some of the meal you made."

Per the plan she had to strike the right balance between reluctance and giving in. It wouldn't do to appear too eager. The problem was that having dinner with him was tempting and it was awfully darn difficult to tamp down her enthusiasm. Because, gosh darn it, she did eat alone most of the time and the prospect of companionship at a meal was awfully appealing. And she told herself any companion would do. Herself almost bought into that thought.

"I don't know—"

"Did you put poison in the casserole?"

"Of course not. Wow, you can take the detective out of Chicago, but you can't take the suspicion out of the detective."

"And you didn't put a gallon of hot sauce in there to sabotage it and get even with me?"

"It was for your dad. I didn't even know you'd be here. The goal is to make Hank stronger and *not* give him another heart attack."

"So stay. It smells pretty good. Have dinner here." His blue eyes darkened with challenge while the beginning of a grin curved up the corners of his mouth.

"If that law-enforcement thing hadn't worked out, you'd have made a pretty persuasive lawyer." She happened to be looking at him and saw the shadows cross his face. They were there for a moment, then disappeared. "I'd like that."

"How about a glass of wine?"

"Sounds good." It actually sounded fabulous, but again, balance. Not too eager.

He opened the refrigerator and pulled out a bottle of Chardonnay, then found two wineglasses in the cupboard. After removing the cork, he poured and handed her a glass.

"Can I help with something?" she asked. "There should be a touch of a green. I could throw some salad together. Microwave some broccoli."

"Yeah, broccoli would be easiest. But I can do that. You've already done more than your fair share."

"Can I at least set the table?"

"If you insist." He'd already opened the freezer and glanced over his shoulder at her.

The look zinged right through her. "I do."

"Okay."

April was here so often she knew where everything was stored. So she got out plates, utensils, napkins and water glasses, then arranged them all on the round oak table in the nook. She and Will moved around the kitchen as if this meal was a meticulously choreographed ballet. But instead of dips, twirls and lifts, they managed to avoid even the slightest touch. Was he on edge, too?

She put hot pads out, then took the casserole from the food warmer and set it in the center of the table with a serving spoon. The bubbling had stopped but the dish was still warm and smelled yummy if she did say so herself.

Will set a steaming bowl of broccoli beside the noodle dish and said, "Let's eat."

April sat across from him, then put food on her plate and dug in. Macaroni and cheese was world-class comfort food, but noodles and chicken came in a close second to her way of thinking. Since Will had come back to Blackwater Lake, comfort was in short supply. Now here she was sharing a meal with him and feeling decidedly *un*comfortable.

"I can't remember the last time we had dinner together," she said.

Will took a sip of wine, then his mouth pulled tight. "I'm sorry, April."

"The thought just popped into my mind. I didn't say that to make you feel bad," she assured him.

"I know. And yet I do." He toyed with the stem of his glass, those big hands dwarfing the delicate crystal that had been his mother's. "I should have told you that I was dating someone. It was a lie of omission and I'm not proud of how I handled it."

April put down her fork and picked up her wine, then took a sip. He was sincerely sorry about what happened and that confused her. The goal was to seduce him and be the one to walk away, but this contrite Will made her question the mission. It was for closure, she reminded herself. That didn't mean she couldn't meet him halfway.

"Look, Will, it takes two to make a relationship. You're not the only one responsible for the way things turned out. If you remember back, communication between us had dropped off by a lot. You're not entirely responsible for that. Phone calls and messages go both ways and I didn't hold up my end of that either."

"Still, I should have—"

"Let it go. Really. Do whatever you need to in order to work through this because I don't see you as good martyr material."

"No?" His mouth twitched.

"Let's file it under 'Not meant to be.' Thinking about that time and wondering what if will drive you crazy." She shrugged. "We'll never know what might have happened if my mom hadn't gotten sick."

"I suppose."

"No supposing," she said. "It's true. That part of our life is in the past. But this is a new time. Maybe there's a chance to salvage a friendship."

"I'd like that." He held up his glass. "To being friends."

She touched the rim of her glass to his. "Friends."

They drank, then smiled at each other. She might be a flirting failure but friends was a start. She could work with that.

Sometimes it was hard for Will to believe he was filling in for his father as the sheriff of Blackwater Lake. Granted it had been less than a week, but that didn't change the fact that he had big shoes to fill. Hank Fletcher had always been his hero and Will wanted to follow in his dad's footsteps. Any law-enforcement job was a big one, but compared to what he'd seen in Chicago, this gig was like maintaining order in the land of Far, Far Away.

The office had one main room with a couple of desks for a single deputy and the dispatcher/clerk. Clarice Mulvaney was in her midfifties, a plump, brown-eyed brunette, friendly and efficient. Deputy Eddie Johnson was Will's height, but skinny. He was barely twenty-one but looked about twelve. Or maybe that was just because Will felt so old. Still the kid was smart and eager to learn.

In the back of the room there was a door that led to two six-by-eight-foot cells, empty at the moment and since this was Tuesday there was a very good chance they would stay that way. Things got a little extra exciting on the weekend when someone was more likely to be drunk and disorderly. Although every day was a weekend now because the official kick-off of summer had been last Saturday. So there was no taking weeknights for granted with tourists all over the place for the next three months.

As acting sheriff, Will took the private office off to the right, which had a closing door. Rank had its privileges.

The phone rang and Clarice answered. "Blackwater Lake Sheriff's Office. This is Clarice." She listened for a moment then said, "Is everyone all right?" After grabbing a pen, she jotted down notes. "Okay. Sit tight. I'll send someone right away."

"What's up?" Will asked.

"MVA on Lake Shore Road. Two cars involved."

Will moved in front of her desk. The sheriff also co-ordinated fire-department services. "Do we need to roll rescue and paramedics?"

"No. Everyone was out of the cars and there are no apparent injuries. But neither of the vehicles is drivable, so we need to alert McKnight Automotive that there will be either a tow or flatbed truck removal."

"Okay. Can you take care of that?"

"Sure thing."

"Eddie," he said to the blond, blue-eyed deputy. "Take the cruiser out there and evaluate the situation. Talk to everyone involved and make a report. Radio in with your recommendations."

"Yes, sir." In a heartbeat the kid was out of his chair and ready to go.

Will held out the keys, and the deputy grabbed them on his way out the door. It didn't escape his notice that the kid's smooth face barely required a shave. Must be a thrill to drive a cop car. If there was another call Will would take his SUV. He stood beside his dispatcher and both of them watched the deputy put on the cruiser's lights before pulling away from the curb. As he'd been trained to do.

Will knew Clarice had worked with his father for over

twenty years and was a valued member of the small department. Hank had always said she made him look good. When the resort was completed, the town was going to grow and law enforcement would have to keep up with it. Not his problem, he reminded himself. After the summer he was out of here. But his dad was going to have to deal with it and that would mean more stress. He would need dependable, dedicated employees.

"What do you think of Eddie?" he asked.

Clarice looked thoughtful for a moment. "He's a good kid. Coolheaded, smart, conscientious. Your dad has an eye for talent." She grinned. "After all, you're here."

"Not because of talent. It's the training."

"Could be both," she said. "And your dad figured Eddie could benefit from your experience and training."

"While I'm here." Will didn't want to give the false impression that he was staying for good and put a finer point on her statement.

"One day at a time." She had a mysterious Zen expression on her face.

"Right."

He was looking out the window and saw the door to the Photography Shop open and April walked out. She turned and locked up, then crossed the street and headed toward the sheriff's office. It was possible she was going somewhere else, but he hoped not. The sight of her lifted his spirits just like she'd done last night when he found her on his porch with a casserole in her hands. It wasn't fancy food but turned out to be the best dinner he'd had in a long time.

That had little to do with the cooking and everything to do with the company. Like every situation, he analyzed it and figured he'd enjoyed the evening because any lingering guilt about hurting her was gone. There were other things that kept him up at night but not her. At least not guilt about her, because he'd lost some sleep wondering if her mouth still tasted as sweet as he remembered.

April walked into the office and saw him standing by the dispatch desk. "Hi."

"Hey."

She looked at the older woman. "Hi, Clarice. How's the family?"

"Everyone is doing great."

"Are you a grandmother yet?" April asked.

"Sandy's due after Labor Day."

"I didn't know you were going to be a grandmother," Will said.

"Because you never asked." Her tone was only marginally disapproving. "She and her husband live in California, a suburb of LA. He's an attorney for a big law firm there. Sandy works at a preschool, at least until the baby's born."

"Congratulations," he said.

"Thanks, boss. By the way, I'll need some time off after she gives birth."

"My father will be back then. I'm sure he already has you covered and it won't be a problem." Then Will remembered she had a son, too. What was that kid's name? Oh, yeah. "How's Mark?"

"Good. I'm surprised you remembered his name." She hadn't missed the slight hesitation. "He's getting a doctorate in marine science from the University of Miami."

"Wow."

"Yeah. A nerd like his dad."

Will knew her husband taught chemistry at the junior college located about twenty-five miles from Blackwater Lake. Where April had gone to school. Damned if even after all this time he didn't still feel a twinge remembering that she hadn't gone with him to Chicago.

Will looked at her now. "So, April, how can we help you? Are you here to report a crime?"

She laughed. "More like crime prevention."

"Oh?"

"Yeah. Would you mind if we talked in your office?" The words were for him, but April gave Clarice a shrug that was part apology, part I-know-you-understand.

"I've got work to do," the dispatcher said.

"Okay. In my office, then." He turned and headed in that direction with April behind him. When they walked in the room he asked, "Do you want me to close the door?"

"Not necessary. I just wanted a little privacy for this conversation."

"Okay." He indicated the two chairs in front of the desk. "Have a seat."

"Thanks." She sat down and the wattage on her smile was probably visible from space. Plus she was doing that weird thing with her eyes again. "I could use your help."

"With what?"

"Crowd control. More specifically teenage make-out prevention."

"A little more information would be really helpful."

"Yeah. Sorry." She laughed again, but the sound seemed more nervous than anything else. "Every year just after school gets out the high school kids get together in that open field a half mile from the high school. The seniors who ruled the school pass on the power, symbolically of course, to the juniors, who are now incoming seniors."

"Okay. But why do you need official backup?"

"That's the thing. It's not official, not technically a school function, so no chaperones are required. But these are teenagers and extra surveillance is the smart way to go."

"Why are you doing the asking?" Apparently his guilt

wasn't completely gone because there was a part of him surprised that she would request anything from him.

"I take pictures that always make their way into the yearbook. It's an annual thing they do. Every year." She cringed. "I already said that, didn't I?"

"Yeah."

"The thing is, I don't want any of them having sex on my watch."

"I guess not." He couldn't stop a small smile.

"Glad you think this is funny."

"No, I don't."

"Yes, you do," she challenged.

"Maybe a little." He shrugged.

"Come on, Will, be serious. These kids are drowning in hormones and they're sneaky."

He remembered. Partly because there was something about April that made him feel like a randy teenager again. The reaction could have been because she mentioned making out and sex, but he didn't think so. It was all her. The playful ponytail, curves that had grown curvier with time and a mouth that would drive a saint insane.

"What time is this photo shoot?"

"Tonight. Eight o'clock. I know what you're thinking," she said.

"I don't think you do."

"You'd be wrong. You're thinking that it would be better to schedule this earlier in the evening before the sun goes down." She shook her head and pressed those plump lips together. Then she seemed to remember something and forced a big smile, followed by some eyelash batting. "The problem is that a lot of the kids have summer jobs and aren't available earlier. Not to mention that I have a business and later is better."

She was wrong. That wasn't what he'd been thinking.

His thoughts ran more along the lines of finding a secluded place to get *her* alone in the dark. "I see."

"I thought you would." Her eyes took on a pleading expression. "So, can I count on you?"

Will was conflicted about what to do. He didn't want to turn her down. This behavior of hers was surprising. First dinner last night and now a request for assistance today. She smiled a lot and did that weird thing with her eyes, which he didn't recall, but they'd toasted to friendship last night. And today she'd voluntarily come to see him and ask for assistance.

On the flip side, it probably wasn't a good idea to be out with her after dark, what with his mind going randy teenager on him. Still, the kids would be around and that would cool his temptation. Friends helped each other out.

"Okay. I'll give you a hand."

"Thanks, Will." She smiled again, but it was the first natural one since walking into his office. And it was a stunner.

He really hoped this wasn't a mistake.

Chapter Three

It was a beautiful night for taking pictures. April had her digital SLR camera on a tripod set up in the meadow and was snapping pictures of the outgoing senior class student-body officers passing a plastic toy torch. Someone held up a handmade sign that said "Class of 2017—we rule the school!" She stopped and scrolled through the images, then adjusted the shutter speed in order to make the shots clearer while allowing for the light from a full moon.

And speaking of that… She counted heads for the umpteenth time. There were supposed to be ten and she tallied eight. "Where did Trevor and Kate go?"

She looked at the group of teens and every single one looked guilty as sin. "Come on. You know my rules. No getting frisky and pairing off during this shoot. I know the seniors who just graduated don't care. But listen up seniors-to-be, if you want me to take pictures next year you'll tell me where they went. Otherwise this tradition will just be a sad memory."

April looked at them and they stared back at her without speaking. "Anyone? Now would be a good time to speak up. You really want to spoil the fun for the other classes coming up behind you?"

"You're right. We don't care." That was Mike Espy, a good-looking football player who'd received a football scholarship to the University of California, Los Angeles. "I can't wait to get out of this two-bit nowhere town. It's big-city excitement for me."

"Oh, don't be such a jerk." Patty Carnegie, a pretty blonde cheerleader who was looking forward to senior year and being captain of the squad, gave him a withering look. Then she met April's gaze. "They took a walk."

Red alert. That was code for finding a place to be alone and unleash all the teenage hormones raging through them. Will was out there somewhere. She knew because they'd come here together in his SUV. Part of her had expected him to back out, but he'd been right on time.

She wondered if he'd felt the same way Mike did about not being able to shake the dust of Blackwater Lake off his shoes fast enough. That didn't really matter now, though. She had two unaccounted-for teenagers who could be getting into trouble on her watch.

"Look who I found wandering around in the woods." And there was Will, walking the two wayward kids back to the group.

There was a lot of good-natured hooting and hollering but Trevor and Kate looked unrepentant. "We had to try," he said.

"And I have to tell you not to do it again."

April shot Will a grateful look. He shrugged as if to say he didn't blame them. Kids would be kids. She and Will had been there once upon a time when his father the sheriff had broken up one of their make-out sessions.

The windows of Will's seen-better-days truck had been fogged up and they felt like the only two lovers in the world. Right up until the moment there was tapping on the driver's door. April quickly adjusted her clothes and Will rolled down the window. Hank peeked inside and ordered him to get her home on time. She never knew if Will's dad had said anything to him privately. Hmm.

"Okay, you guys, let's finish up." April took her place behind the camera again.

"What should we do?" Lindsay was a junior and incoming student-body treasurer.

"Just be yourselves. Hang out. Pretend I'm not here," she advised.

"You just told us not to do that again," Mike reminded her.

Everyone laughed and she snapped a great picture. "I told you not to go walking alone in the woods. Now I want you to relax, have fun. If you think about getting your picture taken, you'll freeze up and be stiff. So act as if I don't have this camera trained on you to record this moment in the history of Blackwater Lake High School."

"Go Wolves," someone called out.

"Let's hear it for the blue and gold," a boy said.

Spontaneously the kids started a cheer. "Two, four, six, eight, who do we appreciate?"

"Kennedy," everyone hollered.

Then a chant started. "April! April! April!"

She smiled, watching them have fun. The innocence of youth that she was capturing forever. She got some great unstructured shots, more than enough to provide the yearbook committee with outstanding choices.

"Okay, you guys. Listen up. This is a wrap." She grinned at all of them. "Great job. Sheriff Fletcher will make sure everyone has transportation home."

A couple of the girls hugged her and expressed the appreciation of everyone, then hurried off with the group to the dirt area where they'd parked cars. Will brought up the rear and the moonlight allowed her to appreciate what a very excellent rear he had. That reaction was a direct result of pent-up big-girl hormones because she hadn't had a real date for a while.

She heard the sound of cars starting then driving away while beginning the task of packing up her equipment. It had been fun as always and her threat to discontinue future photo shoots was an empty one because she enjoyed it as much, if not more, than the kids. Maybe because her senior year in high school had been the happiest time in her life.

When the car noises faded she saw Will walking toward her. The anticipation filling her at the sight of him wasn't too much different than what she'd felt when they'd been together before. Flirting with a toad would be a challenge. But for the purposes of this plan to put him behind her, April knew it was good to be attracted.

"Mission accomplished." He watched her pack up her cameras and lenses and put them in their protective cases.

"Everyone got off okay?"

"Yes. And I have to say it was like herding cats."

"I know what you mean." She looked up at him and her heart stuttered. At some point she was going to have to get a handle on that reaction, but it probably wouldn't happen tonight. "Seriously, Will, thanks for your help. I'm really glad you were here for backup."

"I didn't do much."

"You did a lot. Not just anyone can stand there and look intimidating, but you pulled it off spectacularly."

"It's a gift. Then there were those two who just had to defy authority," he said.

"And you got them safely back to the herd. Bless you."

"Happy to help."

"I appreciate it." She had packed everything up while they talked and now folded the tripod. "I'm all set."

"Let me get that for you." He easily picked up everything that would have taken her two trips to haul.

"Thanks."

In silence they walked back to where his SUV was parked in the dirt area. He opened the rear liftgate and stowed her equipment while she climbed into the passenger seat. Moments later he slammed the door then settled behind the wheel and turned the key in the ignition. The dash lights illuminated his features and the past came rushing back to her. All the dreams, hopes and hurts of that teenage girl she'd once been.

One of the perks of not being together anymore was that theoretically she no longer cared what he thought of her. That meant she didn't have anything to lose by asking him whatever popped into her head. And she did it now. "Do you remember that night we were in your truck, parked right here, and your dad found us?"

"I wish I could say no." The glance he sent her was uncomfortable.

"Did he ever say anything more about it? When I wasn't there?"

"Yes."

She waited but he clammed up. "Care to elaborate?"

"If I said no would you let it drop?" This time he looked hopeful.

"From the perspective of a girl who never knew her father and missed that experience, it's my opinion that you should be grateful your dad cared enough to get involved. To risk alienating you."

"I get that now. At the time he really ticked me off."

"What did he say to you?"

"He told me not to disrespect you."

She smiled. "That sounds like Hank. Did he give you the don't-get-her-pregnant speech?"

"Don't remind me," he groaned, his reaction confirming her guess.

Considering they eventually broke up, it was a blessing there hadn't been an unexpected pregnancy. That reminded her of what Mike had said and she wondered how Will felt. This was as good a time as any to bring it up.

"Can I ask you something?"

"As long as it has nothing to do with my dad making me feel twelve years old."

"No." She laughed. "I don't know if you heard what one of the boys said. You were herding stray cats."

"What?" he asked.

"I said the graduated seniors probably didn't care but I was going to end the passing-the-torch tradition if they didn't follow my rules. He, Mike, confirmed that he didn't care and couldn't wait to get out of this small town, get a taste of the big city."

"Young and stupid," Will muttered.

"So you didn't feel that way when you were around his age?" she asked.

"No, I did."

"But you just said he's young and stupid. Do you regret moving to Chicago?"

He was quiet for several moments. "I just meant the big city isn't just about excitement." His mouth pulled tight for a second. "In a place with so many people there's a lot going on, both good and bad. The years give you perspective to see both sides."

"I guess so."

April had the oddest sensation of disappointment, as if she'd hoped he would admit he had regrets about leaving

Blackwater Lake, and her, behind. And wasn't that just silliness. It was a reminder of why she was here with him in the first place and romance was definitely not involved.

She'd foolishly believed that she and Will would be together always and deliriously happy. They would have kids and be the family she'd always longed for. He was right about years giving you perspective because she no longer had stars in her eyes. As far as she was concerned the only stars on her radar were in the sky and that's where they were going to stay. There was no way she would get sucked in to romance again.

Her assignment was to have a fling with Will and this time be the one to end things. High school had been happy because of Will, but now she had to put it, and him, behind her.

It was time for phase two of the plan. "Do you want to stop at Bar None for a drink? I'm buying. Call it a thank-you for your help tonight."

He didn't say anything for a few seconds and she braced for rejection. Finally he said, "That sounds good."

Here goes nothing, she thought. A friendly drink and that was it. She wasn't going to blow this chance for closure.

The morning after helping April with her teenage photo shoot Will was still trying to forget how beautiful she'd looked in the moonlight. And how eager he'd been to have a drink with her. There'd been a part of him hoping it would lead to more, but no such luck.

"You didn't have to come with me to see the doctor, Will."

"Hmm?" His father's voice pulled him back to the moment.

"I said, I could have brought myself here to the clinic. You didn't need to tag along."

"If I didn't, you know as well as I do that Kim's head would explode."

His dad laughed. He was sitting on the exam table in one of the patient rooms at Mercy Medical Clinic, waiting to see Adam Stone, the family-practice doctor on staff. Adam had consulted with the cardiologist and cardiothoracic surgeon who'd performed the bypass surgery and was now handling the follow-up checks. In fact, he'd stabilized Hank after the initial heart attack, before transport to the medical center in Copper Hill, which was over an hour away.

"Your sister *is* something of a control freak."

"That makes it tough when she can't be in two places at once." Sitting in a chair against the wall, Will grinned at his dad. "It was either doctor duty or her appointment with the manager at Fireside restaurant to consult on the food for her wedding reception."

"I'm glad she picked that one," Hank said. "This wedding is really important to her. And she's been through a lot of tough times. She's way past due for a chance at happiness."

"Yeah." Will couldn't agree more.

"The thing is, she would have put wedding prep on hold to come to this appointment with me if you weren't here, son." His dad's gaze was unflinching.

Will did his best not to squirm like a twelve-year-old in the hard plastic chair. Since coming back to Blackwater Lake it seemed guilt was his new best friend. His sister had carried all the family stuff, including being a teenage single mom while going to college and becoming a teacher.

And then there was April and how he'd treated her. At least he'd squared one out of those two guilt trips. She didn't seem to be holding a grudge about the past. He'd had a great time last night and it seemed as if she had, too.

Bygones went bye-bye. She was friendly and, if he didn't miss his guess, a little flirty.

Since that lightning-rod moment all those years ago when her full mouth and curvy body had grabbed him by the throat, she'd always had the power to get his juices going. As much as he wished that was a bygone, too, it had happened again last night.

But this doctor's appointment was about giving his sister a break so she could finalize details for her summer wedding.

"I'm happy to help, Dad." Will really meant that. "And I hope Kim enjoys everything—up to and including her wedding day. She deserves all the good stuff."

"Who's holding down the fort while you're here with me?"

Will had no doubt this was small talk because Sheriff Hank Fletcher still knew exactly what was going on in his jurisdiction. "Clarice and Eddie. They know how to get me if something comes up they can't handle."

"What do you think of Eddie? Professional assessment."

"Hard to tell. I haven't been here long enough to see him function in a crisis. But he seems bright, eager. He brings a lot of energy."

Hank nodded. "I thought so, too. Things are going to change when the resort and building development are finished. More people will move here, which is a blessing and curse. We'll do our best to anticipate potential problem situations but life has a way of throwing the unexpected at you just when you think you've got it all figured out."

Will didn't miss the sadness in his father's blue eyes and knew he was thinking about losing his wife in a car accident. He'd come home for the funeral but couldn't stay long. He had to get back to his job and proving himself to the seasoned veterans in the Chicago Police Department.

Or was that just what he'd told himself to shut down the guilt he'd felt for leaving the people he loved?

He and April had hooked up and it was the last time they were together. Considering they'd just buried his mother, it was probably the best and worst night of his life. She had made him forget the pain for a little while.

"It's good for Eddie to have you here," Hank said.

"Why?"

"You have a lot of big-city experiences. Blackwater Lake won't be on that scale, but there's a lot you can teach him that I can't."

"I'm happy to do what I can, Dad, while I'm here. But—"

There was a light knock on the door then it opened and the doctor walked in. In his white lab coat over light blue scrubs, Adam Stone greeted them both and shook hands.

"It's good to see you, Will."

"You, too." They'd met a couple months ago during his dad's health crisis.

"So, how's the patient doing?"

"Feeling great, doc." Hank pulled his T-shirt off as the doctor removed the stethoscope worn draped around his neck.

"Take a deep breath." Adam pressed the round thing to various places on his dad's chest and back, carefully listening each time he moved it. "Sounds good. Strong heartbeat and your lungs are clear."

He carefully inspected the scar on Hank's chest and nodded approval. "This looks awesome."

"Chicks dig scars," Hank joked.

"Then you should be very popular, Dad."

Adam laughed. "It's healing well."

"How's the wife and kids," Hank asked.

"Great. Couldn't be better." The doctor smiled broadly.

"C.J. is loving Cabot Dixon's summer camp and has decided he's going to be a cowboy when he grows up. Or Robin Hood. He's been taking archery classes with Kate Scott, actually Dixon now. They got married," he explained to Will. "And C.J. can't make up his mind whether he likes riding horses better than shooting a bow and arrow."

Hank laughed. "And that little girl of yours?"

"Beautiful. Just like her mom." His voice grew marginally softer when he mentioned the two women in his life. "Although I could do without the terrible twos. If she's as good at everything else as she is at that, she'll be incredibly successful in her chosen field."

"Yeah, I remember that stage," Hank said wryly. "My wife handled it and that's why Kim and Will grew up so well."

Will marveled at how his father got people to talk, to open up. He considered it part of his job to know the citizens of his town and the man was a master. That was very different from Will's work in Chicago. There was no way law enforcement could spend the time to get to know everyone.

Adam met his gaze. "How is it being back?"

Will figured he should be used to that question by now but it seemed every day in Blackwater Lake made his feelings a little less clear. So all he said was, "Good." Best to leave it at that and change the subject. "So my dad is doing okay?"

"Pretty remarkable actually. Pulse, heart rate, breath sounds, blood pressure are all where we want them. Anything you think I should know?" Adam asked.

"No. I'm feeling good," the patient said.

"I'm going to order some blood work."

"Heaven forbid I should get out of here without someone sticking me with a needle," his dad joked.

"Man up, Hank. You should be used to it by now," the doc said.

"Not really."

Adam glanced through the chart. "You're still exercising and watching your diet?"

His dad's expression was wry. "Have you met my daughter, Kim? You know, the pretty, bossy one?"

"Okay. Point taken. I'm betting that skill was sharpened by working with teenagers." Adam laughed. "I'll take that as a yes. So keep it up. At this pace you'll be ready to go back to work when your medical leave is over at the end of summer."

"Thanks, Doc."

"I want to see you again in six weeks. You can make an appointment with the receptionist on the way out." He shook hands with both of them again. "Take care."

Twenty minutes later they were in Will's SUV and headed home. After leaving the clinic his dad had grown unusually quiet, a stark difference from the gregarious man who was keeping up with the personal life of someone who lived in his town. The checkup couldn't have gone better. So what was the deal? Will was a police officer and trained detective but without clues he was unable to draw a conclusion.

And then there was this dandy technique that cops used to find out stuff. It was called interrogation. "What's going on, Dad? You're pretty quiet over there. The doc gave you high marks and said you'll be back to work soon."

"Yeah." The flat tone was a clue.

"Is this about work?"

"In a way. I've been thinking about retiring. I knew it was creeping up on me but didn't give it a lot of thought until the heart attack and surgery. Now…"

"What?"

"It's been on my mind. And you know that pretty, bossy sister of yours? She's been relentless about me slowing down. Taking it easy. Traveling."

"You've always wanted to," Will reminded him. "I remember you talking about it when Kim and I were kids."

"Not so much after your mom died."

Will felt a jab of guilt again that he hadn't been around much after the funeral. "I know that was a hard time for you."

"It was. And I'll always love her. But I'm not grieving the loss anymore." A big sigh came from the passenger seat. "Since Josie—"

"The widow who rents a room from Maggie Potter. I met her when you were in the hospital." Nice woman, he thought.

"Yeah. She stayed in Copper Hill to be there for your sister until I was out of the woods."

"I liked her."

"Kim does, too. And if she didn't—"

Will laughed. "It wouldn't be pretty."

"No kidding."

"You should take a trip," Will said. "With Josie."

"I'd like that, but I feel a responsibility to the folks here in Blackwater Lake. Can't just turn their welfare over to a rookie deputy, no matter how smart and eager he is. Not with the hotel and condos getting closer to opening every day."

"Yeah, I can see where you're coming from."

Will knew this was his dad hinting for him to make this temporary sheriff thing permanent. He remembered what that kid at the photo shoot had said about his hurry to get to the big city. In fact Will had told April he understood where the kid was coming from. But it felt like forever since he'd been obsessed with excitement, getting away from this town to do something more important.

"I know you do, Will. And I always knew you wanted me to be proud of your accomplishments. You have no idea how proud I am of you, the man you've become."

"Thanks, Dad."

"And you're older now. Age has a way of making you look at things differently. This town really has a lot to offer a man."

Just like that an image of sassy April Kennedy popped into his mind. She wasn't that skinny little girl anymore, but had grown into a beautiful, confident, accomplished woman. So many of his good memories were wrapped up in her, but she was the girl he'd left behind. It hadn't worked out for them and no matter what Will accomplished in his career the failure in his personal life would always bother him.

"Blackwater Lake was a good place to grow up. Tim is thriving here."

"Yes, he is. He's a great kid." There was grandfatherly pride in his voice, but there was something flat in the tone.

Will glanced over to the passenger seat and saw the look of resignation on his dad's face. He should have known the man wouldn't miss the way Will had deliberately changed the subject. There was no point in taking the idea any further. He would be going back to Chicago at the end of the summer.

That was just the way it was.

Chapter Four

In her kitchen, April peeked out her sliding glass door with its great view of Will's house across the alley. She knew he ran every morning and she did, too. In spite of Kim's dire prediction that she and Will were bound to run into each other, so far it hadn't happened. That was about to change. She hadn't seen him since he'd helped with the teenage photo shoot and that had been a couple days ago. The time had come to give her game a kick in the pants.

It was Sunday, the one day of the week that she didn't open the shop until afternoon. But she got up a little earlier than usual, put on her running clothes, stretched out and now watched the Fletchers' back door. If he didn't show soon she'd have to do her run solo and think of another way to get this flirtation show on the road. Then an ego-deflating thought hit her.

What if he just didn't like her at all?

Before she had a chance to blow that out of proportion

his rear door opened. It was him, and he leaned back inside for a moment. This was her chance.

She left the house and hurried up the sidewalk until reaching the alley, then pretended not to see Will, who stopped at the edge of the grass behind her.

"April?"

She glanced over her shoulder. "Hey, Will. Morning."

He caught up with her and fell into step. "Mind if I tag along?"

"Nope." It took effort not to look smug.

"How far do you go?"

"About six miles. Up Deer Springs to Spruce. Around the elementary school, down Elkhorn Road and back."

"Works for me."

She glanced over at him in his running shorts and snub gray T-shirt with the bold black letters *CPD* written on it. The wide shoulders and broad chest were pretty impressive and that was darned annoying. Why couldn't he be fat? Would it kill him to have male-pattern baldness setting in? But she wasn't that lucky. He was even better looking than when she'd loved him.

"Try to keep up," she said and increased her speed.

Will stayed right with her and it was easy for him because his legs were muscular and so much longer than hers. If he wanted to, he could leave her in the dust. But he didn't, so it wasn't a stretch to assume he didn't mind her company. She would go with that working theory.

"How's your dad?" She happened to look over at him and saw his mouth pull tight. "What's wrong?"

"He's fine." With the baseball hat and aviator sunglasses it was impossible to read his expression. "Had a checkup the other day and doc says he's the poster boy for how to recover from a heart attack."

"Oh, good. You scared me there for a minute." That was

a relief. Hank Fletcher was the father she'd never had. "It's just that you had a weird look on your face and I went to the bad place."

"Sorry. Didn't mean to send you there. Dad passed everything with flying colors. Doc even said if he keeps up the good work he'll get the green light to go back to the job at the end of summer."

"That's great." Then she noticed the muscle in his jaw flex and wondered what he was leaving out. "So why do you look like someone disconnected the siren on your cop car?"

He met her gaze and one corner of his mouth quirked up. "Because someone disconnected the siren on my cop car."

"Okay. Roger that. You don't want to talk about it."

April remembered a time when he told her everything, but obviously things had changed. It shouldn't bother her that he no longer confided in her. The fact that it did even a little was evidence that getting closure was the right way to go.

For about a mile they ran without talking. Then Will broke the silence. "How's business?"

"Good. Summer tourist traffic in the shop is up significantly from last year. Plus weddings keep me busy. 'Tis the season for them."

"Are you taking the pictures when my sister gets married?"

"Of course."

"But you're her best friend. Who's going to be her maid of honor?" Will asked.

"I don't think she's having one." She and Kim had sort of danced around this. If her friend had chosen someone else April would know. "I'm doing the bridal shower and everything the MOH is supposed to do before the actual ceremony. I'll just be too busy commemorating the important moments for posterity to actually take part in the important moments."

As they finished the loop around Blackwater Lake Elementary and headed back, Will asked, "Does it ever bother you to miss out on stuff because you're documenting memories?"

"I love what I do." If she missed out it wasn't because of taking pictures. People left her. Her father did before she ever knew him. Her mom died. Will... He found someone else.

"Now you're the one with a weird look on your face."

As their feet hit the asphalt in a rhythmic sound she glanced over, annoyed again. This time because he still knew her well enough to know when something bothered her.

"I have cramps," she said.

"Do you want to slow down? Walk the rest of the way?"

"No." She kicked up her speed again, enough that it kept them from talking.

April had done this route so many times she knew to start slowing down at the intersection of Deer Springs and Spruce. By the time they got back she was walking and stopped at the edge of her grass to stretch her muscles so she didn't really get cramps. Instead of saying goodbye, Will did his postrun stretching alongside her.

Again she couldn't help noticing how masculine he looked, his T-shirt showing darker spots around his neck and arms from the sweat. And, doggone it, that was sexy. If any health-care professional had checked her heart rate right then she could blame it on the run, but that would be a lie. The spike had nothing to do with exercise and everything to do with the Fletcher effect. It wasn't cause for alarm, just appreciation for a good-looking man. But it was

still more evidence that she needed to ratchet up this flirtation in order to put him in her past where he belonged.

"Do you want a bottle of water?"

Will straightened slowly, clearly checking out her legs
as he did. She was wearing a stretchy pink shirt over her
sports bra and black spandex capris that fit her like a second skin. And she'd give anything to know if he liked what
he saw. Darn sunglasses.

"I can throw in a cup of coffee," she offered, "and a
muffin baked fresh this morning."

"Blueberry? Like you used to make?" There was a
husky quality to his voice that amped up the sexy factor.

"Yes. Did that sweeten the pot?"

"Not really. You had me at water." He grinned. "But I
wouldn't say no to a muffin."

That was why she'd made them. He'd always raved
about her baking. If the spandex hadn't worked, muf-
fins were her fallback strategy. The way to a man's heart
through his stomach and all that.

"Come on in."

He followed her into the house, where she grabbed two
bottles of water from the refrigerator, then handed one to
him. He twisted the top off, then drank deeply, again one
of those profoundly masculine movements that made her
heart skip.

This was where she got it in a big way that the last time
she'd kissed a guy had been longer ago than she could recall. The resulting knot of yearning wasn't a flaw in the
plan, she told herself with a confidence that took some
work.

"I'll turn on the coffee."

"Can I help?" He sat on one of the high stools at the bar
separating kitchen and family rooms.

"No. Thanks."

Water and coffee grounds were ready to go; she only had to flip the switch. As soon as she did a sizzling sound started and almost instantly the rich coffee aroma filled the room.

"You've made some changes since the last time I was here," he commented.

"Yeah." She looked around the kitchen. This place was where she'd spent her teenage years. Now it was part of her inheritance, although she'd give it up in a heartbeat to have her mother back. "I updated the cupboards and changed the countertops to granite. Along with the house, my mom left me a little money and after I got the shop up and running there was enough left to do a few things."

"It looks good."

"I like it." She reached up into one of the cupboards and pulled out two mugs—one that said I Don't Do Mornings and the other sporting the Seattle city skyline, including Space Needle.

"Have you been to the Pacific Northwest?" he asked.

"Yeah. I went with a friend."

"Anyone I know?"

"Don't think so. Joe moved here after you left for Chicago." She poured coffee in the Seattle mug and handed it to him. "Do you still take it black?"

"Yup. Do you still drink yours the sissy way?"

"Of course. Cream and sugar." She smiled at the memory of how he used to tease her about this. "But these days it's nonfat and sugar substitute."

"Why?"

"A girl has to watch her figure."

"Some girls maybe, but not you. Guys will do that for you." Maybe it was wishful thinking but it sounded like there was a slight edge to his voice. "What does Joe do?"

"Construction. While he was here." She handed him a paper plate with a muffin on it.

"Does that mean he's gone?" He folded the cupcake paper down and took a bite of muffin.

"Yeah. He went back to Seattle. It's where he's from. We went there to visit his family."

"Do you keep in touch?" Definitely an edgy sarcasm in his tone.

"No." She poured cream in her coffee, then took the container and put it back in the refrigerator. When she turned back, she caught him staring at her butt and legs. And if her feminine instincts weren't completely rusted out, she was pretty sure he approved of what he saw. "There was no point. Long-distance relationships don't work."

"April—"

She held up a hand. "That wasn't a dig at you. Really, Will. It's just the truth."

He looked at her over the rim of his mug as he took a sip. "Okay." Then he glanced at his watch. "I have to get going. On duty in a little while."

"I guess peacekeeping is a seven-day-a-week job," she said.

"'Fraid so." He stood. "Thanks for the coffee and muffin. We'll have to do this again sometime."

"I'd like that." She walked him to the door. "Bye, Will."

"See you."

She watched him walk over to his house and remembered the approval on his face when he'd checked her out. A glow radiated through her and it wasn't just about the fact that her revenge plan was back on track.

No, this was about the fact that Will wasn't completely neutral where she was concerned. It was personally satisfying and she looked forward to more.

* * *

"I swear Luke and I are going to Vegas for a quickie wedding." Kim plopped herself down on the couch in the family room.

Will picked up the remote and muted the sound of the baseball game on TV. He'd only turned it on to keep himself from thinking about April. It wasn't working very well. The memory of her in those tight black running pants had his mind on things it had no business being on. The White Sox could wait. His sister, on the other hand, was on the verge of a meltdown if not already there.

"What's wrong?"

"Everything." She threw up her hands dramatically.

"Where's Dad?"

"At the movies with Tim. You're it, big brother. There's no one else here to deal with me. I don't need a big wedding. A small backyard barbecue would be perfect, don't you think? Or even something at the park. Easy peasy."

"You know you want a big wedding," Will reminded her.

"Why? What was I thinking?"

"That you've never been married before and you're only doing this once, so it's going to be a blowout affair."

"That's a direct quote, isn't it?" she asked.

"Yup." He looked at her beside him. "You said it the night before Dad had his surgery."

"Talk is cheap. Making a grand pronouncement is a lot easier than taking the steps to make it happen."

"Talk *is* cheap. But I can't help if you don't spit it out, Kimmie. What specifically is making you freak out?"

Tears welled in her blue eyes. "I got a call from the bridal shop. My dress is back-ordered and might not arrive in time."

"So pick out another dress." When big, fat tears started

rolling down her cheeks, he knew that was the wrong thing to say. "Hey, come here."

She slid over and leaned her head on his shoulder. "It's just…I w-wanted that dress."

"And it might be fine. Back-ordered isn't a definite *not going to happen*. But maybe you can pick out a runner-up just in case?"

"That's way too sensible." She sniffled and probably rubbed her runny nose on his T-shirt. "I just wanted to be bridezilla for a day. Throw a tantrum."

"And it was a beauty, sis. Way to be an overachiever." He put his arm around her shoulders and tucked her against him. "The thing is, I can guarantee that no one, including your groom, will know that any dress you wear is not your first choice."

"How can you be so sure?"

"Because you'd look beautiful in a burlap sack."

"Aw. That's sweet." She sniffled again and looked at him. "Makes me feel bad about blowing my nose on your shirt."

"It's yours now."

She smiled as intended. "How do you know Luke won't know it's a second-best dress?"

"Because guys don't care about that stuff. He'd be happy if you walked down the aisle naked." He winced. "I can't believe I just said that to my sister."

"It's okay. I took it in the spirit and all that. It's not a news flash that guys are pigs."

"That's harsh. We just have an acute appreciation for the female form."

"Right." She rubbed at an imaginary spot on the leg of her jeans. "Speaking of female forms, I saw you and April go running the other day and you went in her house when the two of you got back."

Will had forgotten how life was in a small town. Everyone watched what was going on and talked about it. At least Kim was talking to *him* and not someone at the Grizzly Bear Diner, which was ground zero for rumor spreading.

"So," he said narrowing his gaze on her, "your summer job while you're not teaching high school is doing covert surveillance for the CIA?"

"There are times when teaching teens feels like doing covert surveillance. It's not easy to stay one step ahead of those kids." There was a sly look in her eyes. "Speaking of steps, we were talking about you and April running together. What's up with that?"

"She runs. I run." He was having a little trouble concentrating after his naked woman remark, except April was the woman he was picturing naked. Okay, so he was a pig. He was a guy. He could own that. Because April had looked pretty spectacular in those tight black pants she'd worn. That spandex stuff hugged every curve and left little to the imagination, just enough that he wanted to take them off her and see everything. But that was pretty stupid, right? The two of them had their shot and he blew it. "I saw her in the alley before she started her run, so we went together."

His sister said something that sounded like, "Good for her," but Will couldn't be sure. "Afterwards she invited me in for coffee and a muffin."

"Is that what you crazy kids are calling it now?" There was a suggestive note in Kim's voice.

"There is no 'it.' We're friends. I guess."

"What does that mean?"

"I don't know." Will dragged his fingers through his hair. "It's just— When I made the decision to come back to Blackwater Lake for the summer, I knew I'd see her.

When you suggested I make sure the first time was private, I knew you were right. And—"

"What?"

"I was ready for it. I was prepared to deal with her anger. Possibly resentment. Hostility. Even hurt. I was braced for attitude whatever form it would take. That's something I'm trained to handle. After all, I'm Chicago PD."

Kim's forehead wrinkled. "What's your point?"

"My point is that I wasn't prepared for her to be friendly. She was a little resentful that first time I went over to her shop. But since then she's been—"

"What?"

"I don't know. So sweet my teeth are getting cavities."

"You've seen her a lot, then?" Kim looked like she was working hard at acting innocent.

"She brought over a casserole. Then asked for my help taking pictures of the graduating seniors passing the power torch to the incoming class. Before you say anything, I was working crowd control."

"Making sure no one had sex," she clarified.

He nodded. "We got a drink after. Her idea. Then we did our run together and had coffee."

"I still don't get the problem." Kim didn't look puzzled as much as a little self-satisfied. "It's all peace and serenity with your ex-girlfriend. Most guys would be ecstatic. Why are you complaining?"

"I'm not. Just the opposite."

"So, what is the opposite of complaining?" She tapped a finger to her lips. "Praise. Go into rapture over—"

"No one is going into rapture over anyone," he scoffed. "But she's acting pretty cool."

"You should have been more appreciative of what you had before sleeping with that woman."

"The only person you ever call *that woman* is my ex-wife, Brittany."

"Yeah. Her. And I bet she spells her name with an *i* at the end and the dot over it is heart shaped."

"Let me guess. You don't like her." Will knew exactly how his sister felt about his ex. She'd made it clear the first time they met.

Now Kim made a face that looked as if she'd taken a bite out of a sour lemon. "I never liked her."

"And I should have listened to you."

"It's very big of you to admit I was right, Will. I never thought the day would come when I'd hear you say those words. Although I was always aware that you felt like that."

"Don't let it go to your head. For what it's worth, on the divorce papers she spelled her name with a *y* and I assume that's the legal way. She wouldn't have slowed the process down by getting cute with spelling. She couldn't wait to be the ex Mrs. Fletcher."

"Don't tell me." Sarcasm was wrapped around every word. "She had her hooks into another guy. Probably seeing him before you two separated."

Although he had a whole lot of suspicion, Will had no independent facts to confirm it. All he said was, "Probably."

"You're well rid of her, Will." She put her hand on his arm. "Please don't let one bad experience make you gun-shy about a relationship. After all, look at me."

"What about you?"

"I'm the poster girl for what not to do. Pregnant at seventeen and abandoned by the father."

"This isn't getting even, sis, but I never liked that guy."

"Okay. And I didn't listen to you. We need to work on that." She sighed. "But, my point is that I didn't close myself off from love and now there's Luke."

"You're a lucky girl." But this had to be said. "For the record, I'm a detective. I can track that jerk down if you want to get back child support out of him."

"Sweet of you, but no. Someday Tim might want to meet him or the jerk might want to see his son and if it feels right I wouldn't stop it. But if the guy asked my son for a kidney, he'd have to go through me." A fierce, protective, maternal expression settled on her face. "As of now I don't ever want anything from him. Things worked out for the best. Tim is a great kid."

"You'll get no argument from me."

Guilt, but no pushback. Not being there for her was one more thing to add to his list of sins. Will had gone ahead with his career and hadn't been around to support her. That kid of hers, his nephew, was terrific, because he had a terrific mom and a grandfather who was devoted to him.

Her face went soft as all teasing disappeared. "I keep wondering when he's going to show interest in the opposite sex."

"He might not show it yet, especially to his mom, but I guarantee you there's already interest."

Horror widened her eyes. "Should I talk to him about safe sex? I don't want him to make the same mistake I did and for sure I'd phrase it better than that because I don't for one minute consider him a mistake. He's a blessing. But I would much rather not have him be a father before he's out of high school. Or college, for that matter."

"Is there a health class in the high school curriculum?"

"Yes, but I'm his mom. I feel as if I should have a conversation with him. Shouldn't that come from me?"

"He won't want to hear it from his mom."

"Voice of experience?"

"Not exactly. Dad said something to me and I still didn't

want to hear it. That's just the way boys are." He met her gaze. "So, no one special for him yet?"

"He's only fourteen. Too young to date."

"I can talk to him about this if you want." Maybe make up for not being around when he should have been.

"Would you?" She hugged him. "Let him know I'm willing to have a conversation about anything he wants, but didn't want to embarrass him. And tell him that—"

"I'll let you write out the talk on five-by-seven cards if that would make you more comfortable," he teased.

She laughed. "No. Just make sure he's ready for anything when he starts dating. It's important for him, but he also has to protect any young woman he might be with."

"I'll make sure he understands." He cleared his throat. "Speaking of dates… April said she'll be taking pictures at the wedding."

"Yeah. She's the best. Even if I decide to have it in the backyard."

He ignored her little flare-up of nerves. "Is she seeing anyone?"

"She sees a lot of people. After all she has a business and works with the public—"

"I meant is she dating anyone?"

"Of course," Kim said. "She's really pretty and a lot of fun. Guys ask her out all the time. And there's this one. Jean Luc. He's a same-time-next-year ski instructor who's here every winter."

That information was more unsettling than Will had expected. The idea of her with another guy really bugged him. That was something of a surprise, even more than her being friendly.

"So no one right now?" he asked.

"Not that I know of." Again Kim had that overly innocent thing going on. "Why?"

"She tells you everything. What do you think about me asking her to dinner?"

Kim stood and looked down at him, possibly with pity in her eyes. "She's probably not interested, but you've got nothing to lose by asking."

"Okay, then."

"Now that I've let off steam, there are lists to make and stuff to plan." She started out of the room. "Good talk, Will."

"Yeah."

Maybe.

But he couldn't shake the feeling that Kim was wrong—and he had a lot to lose if April said no.

Chapter Five

April put the Back in an Hour sign in her shop window and locked the door. She glanced across the street for a possible Will sighting and was disappointed when she didn't see him. It hadn't been her habit to do that before he came back to town and she wondered how long after he went back to Chicago before she stopped.

That was concerning but fell into the question-for-another-day category. Right now she was going to see Kim. Her friend had called, announced she had some important news and insisted April meet her for lunch at the Harvest Café. Whatever she had to say, it needed to be shared in person and Kim had appointments all afternoon to deal with wedding stuff. Since they both had to eat, it was a two birds, one stone situation. Good thing all was quiet at the Photography Shop.

The café was two blocks away, so she turned right and curiosity made her pick up the pace. She couldn't imagine what was so important that Kim had to call an emergency meeting. Hopefully there wasn't anything wrong.

Main Street was busy with tourists window shopping and leisurely strolling the downtown area. When the new resort was completed with its hotel, condos and retail space, foot traffic would increase and she would have to think about hiring someone part-time. It was an exciting thought.

Almost as exciting as having Will in her kitchen discussing the fact that he thought other guys liked her figure, which, in translation, meant he'd at least noticed and approved. He'd asked more than one question about an old boyfriend and sounded just the slightest bit jealous. That was good. For the plan.

Except that was the thing. After she'd "accidentally" run into Will, the plan never entered her mind again when she was with him. She behaved naturally and enjoyed hanging out with him. No flirting. No skullduggery or underhandedness. Just friendly and fun. She was no actress and trying to be one made her uncomfortable.

She crossed the street with the Grizzly Bear Diner on the corner. It specialized in burgers and sandwiches. After that she passed Tanya's Treasures, a gift and souvenir shop that was now under new ownership. Tanya had moved to Southern California to be with a man, a tourist, she'd met here in town. Way to go, Tanya.

Next door to the gift shop was Potter's Ice Cream Parlor and then the Harvest Café, both owned by Maggie Potter and her business partner, Lucy Bishop.

April nearly ran into another passerby while drooling over the pictures of ice cream sundaes and fighting the urge to go in. Who needed a healthy lunch? But she could still hear her mother's voice in her head—dessert after you finish your dinner. It made her feel as if her mom was still with her.

She walked into the café, which was full of people sitting at the counter and tables scattered around the open room. The decor was country cozy and done in fall shades, with flowered tablecloths and color-coordinated napkins in gold, green and rust. A shelf high on the wall held a copper teakettle, tin pitcher, pottery bowls and dried flowers. The women of Blackwater Lake loved this place and dragged their significant others in frequently.

In fact, just inside the door, Maggie was there with Sloan Holden.

"Hi, April." Maggie was a pretty, brown-eyed brunette who now had a ginormous diamond on her left ring finger. "Have you met Sloan?"

"Yes," he answered for her. "Liam and I were in the Photography Shop looking at cameras. It's nice to see you again." He was a tall, handsome man. And nice.

"You, too." His son was about ten or eleven, April recalled, a polite, curious and funny kid. That said a lot for the dad's parenting skills.

"Kim Fletcher told me you're taking the pictures at her wedding in August. When Sloan and I started talking about setting a date for our wedding he mentioned the photos he saw in your shop." Maggie looked up at him and smiled. "We both want you to handle the photography for ours."

He nodded. "The wedding pictures I saw were really stunning, an excellent representation of your work."

"Thank you," she said. "I'd love to. When you pick a date let me know so I can block it off on my calendar."

"Will do." Sloan looked at his bride-to-be. "I hate to leave, but work is waiting."

"Me, too." She stood on tiptoe and kissed him. "I'm glad you came in for lunch. See you at home."

"Can't wait." Tenderly, he ran a finger over her cheek. "Bye. Nice to see you again, April."

"You, too."

The two of them watched him leave and April wanted to sigh right along with Maggie. She'd been a widow with a young daughter for several years before Sloan rented a room at her bed-and-breakfast. The two fell in love and now they were getting married. She'd gotten a second chance at happiness, and who didn't love a happy ending?

April was only human and couldn't help just the tiniest bit of envy that crept in. She'd fallen in love once upon a time. But a happy ending? Not so much.

Maggie snapped out of it and looked at her. "You're meeting Kim Fletcher, right? She's already here. That table back in the far corner."

April spotted her friend who gave her a wave. "Thanks, Maggie. And let me know about that wedding date."

"Will do."

She picked her way through the full tables, then sat down across from her friend. "Hi."

"Hey, kiddo. Glad you could meet me."

"You said it was important. Is your dad okay?"

"The doctor says he's doing great."

"Will told me." She remembered the look on his face when he'd relayed what the doctor had said. There was something going on with him and his dad, but he'd changed the subject. Still, that had been a couple days ago. "Has there been a setback in Hank's recovery?"

"Not if he knows what's good for him," Kim said fiercely. "And I make sure he does."

"No kidding. You're bossy in the best possible way."

"That's what Luke says."

April hoped there wasn't a hiccup in the relationship and that was the reason for this meeting. "How is your guy?"

"My guy," her friend said dreamily. "Makes me want to burst into song. But don't worry. I know my limitations. No one wants to hear that."

"I think you have a lovely voice," April said loyally.

"That's why I love you." Kim turned serious. "And speaking of love…"

"Oh, God. Who else is engaged?" Not that April didn't like a romance as much as the next person, but this town was swimming in it.

"What does that mean?"

"Let me recap." April held up her fingers to count off the couples. "You and Luke. Maggie and Sloan, who just asked me to take pictures at their wedding. His cousin Burke and Sydney McKnight. Her father, Tom, married the mayor. Then there's Cabot Dixon and Katrina Scott, the runaway bride. They're all recently married or engaged. It's an epidemic. Or something in the water."

No, scratch the last one. If that were the case, April wouldn't feel like a slacker.

"Don't worry, sweetie. Your time will come. The biggest problem you'll have is who's going to take pictures at your wedding since you won't be able to do it yourself, what with being the bride and all."

"You don't have to say that, Kim. I don't need a man in order to be fulfilled." That was true, but she'd loved being in love. "I have my business. In fact I'm thinking of hiring someone part-time."

"That's wonderful. But you don't have to choose between the two. A woman can have a career and a relationship."

April had no doubt that was true except she'd all but given up hope of having both in her life. And that was okay. She'd gone along with this plan in order to have closure. "You didn't call me here for a pep talk. What's up?"

"I'm pretty sure my brother is going to ask you out." Kim waited for a reaction and when one wasn't forthcoming, she looked a little disappointed. "I expected a screech. A smile. Something."

April's heart skipped and stuttered, but the other woman couldn't see that. "How do you know this?"

Before Kim could answer, their waitress appeared. "Welcome to the Harvest Café. What can I get for you ladies?"

"We're kind of in a hurry. I really hate to do that to you," Kim said. "But I have appointments and April has to get back to work. So, I'd like an iced tea and the cranberry Cobb salad."

"Make it two." April handed over her menu.

"Coming right up."

"Okay," April said when the young woman was gone. "How do you know he's going to ask me out?"

"He told me. Practically."

"What does that mean?" This felt a lot like junior high, but April couldn't seem to shut off the need for details.

"He was asking questions. Like are you dating anyone. And I said of course you were since you're gorgeous and smart." Kim took a breath. "Then he put a finer point on it and wanted to know if you were exclusive with anyone, so I told him about Jean Luc, your winter-ski-instructor-lover. Same-time-next-year sort of thing."

"There is no Jean Luc."

"He doesn't know that." Kim's grin was wicked. "He didn't look happy."

Was it wrong, April wondered, that inside she was pumping her arm in a gesture of triumph? "Then what?"

"He asked what I thought about him inviting you to dinner."

"And you said?" April held her breath.

"I told him you probably wouldn't be interested, but he had nothing to lose by asking."

"You didn't." Of course she was interested.

"Yes, I did. You don't have to thank me."

"Good, because I wasn't planning to. What if I am interested?"

"Of course you are. That's what this plan is all about in the first place." Kim stopped when the waitress brought a tray with their salads and drinks, then set everything on the table.

"Anything else I can get you?"

"Just the check," Kim said.

"You got it."

April picked up her fork. "So you don't really know if he's going to ask."

"Oh, he is," her friend said confidently. "And when he does, you need to play hard to get."

"Wait a minute. Isn't this the goal?"

"Well, sleeping with him is the goal, but this is a start. But it shouldn't be too easy. Not only would that make him suspicious, men never appreciate anything they didn't have to work for." Kim took a bite of her salad.

"I don't know," April said. "And I already asked him to go for a drink after he helped me out."

"That doesn't count. And this way you'll keep him guessing. Trust me, sweetie. The end will be much more satisfying if you string him along just a little."

"Look, Kim, you know me better than anyone. You know I don't play games." She pushed the greens topped with dried cranberry, egg, bacon, blue cheese crumbles and avocado around the bowl. "The thing is I want to go out with him. Pretending makes me uncomfortable. Don't you think it's time to just be up front with Will?"

"Absolutely not." Kim gave her a don't-you-dare look.

"Remember why you're doing this in the first place. If you play this my way, everyone in Blackwater Lake will be talking about you and Will."

"But we had our chance and it wasn't meant to be," April protested.

"Did I say anything about my brother proposing?" She shook her head. "I did not. This is all about you moving on. That's going to happen when you get a chance to tell Will that you're not into him. Do you trust me, April?"

"Of course I do. You're the sister I never had. I know you wouldn't steer me wrong."

"Darn straight." Kim smiled. "This is going to work. I just know it."

April hoped she was right. She wanted to put Will Fletcher behind her before he went back to Chicago and put Blackwater Lake behind him.

Will had forgotten what a Blackwater Lake Fourth of July was like.

The shops in town were dripping with red, white and blue decorations. American flags flew on lampposts and residences. There had been a morning parade on Main Street with horses, cars, wagons and kids from elementary to high school. The town fire engine was the finale. Every parade entry was decorated for Independence Day and prizes were awarded for the most artistic, innovative and patriotic. Mayor Goodson-McKnight had picked the winners.

About two o'clock folks started showing up at the park for games of touch football, soccer and water balloon tosses that got fairly rowdy in a wet way. People staked a claim to the park tables by the built-in barbecues, where the town council and volunteers grilled hamburgers and hot dogs.

Blankets and chairs were spread out and arranged under trees as a break from the sun, also keeping in mind the best vantage point for the upcoming fireworks display put on by the fire department. That would happen in about an hour. The whole scene was like a long, cold beer for the small-town patriotic soul.

Being on duty here was, well, a walk in the park compared to a shift in Chicago on this holiday.

Will had seen April turn up everywhere with a camera hanging around her neck and a pocket-sized notebook in her hands. She was alternately taking pictures and getting names of the folks she'd snapped to document the festivities for the *Blackwater Lake Gazette*.

She was the picture of patriotism in her denim shorts, red-and-white-striped spaghetti-strapped top, hair pulled back in a perky ponytail. And he found himself on the alert, constantly watching for those particular denim shorts and top. Her shapely, tanned legs tied him in knots, especially because he remembered how good it felt to have them wrapped around his waist while he was buried deep inside her.

Will snapped his attention back to his job and picked his way through tables, blankets and toddlers, watching for any potential trouble that could mar the celebration. Then he heard his name and recognized Cabot Dixon, a local rancher who also ran a kids' summer camp.

He walked over and shook hands with the man, who stood up. "Been a long time, Cabot."

"Yeah." He indicated the pretty woman beside him with the light brown, sun-streaked hair. "This is my wife, Katrina Scott."

"It's Kate Dixon now." She smiled. "Nice to meet you, Sheriff."

"Will," he said. Pieces of stories he'd heard fit together.

"You're the woman who showed up at the Grizzly Bear Diner in a wedding dress."

"Guilty. I don't suppose I'm ever going to live that down," she said, not looking the least bit bothered.

"Probably not," Will agreed. "It's one of those legends that will be passed on from generation to generation and immortalized with a hammer and chisel on cave walls."

"I was sort of hoping for a Facebook fan page," she teased.

"She's the best thing that ever happened to me." Cabot put an arm around her shoulders and pulled her in closer to him. "Other than Tyler, of course."

"How old is your son now?"

"Going on ten. He's over there." Cabot pointed to a group of boys in an open grassy area playing soccer. "I heard you were the new sheriff in town."

"*Acting* sheriff. It's temporary." No matter how much his dad might want him to be permanent.

His friend looked around the idyllic setting. "This must be really different from Chicago. Will is a detective with CPD," he explained to his wife.

"It's the polar opposite of what I'm used to," Will agreed.

"Must be boring here," Cabot guessed.

"Excitement can be highly overrated." He shrugged. "I keep busy. Today alone I've confiscated enough illegal fireworks to take out a good-sized city."

"Teenagers?"

"Of course." He grinned and his friend returned it. "We did our share of that when we were their age."

"And your dad always caught us."

"Every year," Will confirmed.

"You guys tried it more than once?" Kate's blue eyes went wide.

"It was worth a shot," Will and Cabot said together.

"Men." She shook her head. "They get bigger but never stop being little boys."

"It's basic training," her husband explained, brown eyes teasing. "When Ty gets to be a teenager, he won't be able to get away with anything because I've done it all."

"My nephew complains about that. And he's living with two cops. He'll have to be twice as good as we were to be even half as bad."

"If they're going to pull stuff, and they are," Cabot said, "at least there's a lot less trouble to get into here in Blackwater Lake."

He and Kim had turned out okay and her son was doing great, Will thought. "I suppose it's a good place to raise kids."

"Sure hope so." Cabot looked at his wife who nodded slightly. "Just found out we're having another one."

"Congratulations." Will shook the other man's hand again. He saw the expression of pleasure, pride and excitement on his friend's face and felt a stab of envy.

"We're very excited," Kate said. "Ty is going to be a wonderful big brother. Although he's very vocal about not wanting a sister."

"I know how he feels. Mine's been a pain in the neck since she was born," Will teased.

"You don't mean that," she said.

"You're right. Kim is the best and that reminds me. Her son is fourteen and I need to make sure he's not doing what Cabot and I would have been doing at his age."

Cabot laughed. "Good luck with that. It was really great to see you again."

"You, too."

Will walked away and found his nephew shooting hoops with some friends while a group of teenage girls watched.

Judging by the hormone-drenched looks going back and forth between Tim and one of the young ladies, the talk Will had promised to have with the kid should happen pretty soon, he thought.

Keeping his eyes and ears open, he moved through the crowd, saying hello to old friends and being introduced to recently relocated residents. Learning what was going on. Sydney McKnight was engaged to Burke Holden, who was involved in building the new resort up on the mountain. His cousin and business partner, Sloan, was engaged to widow Maggie Potter. Her brother, computer millionaire Brady O'Keefe, had married his executive assistant.

Envy hit him again, smacked right into him like a bug on a windshield. Perspective was a funny thing. He'd run to something for his career and somehow felt as if he'd been left behind. He figured that feeling was as temporary as filling in for the sheriff.

Keep moving, he thought, making another circuit through the park. He was nearing the parking lot and saw the fire department's red hook-and-ladder truck parked there. In preparation for the holiday, he'd coordinated with fire and rescue to mobilize for the community celebration in the park. There was always a chance that Will would miss confiscating some banned fireworks and they could escalate into a big blaze during the dry summer months. Or someone shooting them off could get hurt.

Walking closer, he saw the fire captain he'd worked with. Desmond Parker. Nice guy who'd been recruited from Lake Tahoe, California, to expand the department as necessary to deal with the resort development.

He looked closer and saw that Des was chatting up a woman in a familiar red-striped, spaghetti-strapped knit top and denim shorts. It was April and she was smiling. Worse, she was looking at the guy the way she'd looked at Will when they were at Bar None, as if she was having a good time.

That started a slow burn in his gut and no high-powered fire hose was going to put it out.

Will stepped off the curb, onto the parking lot asphalt, and walked over to them. "April."

She looked pleased to see him just before her expression shifted into neutral, as if she'd caught herself and dialed down the reaction. "Hi, Will."

He held out his hand to Des. "Good to see you."

"Happy Fourth."

"You two know each other?" April looked at him, then the other man.

"We met at a community preparedness planning meeting," Des explained.

"Oh. Right," she answered. "Of course you would.

Will was no expert on what women found attractive in a guy, but he could see where this particular one could appeal. He was tall, blue eyed and sandy haired with a strong jaw and muscular build. Then there was the dark blue pants and shirt making up the uniform. He knew from personal experience that women liked the uniform.

And damn it. He hadn't sized up a guy like this since... Hell, ever. Even worse, he actually liked Des Parker. He was a stand-up guy and knew his job, but the thought of April with him was infuriating. Will knew why. He was jealous.

"How's it going?" Will asked him.

"So far, so good. On your end?"

"Quiet. I've got a lot of unauthorized pyrotechnics in the trunk of the cruiser. I'll turn them over to you tomorrow."

Des grinned. "The guys and I will have fun getting rid of them."

Will knew they were going to shoot them off. The difference was firefighters knew how to take the necessary precautions and do it safely. He couldn't stop a reluctant smile. "I'm sure you will."

Des looked at his watch. "Speaking of shooting off fireworks, I have to go. We're staging for the town's display now."

"Let me know if you need any help," he offered.

"Will do."

"Thanks for letting me get some photos of you with the truck, Des."

"Anytime." The other man smiled at April. "I'll call you."

"Okay."

Watching the man walk away, Will wished there was some town ordinance prohibiting a guy he actually liked from hitting on another guy's ex-girlfriend. But if that was the case, the sheriff's department would need a lot more deputies.

Alone at last, he thought, looking at April. Was he the only one who felt something simmering between them? Detectives were trained and on-the-job experience sharpened gut instinct about people. He didn't think she was disinterested and it was time to find out if he was right.

"You've been busy today. Taking pictures, I mean."

"Yeah. People enjoy seeing themselves in the paper." She glanced at the crowd in the park. "I should go set up to get some pictures of the fireworks."

"Before you go, there's something I'd like to ask you." Will realized he was nervous. He hadn't been nervous asking a woman out since he was a little older than his nephew.

"Yes?"

"We could both use some R & R after a busy day. I was wondering if you'd like to have dinner with me tomorrow night."

She looked at him for several moments. "It's very nice of you to ask. But I don't think so."

"Okay." He was about to ask for an explanation, but she turned away.

"I have to go."

Will stared at the sway of her hips as she walked toward where the whole town was gathered. Well, slap him silly if that didn't make him hotter than a sparkler even though she'd just rejected him.

Women, he thought, were beyond the understanding of mortal men. Detective skills were not useful in unraveling the mysteries of a woman's mind and that was damned unfair.

Chapter Six

"What's all this crap?" Will had just rolled out of bed and headed downstairs for coffee. Now he stared at the mound of files and paperwork that covered every square inch of the kitchen table. He gave his sister, who was sitting in front of it, a patented Chicago PD glare.

She didn't look the least bit intimidated. "This, dear brother, is my wedding. Files for every phase from reception menu to flowers. Receipts, invoices and samples that combined will make it a perfect day."

He was not in the mood for perfect anything, especially a wedding. Yesterday April had turned him down flat. It wasn't ego talking. Okay, maybe a little. But more troubling was that he might be losing his edge. He couldn't believe he'd read her so completely wrong.

Leaning his back against a counter with his arms folded over his chest, Will wasn't ready to let this drop. "How is a guy supposed to sit at the table and eat breakfast? And forget about opening a newspaper to read."

"Stand up and eat cereal the way you usually do," she snapped back.

There was nothing she could do to make him admit she was right about his normal pattern. "What about the other people in this house who might want to sit down to a leisurely meal?"

"Dad went somewhere with Josie. And Tim isn't up yet." She glared right back at him. "You're certainly in a mood."

"This isn't a mood. This is an attempt to stand up for male freedom and equality in this house. We have a right to use the table. The good of the many outweighs the good of the one."

"Oh, for Pete's sake. This won't be forever. Just a few more weeks then I'll be out of your hair."

"It won't matter then. I'm going back to Chicago right after that." Without getting a chance to spend time with April. That realization did not improve his mood.

"What's wrong?" Kim studied him intently.

"Nothing."

"Come on. This is me. Does your mood have anything to do with April?"

His gaze snapped to hers. "Why?"

"That was just a shot in the dark but I obviously got it right." Her eyes narrowed on him. "You asked her out and she said no."

"She told you."

"No. I swear."

His people radar was malfunctioning and he couldn't be sure, but she looked just a little too innocently sincere. "She must have said something to you."

"I haven't seen her since yesterday at the town picnic in the park," Kim vowed.

"She could have called. You two are BFFs. You tell each other everything."

"Yes. But this is breaking news. She didn't tell me she shut you down."

He winced. "Way to make me feel better."

"I'm sorry, Will."

"Go ahead and say I told you so." Kim had also told him he had nothing to lose by asking but it didn't feel that way right now.

"I would never do that. Not when you're so upset."

"I'm not upset. Why would I be? It's no big deal. April and I are friends and I thought it would be a good idea to hang out. She didn't want to. I'm over it."

"Epic shutdown, Uncle Will." Tim walked into the kitchen wearing a gray T-shirt displaying in black letters *Blackwater Lake High School Football*. His hair was sticking up and there was enough stubble on his jaw to prove he was closer to fifteen than fourteen. Clearly he'd overheard that April had said no. And now he was staring at the table where his mom was sitting. "What's all this crap?"

"That does it." Kim gave them both the hairy eyeball, then let her hostile gaze rest on Will. "You barely know your nephew. Take him and go do something."

"Are you throwing me out?" Will asked.

"Look at it as an opportunity to bond."

Tim backed away. "I think we better do what she says, Uncle Will, or her eyes will turn red and her head might explode."

"Yeah, kid. Sounds like a plan."

Looking like two rejects from a suspect lineup, they left the house. After stopping at the Grizzly Bear Diner for take-out breakfast sandwiches, Will drove out to the Blackwater Lake Marina.

"Do you like fishing?" he asked his nephew.

"It's okay."

"Let's rent some gear at the marina store."

"Cool."

They walked in and looked around. There were circular racks of T-shirts and lightweight outerwear. A cold case against the wall was packed with soda and water with a display case of chips and snacks beside it. Another wall held fishing equipment from poles to lures. Will recognized Brewster Smith standing behind the cash register at the checkout counter. The man had worked there as long as he could remember.

"Hey, Brew."

"Will Fletcher." This guy was close to sixty if he hadn't already rung that bell. He had a full silver beard and a head of hair to match. "I was wondering how long it would take you to get out here. Heard you were back."

"Temporarily. Are you ever going to quit this job?"

"Nope."

"I'm sure Jill Beck appreciates your loyalty."

"Don't work for her anymore. And she's Jill Stone now. She married a doctor from Mercy Medical Clinic and had a baby girl. They sold the property, marina and all, to a famous writer fella and built a big house in that fancy development overlooking the lake."

"Who's the writer?"

"Jack Garner."

"No kidding?" Will had read his book *High-Value Target*. It was a big hit. Spent months at the top of the bestseller lists.

"Yeah, but I don't see him around much. He keeps to himself."

"Must be working on the next book."

"I guess." Brew grinned at Tim. "Hey there, young fella. Been a while since I've seen you out here with your grandpa. How's he doing?"

"Good. Thanks for asking, Mr. Smith."

"Glad to hear it." The older man rested his hands on the counter and looked at them. "What can I do for you?"

"Do you still rent fishing gear?" Will asked.

"Sure do. I'll fix you fellas right up."

The man was as good as his word and fifteen minutes later they had set up at the lake's edge and were sitting side by side in folding chairs that had holders for their fishing poles while waiting for a fish to bite. Their lines were in the water. The sky overhead was a perfect shade of blue and the sun was shining. Uncle and nephew ate their breakfast in silence.

Will figured he was the adult and it was up to him to break the silence that was growing more awkward by the second. When nothing that wasn't lame came to mind he realized two things. First, Kim was right about him not knowing his nephew. Second, the only kids Will had contact with were in trouble with the law. If Tim had been caught stealing or with an illegal weapon he would have plenty to say to him. But he was a good kid.

He looked over. "Are you sure you don't want a soda?"

"No. I'm good. Mom doesn't like me drinking too much of it."

"Right. Good call." Will had been amused earlier that the kid had the same reaction to her pile of wedding stuff on the table as he did. That sparked a conversation topic. "What do you think about her getting married?"

"It's cool."

Will waited for more and when it didn't come, he asked, "So you like Luke?"

"I sort of fixed her up with him. He's the football coach and I'm on the team."

"Don't they both teach at the school?"

"Yeah. But nothing happened until she started picking me up from practice. I hung out in the locker room longer than I needed to and they started talking." He shrugged his thin shoulders. "The rest is history."

"But you like him?"

"He's a pretty cool guy."

"I'm glad to hear it."

Another awkward silence fell. This was not a good time to remember that he'd promised Kim he would have *that* conversation with her son. *Here goes nothing*, he thought.

"You're a pretty good basketball player."

"Thanks. How do you—" Then the light went on. "At the park yesterday."

"Yeah. I saw you in that pick-up game. There were some girls watching. One of them was a cute redhead and she had her eye on you."

Tim didn't look over but his face turned as red as that girl's hair. "Lexie."

"Do you like her?"

"She's okay."

The kid's body language elaborated. There was so much tension he looked ready to snap like a twig.

"I think you like her a lot," Will said. "Have you kissed her?" There was no answer and that was answer enough. "Do you have any questions about anything?"

"Such as?"

"What happens after kissing?"

Tim shook his head. "I know about that."

"What about birth control?" Will figured this would be quicker and easier on both of them if he was more specific. "Condoms."

"What you're saying is that I shouldn't put a girl in the same situation as my mom was with me." His voice was tinged with hostility and a bit of resentment thrown in.

"Yeah. That's what I'm saying." This kid was smart and would know if Will wasn't being completely honest and up front with him. "Just because your mom was young, that doesn't mean she doesn't love you more than anything in the world. I know for a fact she does."

"Yeah. She tells me all the time." He looked over. "And the guy who got her that way ran out on her. And me. He left town and disappeared."

"He did." The rat bastard. But letting his nephew know how ticked off he still was wouldn't help. And he didn't make the same offer he had to his sister to use his detective skills and find him. Will didn't want to put ideas into the kid's head. If he came up with it himself and Kim was on board he would do everything possible to find said rat bastard.

"The thing is, Tim, you and your mom were better off without a guy who would leave like that. And you're lucky. You have family who love you. And that's the most important thing."

"I guess."

"So, if you need condoms..." Will stopped until the boy looked at him. "There are a lot of people for you to turn to. Your mom. But I know that would be weird. Granddad. Luke. Me."

"Okay. Got it."

"Good."

"Can I ask you something, Uncle Will?"

"Sure. Anything." But he braced himself.

"What's the deal with you and April?" Tim glanced over and there was a definite protective expression on his freckled face.

"That's a good question. I wish I knew the answer."

"So you don't know why she turned you down when you asked her out?"

"Nope." Will stuffed the paper their breakfast had been wrapped in back into the bag.

"Well, I like her," the boy said. "And you keep telling everyone that you're only here in town temporarily while Granddad recovers from his surgery. And you said me and my mom are better off without a guy who would walk out on us."

"That's right." It was a good thing he'd braced himself. Will had a feeling he wasn't going to like what came next.

"Maybe if you're not staying you should just leave April alone."

"That would probably be the wisest course of action," Will admitted.

"So, are you going to back off?" Tim asked.

"Can't lie to you, son. I'm not sure."

Because he had a problem. April's rejection made him want to see her even more. Did that make *him* a rat bastard?

After a long day at work, Will walked into Bar None for a beer. It was crowded, apparently the happening place on a summer evening in Blackwater Lake. But, like a heat-seeking missile, his gaze went to a bistro table in the far corner where his sister was having a glass of wine with April. Both women acknowledged him, but April smiled and waved as if she hadn't rejected his dinner invitation a couple nights ago on the Fourth of July. Then she turned her attention back to Kim, clearly shutting him out.

So he headed for the bar and took the only empty stool, which, as luck would have it, afforded an unobstructed view of that corner bistro table where April was pretending she hadn't been acting weird.

Delanie Carlson, the owner of the bar, walked over. The curvy redhead was somewhere in her twenties and had inherited the place from her father. "Hey, Sheriff. How are you?"

"Good." Maybe. He glanced over at April, who was still not looking at him. Forcing a smile, he asked, "You?"

"Oh, you know. Can't complain."

"Looks like business is booming."

"Yeah." Her blue eyes darkened a little as she scanned the place. "What can I get for you?"

"Beer."

"Bottle or tap?"

"Bottle."

"Anything to eat?" When he shook his head, she said, "Okay. One beer coming right up." She walked over to a refrigerator under the bar and pulled out a long-neck bottle. After twisting off the cap, she set it on a napkin in front of him. "Enjoy."

"Thanks." Will didn't want to but couldn't stop himself from looking at April again. If only he could stop dreaming about her, dreams so hot his sheets were practically smoking. He needed a distraction and Delanie was busy.

He glanced at the guy sitting beside him, who was also sipping a beer. Will had never seen him before. "You a tourist?"

"No."

"New in town?"

"Not that new." There was a blank expression on the newcomer's face before he resumed staring at the bottle of beer in front of him.

Will sized him up. He was fit and rugged looking, roughly two hundred pounds with black hair and blue eyes. There was a tattoo on his forearm.

He was starting to get a complex. First April rejected him and now this joker didn't want to talk. It was strictly stubbornness and bad temper that made him pursue this line of questioning. "How long have you been here?"

"More than six months."

"But less than a year," Will guessed. The other guy merely lifted a shoulder. This was starting to feel like an interrogation in that special room with the two-way mirror. "Care to tell me your name?"

"Jack Garner."

"The writer. I read your book."

"Good. I have a mortgage to pay."

"Didn't say I bought it. Just read it."

They stared at each other for several moments and finally Jack said, "Okay. I'll bite. What did you think?"

"It was good." Will was picky about his reading material, but he'd really liked the book. "The action was realistic. I'm guessing you spent some time in the military."

"Army special forces, Ranger division."

That explained why the details were spot-on. "I look forward to the next one."

"Yeah." Jack frowned and took a long pull on his beer.

Will glanced over at April again. She was wearing a pink sweater set with black slacks and had her hair long and silky past her shoulders. She looked so kissable it made him ache. Part of him thought if he stared long enough he'd catch her looking at him. And then what? Even his nephew had advised him to keep his distance. But too often rational thought and hormones didn't see eye to eye. So here he was being pathetic.

"Why don't you just go over there?"

Will met Jack's gaze. "What?"

"You keep staring at that table in the corner. Don't know which one of those ladies you're interested in, but do something about it, man."

"The blonde is my sister and she's engaged."

"Got it." Jack saluted with his beer bottle, letting him know he'd received the warning loud and clear. "So it's the cute brunette."

Jealousy balled in his belly and he wanted to warn him off April, too. But he had no right and that just pissed him off more. "That hasn't been confirmed."

"Yeah, it has. If I were you, I'd just go over there and sit down."

"Who made you my wingman?"

"It's a dirty job, but apparently someone has to do it." Jack looked amused.

"Why would I take your advice?" Will challenged. "Because you know so much about women?"

"What I know about the fairer sex would fit on the head of a pin."

"Then I have to ask: What makes crashing their conversation a good move?"

"It's what you want. You're preoccupied. You're staring at her and it's getting obvious." Jack paused, then added, "And, frankly, you're just not very good company."

Will stared at the other man for a second or two then laughed. "Don't hold back. Tell me how you really feel."

"Will do."

When Jack grinned, Will's gut told him it was something the man rarely did. He held out his hand. "Will Fletcher. Acting sheriff of Blackwater Lake."

"Good to meet you, Sheriff." Jack shook his hand. "Now leave me alone and let me brood."

"Roger that."

Will picked up his beer and headed over to the table where the two women sat. "Mind if I butt in?"

"Hi, Will," his sister said. "Have a seat."

He'd planned to anyway, but it was nice to be invited. "How are you, April?"

"Good, thanks." She gave him a big smile. "So you survived the Fourth of July."

"I did. Here's to that." He held up his beer and they clinked their wineglasses against it.

"I saw you talking to Jack Garner, the writer," his sister said.

"Yeah. Nice guy."

"He doesn't usually talk to anyone when he comes in here," Kim added. "Before you ask how I know that, I should tell you that I don't spend that much time here in the bar. Delanie told me."

"Well he's probably got his reasons for keeping to himself." Will knew some guys on the police force who developed PTSD from incidents related to the job. He figured in army special forces Jack Garner had seen things that changed him, things he didn't want to talk about.

"Actually, Will, I'm glad you're here," his sister said.

That was a surprise. "So I get a pass on crashing girls' night?"

"It's not so much girls' night," April said. "More of an emergency management meeting."

"What's wrong?" He looked from one woman to the other. "You're not calling off the wedding."

"No." Kim's voice was adamant. "But you know all those files and the paperwork on the table the other morning?"

"The crap?" he asked wryly.

"Yeah. That."

"What about it?"

"I'm beginning to be overwhelmed." Kim caught her bottom lip between her teeth.

"You know I was kidding about that, right?" He hadn't meant to freak her out.

"I know. It's just that I'm feeling the pressure. On top of the fact that my dress is back-ordered."

"It just kills me that I can't be your maid of honor," April said.

"I didn't think I needed one. But I also didn't realize there would be this much stuff. Besides, you're my photographer and I know the pictures will be amazing. That's what this is all for. When Luke and I are old we can look at our wedding album and ask who the babies are in the pictures April Kennedy took. It's just the putting-it-all-together part that's getting to me." She sighed. "Maids of honor come and go, but pictures are forever."

Both of the women looked as if they were ready to have an emotional moment that would probably involve tears, and Will was beginning to regret crashing the party. Like most guys, he wanted to fix it. Anything to keep them from crying.

"So pick someone else to be your maid of honor," he suggested. "You have friends, right?"

"Of course I do. But if I ask someone now they'll feel like an afterthought. That might hurt their feelings."

"If they're really your friend, it probably wouldn't be like that," he pointed out.

"Family wouldn't be like that at all," April said. "They would just be there for you because you need them. It's too bad you don't have a sister."

Suddenly there was a gleam in Kim's eyes. "I've got it."

"Unless Dad has a secret baby daughter somewhere, you still don't have one. So what do you have?" Will asked warily.

"A brother and an idea. You can be my maid of honor."

He shook his head. "I don't meet the physical requirements. In case you haven't noticed, I'm not a maid."

"Okay. Man of honor then. Besides, what's in a name? You can be my second, like when duels were fought in the olden days. I think you'd be fantastic, Will."

"He would. What's that police motto? To protect and serve? It takes a guy's guy to be a man of honor." April's voice was pleading.

And Jack Garner was right. She was so cute he wanted her in the worst way. How could he say no to her? "Okay. But if the squad in Chicago finds out about this, I'll get you back," he warned her.

"Oh, Will—" Kim started to cry.

"Oh, for Pete's sake." He handed her a napkin then took her hand in his. "I said yes so you wouldn't cry."

"I'm just happy," she said, dabbing her eyes.

"This calls for a toast," April said. "To Will, the best man of honor you could ask for."

"Probably the only one," he grumbled.

Kim laughed as intended. "To Will."

They touched glasses again and he met April's gaze. She wasn't ignoring him now. She was looking at him as if he'd hung the moon. As if he was her hero.

If he invited her to dinner right this minute would she say yes? Not only did he not want to ask her in front of his sister, a guy's ego could only take so much rejection. Private was better.

He didn't know what April's problem was. Other than the fact that he wasn't staying permanently in Blackwater Lake.

Still, they both knew where the other stood and there wasn't any reason not to have some fun while he was in town. When he got a chance, he planned to pursue that line of questioning.

And he was going to pursue it very soon.

Chapter Seven

April helped Kim carry her wedding dress upstairs. Not only had her first choice arrived without a hitch, it fit like a dream. No alterations required. The bridal shop at Mountain's Edge Mall had offered to store it for her until the wedding, but Kim refused. She'd said everything was starting to feel too out of control and this gave her the illusion of having power over it all.

"I'm guessing this isn't a slip dress." April was wrestling with the bottom half of the heavy, bulky, zippered storage bag.

"Not a chance. I'm a mom, but I've never been married before and this is going to be my dream wedding." There was a note in her voice that hinted at convincing herself more than anyone else.

"Would it be this heavy in a dream?" April asked, trying to tease her friend's nerves into submission. It was obvious that asking Will to be her man of honor hadn't taken the edge off the pressure she was feeling. "How are you going to move in this dress?"

"On my day I will float on air," Kim assured her.

They finally made it upstairs and turned left toward Kim's room. Her son's, which his mother often said could be mistaken for a biohazard waste dump, was right next door. April knew Will slept across the hall.

She forced herself not to look in that direction and check out where he was hanging his hat these days. He hadn't asked her out again, but the other night at Bar None he'd joined her and Kim. He seemed to have a good time and April did, too. It felt a little like a date and she hoped Kim's strategy of making Will work for it wouldn't cost her a chance to go out with him.

"I guess Will isn't home yet."

"If he was, I'd have made him haul this behemoth up the stairs." Kim backed into her room, pushing open the door with her shoulder. "It's the least the man of honor can do."

"It was really sweet of him to agree to do that."

"I know, right?" Kim waited for April to bring the bottom half of the bag into the room. Instead of sliding doors, her walk-in closet had a closing one with a metal hook on the outside. They managed to put the dress's heavy-duty hanger on it. She looked at April and blew out a breath. "It just felt appropriate to ask Will to stand up with me. If it can't be you."

"Could have knocked me over with a feather when those words came out of your mouth," April admitted. "I thought you were kidding."

"I was a little. At first. Then I realized I could really use someone. I'm not even sure what for because you've been there for me, for everything."

April's gaze drifted to the zippered garment bag. "Can we look at it again?"

"Twist my arm." Kim reached up and unzipped the bag, letting the full tulle skirt spill out.

They stared at the strapless bodice, sparkling with crystals and tapering to a fitted waist, where the full skirt flared out. It oozed femininity.

April sighed. "I can just picture it all. The roses and lilies, with a few hydrangeas thrown in for color in your bride's bouquet. Hank, Tim and Will in their black tuxes. Guests gathered for the happy occasion."

"Yeah." Kim's voice was a little shaky.

Time for a pep talk. "Then you walk down the aisle, where the man of your dreams is waiting next to the minister who will preside over your vows."

"That's the plan."

"Are you writing them?" April asked. Her friend was most confident with the written word and loved instructing her students in the art of essay writing. "If Blackwater Lake High School's favorite English teacher doesn't write her own vows, what kind of message would that send?"

"Not a good one, I'm guessing." Doubt crept into her expression.

"Oh," April said staring at the stunningly beautiful dress. "You're going to look so gorgeous in this when you become Mrs. Luke Miller."

"Oh, God—" Kim's eyes widened.

April thought maybe this was a good time to take the focus off the dress. She spotted several boxes in the corner and walked over to peek inside. "The invitations. They're beautiful." She picked one up and ran a hand over the embossed white lily and read the words out loud. "Mr. Henry Fletcher and Mr. and Mrs. Frank Miller request the honor of your presence at the wedding of their children, Miss Kimberly Fletcher and Mr. Luke Miller."

"Do you really like them?"

April had helped her pick them out. "Even better than I thought. These came out so great. It's going to be official."

"Eek—"

There was a knock on the open bedroom door. "Anyone home?"

"Will, I didn't hear you come in." Kim looked at her wristwatch. "It's late."

"Long day. Some tourists having a little too much fun." His gaze was on April when he said the last word. There was a smoky look in his eyes and a rough edge to his voice that hinted at the kind of fun a man and woman needed privacy for.

Or maybe that was just her imagination, April thought, because she'd had that kind of fun on her mind since this dating-and-dumping plan had started.

"Hi, Will," she said.

He nodded, then looked at the dress and whistled. "I guess you got the one you wanted."

"Uh-huh." Kim bit her lip uncertainly.

"And you rode shotgun," he said to April.

"Yeah." Her gaze was on her friend, who'd turned a little pale.

"I'm kind of new at this man-of-honor thing. Is it in my job description to stand guard now over this big, poofy ball of white?"

Apparently those words pushed Kim over the edge because she burst into tears.

"I was kidding." Will looked at April and said, "What did I say?"

"N-nothing. It's me," Kim blubbered.

"What's wrong with you?"

"Everything," she wailed.

"Like I said, I've got no experience with this MOH stuff, but I'm a quick learner." He took his sister's hand, led her over to the bed and sat her on the floral spread before going down on one knee in front of her. "It would help me out a lot if you'd be a little more specific about what the problem is."

"I think I'm making a big mistake." She buried her face in her hands and sobbed.

Will met April's gaze with a look that said he would rather do police paperwork in triplicate than deal with a weeping woman. He stared at the floor for several moments, shaking his head. Any second she expected him to bail. Say something about a hysterical woman being above his pay grade. Or advise his sister to walk it off.

Finally he sighed, then said, "Kimmie—"

"W-what?"

He stood, then sat on the bed beside her and settled his strong arm around her shoulders. "Why do you think getting married is a mistake?"

"It just is."

"So you don't love Luke?"

"Of course I love him." She lowered her hands and stared at her brother as if he were crazy. "He's handsome, funny, kind and loving. Sexy."

"Too much information," Will said.

"The point is that Luke is everything I've ever wanted in a man."

"Okay. Then your son doesn't like him?"

"Tim likes Luke a lot. He played matchmaker for us."

"Okay." One corner of Will's mouth curved up. "He actually told me that when we went fishing. So, moving on. Obviously his parents think you're not good enough for their son."

"Don't be ridiculous." She sniffled. "His family likes me better than him. And they love Tim. Already they're insisting he call them Grandma and Grandpa."

"Okay. Then there's something here that I'm not seeing," he said.

Brilliant strategy, April thought. Will was going through everything step-by-step to eliminate her fears instead of just telling her it would be okay.

"Maybe Luke and I should just go to Vegas," Kim said.

"So it's the big, showy wedding that's freaking you out," he deduced.

"Some," she admitted, meeting his gaze. "There are a lot of details to take care of. What if I forget something? Worse, what if it's all a huge mistake, and Luke and I end up hating each other?"

"That's not going to happen." Will was adamant.

"How can you be so sure?"

"Because you've kissed a lot of frogs and waited for the right guy." He lifted her hand and put it in his big palm, then folded his fingers around hers. "Take it from someone who didn't wait and got it wrong."

His gaze settled on April when he said the last words. Her legs wobbled and she locked her knees to keep from toppling over. His blue eyes darkened to the color of the lake and more than anything she wanted to drown in them.

"I never liked the woman you married," Kim said.

"Yeah." He smiled at her declaration. "You've made that abundantly clear. More than once."

"Sorry."

"Does Luke know you're the queen of saying I told you so?"

"You'd have to ask him." But she laughed for the first time. "I guess it's just everything getting to me. The invitations. The dress. Food and flowers. Writing vows. It's getting real. And pretty darn scary."

"A normal reaction," he reassured her.

"Yeah?"

"No question. Anyone who doesn't have a meltdown and take inventory of the situation shouldn't be doing it."

"I guess you passed the test," April said.

"Tests are good," Kim agreed.

"So says the teacher." Will pulled her in for a bear hug. "You waited for the right guy and deserve to have a big party to celebrate. It's going to be perfect."

Kim nodded. "You're right. Thanks for talking me off the ledge."

"What's a man of honor for?"

His sister smiled and nodded, then said, "I need to go wash my face."

"I was going to say," he teased. "You look a little puffy."

She laughed, then left the room.

April released a breath. "It happened so fast. I was excited about the dress and the wedding and couldn't stop talking. When I realized she was starting to panic it was too late."

"Bound to happen," he said.

"You were amazing with her." His gentle common sense, reassurance and understanding tugged at April's heart. "You even used your own experience to convince her she was making the right choice."

"That's me. A horrible warning." But there was laughter in his eyes when he said the words.

"I didn't mean it like that. You did really good today, Will Fletcher."

And as gooey as she was feeling inside, it was probably just as well she hadn't gone out with him. This was a sweet side of Will, the side that could break her heart again if she wasn't careful.

Just because he admitted that he got it wrong with April before didn't mean the two of them could get it right now.

* * *

April put a low-cal, frozen chicken-enchilada dinner in her microwave to cook and tried to convince herself she wasn't lonely, bordering on pathetic. She had a successful business and loved her work. Lots of people called her friend. But all were married with the exception of Kim, whose single status would change about six weeks from now before summer ended.

The truth was that Kim's approaching marriage hadn't made her think this way; the engagement had happened months ago. These feelings hadn't surfaced until Will came back to town. Along with him came old memories that she'd managed to put away. Memories of runs, dinners, movie dates. Memories of not being by herself.

She was over him. Really. But it had been more than a week since he'd asked her out and she'd turned him down. Kim's reasoning seemed sort of lame now, all things considered. Only three days ago he'd reasoned his sister out of a meltdown. Then April and Will had had a moment alone in Kim's bedroom, which she was certain had been a *moment*. After that…nothing.

"They don't call. They don't write," she muttered, listening to the hum of the microwave. And for real excitement she watched her frozen dinner turning inside the appliance.

Then things got exciting. At the same time the microwave beeped a signal that her cheese enchiladas were now warm and probably rubbery, there was a knock on her kitchen door. That made it official. She might be lonely, but pathetic was off the table because someone wanted to see her.

"Please let it not be a door-to-door salesman," she pleaded.

Although they'd ring the bell beside the front door. It

was probably one of the Fletchers—Hank, Kim, Tim or Will. Her money was on the first three.

After turning on the outside light, she saw Will through the sliding glass door and knew she'd have lost her bet. Her heart started thumping. Hard. But that was only because she was so happy to see *someone*. Anyone. And he had something in his hands that looked suspiciously like a pizza. There weren't many things that could fit in a big square flat box.

April unlocked the door and slid it open. "Hi."

"I come bearing food. And wine." There was a bottle of red tucked under his arm. It was starting to rain and the outside light made drops of moisture sparkle in his dark hair. "In the spirit of full disclosure, I have to tell you it's a bribe."

"Oh?" She stepped back to let him in out of the rain, then closed the door behind him.

"I need asylum."

"Did you say *an* asylum?" she teased.

"If you don't let me in, that's exactly where I'll be headed." He almost looked dead serious, but there was a hint of laughter in his eyes.

It was surprising how well she still knew him, could still read him. "What's wrong?"

"Nothing, I guess. As far as I can tell, there's not a crisis but Kim is making everything wedding into a federal case. It's driving me nuts." He set the pizza box and wine on the island and looked at her.

April remembered the pleading expression from a lifetime ago. It was the one that could get her to do anything. Of course that was a time when it took very little to get her to do whatever he wanted because she'd been blinded by love.

"So, what do you want? Define asylum."

"As God is my witness, I will be the world's best man of honor my sister ever had, but I can only do that if I can recharge my batteries with someone normal and reasonable."

"Where's Kim now?"

"Out with Luke."

"So, last time I checked your dad and nephew were normal and rational."

"They're not home."

So he'd been alone. Did that mean he was lonely, too? Just moments ago she'd been feeling sorry for herself and now those feelings transferred to him.

"Okay." She nodded. "I'll throw together a salad. You open the wine."

"Roger that." He saluted, then frowned at the intermittent noise coming from the microwave. "What's that sound?"

"My frozen dinner."

He made a face and managed to look adorable. "So a case could be made for me rescuing you from a tasteless, plastic meal."

"One could say that, but one would be wrong." She pulled the small, pathetic, individual dinner out of the microwave to stop the annoying sound and dropped it in the trash. "This particular entrée is one of my favorites."

"That's obvious by the way you couldn't get rid of it fast enough."

"Okay." She couldn't stop a smile. "You're the one who set a high bar for full disclosure. Pizza is so much better than what I was going to have. You did rescue me." She gave him an adoring look and batted her lashes. "My hero."

"Aw shucks, ma'am." He picked up the bottle of wine and asked, "Where's your corkscrew?"

"That cylindrical red thing on the counter to the left of the oven."

He walked over and picked it up. "You have an electric one?"

"It's an investment."

"In what?"

"Independence. Women's liberation. Whatever you want to call it. I just needed to know I could get a cork out of a wine bottle without a man around to pull it out with brute strength."

Was that a flirty remark? It felt a little flirty, but lately she'd been pretending with him. And it had been so long since she'd done it with any man, her flirt-meter was rusty. But she was pretty sure she'd just nailed him with genuine, authentic flirtation material.

The thing was, no effort had been involved and that was due in no small part to her attraction, which was completely natural and extremely powerful. The challenge wasn't in flirting with him, but in not letting it be more.

"Okay," he said. "Since I've got nothing to prove regarding my masculinity, I'm okay using the girly opener."

"Good thing. It's the only one I've got. Your other choice would be to get the cork out by hitting the bottle on the edge of the granite and whacking off the top."

He laughed and the sound brought back more memories that grabbed at her heart. When they were together, talking had always turned to teasing and that turned sexy, which led to making love. Since that was her endgame, his need for sanctuary worked to her advantage. But somehow the whole thing felt dishonest.

"Something wrong, April?"

His voice snapped her out of the conscience attack. "No. I'll get the salad made."

She turned the oven on low and put the pizza in to keep it warm while getting everything else ready. In ten minutes they were sitting across from each other at the square oak table in the kitchen nook with a meal in front of them. Slices of pizza on paper plates. Salad in bright orange pottery bowls. Stemless glasses containing a deep maroon–colored wine.

Will held up his glass. "To—" He thought for a moment, then shrugged and said, "I've got nothing."

"How about to friends who are willing to take you in as long as you bring the pizza and wine?"

"I like it." He touched his glass to hers, then took a sip.

April did the same, set her glass down before digging into the pizza. It was like a party in her mouth, as she savored the blended flavors of cheese, tomato sauce, sausage and black olives. With her mouth full, she said, "This is my favorite."

"I know. You think I'd have begged you to take me in with anything less than your beloved first choice?"

"I'm just surprised. I didn't think you'd remember."

"Then prepare to be surprised again." He thought for a moment. "I remember that you don't like ketchup on your fries because it camouflages the exquisite taste of a perfectly good potato. Same goes for flavored chips. You're a traditional-chip girl who doesn't like it messed up."

"Hmm." This was a little disconcerting. Nice. Flattering, but unsettling.

"I also remember no ground pepper on your salad. You like guacamole but a naked avocado makes you gag. Toast or English muffin has to be well done and you credit, or blame, your mother for that. When she got distracted, anything in the toaster burned, but money for a single mom raising a daughter was tight. No food in your house got wasted, so she somehow convinced you the black part was good for you. And now you have to have it that way."

April somehow managed to keep tears from welling in her eyes. It wasn't easy, what with him talking about the mother she still missed terribly. On top of that she was moved that he recalled the silly little things she'd shared with him.

"Wow. Your powers of recall are impressive." And touching. "Okay. Two can play this game."

"This is a game?" One dark eyebrow rose questioningly.

"It's called reminiscing." She tapped her lip, searching through the amazing stack of recollections. "I remember that you like a steak so rare it's practically mooing on the plate. You prefer rice to potatoes, but mac and cheese is the carbohydrate gold standard. And raw spinach in a salad is acceptable, but cooked is slimy."

He finished chewing a bite of pizza. "Gold star for you, missy."

"Thank you very much." She drank some wine, nearly finishing what was in the glass.

Will picked up the bottle and refilled them both. "You cry at sad movies and jump out of your skin at scary ones."

"Busted." She smiled, thinking about how she used to hide her face against his shoulder when they saw a horror flick. These days she just didn't go to that genre. "And you preferred science and discovery channels on TV as opposed to scripted comedies and dramas."

"Still do." He looked at her, something dark and intense in his eyes. "It's nice to know some things don't change."

"Yeah." She drank some wine, a wistful, reflective feeling settling over her.

They finished the meal in relative silence, each of them thinking their own thoughts. Doing the dishes together was another thing that hadn't changed. There weren't many from this meal, but on the rare occasions she'd cooked for him and the two of them were alone, he'd always insisted on helping to clean up. It was the least he could do since she'd done the hard part.

She closed the dishwasher door and finished the wine in her glass. Since the bottle was now empty that meant she was responsible for half of it disappearing and the buzz she was rocking didn't come as a surprise. It was also liberating, as in the censor between her brain and her mouth was buzzed, too. That meant it wasn't functioning efficiently to filter her thoughts.

All this talking about the past brought up good memories but also bad. April hadn't forgotten that he'd cast her aside for another woman. There was a question she'd never had a chance to ask, but she did now thanks to two glasses of wine.

"Why did your marriage break up, Will?"

Chapter Eight

Because she wasn't you.

The thought popped into Will's mind and he was a little stunned. But maybe he shouldn't be. The other day while his sister was freaking out he'd told her she waited until Luke came along and got it right. He hadn't waited and got it wrong because the woman he'd proposed to wasn't April. He hadn't said as much to Kim, but it must have been in the back of his mind.

He would probably regret that decision for the rest of his life.

And now he was lucky enough to be standing in her kitchen after sharing pizza and a bottle of wine. It was more than he deserved.

"Will?" April held up her hands. "Never mind. Forget I said anything. I shouldn't have asked. It's really none of my business and, for the record, I'm blaming it on the wine. Seriously, I'm sorry—"

He touched a finger to her lips to stop the words. "You have nothing to apologize for. I don't mind telling you what happened. More than anyone else you have a right to know. Obviously, you already realize what an idiot I am."

"I don't think it's fair or right to factor in IQ in terms of relationship analysis. Being smart has nothing to do with matters of the heart." She leaned back against the counter in front of the sink and folded her arms over her chest. "For what it's worth, I don't think you're an idiot."

He stood across from her with the kitchen island to his back. "You're very gracious even though I don't deserve it."

"No, you don't," she teased. "But I can't help it. A flaw in my personality."

"Okay. As flaws go it's not bad." He smiled, then wondered how it was that she could do that when he was contemplating this deeply personal disappointment in himself. It was a mistake he still took very hard. Maybe telling her would be a good thing, help put it to rest forever. "The reality is that the marriage was doomed from the start."

"Why do you say that?"

Will didn't expect to hear genuine sympathy in her voice. Probably because he'd treated her so badly and felt fortunate that she was even talking to him. She had every right to be glad things hadn't worked out for him. Who could blame her for it? But he didn't see anything like that in the compassionate expression on her face.

"She was just there, a bar where cops hang out after a shift. She was pretty. Flirty."

"That's not good."

For the life of him he couldn't figure out why she looked guilty all of a sudden. Maybe she did have a little he-got-what-was-coming-to-him going on.

"Anyway, she was there and available. I was lonely."

"I understand." A little sadness crept into her voice.

Now it was his turn to feel guilty. He looked down at her and in the dim light he could see sorrow on her face, a bruised expression in her eyes for just a moment. Because he'd been the one who moved to Chicago and left behind everything and everyone he'd known, he thought loneliness was exclusive to him. Now he saw how selfish that was. He realized April must have been lonely, too, and she'd stayed behind in the town where they'd fallen in love. That must have been a different kind of loneliness.

Alone in a crowd.

"It's no excuse for what I did to you, but it is the truth."

"I really do understand, Will."

He studied her expression, then nodded. "Anyway, I proposed to her and she said yes. There was no cooling-off period. We went to city hall and got married. It was all downhill from there."

"What happened?" She crossed one foot over the other at the ankles.

"I wanted to make detective, so when anyone asked me for anything, any extra work, I was the go-to guy. Special task force on drugs. Working with vice. Stakeouts for illegal weapons trafficking. You name it, I did it."

"Didn't she understand that you were trying to move up in the department?"

"I told her that. More than once."

Will remembered the endless arguments about him not being around. The accusations that everything and everyone was more important than her. His response was standard-issue—he was there now and she'd picked a fight.

"We had some pretty loud discussions," he said.

"Did you try marriage counseling?"

"I suggested it and she came back with something sarcastic like I was never home as it was. I couldn't fit her in, so how could I manage to see a shrink?"

"I hate to say this, Will, but that's a valid point given what you just told me."

One of the things he liked about her was that reasonable streak and he couldn't fault her for it now.

"Yeah." He dragged his fingers through his hair. "I know. And I was about to concede that point to her when she accused me of using work to avoid her."

"Was she right?"

"At the time I was defensive, but now that I have some distance it's fair to say there was some truth to her accusation."

"But nothing changed." April wasn't asking a question.

He'd made an effort to be around more. Turned down some extra assignments. "How can you know that?"

"Because you're not married to her anymore." She shrugged as if that explained it all. And she was right.

"No, we're not married." Duh. And whatever pathetic attempt he'd made hadn't changed the inevitable split. "I approached her about a trial separation, to see if we'd be happier apart. And it took me a while to bring it up. I didn't want to hurt her."

"What did she say?"

"She bypassed the idea of separating and went straight for divorce. Said there was no point in dragging things out longer than necessary."

"How did you feel about that?"

"You sound like a shrink," he commented.

She lifted one shoulder. "When I take portrait photographs, I ask a lot of questions. That brings out emotions that the camera captures. It's a habit."

"I'll remember that. And the truth is that when she wanted to end things permanently I was relieved."

"Obviously that was the right decision, then."

"It feels wrong," he said.

"Why?"

"I always wanted what my parents had before my mom died in the car accident. They were crazy about each other. Held hands and kissed in public. Kim and I used to give them a hard time about embarrassing us, but they didn't care."

"I remember." She smiled fondly at the memory.

"And Kim always said she was the family screwup, getting pregnant at seventeen. The thing is she never made the mistake of marrying the jerk. She waited until she knew it was right."

"Everyone's journey is different, Will," April said reasonably. "No one gets out of this life without regrets of one kind or another."

"I know," he said. "But being the family failure is hard for me."

"Because you've always been the guy in the white hat, righting wrongs and fighting the good fight."

"Truth, justice and the American way. Superman, that's me. But I messed up."

"That's one way of looking at it. Or one could make an argument that you saw things weren't working out and did the right thing for both of you." She straightened away from the counter. "But here's something your father always says. It's not our successes that reveal character. It's how we handle our mistakes that defines us. Your actions don't sound like a failure to me."

"You're cutting me slack I don't deserve."

"Oh, Will—" She hesitated a moment, then took two steps toward him and moved in close, wrapping her arms around his waist. "It really is way past time to stop beating yourself up about what happened in the past."

Will was having a hard time processing her words, what with that sweet little body pressed to his. He could feel her small firm breasts and her soft cheek resting against his chest. The scent of flowers drifted to him from her hair and he couldn't stop himself from wrapping her in his arms.

"April—" There was a hitch in his voice as a powerful yearning ground through him.

When she raised her head and looked up at him, he kissed her. Their lips met for one beat, then two. In the next second they couldn't get enough of each other. She met him more than halfway and above the swishing of the dishwasher he could hear the sound of their heavy breathing and her soft moans that made him hot as a firecracker.

"I never thought I would get a chance to kiss you again," Will said in a husky, edgy whisper against her lips.

The words sent a crushing cascade of guilt down on April that was as effective as a bucket of cold water in destroying the mood. More than anything she wanted to go where this kiss was leading, but she just couldn't do it. She couldn't get past the fact that this was part of a premeditated plan to flirt, fall into bed, then dump him in the name of closure.

Now the plan felt all kinds of wrong.

She stepped out of Will's arms. "I can't do this."

"I'm sorry? What?" He stared at her.

"I can't do it."

"What exactly?" Surprise and frustration merged in his voice.

"Kiss you." She hesitated. "And whatever else might follow after that. I just can't. Not like this."

"Well…" He blew out a long breath. "Just the Cliff's Notes of biology here, but *this* is pretty much the only way to do it."

"No." She twisted her fingers together. "You don't understand."

"You're right. I don't. And, honey, at this moment I don't really want to." There was a lot of lust in the look he settled on her.

"And I don't really want to tell you. But, like I said before, you set a high bar for full disclosure. So whether you want to or not, you have to hear this."

"Okay, then. If I agree to listen, can we pick up where we just left off?"

"Trust me. You're not going to want to do that." When he found out she was a scheming, underhanded, devious witch, he wouldn't want anything to do with her.

"Let me be the judge of that. Because right now I want to kiss you more than anything. And unless you tell me you're a man, which I know for a fact isn't true, there's not much you could say to change my mind." His blue eyes turned darker and focused a lot of intensity on her mouth.

It was so tempting to say "Gotcha" or "Just kidding" and continue kissing him, but she realized the weight of this secret was crushing.

"Okay. Here goes." April stood up straighter and met his gaze. "I'm kissing you under false pretenses."

"I'm not sure what that means." He tilted his head, studying her. "Are you saying you didn't like it?"

"No," she said adamantly.

"Because it sure felt to me as if you were really into it."

"I really was," she assured him.

"Good. No offense, but I don't think you're that good an actress." The corners of his mouth curved up. "I'm a detective. I know when someone's trying to pull a fast one and that's not what you were doing. Trust me on this, you couldn't lie your way out of a paper bag."

"Thanks, I think."

"So, define false pretenses."

"Okay." She twisted her fingers together, trying to figure out how to word this confession. "After you came to see me when you first got back to Blackwater Lake, I had a heart-to-heart talk with Kim."

"I knew she was somehow involved. You two are as thick as thieves."

Kind of an appropriate analogy, but he really had no idea, she thought. "Don't blame Kim."

"I can't blame anyone until you tell me what's going on."

"Right." She didn't want to tell him the whole truth, about how hard it had been seeing him again, the painful feelings he'd stirred up. "Kim and I got to talking. This is a small town and people have a way of knowing everything that goes on. And they have long memories. I realized that since you and I broke up, I've always been the poor girl that Will Fletcher left behind. Your sister was just thinking out loud and remarked that I never got closure from our relationship. It all went down on your terms."

"That's true." He nodded and the shadows in his eyes said he regretted what happened. "I'm sorry, April—"

She held up her hand. "Please don't say that. The thing is that Kim had an idea for how I could get closure." She stopped because as soon as she told him the rest of it, he was going to leave and never speak to her again. April couldn't really blame him, but, wow, this was really so much harder than she'd expected.

"What was her idea?" Oddly, Will didn't look wary or angry. Not even a little upset. More amused than anything else.

She blew out a long breath, then forced herself to meet his gaze. "The plan was for me to flirt with you. Have a fling. Then be the one to end it so everyone in Blackwater Lake would stop pitying me."

"So that's why you looked guilty when I mentioned my ex-wife was flirty when we met."

"Yes." April was surprised he'd noticed, then realized she shouldn't be. He *was* a detective—a good one—and trained to pay attention to reactions. It was probably impossible for him to turn off his powers of observation. "And look how that turned out."

"I knew something was up with you," he said.

"No way." Surely she hadn't been that obvious. "I don't believe it."

"After that first meeting in your shop when we talked, every time I saw you, you acted funny. Did something weird with your eyes. Now I realize that was you flirting. Or trying to." He looked awfully smug. "I guess I should be relieved that you're not very good at it."

That didn't sound like an angry, resentful man who was going to set a speed record for walking out. But it could be payback for her scheming him. Or trying to. "Why relieved?"

"Because eventually you forgot to pretend and behaved naturally. When you flirted, and you did, it obviously was sincere."

She narrowed her gaze at him. "Look, Will, don't be nice to me. I don't deserve it. Just leave. I know you want to. We'll call it closure and move on."

"Who says I want to leave?"

Now she was really confused. "I was dishonest with you. Why would you want to stay?"

There was a smokin' hot look in his eyes when he said, "Because I really want to take you to bed."

"Oh, my—" April's heart started beating so fast she couldn't seem to form words. That required a thought process coming from a brain that wasn't fried. Finally she managed to say, "I don't see how it's possible that you would want me after what I just told you."

"I understand," he said simply. "I get how this town works and what you've been going through. On top of that, you get points for coming clean." He moved closer, until their bodies were barely touching.

"But the fact that I could even do that—" She caught her top lip between her teeth.

"The thing is, you didn't really do it. There's evidence that my sister has been, shall we say involved, since the beginning." There was the steely-eyed detective. "Do you have an on-again, off-again thing with a ski instructor named Jean Luc?"

"No." But she couldn't help smiling.

"My sister has always been good at making stuff up." He nodded. "And when I asked you out— There's a reason you said no, isn't there?"

She sighed. "I hate to rat out your sister, but she convinced me that playing hard to get was the best way to get a man to notice you."

"Not in your case. All you have to do is walk into a room." His voice went all husky and deep. "So, my sister has been more invested in this mission than you are probably aware."

"Please don't be mad at her."

"I'm not." And he truly didn't look peeved. "But it shows how much you need to convince this town that you're here because you want to be and not because you were left behind."

"That's true." Pretty much.

He stared at her for several moments. "So, I have an idea."

"Your sister had one, too. Apparently it's in the Fletcher DNA." She blew out a breath. "I'm afraid to ask what it is."

"You don't have to ask. I'm happy to share." He reached out and tucked her hair behind her ear. "If you want a fling, I'm completely open to that."

"Wow, you're such a giver." Her pulse was going wild at the suggestion. But rational thought managed to break free of the sensual haze. "There's just one problem with your idea."

"And that is?"

"At the end of the summer you're leaving Blackwater Lake. I'll still be the girl you left behind. Twice."

"I see your point." He nodded thoughtfully. "Okay. How about this? We have a fling and before I leave, you can publicly dump me."

"Where's public?" she asked skeptically.

"You pick the place."

"Main Street? Farmer's market on Sunday morning? The Grizzly Bear Diner?"

"Any or all of the above," he agreed.

She thought it over and deemed the terms to be very generous. Besides, she really wanted him and the yearning inside her was turning into an unbearable ache. She held out her hand. "You've got yourself a deal."

He took her fingers into his large palm and squeezed, then released her and scooped her into his arms. When she wrapped her arms around his neck, he nuzzled her cheek and whispered into her ear, "I've got something else in mind to seal this deal."

His breath on her ear sent tingles skittering through her body. They'd been heading in this direction ever since she'd brought him that chicken casserole and he'd invited her in for a glass of wine.

He carried her as if she weighed nothing and she knew

that wasn't true. But the gesture made her feel safe, protected, not alone. And, being completely honest, it was romantic. He swept her away, literally, into her bedroom. As long as she didn't get swept away for real, where was the harm? She was no longer that young girl who was barely a woman. She was fully grown with a mind of her own and knew what she wanted.

And she wanted Will.

He set her on her feet beside the bed and cupped her cheek in one hand as he lowered his mouth to hers. The fire she'd banked in order to get her confession out burst into flame once again. They kissed and kissed, trying desperately to get closer, but it wasn't enough. He was a great kisser and she could do it forever, preferably without clothes.

In the next moment, as if he could read her mind, he was pushing at her shirt, yanking it up over her head. Before it hit the floor, she was shoving at his T-shirt and he pulled it free and threw the thing somewhere. Shoes were kicked off and the rest of their clothes were tossed anywhere. Will reached around her and hauled the quilted bedspread down to the foot along with the blanket and sheet.

Then his hard-muscled body and heat were pressed up against her, nudging her toward the mattress. She sat and scooted over to make room for him, but before joining her he reached for his jeans and took something from his wallet.

Condom. Thank you, God.

He slid in beside her and gathered her close, letting their bodies come together, bare skin to bare skin. The feeling was indescribable and the dusting of hair on his chest tickled her breasts in the most erotic possible way. She leaned back far enough and brushed a hand over the contour of muscle and grazed his nipple with her thumb, causing him to hiss out a breath.

"Problem?" she teased.

"Not unless you stop." His voice was ragged.

So she did it again and he groaned before nudging her to her back. He kissed her neck, then moved lower and sucked the tip of her breast into his mouth. With his tongue he flicked the nipple, then pulled back to blow softly on the wetness. It drove her wild and she'd forgotten how much she loved him doing that. She couldn't believe he'd remembered. And that wasn't all.

He kissed and nipped his way down her body until she was writhing with need.

"Will, I don't think I can wait—" She could hardly breathe. "Please…"

"Your wish—" His voice was so low it was barely audible.

He reached over to the nightstand and grabbed the packet, then ripped it open. After rolling it on, he came back to her and settled himself between her legs.

Slowly he filled her and the sensation simultaneously stole her breath and made her sigh. He moved inside her, a measured rhythm meant to retrace steps from their last time together.

But April wanted more. She wanted now. And she wanted new.

Her hands wandered over his body, tracing lightly over his abdomen until he groaned. He lowered his body closer to hers, limiting her wandering hands. She smiled, knowing he didn't want to be rushed but doing it anyway. Lifting her head, she drew close enough to kiss his neck, tracing his earlobe with her tongue.

"April—"

"I know."

And then she lost track of everything, preoccupied with her senses, just letting her body feel and build slowly, breathing faster and faster. Without much warning she went right over the edge and cried out as pleasure rolled like a thunderstorm through her. He held her close and pressed deeper, then deeper still until he groaned and followed her over that sensuous cliff. They clung to each other until their breathing returned almost to normal.

Will exhaled slowly then kissed her forehead before rolling out of bed. "I'll be right back. Don't you dare go anywhere."

As if, she thought.

She didn't think she could have moved if her life depended on it. Her body was happy and relaxed. She closed her eyes, but was aware when the light in the bathroom went on. A minute later the room was in shadow again and Will was back.

He slid into bed, pulled the sheet up over them then drew her to his side with one strong arm holding her close to him.

"And that's how you really seal a deal."

"I like it," she said drowsily.

She was too sleepy and sated to realize all the implications of sex with Will. Her only thought before falling asleep was how very much she liked this fling thing.

Chapter Nine

After closing up shop for the day April drove home, parked her compact car in the driveway, then walked straight across the alley to the Fletchers' back door. Kim had called and said they needed to talk, so here she was, knocking on the door.

Almost instantly her friend answered and grinned. "So, my brother sneaked out of your house late last night. Or was it early this morning?"

"More like late last night," April confirmed.

She smiled and felt as if she'd been doing that all day. Surely everyone she'd seen had known that she had sex with Will Fletcher last night and didn't regret it.

"Is it safe to assume that the two of you didn't spend all those hours discussing old times?"

"It is safe to assume that." April sighed. "There was physical activity involved."

"You slept with Will." Kim looked both pleased and aggravated. "He's never even taken you out to dinner."

April followed her into the Fletchers' kitchen. "Keep your voice down. It's possible they didn't hear you in Cleveland and I'd like to keep it that way."

The two of them stood by the island. "Dad and Tim are out and Will isn't home from work yet."

"Seriously, Kim, he actually has taken me out to dinner."

"Not since you set out to seduce him."

Wow, April hadn't really done that, at least not by herself. If seduction had been involved, both of them were guilty. A little pizza. A little wine… Will kissed her and they both went up in flames.

"To put a finer point on it," she said, "He did buy dinner. He brought over a pizza because the wedding stuff was getting to him and he needed a calm place to decompress."

"Oh, please. He's not that delicate. And, just so we're clear, that's not the same as going out and doesn't count." Then Kim tsked before grinning broadly. "Was it awesome?"

April felt heat creep into her cheeks when she thought about the way he'd touched her. Everywhere. And she'd been like putty in his hands. "Yes."

"And?"

"I'm not sure there's anything more to add."

"Where do things stand between you? Where do you go from here? What are your expectations?"

"We're just going to have fun." Then April decided her friend should know the whole truth. "Don't be mad, but—"

"That's never a good way to start a sentence."

"I told him about the plan to dump him. And that it was your idea. For the record he guessed that you were involved. I'm sorry." She studied her friend's expression, trying to gauge her level of annoyance. "I just couldn't go to bed with him and not tell him about the plan."

"I knew you couldn't do it." Kim smiled. "You're so honest and it's why I love you. But I knew if things headed in that direction you'd never seal the deal without spilling the beans."

"So you're not mad?"

"Did you have a good time?" the other woman asked.

"Yes." April felt the glow from deep in her soul and wondered why Kim even had to ask.

"Then no way I could be mad. You haven't looked this happy in a very long time and it's wonderful to see." She turned serious. "Are you okay with this just being a summer thing?"

"I know he's leaving when Hank goes back to work. This time I'm going into it with my eyes open. So, yeah, I'm okay with it." She snapped her fingers. "I forgot the best part. He agreed to let me publicly dump him before he leaves."

"He's a good man," Kim said fondly.

The front door opened and closed. Moments later the man in question walked into the kitchen. He smiled at April. "Hi."

"How was your day?" She smiled back, fully aware that the glow she'd been rocking all day had just amped up by a factor of a hundred.

"Good."

"Don't mind me," Kim said. "Just pretend I'm not here."

Will looked at her. "Hi."

"Hey." She looked from him to April. "Luke is picking me up in a few minutes. We're going to Bar None for a drink and dinner. You guys should come with us. We'll make it a double date."

"And why would we want to do that?" Will asked.

"Because you owe her a dinner after what you did last night."

April looked at him and shrugged. "She saw you coming out of my house at an indecent hour."

"Who put you on sibling surveillance?" It was hard to tell whether or not he was annoyed at getting caught.

"I made her tell me what happened," Kim confirmed. "And, just so you know, I approve."

"I'd expect nothing less." Will's expression was wry. "After all, it was your idea."

"You don't have to thank me." His sister waved a hand dismissively. "Just say you agree to a double date. You and April. Luke and me. It will be fun. We've never done that before."

"So why should we do it now?" he said and sent April a look that said he was deliberately giving her a hard time.

"If you don't," she warned, "I'll tell Dad you spent the night at April's."

"I'm willing to take my chances." The look on his face was one that he reserved for torturing his sister. "On second thought we should go with her and Luke."

"I'll bite," April said. "Why?"

"I haven't had a chance to really get acquainted with the man my sister is going to marry. Maybe he should know what she's really like."

"Do your worst," Kim challenged. "You don't scare me."

"What do you say, April? Are you up for a double date?" he asked.

She had the ridiculous feeling that she would follow him anywhere. And this wasn't the first time she'd experienced it. When he went to Chicago, she'd so wanted to go with him but couldn't leave her mother. For whatever reason, fate had deemed that the two of them were not destined to be together forever. Just for this summer. And the only ridiculous thought she had right this second was that they were wasting precious time.

"Yes, I'd like to double date."

"Okay. April wants to go, so that's what we'll do," Will declared.

"Good choice," Kim said. "I was about to play the man-of-honor card."

Will groaned. "You're going to make sure I regret saying yes to that, aren't you?"

Kim just smiled.

Thirty minutes later the four of them were sitting around a bistro table at Bar None. Delanie Carlson had taken their order of beers for the guys, white wine for the women and burgers all around. The place was packed and not only because it was Friday night. It was also summer and the tourists were out in force.

April watched Will make conversation with Luke. The high school football coach was a good-looking man with nearly black hair and brown eyes. He was physically fit, muscular, smart and completely crazy about Kim. Fortunately he was also a local boy and her friend wouldn't have to choose between the man she loved and the town that was woven into the fabric of her soul.

With a server in her wake, Delanie carried over a big tray. The two women set out drinks and food. "Anything else I can get you?"

"I don't think so," Kim answered.

"Okay. Enjoy. And just holler if you need anything."

"Thanks, Delanie," all four of them said together.

Her mushroom Swiss burger was as big as a Toyota, so April cut it in half, then took a bite. After chewing and swallowing she said, "I didn't realize how hungry I was. This tastes really good."

"It sure does." Will's eyes gleamed as if to say it didn't

taste as good as *she* did. Then the look faded and he turned his gaze on his sister's fiancé. "So, Luke, did you know that you're marrying a world-class meddler? As in my sister interferes in other people's lives."

"That's a little harsh," she defended. "I'm more of an idea person."

Luke didn't appear to be the least bit surprised or put out. "What did you do now, love of my life?"

"I came up with a brilliant plan. April's mission was to flirt with Will, have a thing for the summer, then be the one to end it before he goes back to Chicago. If she pulls that off, no one will feel sorry for her when he leaves."

Since everyone in town knew the story, April didn't bother going into her disastrous history with Will for Luke's benefit. "What Kim didn't factor in is that I'm not a skilled flirt. Give me a camera and I'm good. Give me a man and…" She shrugged as if to say "Insert appropriate slacker word here."

"I thought there was something wrong with her eyes at first," Will said.

The heated look he turned on April made her toes curl. "I tried to bat my lashes and it wasn't pretty."

"Yet here you two are," Luke pointed out. "So apparently my winsome and wonderful wife-to-be came up with an idea that had merit."

"And then some, my handsome, heroic husband-to-be." Kim looked at her man and raised an eyebrow. "He spent the night with her."

"Oh."

Will set the remaining half of his bacon cheeseburger down on his plate. "That's not the point, Luke. Before it's too late you should know that my sister is an epic interferer. And she's not likely to change, so beware. If she turns her powers on you, my friend, there could be hell to pay."

"Another way to look at it is that putting so much effort into the people she cares about is part of her charm," Luke said.

"Oh, my." April sipped her wine. "He's such a good man."

"I have to ask," Will persisted. "Does Tim know that you're going to side with his mom all the time?"

Luke laughed. "He does if he's as smart as I think he is."

"You've really got it bad," Will observed.

"Oh, you're so dramatic," Kim scoffed. "I bet you're really good when you go undercover."

Will's expression hardly changed, but there was something cold and intense in his eyes. "I try to do the best possible job whatever the assignment."

"I'm glad you appreciate me." Kim leaned over and kissed her intended's cheek. "My brother puts most of his energy into the police force. I wish he could find balance."

"Life and death, sis. That's the balance."

It didn't seem as if the other couple noticed, but April felt the shift in him, the darkness. He'd told her that dedication to his job had been responsible for his failed marriage, at least partially. And he'd also revealed that he'd married the wrong woman.

What if he married the right one? she thought. Would that balance him? Or was he unbalanceable?

She would probably never have an answer to that question because all he'd promised was a summer fling ending in a public breakup.

Will parked his SUV in the lot behind the sheriff's office and exited the vehicle. He looked at the spectacular blue sky and the towering Montana mountains and dragged in a deep breath of clean, fresh air, then grinned. This was the best he'd felt in probably years, a little carefree and a lot relaxed.

Sex with April no doubt had something to do with the relaxation. That particular tension had been gnawing at him since seeing her again. But it was even more than that. It was talking to her, being around her. Laughing. He hadn't realized how much he'd missed that. And dinner last night with Kim and her fiancé had been fun, and fun had been in short supply for a while now.

When he walked inside the office, Eddie and Clarice were already there. "Morning," he said.

"Hey, Sheriff." Clarice looked at him more closely. "You look perky today."

"Do I?"

"Yes, sir. Does it have anything to do with April Kennedy?"

"And why would you ask that?"

"Word around town is that the two of you were seen at Bar None last night," the clerk explained.

He really should have expected this. After all, his sister was the one who'd warned him to make sure the first time he saw April again was private and away from prying eyes. For some reason, today he couldn't muster the will to care that it was all over Blackwater Lake that he and April were dating. And under the conditions of their arrangement the more public their relationship, the more satisfaction April would get out of ending things.

"We were there last night," he admitted. "Had a great time with my sister and Luke. But you probably already know that, too."

His dispatcher smiled broadly. "That was brought to my attention, yes."

"Okay, then."

"I just made a pot of coffee, Sheriff," she said.

"I could use a cup." There was a table in the back of the room where the pot was kept along with supplies to keep it full. He walked back and grabbed one of the mugs sitting rim down and poured the hot black liquid into it. Clarice made it a point to wash up the mugs every day before she left and that was much appreciated.

Will walked back to her desk and leaned a hip on the corner. "What's up? Anything going on this morning that I should know about?"

"Pretty quiet. Got a complaint from out at the Harris place. During the night the barn was spray painted with words I refuse to repeat even though I know you've heard them all. Seems every summer we have to be the graffiti police. Eddie's going to check it out."

"Probably kids," the deputy said, joining him by the desk. "But I'll go out there and file a report."

"We'll need pictures. Do you want me to give April a call?" He wouldn't mind talking to her. Just hearing her voice always made him smile. Interesting because when she took pictures, she never told the subject to smile but clicked away while chatting with them, just capturing honest emotion.

"Sheriff?"

Will looked at the deputy. "Hmm?"

"I said I don't think it's necessary to bother April. This is the third call we've had with the same complaint. So far there's been no real evidence, but I'll take a couple pictures with my cell phone for the report. Just to be thorough. Unless someone catches them in the act…" Eddie shrugged.

Will nodded, then sipped his coffee. "Everything quiet at the campground out by the lake?"

During the summer there'd been a number of noise complaints. It was inevitable what with the campers living in close quarters. Usually too much alcohol was involved. But he'd instituted regular patrols because there was something sobering about a black-and-white sighting.

"Haven't had any calls, although it's still early," Clarice said. "But I think the drive-throughs make people stop and think. So far this summer the number of complaints from out there are down."

"Good." He looked at Eddie. "So when you're finished at the Harris place you'll swing by the campground?"

"Sure thing."

"Okay. Then I'll go catch up on paperwork—"

The ringing phone interrupted and Clarice answered. "Blackwater Lake Sheriff's Office, Clarice speaking. How can I help you?" She listened for several moments and the expression on her face changed from carefree to concerned. "How long since anyone has seen her? How old is she?" She jotted some notes then said, "I'll send someone right over."

"What's wrong?" Will asked.

"That was Mimi from the front desk at Blackwater Lake Lodge. There's a kid missing. Six-year-old girl. Been about an hour and a half since her parents saw her."

"Do you want me to go to the lodge first, Sheriff?" Eddie asked.

"No. I'll go." He set his half-empty mug down on Clarice's desk. "By the time I get there she'll probably turn up."

But when he got there, she still hadn't been found. Will interviewed the parents and each thought she'd been with the other. He believed them. Another thorough search of the property under his supervision was conducted without success.

Then he considered his options as a law-enforcement officer. This wasn't a custody dispute situation and after interviewing the staff there was no evidence of anyone or anything suspicious. That meant he couldn't make a case that the little girl was in imminent danger, which would meet the criteria for issuing an Amber Alert.

For now he would keep the search confined to the town of Blackwater Lake and the immediate area surrounding it. The parents had a recent picture of the little girl, Riley Shelton, and a description of the clothes she was wearing when last seen. Will assured them that everything possible would be done to locate their daughter. He didn't use the word promise because a long time ago he'd learned that too many things were out of his control and he wouldn't give them false hope.

When he returned to the office, Clarice took the picture and description to April so she could scan it and make up fliers to distribute around town. Will made phone calls and organized volunteers to search.

Fifteen minutes after that call his father walked into the office. "Hey, Will."

"What are you doing here, Dad?"

"Cabot Dixon called me and said there's a little girl missing up at the lodge."

"Yeah." Things sure didn't move that fast in Chicago.

"I'm here because you need all hands on deck. I'm on medical leave, not an invalid."

Will nodded. "Glad to have you on this."

After that, men, women, teenagers, anyone who could showed up at the office. Will organized them into groups of two and three. He had maps of the surrounding area broken up into grids and assigned one to each group. Clarice made sure each one had a cell phone and water.

The office door opened and April came in with a stack of papers and put them on the dispatcher's desk. "Here are the fliers."

Will picked one up and looked at the blue-eyed, blonde, freckle-faced little girl last seen wearing denim shorts and a lavender T-shirt with two characters from the movie *Frozen* on the front. "These are great."

"I already put one up in the window of my shop. Is there anything else I can do?" she asked.

He looked around the room, which was now nearly filled with volunteers who were grabbing up the fliers. "I'm going to assign one of the volunteers to take some of these and distribute them to the business owners around town. Then I'll head out and keep looking. I think we've got it covered for now."

"Those poor parents must be frantic with worry."

"Yeah." Will had seen that look too many times. Chicago or Blackwater Lake, it didn't matter. The fear was the same. But he would rather see that than grief and despair if they didn't locate this child.

Her eyes were full of concern. "I can't even imagine how they feel."

"I know."

"You'll find that little girl. I'm sure of it." She put a hand on his arm.

The warmth of her fingers felt good, reassuring, but he wasn't so sure about the success of this operation. Where he worked, too many kids didn't get a break. It was hard not to think the worst.

"We'll do our best," he said.

She nodded. "I'm thinking good thoughts."

"Okay. Thanks." He took a flier. "I have to brief the volunteers before they head out, then get to my search area."

"Good luck." She gave him a reassuring smile, then left the office.

Will stood by the dispatcher's desk and looked around the nearly filled-to-capacity room. "I need everyone's attention."

Almost instantly chatter stopped and you could have

heard a pin drop. "You all have your assignments. I need you to call in every hour whether you have news or not. Clarice will be here coordinating communication. Everyone stay together. We don't want anyone else lost out there."

"What if we find her?" one of the teenage girls asked.

"Call into the office and let Clarice know your position. She'll dispatch emergency personnel to you." He looked around again. "Any other questions?" When everyone shook their heads he said, "Thank you all for your help. Now, let's get out there and find Riley."

Will headed back out to the lodge and one more time searched the grounds immediately around the building, then expanded his perimeter, driving slowly. She was so little, he thought, and could be almost anywhere. He was alert to any flash of color and fervently wished she'd put on something that morning the color of the vests that construction and road employees wore to be visible.

He parked the SUV at the lodge and followed the paths on the grounds, trying to guess which way a curious six-year-old would go. What would attract her attention?

Just beyond the lodge property trails there was a clearing in the dense trees and underbrush. From here you could see some of the tallest mountains in Montana, where the very top had snow all year round. Will remembered Riley's mom telling him what she was wearing that morning, nerves compelling her to add that the characters were sisters from her favorite movie. One of them froze everything and went to the snowy mountains in order not to hurt anyone.

What if...

After calling dispatch to check in with Clarice and give her his position, he started walking toward the mountain. The trees quickly closed in and a child could easily become disoriented. Will had hiked and camped in here with his dad and knew the area well.

Every ten minutes he stopped and called out. "Riley? I'm a police officer. Can you hear me?" Then he'd carefully listen for a response.

For about an hour he kept at it, then checked in with the office for an update. Clarice had no news and the bad feeling that he always carried around with him got a little bit worse. That drove him on.

"Riley?" He listened. "It's Sheriff Fletcher. Can you hear me?" He stopped talking and listened again. There was a noise off to his right that didn't belong in the woods. He moved slowly in that direction. "Riley? I'm here to help you."

He heard the sound again. It was like whimpering, and exhilaration pumped his adrenaline. "Riley, honey, make some noise. Let me know where you are. I want to take you back to your mom and dad."

"Over here."

The words were faint and Will had trouble judging the direction. "Louder, honey. Shake the bushes so I can see where you are."

He heard her and moved steadily toward the sound. Finally he saw a flash of lavender and blond hair through the trees. Thank God. She was shaking a blackberry bush for all she was worth.

He moved beside her and went down on one knee. "Hey, Riley. My name is Will. Good job with that bush and helping me find you."

"I'm scared." Her mouth trembled.

"I bet you are. Don't worry. I'm here to help you." He gave her a quick once-over. "Are you hurt?"

"A little." She pointed to scratches on her shins. There

were some on her face, too, along with streaks where tears had tracked through the dirt. "I want my mommy."

"You got it, kiddo. But first, are you thirsty?"

"And hungry."

"I don't have food, but you'll be back at the lodge pretty soon and we'll get you something to eat. Here's some water." He took an unopened water bottle from the holder at his waist. When she'd had enough, she handed it back. He smiled at her, trying to put her at ease. "I like your shirt."

She nodded and looked down at her front, pointing to the blonde character wearing a long sparkly turquoise dress. "That's Elsa. She made everything frozen and thought she hurt her sister, Anna, so she went to the mountains where she couldn't hurt anyone ever again."

"Is that what you were doing when you wandered away? Trying to get to the snow on the mountain?"

She hesitated, then nodded. "I hurt my brother, then I felt bad. I didn't think it was far, but then I walked and walked. My legs are really tired."

"Do you want to ride on my shoulders?" he asked.

She nodded. "I really want my mom."

"Roger that."

He called Clarice and instructed her to notify the parents that he was bringing Riley back to the lodge. Then he wanted her to notify fire department search and rescue and have them standing by to check her out, although she seemed to be in good condition. After that she should call the volunteers back in and cancel the missing child alert.

After finishing his orders and hanging up, he held out his arms. "Come on. I'll give you a lift."

The walk back, even with the little girl on his shoulders, was completed in half the time. As he approached, he noticed a crowd gathered on the lodge's rear lawn. The group included the Sheltons, the hotel's general manager, some of the volunteers including his dad and a photographer from the *Blackwater Lake Gazette*.

Will handed Riley into her mother's waiting arms and her father shook his hand. When that wasn't enough thanks for bringing his child back safely, the man bro-hugged him. Really, no words needed to be spoken; the expression in their eyes said how grateful they were to him for bringing their child back safe and sound.

It felt good, really good, to get a positive outcome. In Chicago detectives were called in when someone broke the law. At that point there was no prevention and all he could do was try and find justice. Nothing wrong with that, but today it didn't compare to what he was feeling. It had been a very long time since he'd experienced this kind of job satisfaction.

He didn't know what it meant and deliberately refused to analyze the feeling too closely, but all he could think about was talking to April. He wanted to tell her about his really good, totally awesome day, share the excitement with her.

The way he used to.

Chapter Ten

April got home from work later than usual. It had been an exciting day, in the best possible way. Crisis averted and all was well in Blackwater Lake.

After changing out of her work jeans, putting on pink shorts and a white spaghetti-strapped top, she walked barefoot to the kitchen. "Now my biggest problem is what to have for dinner," she said to herself.

She opened the refrigerator, hoping to find something for a meal, which would, in fact, be a miracle since she hadn't bought groceries in a while. Or maybe the food elves had provided provisions, but no such luck. There was some celery in the crisper along with nasty-looking lettuce, fuzzy tomatoes and a shriveled-up cucumber. That eliminated salad as a possibility. But she did have a half dozen eggs, some mushrooms and cheese that could be rescued.

The freezer wasn't very bountiful. Just vegetables that were more ice than anything else. A container of ice cream with about two tablespoons left and a bag of frozen peas she kept for muscle aches after a run.

She had two choices besides going to the grocery store, which wouldn't happen tonight. One—a trip to the Fletchers where she might throw herself on their mercy. Two—dry cereal because there was no milk. Will was probably at home, which was both good and bad news for the same reason.

She wanted to see him, but getting too attached was a bad idea. For her own good she was confined to quarters and needed to fend for herself.

"I guess it's dry cereal." She sighed and went to the pantry, pulling out the box of Cheerios. "Mental note—tomorrow grocery shopping."

She opened the top flaps of the box and unrolled the plastic inner bag, then grabbed a handful of toasted oats in the shape of an *O*. There was a knock on the kitchen's sliding glass door and she looked over. Will was standing there. The rush of pleasure she felt at the sight of him put a hitch in her breathing that nearly made her choke on the cereal. It was a really good idea to keep her distance, but she didn't have the willpower to send him away.

Spineless? She preferred to think of it as being neighborly.

Box in hand, she walked over to the door and unlocked it, then slid it open. He had a brown bag in his hands with the logo of the Harvest Café.

"Hi." She smiled and knew that the joy of it came from deep inside. "This is getting to be a habit."

Not necessarily a good one. It would be too easy to get used to seeing him every day.

"What is?"

"You coming to my back door with food to rescue me from starvation."

"And not a moment too soon," he said, eyeing the big yellow box in her hands.

"I love it for breakfast. And yeah, I know it's dinner time, but it's good now, too," she said. "Come in. If you're up for it, one thing I do have is a bottle of wine."

"Your survival instincts are something to behold," he teased.

"It's about priorities." She pulled two stemless wine-glasses from the upper cupboard and an unopened bottle of Cabernet out of the pantry. "Wine comes from grapes, so you've got your fruit. It pairs with anything, including cereal."

"It does if you're not particularly fussy," he pointed out. "And apparently you're not."

"Nope." April grinned happily, already drunk on just the sight of Will Fletcher. It was really good to see him and she couldn't find the energy to remind herself why it was a bad idea to be this happy. "And think of it this way. If there's an alien invasion or some other sort of crisis, after a glass of Cabernet I really wouldn't care."

"You'll get no argument from me." He set the brown bag on the island and pulled out several cardboard to-go boxes.

"What have we got here?" She opened the containers and found meat loaf, mashed potatoes, green beans, Caesar salad and chocolate cake. Her mouth started to water. Then she looked at the smile on his face and her heart melted. "This is hands down my favorite thing from the café. How did you know?"

"I walked in and asked for two meals to go. Lucy Bishop, one of the owners of the place, wanted to know who the second one was for. When I mentioned your name, she told me what your favorite meal is."

"So she knows you're bringing me dinner. I guess you and I aren't a secret around town?"

"Good guess." He opened the bottle of wine with her electric opener. "Clarice mentioned us being at Bar None with Kim and Luke. So, all evidence points to the word being out."

People in this town tended to become invested in the current community romance. They were going to be bummed when April broke up with Will. But that was a problem for another day. They still had some summer left.

"I'll set the table while you supervise the wine breathing," she said.

"Okay."

Five minutes later they were sitting across from each other at her kitchen table with full plates and wine.

April took a bite of the meat loaf and sighed with enjoyment. "My taste buds are doing the dance of joy thanks to you. This is the second time today that you're a hero."

"That seems a little overstated. All I did was walk in the diner, order and pay. It really was nothing." He shrugged, a no-big-deal gesture.

"Modesty." She sighed at the creamy taste of the mashed potatoes. "It's the hallmark of a hero."

"That's the thing. I'm not a hero."

"There you go again." She pointed her fork at him. "What do you call finding that little girl, carrying her for miles out of the woods and back to her family?"

"My job."

"Modesty," she said again. "On the local news they're calling you the hometown hero. Must feel pretty awesome being the guy in the white hat."

"All I did was act on a hunch." He lifted one shoulder. "I got lucky."

"I think it was more than that, and finding her unharmed must have felt great."

He looked thoughtful for several moments. "You know what feels good?"

Memories of the two of them in her bed came to mind, but she knew that was not what he meant. "Tell me."

"There was a positive outcome today."

"Isn't that what I just said? You found that little girl and brought her home." She sipped her wine.

"It's more than that." There was an expression on his face that was boyish and carefree. "The community came together. People dropped what they were doing to assist in the effort to find a missing girl."

Holding her wineglass in both hands, she watched him as different looks moved across his handsome features. "It's just how folks in Blackwater Lake roll."

"I know, at least on some level. But it's been a while since I experienced that small-town spirit for myself. That sense of pulling together. In Chicago it so often feels like us against them."

"Must be hard."

"It is sometimes. I'm part of a team that investigates, builds a case of evidence that may or may not go to trial. That's up to the city attorney."

"So it can happen that you put in hours of work without any charges being brought?"

"Yeah. The end result is taken out of our hands." He looked at her for several moments, then continued eating.

"I bet that's frustrating."

Her mind was racing as she dug into her food. She wanted so badly to ask whether or not he was happy where he was. Every job had its pros and cons, and she didn't want to hear him say that being a detective for CPD was everything he'd ever dreamed it would be.

She finished the last bite of meat loaf and put her fork

down. "How about you just focus on the positive. Today you got the *W*."

"A win." He pushed his empty plate away. "The sheriff's office took the call, mobilized the community, handled the search. From beginning to end we ran the show and it felt good to see the operation through to a positive conclusion."

April held out her glass. "To happy endings."

"I'll drink to that." There was a crystal, bell-like sound when he tapped the rim of his glass to hers. "Everyone who took part is a hero. You for doing the fliers with Riley's photo. Clarice for sitting in the office taking calls, coordinating information. My dad for leading his group. And everyone else who showed up to walk an assigned grid and look for her."

"You left out yourself for finding Riley."

"I wouldn't have been able to look where I did if everyone else wasn't searching somewhere else."

"That's true." She decided his look of satisfaction would have to be enough. "It's really something to celebrate."

"It's more than that. I really wanted to share the good news with you. For old time's sake."

April watched a smile turn up the corners of his mouth. She'd seen him do that more than once since he'd come back to town, but this time she saw genuine pleasure and it actually reached his eyes. He looked younger, as if the problems of the world had lifted from his shoulders. For the first time since he'd started his temporary duty in Blackwater Lake she saw the old Will. The man she'd fallen in love with.

"I'm glad you came over." She was feeling so much more than that but didn't have the words to tell him. Instead she stood and walked around the table, then held out her hand to him. "How do you feel about taking this celebration into the bedroom?"

Just like that his eyes went smoky and hot. He took her fingers in his and slowly got to his feet. "That sounds like the best idea I've heard all day."

Side by side they walked down the hall. She looked up at him. "Would you do me a favor?"

"If I can."

"Would you wear your white hat?"

He grinned. "If I had one I'd be glad to."

"Can we pretend?" she asked.

"Anything you want."

Will took her in his arms and kissed her until she could hardly breathe. They *celebrated* more than once and this time he didn't get up and sneak back to his house.

He spent the night in her bed, like he had before everything fell apart between them. Just like old times, he'd said.

Unfortunately that was a shadow hanging over her. He was like the old Will and could crush her heart for the second time.

April felt something move against her and opened one eye.

Will.

He was spread out all over the bed, which meant he probably wasn't used to sleeping with someone. That pleased her. More than she wanted it to. Waking up beside him and watching him sleep was pretty awesome, too. He was so handsome, so unguarded that it made her ache inside. She honestly couldn't believe that he was here. If she couldn't see, touch and taste him, she'd chalk this up to imagination.

"Are you staring at me?" His voice was hoarse and scratchy from sleep.

"Your eyes are closed," she said. "How can you possibly know that?"

"I can feel you looking." One eye opened just a little. "What's wrong?"

"I look hideous. Now that I know you're awake I'm just waiting for you to jump up and run screaming from the room."

"You'll be waiting a long time. You look beautiful."

"That's a lie." She smiled. "But I'll take it."

"If you knew what was good for you, you'd be the one running away from me." The guarded look was back. "I'm no hero and you shouldn't look at me like I am."

"Yes, sir." She saluted. "And speaking of a run, I was planning one this morning."

"I know."

"How?" She sat up in the bed and clutched the sheet to her chest.

He grinned. "That's such a girl thing to do since I saw every beautiful, naked inch of you last night."

Yes he had and the words made her smile. "How did you know I was going to run today?"

"You do every other day." He sighed at her look. "My bedroom faces the alley."

"So you spy on me?"

"I keep an eye on your house," he clarified.

"Are you a stalker?"

"Maybe. But it takes one to know one." He lifted one eyebrow and the expression was decidedly accusatory.

She got his drift. "So, you know that morning I 'accidentally' ran into you it was actually deliberate."

"It's pretty hard to get anything past me."

"Because you're a hotshot detective. Yada yada." She made a face at him. "You know, smugness is not a very attractive quality in a person. Decidedly not heroic. And you only pieced that together in hindsight because I told you the truth."

"Maybe." There was a gleam in his eyes when he started pulling on the sheet. "Or maybe I suspected from the beginning because you were nicer to me than I had any reason to expect."

"Kind of like now," she said, holding tight to the five-hundred-thread-count material covering her breasts.

"When do you have to open the shop?"

The soft, sexy, seductive tone in his voice had tension and heat coiling in her belly, making her thighs quiver. "Noon. This is my late day." And a good thing, too, because she had a feeling this was going somewhere she wanted to follow. "When do you have to go into the sheriff's office?"

"I've got time."

She relaxed her grip and let him pull the sheet away. "Okay, then."

His eyes went dark with desire as he pulled her into his arms. "Your run will just have to wait."

"Schedules were made to be flexible."

April loved being loved by him and couldn't seem to get enough. Afterward he went back to his dad's house for a shower while she took one at hers. Barely forty-five minutes later he was back and had extra clothes in his hands.

"Mind if I leave these here?" he asked. "I still need a sanctuary from wacky wedding stuff."

"Kim's not really that bad, is she?"

"You saw the meltdown," he reminded her. "She's normally levelheaded, but when a wedding is involved apparently a woman becomes schizophrenic."

"I really hope you're not profiling brides," she teased.

"Not at all. I'm just making a case for having a drawer at your house."

Her heart skipped and her stomach fluttered, which apparently shut down all the early warning signals from her brain. "I think that can be arranged."

He grinned. "You just saved my life."

"And don't you forget it. Let's put those away." April went into the bedroom and cleared out a space in her dresser for his clothes. Then they went back to the kitchen and she asked, "Do you want some breakfast?"

"I was hoping you'd ask."

"What would you like?"

"Besides you?" The heated look flashed through his eyes for the second time that morning.

Be still my heart, she thought. "If eggs aren't okay, we'll be making a trip to the Harvest Café because I don't have much of anything else. Getting supplies in here is quickly becoming a priority. I have to start a list."

"Do you still make those enchiladas with the green chili sauce?"

She hadn't for a while. Mostly she'd made them for him because he liked it so much. That brought back memories of him coming over when her mom had a girls' night out. April would cook and they loved being alone. It was a preview of what their life together would be like and she'd looked forward to that so much. But it had only ever been a preview, because they never had a life together.

"April?"

"Yes." She shook off the dark memories and concentrated on right now. He was planning on spending a lot of time here and she would focus on enjoying it. "I can make the enchiladas. Anything else I should put on the list?"

"Not unless you take me with you to lug the bags and chip in for the groceries."

"Sounds like a deal."

"I'll clean off the table." He was looking at the take-out containers and plates still sitting there from last night. "We got a little distracted."

"I won't tell if you won't." She met his gaze and grinned, not the least bit sorry that the lingering mess was her fault. The truth was, all things being equal, she would do the same thing again. "I'll make omelets."

It was really tempting to just stand there and watch him. The play of muscles across his back and shoulders when he worked was mouth-watering. That black Chicago PD T-shirt pulled tight around his biceps could occupy her attention for hours. And don't even get her started on the way his butt looked in those worn jeans.

She'd given him space for some of his clothes and they were going food shopping, splitting the bill. This was one notch below actually formally agreeing to move in together. It felt natural and right, like it should have been the first time.

Better than she'd imagined it could be before she'd found out they wouldn't last forever.

But this time she had a safety net. The relationship had an expiration date and their Labor Day breakup appointment was coming faster than she wanted to think about.

That was a reminder, as if she needed it, that she'd better hold on to her heart with both hands.

Chapter Eleven

"Holy crap."

Will looked at the calendar on his desk in his office and whistled. It was already August. Time flew when you were having fun and he definitely was. Days were busy, filled with the routine problems of the summer tourist season when the population in Blackwater Lake doubled. Nights he spent at April's. It had been several weeks since she'd given him a drawer in the dresser and the empty space beside her in the bed.

Mostly they hung out in the middle, wrapped in each other's arms.

Too bad it couldn't last. And looking at the calendar he could see in black-and-white how short his time in town was. And more significantly, his time in her bed. It had been perfect. Had him thinking about things he hadn't for a long time. But they couldn't make it work before and the same issues still stood in the way. If he was being honest there was another one. He'd failed at marriage and taking another chance wasn't high on his list.

He could only make the most of the time he had left. And speaking of that, through his open door he saw April walk into the outer office. They'd ridden into town together this morning because her car was at McKnight Automotive for an oil change. It was just about quitting time for him, so she must have locked up her shop for the day.

Will shut down the computer, grabbed his keys from the desk drawer and walked out of his office, closing the door behind him. He met April in front of Clarice's desk.

"Hi." He leaned down to kiss her lightly.

"How was your day?" she asked.

Better now, he thought, but didn't say that out loud.

"Busy." He looked at his dispatcher, who was observing them and approving of what she saw if he didn't miss his guess. "Just ask Clarice."

The woman nodded. "A couple of car accidents. Drunk and disorderly on the beach at the lake. Illegal fireworks in a restricted area. Must have been left over from the Fourth."

"That's not good," April said. "It's been too long since we had a really soaking rain, and the hills and mountains are pretty dry. The last thing we need is a forest fire."

"That's for sure," Clarice agreed. "Dry lightning is dangerous enough. We don't need stupid humans messing up. There was a bad one about twenty years ago that came too close to Blackwater Lake for comfort."

"I remember." Will's dad was the sheriff and didn't come home for days because he was setting up detours and keeping curious spectators away for their own safety.

"That was before I moved here." April met his gaze. "But I came from Southern California and there were some scary fires there."

"The locals in this town watch out for the flakes who aren't paying attention." Will didn't say it out loud, but there was no way to prevent some nut job who waited for the perfect set of circumstances—windy weather, motivation, opportunity—and deliberately set a fire. But he'd meant what he said. "Folks are vigilant and pick up the phone if they notice suspicious behavior."

"They watch out for people in general," April said. "I'm a perfect example. Your family sure took my mom and me under their wing."

A couple years after the Kennedys moved in across the alley from him, Will *really* watched April. That old bedroom window of his was a great vantage point to observe the cute little girl who had suddenly grown up and blossomed when he wasn't looking.

Then he'd gone and messed it all up. In a million years he never would have expected to even kiss her again, let alone be invited into her bed. It was a relief to have a plan in place so he didn't hurt her like last time. They were enjoying each other with no strings attached. Although, for reasons he didn't really understand, turning that page on the calendar just now had put a knot in his gut.

"You ready to go?" he asked her.

"Yup. Oh, I almost forgot—" She met his gaze. "I talked to Tom McKnight and the car has to stay there. He noticed the timing belt was slipping and he had to order the part he needs. It could take a couple of days to come in."

"No problem."

Will wouldn't put it out there for the nosy woman in front of them to spread around town, but they were going to the same place. Heck, now that he thought about it, Clarice probably already knew that, too. His sister, father and nephew were aware that he wasn't sleeping under the same roof they were. Again he was relieved that there was a plan in place to save April from being pitied by her well-meaning neighbors.

"Let's roll," he said.

The phone on the dispatcher's desk rang and Clarice picked up. "Blackwater Lake Sheriff's Office, Clarice speaking. How can I help you?" She listened for several moments then frowned. "Where?" After writing something down, she said, "I'll send someone over to check it out."

"What's going on?" Will asked when she hung up.

"That was Jeannie Waterman. A couple of teenagers are acting suspiciously. In your neighborhood actually."

"Did she recognize them?"

"Yes, as a matter of fact. Doug Satterfield and Mike Hutak."

When law enforcement knew your name it wasn't a good thing and he recognized these two. He held out his hand for her notes. "I'll check it out since I'm going that way. See you in the morning."

"Bye, Clarice. Say hi to your hubby for me," April said.

"Will do."

They walked to the rear of the office and went out the back door of the building. Will's SUV was parked right there and he opened the front passenger door for April. After she climbed in, he shut the door and walked around to the driver's side.

He got in, then turned the key in the ignition. "I really hope Jeannie Waterman is overreacting. That it's a couple of boys just hanging out."

"Me, too." She flashed a grin. "I feel like a sidekick. Can I be yours?"

"My what now?"

"Come on, Will. Don't be a stick in the mud and go all law enforcement-y on me. Every hero has a person he can count on in a crisis. A sidekick. You have one in Chicago."

"Yeah. But I call him a partner."

"Same thing." There was pleading in her voice. "Please. Don't drop me off. That will cost you precious time."

He had to admit she was right about that. A minute either way could mean catching these kids—or not. But if they'd really done something wrong, they were probably long gone. "Okay, you can come with me. But stay in the car."

"It's hard to be an efficient sidekick from the right front seat of a vehicle," she protested.

"Take it or leave it."

"You're very bossy," she said.

In the part of town where Will and April lived the houses fronted well-traveled streets with an alley in back for the garage. Unless these kids were complete idiots, that's where they'd be pulling their crap. So, he drove slowly up and down the back ways near the address Clarice had given him.

"There," April said, pointing.

Will didn't see anything. Hedges in this area were nice for privacy, but could easily hide mischief in progress. "What did you see?"

"Believe it or not, an egg went flying through the air." She peered steadily through the front window then pointed again. "There," she said again.

"Okay. I saw it." He pulled the SUV to a stop several houses away. "Stay in the car. I mean it."

He got out quietly, then soundlessly picked his way to the hedge that was almost as tall as he was. He peeked around it and sure enough the teens in question had egged the car in the driveway and were working on the garage door. Parked just two houses down was a beat-up old truck that he knew belonged to the sixteen-year-old Satterfield kid. Hutak didn't have a driver's license yet.

Will walked into the open and stopped in the best place to block their exit if necessary. "Hey, boys."

They both whirled around and the younger one dropped the cardboard egg carton in the driveway, breaking the few that were left. The two of them looked guilty as sin.

"Don't even think about making a run for it. I know where you live."

"Are you going to arrest us?" Hutak was skinny, blond and scared.

"Maybe." Will watched their body language for any sign of running. "You want to tell me why you did this? You got a beef with someone who lives here?"

"Maybe." Satterfield had black hair and eyes with an attitude to match.

Will didn't miss the fact that the kid threw his own words back at him. "Smart ass."

He shrugged. "Or maybe we were bored."

That was probably more like it, Will thought. "Well, before I call your parents, you're going to be busy cleaning up the mess you made."

"No way—"

Will held up a hand to stop Hutak's protest. He liked these two for the profanity-laced graffiti on the barns, too. "Before your mouth writes checks you can't cash, I've got another question. If I search that truck of yours, Satterfield, am I going to find cans of spray paint?"

The two exchanged another guilty glance. "That's what I thought," he said. "Seems like you're going to have a lot to do for the rest of the summer painting over the stuff on the barns you vandalized."

"You can't make us," Hutak said.

"You're right about that," Will agreed pleasantly. Behind him he heard the sound of sneakers and figured his "sidekick" had disobeyed orders. "But I can make the alternative to it feel like the lowest level of hell. Now let's get this mess cleaned up before it dries and you're looking at charges."

He marched the boys to the back door and a woman he didn't know answered. After he calmed her down and explained the boys needed soap, water and rags to undo what they'd done, she was more than happy to oblige and leave him to supervise them.

Satterfield hosed eggshells and slime off the garage and car. "Slave labor is against the law, you know."

"This is more in the neighborhood of punishment fitting the crime." Will folded his arms over his chest.

"You're not really going to call my parents, are you?" Hutak was looking pretty sorry for himself. "If you do, I'm never going to get my driver's license. I'm not even going to have time to learn to drive because I'll be grounded for the rest of the summer."

"Look on the bright side. You'll only be grounded when you're not painting barns," Will said. He heard laughter from behind him.

"My life is over," Hutak said to his friend. "I'm never listening to you again."

"You're such a candy-ass." But Satterfield didn't sound quite as defiant anymore.

When they'd finished, returned the cleaning supplies and apologized to the woman, Will called the parents. Within ten minutes both sets showed up. None of them gave him any excuses for their sons' behavior. They expressed regret and appreciated him taking the time to teach the kids a lesson, saying they had the situation from here.

After they left he joined April in the SUV. "You didn't stay in the car."

"In sidekick school you'd flunk out for not backing up

the hero." She didn't look intimidated like the teens. "I was making sure you didn't need help."

And speaking of help, the parents of those kids had thanked *him* for helping their children. He'd responded that he'd been happy to do it. Just now he realized that was the honest-to-God truth. It was the second time in the past few weeks that he'd found satisfaction in doing his job.

He shouldn't get used to the feeling. Since he'd arrived, he never missed an opportunity to remind people his status was temporary.

His sidekick was temporary, too, besides being a whole lot cuter than his partner in Chicago. And wasn't that a bitch and a half.

Will wasn't quite sure how his dad had talked him into going fishing on his day off, but here they were at the Blackwater Lake Marina. He parked his SUV in the paved lot and they both got out. Just up the small rise he saw the house where the previous owner had added on an upstairs apartment to rent out. Jack Garner owned the whole property now and word was he used one unit for an office and lived in the other one. Just then the bestselling author walked out the front door following after the ugliest dog Will had ever seen.

Jack glanced over, lifted a hand in greeting, then headed in their direction. He stopped in front of them and shook hands. "How are you, Hank?"

"Better. Best shape of my life according to my daughter." He bent to pet the dog's homely, hairy head. "What kind of dog is this?"

"Chinese crested. Harley, say hello." He grinned when the dog barked.

Will stared at the skinny creature that was hairless, except for his head, tail and paws. "Seems...good-natured."

Jack met his gaze and there was something just shy of warning in his dark eyes. "That's like telling a woman she has a good personality. I know he's not the handsomest canine in the kennel, but he picked me out. And I wasn't even looking for a dog." Harley took off. "We're finished being neighborly. Gotta go."

"The writer doesn't waste words." His dad watched Jack follow his dog around the lake.

"I guess you've met him before," Will said.

"Yeah. In town. Never met the dog, though." He shook his head. "Let's go fishing."

They walked up a couple of steps and into the marina store. Brewster Smith was putting Summer Clearance signs on the racks of T-shirts, tank tops, bathing suits and light-weight jackets. Will didn't much appreciate the reminder that summer was quickly coming to an end.

It meant saying goodbye to April and he was nowhere near ready to do that. She was sunlight and magic and heat. Chicago winter was gray and dark and cold. Who wouldn't want to stay here longer?

"How are you, Brew?" Hank greeted the other man.

"Dandy, thanks. You're looking fit as a dang fiddle." He checked Hank out from head to toe. "Recuperation agrees with you."

"That it does."

"How you doin', Sheriff?"

Will shrugged. "Can't complain."

"How's that nephew of yours?"

"He's a great kid." Thanks to everyone but him, Will thought, because he'd been career focused. "Kim's done an amazing job with him. And she couldn't have done it without Dad."

Hank nodded. "I wouldn't have chosen this path for her,

but I couldn't be prouder of the way she handled a difficult situation. And she gave me my grandson."

"Now she's getting married. The years sure have gone by fast." Brew shook his head in amazement. "How's the weddin' stuff coming along?"

"Good," Will answered. "I guess."

Hank laughed. "If you spent more time at the house instead of escaping to April's every night, you'd know for sure that all is well. And you're her man of honor." Before Brewster could ask, he added, "That's like a maid of honor except a man is doing the honor stuff."

Brewster rubbed a hand across the full beard on his chin. "I'm not sure what to say about that except that you'll look fetching in the dress."

"Very funny." Will was glad he'd picked that to comment on and not his relationship with April. He didn't want to put a finer point on what was going on with them.

"I'm a regular comedian." Brew grinned. "So you're spendin' a lot of time with our favorite photographer?"

So much for dodging the subject. "We're friends."

"Hmm." The older man looked at his dad. "You buying that?"

"I stay out of things unless invited in," Hank said.

"Fair enough." The other man looked from one to the other. "What can I do for you fellas today?"

"Going fishing," Hank said. "We need to rent equipment and a rowboat."

"How come you don't have your own?" Brewster asked.

"Never had time. Now I'm recuperating." He looked at Will. "We need two rods, tackle, lures and the whole nine yards. And that rowboat. I'll handle the oars. It's part of my cardiac rehab."

"Good," Will said.

"Okay, then."

Brewster gathered a couple of fishing rods and a tackle box with everything they'd need, then wrote up a receipt and took Will's credit card for all charges. They carried everything to the slip on the dock where the boat was tied up and his dad rowed them out of the marina and to a place not far away that most tourists didn't know about. Cutter's Cove was a locals' secret and shared only with a trusted few out-of-towners. Hank stopped and stowed the oars, then each of them took a rod and got it ready. In a few minutes they'd dropped their lines, then sat in companionable silence.

Will adjusted the baseball cap he wore and looked up at the blue sky. Not a single cloud to break up the expanse— only the mountain peaks did that. The surface of the water was like blue glass while birds chirped and called overhead and from trees on the shore. He let out a breath and with it went a whole lot of accumulated tension.

"This was a great idea, Dad."

"Thought you could use it, son." Hank reeled in his line, then cast it out again in an easy, experienced single movement of his wrist.

"Yeah. I've missed this."

"How's the job going?"

"Good, I'd say. Why?" He looked at his dad. "Are people complaining about me and begging you to come back?"

"No." He laughed. "It's just you haven't said much. I'm feeling a little guilty for pulling you away from big city detective work. Do you miss it?"

Did he? Will hadn't really thought about it. His time and energy had gone into taking care of Blackwater Lake and...

April.

"It's not a good sign when that much time goes by without an answer."

Will looked at his father, who was also wearing a base-ball hat and aviator sunglasses. Even with all his detective experience he couldn't tell what this man was thinking. And he didn't know how he felt, but his dad hadn't asked him to compare and contrast his job in Chicago with the one here in Blackwater Lake. So he'd decided to focus on how the current assignment was going instead of whether or not he missed his job in Chicago.

"I helped two teenagers see the error of their ways," he started. "Caught them in the act of egging a car and they pretty much admitted spray painting barns because they were bored."

"Yeah. Heard that before."

"I bet you have." Will grinned. "The cool thing is that I got their confession while making them clean up their mess."

"Very badass of you, son."

"I'm glad you approve." Will chuckled, then his amusement disappeared as he thought about what might have happened in CPD jurisdiction. His dad hadn't asked him to compare and contrast, but he did automatically. "I didn't have to arrest those kids and start a paper trail that could follow them for a long time. There were no loopholes in the law or plea deals with a prosecutor that put danger-ous people back on the street who should stay locked up."

"We're not talking Blackwater Lake now, are we?"

Will sighed, but all he said was, "Justice and punish-ment aren't so swift and tidy in Chicago. Here I made a difference on a basic level. I made a positive difference in two lives and didn't have to jail a couple of juveniles and put them in the system. That carries a lot of satisfac-tion for me. I called their parents and something tells me that will be enough."

Hank nodded thoughtfully. "If they reoffend, you won't know. You'll be back in Chicago."

He waited to feel the thrill of excitement at the thought of going back, but it never came. Without much enthusiasm he said, "Yeah."

Hank set his fishing rod in the bottom of the rowboat and braced it against the side, then reached into their rented cooler filled with ice and pulled out two cold bottles of water. He handed one to Will.

"Is it possible that you're experiencing job burnout?"

"I don't know."

Will liked being a detective. Putting forensic evidence together with witness statements and interviews to come to a conclusion and take a bad guy off the street. It was a satisfying career. At least it had been. But since coming back home, he'd seen that there were holes in his life, gaps that he'd been successfully able to ignore for a long time.

An image came to mind of the pleasure on April's face when he was buried deep inside her. Her beautiful dark hair spread over the rose-print pillow case. Their naked bodies pressed together, becoming one. It was going to be hard to walk away from her. And he'd seen for himself how people cared about their *favorite photographer*. In the end, she would dump him and avoid the town pity party. But in Chicago, no one would give a damn that he'd been publicly put in his place. He opened the bottle and took a long, cold drink.

"The thing is, son, that heart problem I had made me realize a lot of things."

"I bet," Will said. "Anything specific?"

"Yeah. How much I love my family and that I'd like to be around for a while. I'm willing to go along with the good Lord's plan when He's ready to take me, but I can't think of any reason to make it easy on Him, or go sooner than necessary."

"You're taking care of yourself now," Will said. "Eating right and exercising."

"There's something else." Hank rested his elbows on his knees and dangled the water bottle between them. "I'm giving a lot of thought to retiring."

"Makes sense." But Will remembered his dad talking about this and knew where he was going.

"I think so. The thing is, though, I want to leave the town in good hands. Your hands, son."

"You can find someone better than me," he said.

Here's where the compare-and-contrast thing went the other way. In Chicago the system was so big that the general population had no clue what went on unless it was breaking news. You put your nose to the grindstone and worked hard. In Blackwater Lake it was personal. If he let people down, they were friends and neighbors.

"I don't think there is anyone better," Hank said. "Folks know and trust you because you were born and raised here."

"That doesn't automatically qualify me to be the best person for the job. What about Eddie?"

His father snorted. "He's smart and eager, but young and green. He could grow into the job but not soon enough. And I believe you have more experience and training."

"Even if I wanted to do it, don't folks get a vote?"

"There would be a special election, but half the people in town won't even know it isn't me on the ballot."

"Yeah," Will said wryly, "because we look so much alike."

"Actually, I'm better looking," his father teased.

This was a lot to think about. That day he'd gone to Mercy Medical Clinic with his father for the checkup, his dad had hinted that this was coming. Now that he'd voiced it to the universe, Will couldn't ignore the subject any longer.

"I don't know about this, Dad." He waited for the same arm-twisting guilt trip his sister had put on him when his father ended up in the hospital before the surgery.

"Just one more thing, son." His father took off his sunglasses and there was a look in his eyes impossible to ignore. "I know you always wanted a career in law enforcement since you were a little guy. As you grew up it became clear that you didn't want to do that in my shadow, so Chicago was where you set your sights. And you've done that. I'm real proud of you, Will. Always have been and always will be."

That meant a lot to him. Will made every decision by asking himself whether or not it would make his dad proud or disappointed in him.

"Thanks, Dad."

"Just think about the sheriff's job, Will. Maybe it's something you didn't even realize you want."

Will waited for more, hoping to have something to get defensive about. He should have known better because that had never been his dad's style.

Damn it.

Chapter Twelve

April thought Kim was surprisingly calm considering this was her wedding day. She'd gotten dressed at the Blackwater Lake Lodge where the ceremony and reception would take place soon. This suite was where she would spend her first night with her new husband. Her family was all here: the man of honor, her dad and son.

It was April's job to take candid photos, so that's what she was doing. Trying to be like a fly on the wall and not attract notice. She was constantly adjusting the lens and depth of field to bring one or another of the Fletchers into sharp relief while blurring the background of the shot. The four of them were laughing, teasing, joking. *Family.*

Something April had longed for all her life. But no matter how much she wished it could be different, she was on the outside looking in. And that sounded pathetic. She didn't mean it to be. Her best friend was happy and April couldn't be more pleased.

She took some random shots of the suite's living room with its sofa, love seat, and mahogany coffee and end tables. There was a wet bar and small kitchenette with microwave. A doorway led to the bedroom, which she knew looked like a tornado had hit it. There were pictures as proof. It was important to her that Kim have photographic evidence of every part of this day, even the untidy parts because that's what made the memory real.

When her view was suddenly blocked, she lowered the camera. Will was standing in front of her looking so handsome in his traditional black tuxedo. *Be still my heart*, she thought, then adjusted her own attitude the way she would a lens on her camera. It was important he not know how profoundly he affected her.

"You need a break," he said. "Stand down for a few minutes. It's going to be a long night."

"But I might miss the perfect shot," she protested.

"If you do, no one will ever know. Put down the camera."

"Or what, Sheriff?"

"I'll have to take you in." His voice was slightly north of normal, tipping into seductive territory.

"That could be interesting." But she set down her camera on the coffee table.

Behind them came the sound of metal on glass. Kim was signaling for attention. Her blonde hair hung to her shoulders in layers that framed her pretty face. A crystal-encrusted comb secured the veil that hung to the middle of her back. She looked like a princess in her full-skirted white gown with the lace bodice, sweetheart neckline and cap sleeves.

"I'd like to make a toast if someone will open the champagne."

"I can handle that." Hank twisted off the metal wire on

the mouth of the bottle, then used his thumbs to pop the cork. After pouring some into five flutes, he handed them out, including one for April. He looked at his grandson. "Just a sip for you."

"I know, Granddad." But the teenager looked eager.

As Kim held up her glass, the emotion in her eyes bordered on tearful. "In this room is everyone I love."

"What about Luke?" Will asked.

"Everyone except Luke, smart aleck. I wouldn't be here without you guys." She looked at each of them. "Here's to all of you. Especially to Will for carrying a bouquet when he walks down the aisle in front of me."

"To Will," they all said.

"They" included everyone *but* Will. "I'm not drinking to the bouquet part of that toast, only to the love and walking down the aisle in front of you part. And, in my opinion, that's going above and beyond the call of brotherly duty."

"It wouldn't hurt you to get in touch with your feminine side," Kim teased.

"Are you sure about that?" Will asked. "It could be psychologically damaging to me. Therapy's looking pretty attractive right now."

"Oh, man up, Will." Kim grinned at him.

"That's the problem," he said, clearly enjoying the pushback. "It's bad enough that you talked me into filling a traditionally female role in your wedding, which, by the way, goes against all the rules of manhood. Then you spring this bouquet thing on me in a family toast. That's very underhanded, by the way. I draw the line at carrying flowers. It's just not manly."

"Really, Will—" Kim tsked.

"Dad, help me out here." He looked from his father to his nephew. "Tim?"

"You're on your own, dude." The teen shrugged. "She's my mom. I'm not stupid."

"Okay. I understand." Will nodded. "I get the parent/ child bond. So, Dad, feel free to jump in here anytime and back me up on this."

"Well, son—" There was a twinkle in his father's eyes. "The things we don't want to do are usually the ones that build character."

"Since when is a wedding a teachable moment?" Will looked at his family. "It's a conspiracy. I'm ashamed of you guys." He met April's gaze. "I know my sister is your best friend, but you're sensible. Probably the only one in this room besides me who is. You don't think I should carry flowers down the aisle, do you?"

Four pairs of eyes belonging to the people she cared most about in the world were watching her. She knew this whole silly conversation was a tension reliever for the bride, who in five minutes would descend the lodge staircase and take her vows. The Fletcher family didn't take it lightly. Will had told her as much when confessing his own feelings of failure about his marriage. Kim intended to only do this once, hence the tension.

So, April responded in the spirit of fun. "Come on, Will. You face armed criminals without batting an eye. It's flowers, not pantyhose, high heels and a tiara."

All of them stared at her for a moment, then cracked up. Will laughed the hardest.

Kim waved her hand in front of her eyes. "Laughing till you cry is still crying. I'm going to ruin my makeup."

Just then there was a knock on the door and Hank opened it. Hadley Michaels, Blackwater Lake Lodge's manager and events coordinator, stood there. She had auburn hair and turquoise eyes. In her navy jacket, skirt and matching low-heeled pumps she exuded an air of prim and proper that was far more mature than she should be at twenty-six. "Five minutes, everyone. We need to get you all in the staging area. There's a schedule to maintain."

April grabbed her camera and followed the others out the door of the suite, snapping pictures of their backs as they walked down the hall to the elevator.

Will took his sister's hand and tucked it into the bend of his elbow. "I'm drawing a line in the sand. No bouquet carrying."

She touched the white rosebud boutonniere on his jacket. "Okay, but you could pull it off no problem. Next to Luke, you're the manliest man I know."

The tender brother/sister moment brought tears to April's eyes. Fortunately the lens didn't have emotions to cloud the issue and clearly captured the moment for posterity.

They rode down to the second floor and April got out first, then backed up to take pictures. She got one of them lined up at the top of the stairs with Will waiting to lead everyone down.

She looked at him. "Okay, give me a couple of minutes to get in position."

Will winked at her. "Roger that."

Something about the way he looked, the man himself, slammed her heart and her first thought was, *This can't be.* Anything more than friendship was against the rules. But when she hurried downstairs, the area around the fireplace was filled with friends who were there to wish Kim and Luke every happiness in their married life. Weddings were a seething cauldron of emotion and that's why she'd suddenly been overwhelmed with feeling something deeper for Will. It would pass.

She focused on the minister and Luke, who were waiting in front of about thirty people sitting in folding chairs set out for the event. To the left was a trio of female musicians, one on violin, another playing the flute and a harpist. There were flowers everywhere—roses, lilies, baby's breath. It smelled like a garden and her only regret was that her camera couldn't capture the wonderful, sweet scent.

April did a quick pan around the room to capture the spectators, knowing Kim wouldn't be able to take it in now. Then the trio started the wedding march and the bride began her stairway descent with her brother in the lead and flanked by her father and son. She adjusted her lens and settings to get close-ups of their expressions, then pulled back to take in the flower garland and white bows decorating the banister.

April moved quickly to get a signature shot. Everyone was looking at the bride and she wanted to capture the expression on her groom's face when he got his first glimpse of the woman who would be his wife. Money shot, she thought, snapping the exact moment Luke looked dazzled, happy and head over heels in love. Then she zoomed in on Kim's face filled with absolute joy at the sight of the man she was about to marry.

Will was first down the aisle between the chairs and took his place beside Reverend Owen Thurmond from the nondenominational church in Blackwater Lake. The pastor was in his midforties and had kids who went to the local high school where the bride and groom worked.

Then Hank and Tim escorted Kim down the aisle, stopping right where they were supposed to.

The pastor asked, "Who gives this woman to be married to this man?"

Hank smiled lovingly down at his daughter, then kissed her cheek. He nodded at his grandson before meeting the minister's gaze. "Her son and I do."

Luke moved closer, held out his hand and her father

tucked his daughter's fingers into it, into the safekeeping of her husband-to-be. They walked the several steps and stood facing the minister.

"We are gathered together in the sight of God to join this man and this woman in marriage. I think I speak for the whole town of Blackwater Lake when I say that in terms of finding a soul mate right under your nose, it took you two long enough."

"We needed a little push," Kim said, blowing a kiss to her son, who now stood beside the minister in the best-man spot.

"I don't have to tell you both that marriage is an institution of respect because the fact that you waited so long for the right person speaks to your high regard."

April happened to have her lens on Will and pressed the shutter. For just a moment there was a look in his eyes that she now knew was about his regret at the failure of his own marriage.

"Still," the minister continued, "relationships are like a garden—pleasing at first bloom but eventually needing attention to maintain its lush beauty. In other words it needs work." He looked at each of them. "I understand you've written your own vows?"

"We have," Luke said.

Kim held out her bouquet to Will and shrugged. "I swear holding this is in the job description."

"Okay." He gave her a grin.

April took multiple shots of that, wishing some of the criminals he'd put away could see the badass detective in touch with his feminine side.

Kim had unfolded a sheet of paper and started to read. "Please indulge me in my cheat sheet but I was afraid nerves would make me draw a blank. I'm only doing this once and wanted the vows to be as perfect as I could get them." She turned and smiled at her groom. "On top of that pressure, there's also the fact that I teach English and I struggled to make my vows as eloquent as I urge my students to be. I wanted to do justice to what I feel in my heart. As much as I respect language, there are no words to tell you how much I love you. But I promise to show you every day how deeply I care. I will support you and take care of you the best way I know how. And I will go to every football game, and cheer for you and the team more enthusiastically than anyone else."

Luke laughed but his eyes were suspiciously bright, which would be a fantastic picture. "I'm a football coach, which makes me competitive, so I memorized my vows. Not the best game play because, Kim, you're so beautiful that I'm at a loss for words. I've completely forgotten what I planned to say." There was a chorus of laughter and *aww*s from the guests. "But here's the substance of it. I'm the luckiest man in the world. I promise to be the best husband possible and a father to your son. I love him as if he were my own. And I love you. I will cherish you as long as I live. And yeah, I'm going to put a spin on the traditional vows because I promise to obey."

"Brave words, Luke." The minister chuckled along with the guests looking on. "May the spirit of your words as you promise to love each other sustain you throughout your life together. Do you have the rings?"

"I do." Will smiled, then said, "Yes."

Owen took them and gave the smaller one to Luke. "Do you take Kim to be your wife?"

"I do." He slipped the simple band on her left ring finger.

"Kim, do you take Luke to be your husband?"

"I do." Her hands trembled as she slid the band on Luke's finger. Then he took her hands in his to steady them.

"It's official." Owen looked at everyone gathered to witness the ceremony. "I present to you Mr. and Mrs. Luke Miller. Luke, you may kiss your bride."

When he did, the spectators stood and applauded. April captured everything she could, but found she kept straying back to Will. She reminded herself to be professional. Newlyweds first, family second. But her eye kept searching out Will.

Because he would be gone soon and she wouldn't be able to search him out at all.

"This dress cost me blood, sweat and tears, not to mention sleep," Kim said to her new husband. "I'm not taking it off."

"No, that would be my job now." Luke smiled, a suggestive look in his eyes.

April was standing right there at the edge of the dance floor where they'd had their first dance as husband and wife. He'd made a comment about the impressive circumference of her gown and the challenges of navigating it gracefully. She continued to snap pictures and got the laughter, love and intimacy after this brief back-and-forth. Now the new Mr. and Mrs. were working the room, which was beautifully decorated with white linens on the tables, flowers and flameless candles everywhere. In the corner, a table for wedding gifts was full and people had put presents on the floor surrounding it.

She was looking around for more candid shots of people sitting at the circular tables chatting while some couples were making their way to the dance floor when the DJ started playing a slow song. She noticed two of the Fletcher men walking purposefully toward her. Since she was alone, the two of them probably had something to say to her.

"Hank," she said, then looked at Will. "Hi, great party."

"Yeah. It's a shame you're missing it. But Dad and I came up with a plan to fix that."

"I don't want to hear this, do I?"

"Probably not. But we don't really care." Hank looked at his son. "Tell her, Will."

"Coward." But he grinned. "Okay. Everyone has eaten but you, missy."

"Missy? What are you? The food police?" She shrugged. "Sorry. Couldn't help it."

"You're hilarious," Will said. "As it happens we've been deputized by the bride, who wants you to take a break and eat. She said to tell you it's selfish on her part. If you don't keep your strength up the pictures won't be any good."

April laughed. "That sounds like her. But—"

"I know what you're going to say. And if you trust me with your camera," Hank said, "I can fill in. If they're not good you can work your Photoshop magic on them."

She stared lovingly at the camera in her hands, then gave him an apologetic look. "It's really expensive. Not that I don't trust you—"

"But you don't. I understand." Hank slid his hands into the pockets of his tuxedo slacks.

"I have a compromise. There's an inexpensive point-and-shoot in my equipment bag on that chair in the corner. Would that be okay?"

"A relief, actually. That one—" he indicated the bulky, impressive apparatus in her hands "—is too much responsibility for a rookie."

"Okay, then, it's settled," Will said. "I'll make sure she gets something to eat and you take over photography duties."

"Done." Hank headed over to where she'd pointed out her bag.

Will put his hand at the small of her back and guided her

to a table with one pristine setting left. The other places had wadded-up napkins, half-filled coffee cups and partially eaten slices of wedding cake. He sat her down, then signaled to one of the waitstaff to bring food. Moments later she had a Waldorf salad, petite filet, rice pilaf and asparagus.

"Looks yummy. I'm starving." She dug in to the salad, then started working on the rest. Will sat beside her and watched, a bemused look on his face. She chewed a bite of meat, then swallowed and said, "What?"

"You're really enjoying that."

"You bet. Best food in town here at the lodge." She ate the vegetable as he continued to stare. He was making her nervous in a sexy, take-me-to-your-bedroom way. So not appropriate right now. "Don't you have things to do, Mr. Man of Honor?"

"Yeah. The toast. But Kim wanted everyone fed and relaxed before that and the rest of the traditional stuff. So I don't have anything right now. Except take care of you."

"Babysitting me, you mean." There was a quiver in her tummy that had nothing to do with food and everything to do with *him*.

"It's a dirty job." He shrugged. "But someone has to do it."

"Wow. Feel the love," she said wryly.

In the next moment she wanted those words back. Their plan had evolved in order to avoid that messy *L*-word complication. No way she wanted to change the rules. But she wished he didn't look as tempting as sin. So very James Bond-y in his tux. And this being sweet to her just had to stop. None of that was part of their deal.

"Really, Will, you're part of the family and should go mingle."

"Those were not the orders given to me by the bride. I'm supposed to make sure you eat and have some fun."

When the word *fun* came out of Will's mouth all kinds of things came to mind, but not one of them would be suitable in a room full of people at a wedding reception.

She put down her fork. "I have to get back to work."

"Dance with me first." He touched a finger to her mouth when she started to protest. "You should be aware that I'm not taking no for an answer." When his nephew walked by, Will grabbed him. "Tim, watch April's camera."

"No sweat," the teen answered.

Will held out his hand to her and she only hesitated for a moment before she took it. After tugging her to her feet, he led her to the dance floor and slid an arm around her waist before settling her snugly against his big, hard body. There was nowhere on earth she would rather be, April realized, and she needed to savor every second since their time together would be over very soon.

She slid her arm around his neck and he rested his chin against her temple. In time to the slow song playing, he guided her around the floor and for a few minutes she could pretend they were alone. His heat and strength surrounded her and made a protective cocoon she wanted to stay in forever.

But when the music ended, so did her quiet moment. The DJ announced that all single ladies, regardless of age, should come out on the dance floor because the bride was going to throw the bouquet.

"I have to get my camera," she said.

Will blocked her exit. "You're single. Jean Luc doesn't count."

"No, I need to—"

He took her shoulders and turned her, then gently nudged her toward where Kim was standing with a growing group of females from eight to eighty. "Dad will get these pictures."

April moved toward the group and took a spot at the back. As the tradition went, whoever caught the bride's bouquet would be next to get married. The chances of that happening to her were about as good as a hookup with Jean Luc, she thought.

The DJ announced last call for the ladies before Kim took her place, turned her back and prepared to toss the flowers over her head. Flashes went off as the guests took pictures. Then the bride lowered her arm and turned toward the group of ladies.

"I hope everyone will forgive me," she said. "But I'm going to cheat." The women parted as Kim walked over to April and stopped. "You're my BFF. I want this day to be perfect, which by my definition means you have to have this."

"But, Kim—"

"No *but*s. I can't control everything. All I can do is make sure you get this. The rest is up to you." There was a determined look in her friend's eyes.

April sighed and took the flowers, then hugged her friend. "Luke's right. This dress has an impressive circumference."

"I'll take that as a thank-you."

"And so much more. I love you, my friend. You're going to be so happy."

"I love you, too. Thanks, and you're welcome." Kim pulled away and said, "Now Luke is going to throw the garter."

The DJ made the announcement and then the bride sat in a chair with her groom on one knee in front of her. She lifted her impressive skirt just enough for him to find the lacy garter with the powder-blue bow and slide it down her thigh and off. The single guys, including Will, gathered like the women had and the groom turned his back and tossed it over his head into the crowd.

A young guy beside Will grabbed it, then seemed to realize what he'd done and the ramifications of his athleticism. Horrified, he pushed the lace into Will's hands as if it were a hot rock.

"No way, man," he said, before quickly exiting the area.

Will walked over to April and studied the bouquet in her hands. "I think any superstition is null and void if the rules are bent to the breaking point."

"I'm sure you're right."

"Smile, you two." Hank was there with her less complicated camera. "I'm the acting official photographer. Ready? Say cheese."

Will let his dad snap a couple of photos while they stood side by side. Then he stuffed the garter in his pocket, took April in his arms and bent her back before kissing her soundly. Flashes went off around them, proving this impulsive act did not go unnoticed.

He met her gaze and his own was hot and bright. "Take that, tradition."

"You're just full of surprises," she said breathlessly.

The microphone crackled before the DJ said, "Listen up. The waiters are circulating to make sure everyone has a glass of champagne. It's time for the toast."

"That's my cue." Will pulled her upright.

April caught her breath and watched him head back to the bridal table. Pulling herself together with an effort, she retrieved her camera and thanked Tim for his excellent guardianship. Through her lens she watched and recorded Will's speech.

"Ladies and gentlemen, I hope you're having a great time." There was a round of applause and he smiled. "My sister, Kim, is a remarkable woman. If my mother were here, she'd be extraordinarily proud. The thing is, not just anyone could have talked me into being her man of honor, but she managed it. I'm still not sure how, but I think blackmail and tears were a part of the pitch." He paused as everyone laughed. "She's a warm, caring, good person. That's because of my parents. And then my dad's guiding hand after our mom died. They taught her to be honorable, courageous and loving.

"She was raised in this town where folks aren't just people who interact, but friends and neighbors." He let his gaze wander over everyone in the room. "So all of you are in some way, a good way, responsible for the amazing woman she is. I propose a toast to my sister, Kim, her new husband, Luke, God help him, my father and all of you who are the heart and soul of Blackwater Lake, where folks bring out the best in each other."

April listened to cheers and clapping as she looked at Will. He was relaxed and completely at home. Happy. Whether he realized it or not, he fit in here and his speech could reflect his subconscious desire to make a life in a place where folks brought out the best in each other. Was it possible he could be content in this small town instead of the big city? Content with her?

Against April's better judgment, hope sparked to life inside her. With luck it wouldn't bite her in the butt.

Chapter Thirteen

Will knocked on April's sliding glass door with an elbow since his hands were full of flowers and wine. The sound wasn't loud, but she was in the kitchen and answered immediately.

"Hi." When she noticed the bouquet, there was a pleased, sort of soft expression in her eyes, the one he'd been hoping to see. "For me?"

"I think I made it clear at the wedding how I feel about carrying flowers. So they're definitely not for me." He handed over the cellophane-wrapped blooms.

"I love daisies. Baby's breath, and all the red and purple stuff in here I don't know the names of." She buried her nose in the blooms and sighed. "They're beautiful. Thank you, Will."

"You're welcome." When she tilted her face up he kissed her mouth softly.

"Come on in." She stepped back and let him by but

there was a puzzled expression on her face. "*Why* did you bring me flowers?"

"Because the bouquet Kim gave you is looking kind of—"

"Sad?" she finished for him.

"Yeah."

"Well, that's very sweet of you. Don't let the bad guys in Chicago know about this," she teased. "You'll lose tough-guy points in a big way."

"I'll take that risk." The happy look in her eyes was worth it.

He looked forward to seeing her every day after work and today was no exception. The wedding had been a couple of days ago, so the chaos was over and so was his excuse for coming to see her. The only one he had was that he wanted to.

"So why are you here?" she asked.

Will was beginning to wonder if she could read his mind. He was here because he liked her. She was beautiful, honest and never failed to call him on his crap. That was important and he wasn't even sure why. But she continued to look at him, waiting for an answer.

"I'm here hoping you'll take pity on me and feed me. Dad and Tim went out because there's no food in the house. Apparently Kim didn't shop the week before the wedding. Mani, pedi and hair appointments were more important than basic survival rations."

April stared at him. "Is that pouting? I think you're pouting."

"It's your imagination."

He stared right back at her and figured he got the better end of the deal. She was wearing khaki shorts and a spa-ghetti-strapped olive-green knit top that brought out the green in her eyes. Her sun-kissed brown hair was loose around her face and fell past her shoulders. God knew why he thought so, but her bare feet were so damn sexy. Probably should see a shrink about that because the feeling had nothing to do with sex. Okay, maybe a little. But mostly he got a sensation in his gut that drew him to her in a primitive, profound way.

"I don't believe you," she said, calling him on his crap. "The thing is, Kim is married now. She's going to live in her husband's house. Buy groceries for him. Someone across the alley is going to have to do the grocery shopping while she's on her honeymoon and Tim is too young. Not only does he not have a driver's license, which makes getting the stuff home a problem. But if he was turned loose, your dad would be on a steady diet of chips and Twinkies. Maybe an occasional candy bar with nuts in it just to get some protein. That's not the kind of food plan his doctor put him on."

"Dad's a big boy. He can shop."

"So can you." There was a sassy look in her eyes just for a second, then it disappeared.

Will knew the exact moment when she remembered he was leaving in about a week. He hated seeing the sunshine fade from her eyes. The thought of leaving her for good bothered him even more.

"You're right," he said. "I can shop."

She nodded and busied herself unwrapping the green cellophane from the flowers. Then she walked over to the cupboard. "I need a vase."

There was one on the top shelf, which she couldn't reach without a step stool. It was the place you put things not often used. Pretty soon what simmered between the two of them would be a top-shelf thing and it seemed like a colossal waste.

He moved behind her, close enough to feel the heat from her body without touching her. "I'll get that down for you."

"Thanks."

It was easy for him to reach up and carefully grab the crystal. "Here you go."

She took it from him and looked at the glass, a wistful, sad expression in her eyes. "This was my mother's."

"It's beautiful."

"I love it. Buying this was a splurge for her because there wasn't a lot of money for something that wasn't a necessity." April arranged the long stems in the vase and added water from the tap. "You know she always blamed herself for our splitting up."

"Why?"

"Because she got sick. I just couldn't go with you to Chicago."

"It wasn't her fault."

She nodded. "I could never quite convince her of that, though. Over and over I told her she was my mom. I couldn't be happy with you if I left her to face being sick alone. Someone had to help her fight the cancer."

"I know." That love and loyalty was one of the qualities he most admired in her. And if he'd waited…

This time with her in Blackwater Lake had been a do-over, a flash of what might have been. He'd screwed things up with her royally in the past, but she'd forgiven him. And these weeks of their fling were some of the happiest he could remember. In so many ways he felt like a new man.

She picked up the vase of flowers and put them on the kitchen table, which was already set for two. Meeting his gaze, she smiled. "It would please her to know I'm using the vase she loved enough to blow her budget on. Thanks again for bringing these, Will."

"You're welcome again." He pointed to the place settings on the table. "I see you were expecting me."

"Yeah. You've kind of gotten to be a habit." She shrugged.

"What are we having for dinner?" He sniffed. "Something smells really good."

"Oven-fried chicken, green salad, fruit." Her eyes sparkled. "And I stopped at Harvest Café and picked up two slices of strawberry cheesecake from their bakery case for dessert."

His empty stomach growled, but his heart was full. Part regret, part reluctance to leave her. When he'd agreed to her plan and a summer fling, it had felt like there was all the time in the world, but now it was nearly up.

A timer went off and she grabbed the potholder on a hook beside the microwave. After opening the bottom oven, she pulled out a cookie sheet filled with golden brown, sizzling chicken and placed it on the countertop to cool with a wire rack beneath.

"That looks as good as it smells. Better," he said.

She smiled. "I'll put everything on the table and we can eat."

"I'll open the wine. Apparently I'm channeling your culinary selections because it's a Chardonnay."

"Yum."

They worked together and in a few minutes took their usual seats at the table.

April moved the tall flowers aside. "I can't see you."

"Maybe that's not such a bad thing."

"I disagree." Her voice was quiet but the expression in her eyes said what she didn't put into words. She would miss him, too.

Will remembered what his dad had said about wanting to retire, but he couldn't or wouldn't unless Will took over the responsibilities of the job. But that wasn't the path he'd chosen for himself. No matter how much personal satisfaction he'd felt at making a difference here in Blackwater Lake, coming back meant failure to achieve a goal he'd worked very hard for. As long as he could remember, he'd wanted to be a Chicago PD detective. He'd had stars in his eyes about the job then, but after working it awhile, frustration set in that he couldn't catch the bad guys or get justice every time. Still…

He'd already failed at marriage. Failing in his career, too, made him a two-time loser. How was that anything to be proud of?

He poured some of her homemade oil-and-vinegar dressing on his salad, then mixed it in. Before he could stop himself, the words came out of his mouth. "Are you happy here in Blackwater Lake?"

Her fork stopped halfway to her mouth and her gaze lifted to his. "Why?"

"Just curious. I guess it was talking about your mom and staying here that triggered it." The thought had popped into his mind that she might have regrets about the path not taken. "I just…wondered."

She chewed a bite of salad, a thoughtful expression on her face. "My business is thriving and I really like what I do. People here are the best. If you need them, one phone call brings the posse. No questions asked. Family values are important to everyone. I love it here. There's nowhere else I'd rather be. I can't imagine living anywhere else."

He hadn't even realized he'd been holding his breath for a different answer until his bubble of expectation burst. "I'm glad for you."

She met his gaze. "I know you, Will. It surprises me sometimes how well I still do. I can tell by your expression that what I just told you isn't exactly what you wanted to hear."

"No, it wasn't." He'd been on the edge of asking her to go with him to Chicago. Again. Fortunately he kept those words to himself.

"You deserve all the best in life," he said, meaning that sincerely. "I'm happy that you have everything you want."

At least one of them did. She got under his skin and became a habit in the very best way possible.

But she was happy here and he couldn't ask her to leave.

He was going to have to break himself of her and it wasn't going to be easy.

"April, you're too good at this photography stuff," Lucy Bishop said. "I can't make up my mind between sunset over the lake or twilight on the mountain."

April smiled at her friend's praise. Business was slow at the Harvest Café this time of day and she'd dropped in to browse. "So when is your condo up on the mountain going to be ready for move-in?"

"They're starting to frame the building soon, so I'm being told six to nine months."

"But you're shopping now?"

"It makes me feel as if I'm making progress. Because, frankly, waiting for the first home I've ever purchased to be ready to move in to isn't going well."

"Patience is a virtue," April reminded her.

"Apparently not one that I have in abundance."

"At least you have a house to rent in the meantime. That's not easy to find."

"Yeah," Lucy said. "If Olivia Lawson hadn't fallen in love with Brady O'Keefe and moved in with him, I'd be homeless."

"Wow, Burke and Sloan Holden were onto something

when they decided to develop the land at the base of the mountain."

"I hear presales are through the roof," Lucy answered with a grin. "No pun intended."

April laughed. "Right."

After studying all the pictures again, she said, "I love this one with the sun just going down and the light painting the clouds pink, purple and gold."

"Shouldn't you wait to buy anything until you have a color scheme, not to mention a wall to hang it on?"

"Oh, I've chosen colors. Olive green, plum and rose."

"Sounds very feminine."

"What can I say? I enjoy being a girl. And I've been told that wall hangings don't need to fit in with the other colors of a room but should be something you love." She tapped her lip and gave the picture one more long, appraising look. "I'll take the sunset. It speaks to my soul."

"Thank you, Lucy. No one has ever paid me a nicer compliment." April gave her a hug. "Now it feels wrong to take your money."

"Oh, please—" Lucy waved her hand dismissively. "If I gave food away for free every time someone told me my meatloaf was a religious experience, Maggie and I would go broke. Then where would we be?"

"Well, she'd still be with Sloan Holden, but you wouldn't be able to pay your rent to Olivia," April said.

"Like I told you. Homeless," her friend agreed. "So, let that be a warning, missy. Don't give your work away."

"Roger that." April removed the picture from the wall and folded Bubble Wrap protectively around it. Then she rang up the sale and ran the credit card Lucy handed her. "So, what's new besides the condo?"

"That's code for am I dating anyone."

April laughed. "Are you?"

"No. And that's fine with me."

Come to think of it her friend hadn't been linked to any guy in Blackwater Lake since she'd arrived a few years ago. "I hear that writer comes into the café a lot."

"Jack Garner." Lucy looked thoughtful. "I wouldn't say a lot, but he comes in. Kind of keeps to himself. I respect that."

"You haven't flirted with him?" It was hard to believe this beautiful blue-eyed strawberry blonde was unattached.

"I flirt with everyone. It's called customer service. But he's a brooder. Good-looking, but trouble." Lucy's eyes narrowed. "Look at you peppering me with questions to distract me from asking what's up with you and Will Fletcher."

"I sincerely want to know what's going on with you." But April knew her protest was pointless since she'd been busted.

"And now you do." Her gaze turned curious. "So, you and Will. Details, my friend."

"*Friend* being the operative word… That's what Will and I are. Just friends. And when summer is over he's going back to Chicago to resume his detective job."

"The rumor is you two are really close. Are you getting serious?"

"No."

But last night April had gotten the feeling that he was thinking about asking her to go with him when he left. His question about whether or not she was happy in Blackwater Lake seemed more than idle chitchat. Talk about conflicted. To know that he felt more for her than casual friendship or a convenient hookup would have her doing the dance of joy. But if he'd actually asked her to go with him… Impossible choice.

When they were barely out of their teens, the decision had been easy. More than anything she'd wanted to be with Will. Now there was a whole lot more to consider. She had roots—a business, house and friends.

"But you're going to visit him in Chicago?" Lucy asked.

"I'm not planning to." She would never again risk finding him with a woman who was naked under his shirt. "Will and I have a past. A lot happened before you came to Blackwater Lake."

"I've heard."

Of course she had. "We tried the long-distance thing before and it didn't work out."

"Too bad." Lucy tsked. "You two are so cute together."

"We get that a lot."

They were a whole lot more than just cute together and she knew it by the way her heart squeezed painfully at the thought of him not being across the street at the sheriff's office. He spoke to her soul, April thought, and he had since she was sixteen years old. Soon they would have a public breakup and that would be that. This time she wasn't supposed to get hurt, but more and more that looked unlikely.

Lucy glanced at her watch, then picked up her purchase. "I have to get back to the café and supervise. The dinner rush starts about six and I've got an hour to get ready for it."

"Okay. Good to see you. Enjoy the picture."

"I plan to leave it wrapped. When I finally move, it will be like a surprise." Lucy waved on her way out the door.

April walked over to her big window that looked out on Main Street and the sheriff's office across the way. In a few more days Will would be gone and she would lose him for the second time. Technically she'd only had him once since this was simply a summer fling. Except tell that to her heart; this felt like more than a superficial flirtation.

She was restless, and business always dropped off around now because people were thinking about dinner. It couldn't hurt to close the shop a little early, so she put up the sign and locked the door. After looking both ways to make sure no cars were coming, she walked across the street and into the sheriff's office. Might not be the smartest thing she'd ever done, but soon she wouldn't be able to walk over and see him.

"Hey, April." Clarice's desk was a few feet inside the door. "Hope you're not here on business."

"No. Just wanted to stop in and say hi."

"Will's on the phone." Clarice obviously assumed, correctly, that he was the one she wanted to say hi to.

The door to his office was open and April could hear him talking and see him behind his desk. "How are you?" she said to the dispatcher.

"Great. Looking forward to end of summer and a little quiet time before tourists come in for ski season."

"Yeah."

"Been nice having Will here. When Hank got sick, I didn't know what we were going to do but Will sure stepped up."

"Yeah. It has been nice." She was going to miss him coming to her back door with pizza and wine. And nights without him in her bed were going to be lonely. Heck, just looking from her shop to the sheriff's office and knowing he wasn't here would be sad.

Then Will came out of his office and smiled when he saw her. He walked over and kissed her lightly on the lips. "This is a nice surprise."

"Glad you think so." She knew his behavior was part of the plan and when she was the one to give him the heave-ho, no one would pity her. Still, she felt the familiar flutter in her stomach that being around him always produced. "How's your day?"

"Let's just say the kids are ready for school to be back in."

"Bored?"

"Big time," he answered. "But I have to admit I'm a little on edge. Dad has his checkup with the doctor today for medical clearance to come back to work."

"Oh, Sheriff," Clarice said. "That reminds me. Buck Healy and Fred Turner are squabbling. Buck is coming in to fill out a formal complaint. But Eddie is out on patrol. Do you want me to dispatch him out there and save some paperwork?"

Will shook his head. "This needs a delicate touch. Those two have been bickering for years. If there was a God in heaven, they wouldn't share a property line, but they do. Somebody's cow, horse or goat probably ate someone's garden, grass or tractor. I'll go out and talk to them myself. It's easier if you know the history."

He sure did, April thought. The two feuding neighbors would listen to him because he was one of them, not an outsider. And, unlike Eddie, he was intimidating.

"Come on back to the office," he said to her.

"Don't you have to go and see Buck and Fred?"

"They'll keep for a few minutes."

"Okay." Her tummy did a happy little shimmy that he put off something for her.

She followed him into his office and he closed the door, then backed her against it. He pressed his body to hers. "I'm really, really glad you came in."

"Me, too." Her voice was a wanton whisper.

He lowered his head and touched his mouth to hers again, but this move was full of passion and promise, not meant for anyone else to see. His hands were braced on either side of her head and with his tongue he traced her mouth, urging it open. Her lips parted and he entered, sweeping inside with a groan. Their harsh breathing filled the office until another sound bled through it.

He pulled back, his eyes full of annoyance at the interruption. "Please tell me that's not my cell."

"Can't." She swallowed hard, not able to say much of anything at all.

"Damn." Reluctantly he moved away and walked over to his desk where his cell phone sat on a stack of files. He looked at the caller ID and there was an apologetic expression on his face. "I have to take this."

"No problem."

He hit a button and put the device to his ear. "Hey, Crash, how the heck are you?" After listening he said, "Sorry to hear things are falling apart without me."

Obviously the person on the other end was his detective partner from Chicago. It had been easy to pretend that life didn't exist for him until now, but this reminder tightened a knot in her stomach.

April drew in a deep breath and with a gesture asked if he wanted her to step out while he talked. Will shook his head and leaned a hip on the corner of his desk. She sat in one of the chairs in front of it.

"Things here?" Will asked. "This is a sleepy little town where littering the sidewalk is major crime."

That was just the way April liked it, but he sounded bored. Work in Chicago no doubt was more exciting than spiteful, decidedly *un*neighborly neighbors. But excitement wasn't all it was cracked up to be. Some things were more important. Except she knew him pretty well and he'd always craved excitement. Same old, same old day after day didn't thrill him.

"Hang in there, my friend." Will grinned at whatever his partner said. "Don't worry. It's not that much longer until I'll be back to bail you out. Just a couple more days." He listened and nodded. "Yeah, after Labor Day."

And from the tone in his voice it sounded as if that couldn't be a moment too soon for him. Obviously he couldn't wait to return to his job. It was also obvious by the pain in April's heart that she'd hoped he wanted to be with her enough to stay.

She'd fallen in love with him again. Or, more precisely, she'd never fallen out of love. He'd asked her the night before if she was happy here in Blackwater Lake. She'd said she had everything right here.

But that wasn't exactly true.

She didn't have everything she wanted because she couldn't have Will.

Chapter Fourteen

April paced her kitchen, waiting for news on Hank. He'd seen the doctor that day to determine whether or not he could return to work. And here was another classic conflict. She sincerely hoped the man got a clean bill of health and could go back to doing whatever he wanted to do—being sheriff or running a marathon. Although that would be a miracle since, to her knowledge, he'd never run one before. She loved him like a father and wished him all the best.

On the other hand it would also give Will the green light to leave town. Not that he could stick around indefinitely, but a little longer would be nice. He wouldn't stay for her, but he might for his dad.

She'd been home from work for a while now and if someone didn't tell her something soon…

Just then there was a knock on the sliding glass door and she saw Will standing there. Thank God.

After hurrying over she unlocked and opened it. "What's the verdict? How is he?"

"The doc said he's doing great. He's in arguably the best shape of his life. Returning to work is not a problem." There was an odd look on Will's face.

"What's wrong?"

"Nothing." He forced a smile. "It's great news."

"It certainly is." She forced cheerfulness into her voice and felt as slimy as polluted water for not feeling 100 percent happy. "He gave us quite a scare and it's wonderful how he completely turned everything around."

"Yet another way my father leads by example."

"Your father is a truly amazing man who is admired by all. I'm so lucky to live across the alley from him."

Or unlucky, one could argue.

If she'd never met Will, her heart might not have been broken even once, let alone twice by the same man. Someday she might embrace the sentiment that it was better to have loved and lost than to never have loved at all. But today was not that day.

"He's a good neighbor," Will agreed.

"He's a good man," she said again, mostly because she didn't want to say anything about their next step.

"Yeah." He dragged his fingers through his hair. "If we keep this up, he should qualify for sainthood pretty soon."

"I guess." What they were doing was called procrastination, putting off what they really needed to talk about. And that was just fine with her. "He must be looking forward to getting back to work."

"I suppose."

"He hasn't said?" That surprised her and actually wasn't really an answer. She got the feeling there was something he wasn't telling her. "Well, I'm sure folks will be glad to have him back. Not that you aren't doing a great job, Will. I didn't mean to imply you weren't. It's just that everyone wants normal, whatever that is. And normal is him wearing the badge. And for you to…not." She shrugged. "I'm babbling."

"Really?" His smile didn't quite make it to his eyes. "I didn't notice."

"Some detective you are," she said wryly.

She could banter with him all night and maybe that would squash the pain that was scratching to get out. From experience she knew how bad it would be when that happened.

Unfortunately when she said the word *detective*, that burst the protective bubble they were both working to keep inflated. Regret settled in his eyes and there was tension in his jaw. The Band-Aid was getting ripped off, ready or not.

"April…"

She turned away. "All joking aside, Will, this really is good news. It's also your cue to go back to Chicago."

"Yeah, it is."

"Your partner will be glad to have you back." She took a deep breath and faced him again. "I couldn't help overhearing your end of the conversation earlier in your office."

"So you *were* eavesdropping."

"You told me to stay." She shrugged.

"I know. And, yeah, Pete seemed ready to have me back."

"You must be beyond ready to go back," she said, sort of hoping he would say she was wrong about that.

"Like you said. Normal. Chicago is that for me." He was wearing his law-enforcement face, the one that didn't let on what was going through his mind. The one he'd probably perfected during criminal interrogations.

"Normal is good. I'm a strong advocate of normal."

"It's time to implement the final part of the plan," he gently reminded her.

If everything had gone according to the plan Kim had

suggested, April wouldn't feel like this. Her job was to get him to fall in love with her, then publicly dump him. It wasn't part of her agenda to be the only one falling in love. So, when had things gone so horribly wrong?

Okay, she told herself, grow a spine. The endgame was to put herself back in the driver's seat and not be pitied because Will Fletcher got away again. Growing a spine started here and now.

She met his gaze and put as much spunk into hers as possible. "So, before we take the end of this fling public, I have to ask. You didn't fall for me at all?"

He looked away for a moment, then said, "That isn't the way you pitched me the plan."

Something told her that was all the answer she was going to get. "Any idea how to pull off the final scene of our charade?"

"Actually, I do." He folded his arms over his chest.

Maybe it was hope on her part, but she thought that pose might be to keep from touching her because he didn't trust himself to do that and no more. Maybe she was a little irresistible to him. Without a doubt she knew if he put his hands on her she'd be lost.

"So, you have thoughts. Care to share?"

"There's a spur-of-the-moment celebration of Dad's good news and it will be at the Grizzly Bear Diner."

"I wonder if his heart doctor would approve of him having a hamburger," she mused.

"I believe he's a salad convert even though my sister isn't around to be the food police. She's still on her honeymoon," he added.

"Right. So when is this get-together taking place?" she asked.

"Now. The mayor will be there. The town council. All

the Blackwater Lake movers and shakers. Word is spreading and I'm sure there will be a lot of people."

"In other words it will be gossip central."

"Right." His eyes went blank, grew darker. His cop face. "It should get the job done. I'm thinking it will work better if we walk in together and break the news."

"Okay."

"You say whatever you want to. Although I'd appreciate it if you didn't make me out to be too big a jerk."

She smiled and did her best to keep sadness out of it. "We've already established that I'm not a good liar, so staying close to the truth is best. And the truth is you're not a jerk."

"Thanks for that." He nodded resolutely. "I'll just follow your lead."

"Okay, then."

He moved close and curved his fingers around her upper arms then hesitated before kissing her forehead. "Let's do this."

Let's not, she thought, although it was obvious he'd just said goodbye.

Thirty minutes later they walked into the Grizzly Bear Diner, which was filled to overflowing. The crowd was probably beyond capacity, but no one seemed inclined to enforce any ordinances on an occasion like this.

People parted for them as they made their way to a booth in the center of the establishment where Tim sat with a friend while his grandfather stood and shook hands. Hank was generally soaking up congratulations and good wishes.

April really hated to rain on his parade, but this venue was better than the Labor Day parade to get the word out. Everyone was under one roof and this news would spread like the flu virus. She just needed an opening, then would make it as quick and painless as possible.

Hank grinned when he saw them and opened his arms to hug her. "Glad you two finally showed up."

"Sorry." She stepped away from him and rubbed the side of her nose. "Will and I had some things to discuss."

The older man frowned. "What's wrong?"

And there was her opening. "First I want to say how happy I am that you have medical clearance to return to work."

A cheer erupted around her proving that not only did her words carry, but people were listening. She wondered if there would be any sound to hear when her heart cracked.

When everyone quieted down, Hank said, "What else do you have on your mind? Something's bothering you, April."

All of a sudden she got cold feet. This was his party, a celebration of his hard work to get back up and running. This grand gesture was all about her, so she should be the one to decide whether or not to do it. "It's okay. I'll tell you later."

Hank shook his head. "Maybe I can help. You'll feel better if you get it off your chest."

Usually when she unburdened herself to this man she did feel better, but that wasn't going to happen with this news. "It can wait."

"No. The doctor says I need to keep stress to a minimum. And now you've got me worried. So spill it."

Oh, brother, she'd really stepped in it and had no choice. *Quick and simple*, she told herself. "The thing is, I called it quits with Will tonight."

Hank studied her as a whisper started through the crowd. "I see. Why is that?"

"He's not the right man for me." Keep it simple like he'd

said, she thought. Make it all about her and don't embellish. "We had fun this summer, but that's all it would ever be with us. I want more. And he doesn't define 'more' the same way I do."

The father looked at his son and there was no mistaking the disappointment in his eyes. "That true, Will?"

"Yes. She's a remarkable woman and deserves a man who can make her happy. Someone who won't hurt her."

"I'm the one walking away." She raised her voice, making it determined, definite. No one should doubt that she was in control even though it didn't feel that way. "It's what I want and that makes it best for both of us."

It was quiet enough to hear a pin drop, which was unusual for the diner, then everyone around them started whispering.

Hank was silent for a moment before reluctantly nodding. He cupped her cheek in a big hand. "I guess you know best, honey."

"Thanks for understanding," she said. Wow, she'd never anticipated the effort it would take not to cry. But tears would dilute the effect of what she was trying to accomplish.

At least fate was on her side a little bit because at that moment one of the servers brought a pitcher of beer and some glasses. "Chicken wings and nachos are coming. And a salad for you, Sheriff," he said.

April gave Will one last look and nodded him a thank-you as she backed away. Right now she was numb to the murmurs of sympathy directed at her as she slowly moved toward the diner's exit. She tried to be proud of herself, but this didn't feel at all like the win Kim had promised when hatching this plan.

Lucy Bishop was standing in the waiting area by the front door. "April, I just heard."

"What?" Could news of the breakup really have spread that fast?

"You dumped Will Fletcher." Sympathy welled up in her eyes. "I'm sorry things didn't work out for you two."

News *had* traveled that fast. "I didn't want to give him false hope."

"You're really strong. And wise."

April waited to feel some satisfaction but there wasn't any to be had what with her heart breaking. The only win was that in Blackwater Lake she would no longer be that poor girl Will Fletcher left behind.

April took the fresh batch of her healthy whole-wheat macaroni and low-fat cheese out of the oven and set it on a warming tray. Cooking was her desperate attempt to fill the void Will had left in her life when he went back to Chicago a week ago. So far cooking wasn't helping all that much. And she wasn't eating much of it. Mostly the food was going across the alley to Hank Fletcher. Hence the health-conscious alterations.

He was lonely, too.

Will had only been back in her life for the summer, but she missed him terribly and felt more alone than she ever had in her life. But her neighbor had seen his daughter married, then stood by while she and her son moved out of his house and in with her husband, where they would start their new life as a family. Hank had supported April through so many changes, good and bad, so she planned to return the favor. This time they could help each other.

She got out her casserole carrier and food warmer, then slid the dish inside before letting herself out the kitchen's sliding glass door. It was hard not to picture Will here, not to remember the first time he'd stood there looking completely adorable holding a pizza box and bottle of wine.

Hard to forget every moment with him after that night. There were memories everywhere she turned and each one was like a blow to her soul.

Tears filled her eyes as she walked across the alley to Hank's house. Lights were on inside that indicated he was home from work so she knocked.

The door opened and Hank stood there in suit pants, a white dress shirt and snappy red tie. "Hi, kiddo."

Looking past him she saw a matching suit jacket slung over one of the kitchen chairs. "Are you going out?"

"I'm taking Josie to Fireside for dinner," he explained. "I wanted to thank her for being there for Kim when I went to the hospital."

"Is it more than a thank-you?"

"Maybe." He opened the door wider. "Come on in."

She hesitated. "I don't want to make you late."

"Don't worry about it." He indicated the dish in her hands. "I guess that's for me."

"Yeah. But obviously you don't need it."

"If it's good warmed up, I need it," he said.

"All right, then." She handed it over and walked inside.

"Thanks, honey." He took the dish, then frowned at her when their gazes met. "What's wrong?"

"Nothing. I'm fine."

"The hell you are." He set the macaroni and cheese on the island, then took her elbow and guided her to the kitchen table where he sat her in a chair. "You're going to tell me all about what's bothering you."

"But you have a d-date." Then the sobs started and she felt horrible because she was really happy for him. Dating was a good thing.

He pulled one of the other chairs closer and sat in front of her. "It can wait. But you need to talk to me, April. I can see how unhappy you are. Hell, you've been unhappy since that night at the diner. You said breaking up with Will would be the best thing, but I'm not seeing it."

She drew in a shuddering breath and brushed tears from her cheeks. "Gosh, and here I thought I'd been hiding it pretty well."

"You don't have to do that with me, honey." There was sympathy in his eyes. Will's eyes. "And it's pointless to try. I can see through you. Always could."

"Good to know." She sniffled.

"This is about Will." It wasn't a question.

"Since I can't hide anything from you… Yeah," she admitted. "This is about Will. I really miss him."

"Me, too."

"This is so stupid. *I'm* so stupid." She shook her head. "Here I am feeling sorry for myself when you've suddenly got an empty nest."

She looked at him, really looked. He was still a handsome man who had the passage of time stamped on his face and silver in his hair. This is what his son would look like, but she wouldn't be there beside Will to share the good and bad things that left a mark on a life. The realization made her deeply and profoundly sad.

"Look, April, I love my family. You know that. But—" He stopped and listened for a few moments. "Do you hear that?"

"No. What?"

"It's called quiet. That's the absence of noise. And there's something else."

April glanced around the kitchen and tried to figure out what he meant. But she had no idea what he was talking about. "I don't feel anything."

"The energy level is as it should be."

"I don't understand."

"Because you're young." He sighed. "It's like this. A

man of my age likes his peace and quiet. Some would call it boring. I prefer to think of it as tranquility."

"Okay," she said hesitantly.

"Do I miss them?" He shrugged. "I would if they moved halfway around the world, but right now not so much. If I need a dose of chaos, I can pick up the phone and see if it's okay to drop by their house. Then I come back here to chill out."

"Or go out. With Josie," she teased.

"That, too." He grinned. "Don't get me wrong. I wouldn't trade the experience of having my daughter here and getting to know my grandson so well. I would do anything for them. But I'm fine being by myself."

"I'm glad."

"But you're not. Fine, I mean." He took her hand in his big warm ones. "Just so you know, I'm aware of the little scheme Kim came up with to get you and Will together."

"How?"

"Not much happens in this town that I don't know about. I heard things and put two and two together. Then she confessed everything when she got back from the honeymoon and heard he left town."

His words finally sank in. "Wait, she was pushing Will and me together? She claimed it was about closure for me. So I could move on." And it all worked out so well, she thought.

"Yeah, that was her cover story. But she was match-making. You and Will are pretty stubborn—"

"Will might be." After all they'd been to each other he still left. "But not me," she protested.

"Right." He smiled and apparently decided not to argue that point. "Anyway, she felt strongly that if you two gave it another chance, you'd see that you belong together. That's why she talked you into making him fall for you. It meant you'd have to spend time with him and rekindle what you had before. But she didn't expect that you would actually dump him."

"If you suspected, why didn't you tip Will off to what was going on?" Although she remembered when she confessed the ruse, Will had said he suspected something was up. Like father, like son.

"I thought this whole conspiracy had a decent shot at succeeding," Hank admitted. "And I wouldn't mind you and Will together. I'd have liked that very much."

"Me, too." Unexpectedly she smiled. "But your approval means a lot to me. Even if there's no Will and me to approve of."

"Of course I approve. You're a very special woman. Not like that one he married. I never liked her."

"Neither did Kim." She would have to conclude that was a family thing.

"I know." Hank looked down for a moment, then met her gaze. "My kids think I'm not observant, but they'd be wrong. I just pick and choose what I say and when I say it."

"Probably smart."

"I'm a cop and have been for a lot of years. Details are important and I don't miss them."

"I've always suspected that about you," she said.

He gave her a small smile. "I'm not blowing my own horn here, just stating facts. And I have a point."

"Which is?"

"From the time you turned sixteen years old I've seen the way my son looks at you, April. He's loved you since then and I don't think he's ever stopped."

"Then why did he go—?" Her voice cracked and she caught her bottom lip between her teeth.

"Some misguided sense of honor. The boy knows I want to retire and that the job is his if he wants it."

"I wasn't aware. Will never told me the sheriff's job could be his."

"I've always taught him and his sister to finish what they start. The lesson took real well with him. He's got this thing in his head that leaving Chicago is something to be ashamed of on top of his marriage not working out."

"I see. Then it's really up to him, isn't it?" She nodded sadly. "Thanks for telling me this, Hank."

"I thought you should know." He stood up and folded his arms over his chest. "You're like a daughter to me and I want the best for you."

"That really means a lot."

"And this has to be said. Will is my son. I love him and mostly I'm proud of him." He shook his head in exasperation. "But when it comes to romantic relationships he's not the sharpest knife in the drawer."

"He loves his career and I love mine. We just aren't meant to be." She smiled sadly. "I guess we are both stubborn. Neither of us would bend."

"He just can't see what's in front of him, what's good for him," Hank said. "And it's not easy for a father to watch and not say anything, to let him figure it out for himself. Sometimes you have to walk around with duct tape over your mouth. Metaphorically speaking."

"Well, you're a wise man, Hank Fletcher. And I'm glad that you know I didn't really mean it when I said he's not the man for me. The thing is, he never asked me to go with him…" She lifted her shoulders in a shrug. "On the bright side, at least no one in town pities me this time."

"I didn't pity you last time," Hank said. "It's Will I feel sorry for. I think that job in Chicago is sucking the life out of him and there's nothing I can do. I was hoping you could talk him out of going back."

"I didn't try. If I had, he would only resent me and that

would ultimately destroy us. He had to want to be with me enough and—" she shrugged "—he didn't."

"I know it. Don't like it," he added, "but I know it's true."

April stood and hugged him. "Thank you for listening to me whine."

"Didn't sound like complaining to me, but anytime you need to talk, I'm here for you, honey." He gave her a good squeeze, then stepped back. "You're not alone, you know that. I'm always here for you. You might not be family by blood, but you are by choice and heart. Sometimes that bond is even stronger."

Tears gathered in her eyes again, but this time she smiled. "I'm so lucky to have you."

"I'm the lucky one."

"It's possible you'll get even luckier tonight," she teased. "Say hi to Josie for me."

"Will do."

April left and walked across the dark alley, letting the tears roll down her cheeks unchecked. There was no one to see now. No one to put on a front for. The good news was that she hadn't lost the family who'd taken her under its wing so many years ago.

The bad news was that she was finding out that losing Will for the second time was twice as painful.

Chapter Fifteen

Will looked around the Chicago squad room of the Twelfth Precinct. There were rows of desks with phones, files and computers. The walls had multiple bulletin boards with wanted posters and notices. Activity and excitement hummed in the air. He waited to feel excited about being back, but there was nothing. Since he'd returned a couple weeks ago, he figured the feeling probably wasn't going to happen. There were no windows and even if he could look out one, he would see brick buildings and dingy storefronts in this area of the city. No mountains and clear, blue sky.

Everyone had greeted him with assurances that he'd been missed and there were case files stacked up on his desk to prove it. If all went well, one of them would be closing in a little while.

He'd received an anonymous tip about a drug deal going down and it had turned out to be reliable. He and Pete had made three arrests and the perps were cooling their heels in holding. That would soften them up for interrogation.

During the takedown a crowd had gathered. That always happened, but this time there was something different. As he was cuffing a kid only a little older than his nephew, there'd been a woman in his peripheral vision. His heart had jolted as if he'd been smacked in the chest. For a split second he'd thought she was April. And in that second his emotions ran the gamut from pure exhilaration that she'd changed her mind and followed him to fear for her safety in a fluid and dangerous situation.

His concentration slipped and the kid obviously felt it because he'd twisted away and run. Will chased him and easily brought the kid down. In a slimy puddle. His jeans and T-shirt were never going to be the same. Even worse, the woman wasn't April.

"Welcome back to the Twelfth," he muttered to himself.

Pete Karlik walked over and sat at his desk that faced Will's. "They just brought the drug seller up from holding. He's in interrogation room one."

"Okay."

Pete's sharp blue eyes narrowed. "Something bugging you?"

"Nope."

His partner was thirty-five years old, smart and built like a bull. He'd been married to his high school sweetheart for fourteen years and they had two kids—a boy who was thirteen and a ten-year-old girl. As far as anyone here at the precinct knew the guy had never cheated on his wife. Chicago born and bred, Pete was a good cop who loved his city and would do anything to keep it safe. Dedication like that was something special, something reserved for a hometown boy.

After studying Will for several moments, he nodded. "So, how do you want to handle this? We both know this kid is a low-level flunky. He's expendable to them but could give us information, names, to bring down the organization. Or at least put cracks in it. If we can get him to crack."

"Good cop, bad cop?" Will suggested. He'd played both roles and so had Pete.

The other man looked doubtful. "He's young, but I'd bet the farm he doesn't scare easy. He's hanging out with some really bad guys."

"Okay. You don't think we can rattle him." Will thought for a moment. "We can lay out his options. Reality check."

"Maybe." His partner mulled that over. "If we can imply that the other two scumbags are rolling on him, it could give us leverage to make him see the light."

Will nodded. "Only one of them gets a deal and that would be the first one who talks."

"Okay. Let's work it that way." Pete pushed his desk chair back to stand up when his phone rang. "Karlik." He listened and the frown on his face said there wasn't going to be meaningful information forthcoming from the perp. "Okay, Sarge. Thanks. You just saved us a trip up there."

After his friend disconnected from the call Will said, "He lawyered up."

"Yeah." Pete's expression grew darker. "You're good, Fletcher. Keep it up and you might just make detective someday."

"You're a funny guy." But this situation wasn't the least bit funny. "So much for taking down the big boys."

"Sometimes I wonder why we bother." Pete pounded a fist on his desk. "Do you ever feel like you're one step behind the bad guys?"

Will folded his arms over his chest. "Try five steps."

"And we'll never catch up."

He'd never heard his friend so pessimistic. "Since when did you turn into a glass-half-empty kind of guy?"

"Mine's not half-empty," Pete said. "I don't even have a glass."

This wasn't like the "Crash" Karlik Will knew. He suspected whatever was causing it was bigger than the job. "What's bugging *you*, pard?"

"It's Ryan." The man rubbed a hand over his face. "He was at a party that was raided by the cops. They found drugs. A lot. Regular pharmacies should be so well stocked. Street stuff there, too. The guys who answered the call knew me and gave me a heads-up. Abbie and I decided to let them bring him into the precinct and scare the crap out of him."

"Geez, man." Will's closest experience to having kids was his nephew. They'd had a very short discussion about girls and birth control. He felt guilty for not being more a part of the boy's life. But if Tim had been arrested at a party where illegal substances were found, he'd probably freak. And there was one question he'd ask. "Did Ryan use?"

Pete met his gaze, worry stark in his own. "He swears he didn't. His mother and I tend to believe him. Yeah, I know all parents say this, but he's a good kid."

"Of course he is. You and Abbie raised him."

"I don't want to stick my head in the sand either. If he's got a problem we need to know so we can help him."

"Yeah."

Will thought about the teens he'd busted in Blackwater Lake for spray painting structures and egging cars. Neither of them had asked for a lawyer and didn't know to do it because they'd never been in serious trouble. Things didn't get complicated with arrests and paperwork. He'd been in front of the situation and made a real, positive difference. It felt good.

"He's grounded now and we have to go to court. If the

judge wants to throw the book at him we're okay with that. Scare the hell out of him. It's a juvenile record and can be erased. He can learn from this and with luck it will be a cheap lesson."

"Sounds like a good plan," Will agreed.

Pete sighed. "But what if he doesn't learn? What if he goes to another party when he's not grounded and there are drugs? He was at a friend's house this time. Someone we know and thought was okay. These are the kids he's hanging out with. What if—"

"Those two words will make you crazy, man." Will held up a hand. "Don't go there."

"I wish it was that easy."

"Look, you shouldn't listen to me." Will blew out a long breath. "I don't have kids."

"Why is that?"

"What?"

"Why don't you have kids?" Pete asked.

"Because I married the wrong woman."

"Yeah, you did, buddy. I never liked her. No offense."

"None taken. My dad and sister said the same thing." Will laughed. "It seems to be the prevailing sentiment."

"How's your dad doing?"

"Great." Will missed him. He'd enjoyed having coffee in the morning, discussing things that happened on the job with the man who knew the challenges better than anyone. The man who'd offered the job to him.

"Must have been nice to spend some time with the family," Pete said.

"It was." And April.

Just thinking about her made him smile. Then the emptiness inside him opened wider because he couldn't walk across the alley and knock on her sliding glass door. He couldn't watch her beautiful face light up with pleasure at the exact moment she recognized him. There wasn't going to be an "accidental" meeting outside their back doors that would result in a run together.

He missed her so damn much.

"What's her name?" Pete asked.

"Who?"

"The one you left behind. The one who should have been your baby mama?"

Will knew better than to blow off the question. This man had taught him a lot about interviewing people and could see right through him. "Her name is April. What gave me away?"

"Besides the fact that you say her name as if you're in church?" Pete shrugged, the gesture saying it was easy to figure out. "And you've been different since you got back. It's not job burnout. I know that when I see it. But your heart's not in it anymore. You had the fire in the belly when you first got here, but it went out a long time ago." Pete thought about what he'd just said. "It's like your heart is somewhere else entirely."

"Someday you're going to have to tell me how you get into my head like that."

"No big secret, man. You let that kid slip away today. That's not like you. I just knew you were thinking about her." He grinned. "April. Like spring."

"Yeah."

"And I'll tell you something else, Will. Remember it's worth what you paid for it." Pete leaned forward and rested his forearms on the desk. "I vent about stuff, but I wouldn't change it. Chicago is in my blood. Abbie's, too. We'll raise our family here and the kids will be fine. But your heart isn't here anymore. You need to be where you left it."

"But—"

"No *buts*." Pete pointed a finger at him, all Chicago attitude. "That's not a career failure. It's a choice. There's a difference."

Will's life flashed before his eyes, but it had nothing to do with near-death experience. This city was big and there were parts that were like nowhere else. Beautiful parts. But it was also crowded, noisy, dirty. And most of all April wasn't here. Pete was right. He had a choice.

"You know," his partner said, "while you were gone the captain had me partnered with Jimmy Gutierrez. He's a good cop and has a lot to learn. Reminds me of you."

Will nodded. He got what his friend was saying and pulled out his cell phone, then speed-dialed his sister. The call went straight to voice mail, but he left a message.

"Kim, I need you to do something for me."

April let Kim drag her from the parking lot just inside Blackwater Lake town limits to the sidewalk on Main Street. Come hell or high water they were going to the farmer's market and her friend wouldn't take no for an answer. April wasn't very happy about it, but she wasn't happy about much these days.

"I could have slept in today," she complained as her friend tugged her along.

"Not if you want to get the freshest fruits and vegetables."

"I don't. Old and stale is fine with me." When Will left, he had taken with him all the color in her life. These days her world was black-and-white.

"Old and stale isn't healthy." Kim pointed to the crowd assembled a distance away at the end of the street where it was blocked off. "Look at all those people. They're taking the fresh food right out of your mouth."

"I'm okay with that. Hey, slow down," she protested when her friend linked arms and increased the pace.

"The good stuff is going fast."

"You should have come by yourself. I'm just slowing you down."

"I didn't want to come by myself. I wanted you here." There was an edge of aggravation to Kim's voice, but she seemed determined to project cheerful, friendly enthusiasm.

"What's wrong with you?"

"I'm sure I don't know what you mean."

April looked sideways, wondering who this woman was and what she'd done with Kim. "When did you start talking like Scarlett O'Hara?"

"Well, fiddledeedee." She grinned then drew in a deep breath. "Isn't it a beautiful day for a—" She stopped and for just a moment there was a horrified expression on her face.

"For what? Kim, what the heck is going on with you today? Seriously, you're acting a little weird."

"Nothing. It's just a beautiful day to go to the farmer's market with my best friend. I've been busy with back-to-school stuff, and settling Tim and me into family life. You and I haven't had a chance to really talk since before I got married. Sensational pictures, by the way. Luke and I are still trying to make up our minds which ones to order for the album."

"Take your time." April felt a little guilty about being such a grump.

Black-and-white was a very narrow palette. She sighed and tamped down the tiny bit of envy that wouldn't go away. Just because Kim had gotten everything she'd ever wanted and April had lost the love of her life for the second time, that was no reason to compromise a beautiful friendship. She chalked it up to a very human flaw and resolved to work on it.

"How is married life?" she asked.

"Pretty great." Kim positively glowed. "I like being a Mrs. It's nice to have someone to count on. Oh, I know my family is there, but this is different."

"I'm really happy for you." April filled the words with a lot of phony eagerness and topped it off with a big, fake smile.

"No, you're not." Kim scoffed. "And I don't blame you. It's hard being this happy when my best friend in the whole world is miserable. I can't believe my brother is so stupid."

"Yeah. About that… Your dad told me your plan," she put air quotes around the word, "was nothing more than an attempt at matchmaking."

"Nobody's perfect." Kim shrugged. "I was so sure it would work. I'm so very sorry he hurt you, sweetie."

"You meant well." As they continued walking, April leaned her head on her friend's shoulder for just a moment. "Not your fault Will didn't cooperate."

"He'll come around. You watch. And I'll bet you twenty bucks that he'll be back." There was such confidence in her voice.

"I'll take that bet." April wanted to be a believer, but it was too hard to be wrong. "Because I'm not going to live in False Hope–ville anymore. That painful episode is behind me."

They were passing the Harvest Café where Lucy Bishop had just walked out the door. She smiled. "Hey, you two. How's it going?"

"Good," Kim said. "We're on our way to the farmer's market."

"Me, too. Mind if I join you?"

"That would be great." Kim sounded too eager, almost relieved to have company.

"I go every week, but I'm running late today," Lucy

shared. "I like to beat the crowd and pick out the best fruits and veggies for the café." She glanced up the street. "This is the most crowded time to go."

"True," Kim agreed. "Most of the town will be there now."

"How are you holding up?" Lucy said to April. "I mean with Will gone?"

She heard the pity in her friend's voice. So much for the brilliant plan to change that. It had been too much to expect that if she broke up with him she'd no longer be the girl he left behind. Because he went to Chicago and she was still here, that made her—wait for it—the girl he left behind *again*.

"I'm great," April said. "Just peachy. At least, I will be."

"Good for you," Lucy said.

They were now a block away from their target destination. In the cordoned-off street there were several big blue tarps set up. Beneath them were tables holding crates filled with seasonal fresh produce. Lettuce, zucchini, squash, mushrooms and carrots. Beside them apples, pears and yams were displayed. The crowd was so thick you had to wait your turn to even get close to the bins.

The three of them stopped just outside the first tarp and listened to the hum of voices. The closest people to her waved, said hello and gave her pitying looks. She was just about to turn around and go back the way she'd come when Hank Fletcher walked over with Josie Swanson.

The trim older woman had big blue eyes and a warm smile. Her silver hair was cut in a flattering pixie style. "Hi, April. Haven't seen you for a while."

"How are you, Josie?"

"Great. If you don't factor in that I'll be homeless soon."

"Is Maggie Potter kicking you out?" April asked. The older woman was a widow and rented a room from the recently engaged single mom who'd fallen in love with Sloan Holden.

"Maggie would never do that," Josie said. "It's my decision. Young couples need their privacy."

Hank put his arm across her shoulders. "She's teasing. Actually she's moving in with me. I'm renting out Kim's old room." He winked at his daughter, a sign that he knew he wasn't fooling her with that story.

"You don't waste any time, Dad. My bed is hardly cold."

April knew her friend approved of the relationship. Josie had been there for the family during Hank's health crisis, and his daughter liked her very much. She sighed. Another happy couple.

As they waited their turn to walk under the tarp, the five of them talked, their voices raised against the backdrop of buzzing chatter all around them. April realized it was slowly quieting and finally stopped just as the crowd parted to let a man through.

It was a man who looked an awful lot like Will!

He walked right up to her. "I'm not okay with you dumping me."

Surely a heart couldn't beat as fast as hers was without some kind of consequence. "I thought you were in Chicago."

"I came back. For good," he added.

"I don't understand. What are you doing *here*?" Why hadn't he walked across the alley and knocked on her sliding glass door to tell her this?

"You broke up with me in public and I need to get you back the same way." There was a mother lode of determination in his blue eyes. "Besides, I have a better chance here with the whole town on my side."

"But how did you know I'd be here?" April glanced at Kim, who was looking awfully self-satisfied. Then it hit her. Why her friend had wheedled and bullied her into coming. "You forced me into this. You knew he'd be here."

"Actually he ordered me to get you here," Kim clarified. "And when the sheriff of Blackwater Lake gives you a direct order, it's always best to do what he says."

April thanked her friend with a look that she knew would be understood. "So when you bet me twenty bucks he'd be back—"

Kim shrugged. "Sucker bet."

"I'm not paying you," she vowed. "You should have warned me he would be here—"

"I told her not to tell you. I was afraid if you knew, you wouldn't come," Will said. "And I really wanted—no, needed—you to."

"Why?" Wariness warred with hope inside her. She was stunned and shocked and so darn happy to see him.

"I thought a career in a big-city police department was running *to* something, but I was wrong. Everything in the world that's important to me is right here. I wanted to ask you to come with me when I left, but you're so happy here." His gaze never left hers and his eyes were filled with intensity. "The thing is, you're the smart one. You stayed. But I finally wised up and came back. Not just for you, but this town. It gets into your blood in the best possible way."

"That it does," she said.

"And you got into my blood. You stole my heart when you were sixteen years old and you have it now."

April actually heard a collective sigh from the women in the crowd. "I don't know what to say."

"A simple yes would be just about perfect," he said, his voice low and deep. "Because I love you, April. And I'd really like it if you'd marry me."

Before his words even sank in everyone gathered around them started chanting, "Yes! Yes! Yes!"

How could she say no when he was offering her everything she'd ever wanted in her life? She needed no encouragement from the crowd and threw herself into his arms, then said for all to hear, "Yes!"

"And we got an affirmative." That was Hank's voice and the words incited applause and cheers.

She smiled up at the man she'd loved for as long as she could remember. "Sounds like your dad approves."

"I'm glad. But it wouldn't matter if he didn't. I can be a bonehead sometimes, but of course you know that better than anyone. On the upside, I don't very often make the same mistake twice."

"No you don't," she agreed. "Kim was right. I've never stopped loving you."

"I told you everything would work out." Kim sniffled loudly. "Happy endings always make me cry."

April had just about given up on living happily ever after but this was definitely worth waiting for. She gave Will a sassy look. "Does this mean I get to be your sidekick?"

"For as long as we live," he promised.

She would never have guessed it was possible to be this happy and wished her mother was there to share in it. But she had a strong feeling that her mom was smiling down on them. And just maybe had a hand in making her dream of a family with Will come true.

April was no longer the girl he'd left behind, but the one he'd come home to.

* * * * *

MILLS & BOON®

Why not subscribe?
Never miss a title and save money too!

Here's what's available to you if you join the exclusive **Mills & Boon® Book Club** today:

- ✦ *Titles up to a month ahead of the shops*
- ✦ *Amazing discounts*
- ✦ *Free P&P*
- ✦ *Earn Bonus Book points that can be redeemed against other titles and gifts*
- ✦ *Choose from monthly or pre-paid plans*

Still want more?
Well, if you join today, we'll even give you
50% OFF your first parcel!

So visit **www.millsandboon.co.uk/subs**
to be a part of this exclusive Book Club!

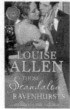   

MILLS & BOON®

Cherish™

EXPERIENCE THE ULTIMATE RUSH OF FALLING IN LOVE

A sneak peek at next month's titles...

In stores from 7th April 2016:

- **The Billionaire Who Saw Her Beauty** – Rebecca Winters
  and **Fortune's Prince Charming** –
  Nancy Robards Thompson
- **In the Boss's Castle** – Jessica Gilmore *and*
  The Texas Ranger's Family – Rebecca Winters

In stores from 21st April 2016:

- **Rafael's Contract Bride** – Nina Milne *and*
  James Bravo's Shotgun Bride – Christine Rimmer
- **One Week with the French Tycoon** – Christy McKellen
  and **The Detective's 8 lb, 10 oz Surprise** – Meg Maxwell

Available at WHSmith, Tesco, Asda, Eason, Amazon and Apple

Just can't wait?
Buy our books online a month before they hit the shops!
visit www.millsandboon.co.uk

These books are also available in eBook format!